DAIKAIJU!
GIANT MONSTER TALES

This book is dedicated to

Gojira (on his 50th birthday, 3 November 2004)

and to

Ishiro Honda (1911–1993)
Eiji Tsuburaya (1901–1970)
Noriaki Yuasa (1933–2004)
Merian C. Cooper (1893–1973)
Ernest B. Schoedsack (1893–1979)
Willis O'Brien (1886–1962)
Eugène Lourié (1903–1991)
and
Ray Harryhausen (1920–)

for unleashing their assorted giant monsters
onto our imaginations

Other titles by Agog! Press

Agog! Fantastic Fiction: 29 Tales of Fantasy, Imagination and Wonder,
edited by Cat Sparks, 2002/2006

AustrAlien Absurdities, edited by Chuck McKenzie and Tansy Rayner
Roberts, 2002

Agog! Terrific Tales: New Australian Speculative Fiction, edited by Cat
Sparks, 2003/2006

Agog! Smashing Stories: New Australian Speculative Fiction, edited by
Cat Sparks, 2004/2006

Agog! Ripping Reads, edited by Cat Sparks, 2006

DAIKAIJU!

GIANT MONSTER TALES

edited by
Robert Hood and Robin Pen

Published by Agog! Press
PO Box U302, University of Wollongong NSW 2522, Australia
agogpress@gmail.com

in partnership with Prime Books:
www.prime-books.com

ISBN:
0-8095-5759-2 (hc)
0-8095-5758-4 (pbk)

Anthology website: www.roberthood.net/daikaiju-antho

Contents

Random Observations
from the Editors

As a term, *daikaiju* (Japanese, *"dai"* = giant + *"kaiju"* = monster) is usually applied to a distinctive form of fantasy film—a pseudo-SF sub-genre that began with Ishiro Honda's original *Gojira* in 1954 and was elaborated over subsequent decades, principally by Honda himself and his film studio Toho. Stylised, spectacular, colourful, both loved and derided, yet perennially popular (Godzilla's 28th film, made to celebrate his 50th anniversary, was released in 2004), it is a sub-genre that is distinctively Japanese despite its original inspiration in such Western movies as *King Kong* (1933) and *The Beast From 20,000 Fathoms* (1952)—and despite the fact that giant monster flicks have proliferated in Hollywood and around the world ever since. (For a fuller history of giant monster cinema, see Brian Thomas' excellent article at the conclusion of this book.)

Of course, in the context of an anthology such as this, we have no business appropriating the term "daikaiju" at all. But when we began, we were aware of the fact that the project's impetus came from the editors' enjoyment of *daikaiju eiga* (Japanese giant monster films) and the knowledge that no coherent literary translation of the cinematic tradition had, as far as we knew, ever been attempted. There are a number of isolated stories that most of us could point to, novels based for the most part on particular films, even comic-book tales such as those in such series as Marvel's *Strange Tales*. Fan magazines and websites occasionally publish giant monster stories. But an anthology of specifically *daikaiju* tales? We don't think there has been one (though are keen to hear otherwise). Remember we are not talking about simple largeness here. There have been anthologies of dragon, sea-serpent and dinosaur fiction. While these creatures are giant-sized and therefore related to daikaiju (again, see Thomas' article), they are not the sort of classic daikaiju we're referring to in this collection of stories. For a start, they are relatively small. To us, daikaiju tales require monsters of unreasonable size, impossible and outlandish dimension, relativities that border on (and sometimes cross into) the utterly absurd. Despite whatever rationalisations might be applied within the narrative, daikaiju are fantastical and provoke awe through the sheer audacity of their conception.

But surely size is not all? We didn't think so even when we started. At first we weren't too clear about what *was* daikaiju and what *wasn't*. We (and the authors who submitted stories) defined the literary version of the sub-genre (for our purposes, at least) as we went along. But there were some elements that, if not essential in toto, seemed characteristic. A penchant for city-trashing and apocalyptic destruction. Metaphorical undercurrents. A sense that the kaiju are more than just Beasts—personality, in other words, albeit of a non-human kind. Pseudo-scientific and metaphysical pretensions. Vast scope. Incredible power. A certain cosmic inevitability. Daikaiju are not scared of Man. They don't duck and weave and die as soon as the fighter pilots get a clear shot, like hunted animals. No, classic daikaiju scorn humanity's military might. If they are often the unnatural product of human arrogance, they manage to transcend that heritage and become supra-natural. They are more like inhuman gods than unnatural beasts. They are impossible, yet they *are*.

Of course, not all of the stories that you are about to read contain all these elements. They mix-and-match and experiment with the possibilities. Many refer, one way or another, to the film tradition, often alluding to Godzilla, the King himself, then breaking off from there into personal imaginative forays. Others more-or-less ignore the films (except as an unstated template) and draw upon alternative traditions. Some might not, in your view as a reader, be daikaiju stories at all. But they all, to the editors, contain enough of the elements to qualify, and take an individual approach that illuminates, in their unique way, important aspects of the "tradition" and its relation to human experience.

On top of that, of course, is the fact that we chose these particular stories because we enjoyed reading them—and thought others would, too. Like most fiction, daikaiju stories might address serious issues (the original Godzilla was an embodiment of the Bomb and illuminated the many moral and eschatalogical issues surrounding it), but in the end it is entertainment value that we look for in them.

When we planned the anthology, however, we had a sneaking suspicion that interest in prospective writers might be limited, that we might not get sufficient stories of sufficient quality to justify an anthology. This is, after all, a rather specialised, almost non-existent field, and likely response was very much an unknown quantity.

We were, we're happy to say, profoundly wrong. Levels of interest, of enthusiasm, far exceeded our expectations. "It's what I've waited for all my life," wrote one author—and the attitude was typical. We quickly realised that the possibility of writing a daikaiju story, and the hope of having it published in a dedicated volume, inspired the fan in writers and the writer in fans. Stories flooded in. And not just ordinary stories, covering a narrow range of themes and approaches. Not just stories that attempted to replicate their cinematic ancestors. And not the sort of trashy pop writing that some might have expected. Invention and imagination went wild.

As you will discover when you read these stories, authors took an amazing variety of approaches, everything from full-on blockbuster-style adventure thrillers to humorous postmodern critiques, meditative fantasies, uneasy character studies, stories of personal crisis, surreal hallucinations, satires (including one that is likely to offend everyone equally) and jokey interludes—even a haiku or four. It's extraordinary how "serious" all this "silly" business about giant monsters can be! Some of the stories are universal in approach, some redolant of the nationality of their authors, be that Australian, American or British. In the end, we can truthfully say that there is nothing ordinary about this anthology. We think you will find it as extraordinary—and as entertaining—as the daikaiju themselves.

But there's more! What you will find here is merely the tip of the daikaiju iceberg. We were forced to leave out many stories we thought deserved publication, helpless in the face of publishing logistics. However, thanks to Prime Books there will now be a second and third volume of giant monster stories for those who can never get enough!

Apart from the many authors who submitted stories, there are others we need to thank. Bob Eggleton is a multi-Hugo-Award-winning artist whose work is in considerable demand, yet his desire to do an original cover for the anthology was a product of enthusiasm for daikaiju and this project, and displayed a spontaneous generosity that matches his amazing talent. Similarly Todd Tennant, whose work on the website *American Kaiju* we greatly admire, was eager to contribute an original piece of artwork—and the fantastic result can be seen on the back cover.

It was while toying with the idea of including a cinema supplement that we were inspired to ask Brian Thomas—a regular Cinescape contributor and author of *Videohound's Dragon: Asian Action and Cult Flicks*—if he'd like to contribute a non-fiction piece on daikaiju cinema. He was more than willing to do so. Finally, J.D. Lees, famed as long-time editor and publisher of the leading kaiju magazine *G-Fan*—and organiser of the annual G-Fest that celebrates giant monster culture in the US—has also been generous in his support. It was only with the enthusiastic generosity and talent of people such as these—not to mention publisher Cat Sparks of Agog! Press and Sean Wallace of Prime Books—that this unique anthology was able to come into existence at all.

Robert Hood
Robin Pen

Lullabye

DOUG WOOD

The young girl hid beneath the bed covers, watching the blur of the night-light that shone across the dark room. She sniffed back tears and wished for sleep. Bedtime was far past and Mother would be cross, but she was too scared of the storm outside. Every time she shut her eyes, the sky rumbled with thunder. Wind rattled the shutters and rain tapped at the window like nervous little fingers trying to pry it open.

She had known a storm was coming. That afternoon, she was picking vegetables for dinner with her Mother in the backyard. The lake, smooth as glass one moment, suddenly went choppy and the wind cold from the tree-lined far shore. She ate little during dinner when the first rain drops began to fall. Afterwards, during homework, she listened more for the tornado warnings from the TV in the other room than to the warm voices of the recorded study guides. The first crackle of thunder erupted as she was going upstairs to bed.

Tucking her in, Mother had asked if the girl would be all right. She nodded; she was a big girl now and she wasn't afraid anymore. Mother kissed her good night and turned out the light as she left. The girl waited a few moments for the sound of footsteps to recede down the hall; then she hurried over to the nightlight and switched it on. Back in bed, she threw the covers over her head.

The girl hated storms, but when she hid beneath the covers, it was better. Still scary, but okay. For there, the sounds were muffled, and she could play a little game she'd thought up, pretending they were something else. The rain on the windows could be the tap of a friend come over to play, the wind a whistled song while she waited for the door to open, the creaking shutter the squeak of the floorboard on the back porch, the rattling branches the door knob being tried.

Sometimes the pretending other things was enough and she could fall asleep eventually. But not when the storm was really bad, as this one was, when the thunder was booming and couldn't be imagined as anything other than what it truly was—a terrifying thing that always made her feel smaller than she was. Many times, she had woken in tears during a storm that broke after bedtime.

The sky flashed white, a brilliance no match for a night-light. She tightened her eyes and clamped her ears. Thunder boomed a few seconds later, rumbling like a boulder down a hill and fading in the distance. She listened intently for a change in the wind, not knowing how a tornado sounded, but sure she would recognise one if she heard it.

The door creaked open and a soft voice called out. "Honey? Are you all right?"

The girl threw back the covers and ran, burying her face in the pleasant softness of her Mother's nightgown. They had the same almond eyes and dark hair, and in each face could be seen the trace of one and the promise of the other.

"Mommy!" she cried, her cheeks damp, "I know you said I shouldn't be afraid, but I can't help it!"

"It's okay, honey," she shushed, patting her head. "I'm here. I won't leave you. Let's go back to bed, okay?"

Mother tucked her in again and then lay down beside, cradling her in her arms, stroking the girl's long brown hair. The thunder that came as they lay there was just as loud as before, the lightning as sudden and harsh; but the girl wasn't as frightened in her tight embrace and she was able to relax at last.

"Mommy?" she asked.

"What is it, honey?"

"Were you ever scared?"

At first, Mother didn't say anything. The girl looked up curiously just as another searing flash of white filled the room. She cringed against Mother's breast, who continued stroking her hair absently. There was thunder; and then Mother said, quietly: "Yes. It was a long time ago when I was your age."

"And did Gramma…did your Mommy…make you not scared?"

Mother kissed her forehead. "Yes, she did."

A streak of lightning flashed across the sky again.

"I can't find Puppy," a girl said. She was almost in tears. "I looked everywhere and I can't find him!"

"Don't worry about Puppy," said her Mother, gripping the girl's hand. "He'll be fine, you'll see. He'll be waiting for us when we get back. Come, we have to go now."

In the entryway, Mother helped the girl on with her coat. She usually liked it when Mother dressed her to go outside, liked the grown-up scent of her perfume as they stood close. This day, though, Mother wasn't wearing any and her fingers worked fast and rough. She missed a few buttons that the girl had to fix herself while Mother pulled on her own coat.

Mother handed the girl the book bag she took to school and told her she had to bring it, too. When she tried to sling it on like always, however, it nearly fell. Whatever Mother had put inside weighed more than all her schoolbooks at once. However, Mother was bringing a suitcase along and the girl was determined to carry the book bag all by herself. She knelt and worked her arms through the straps. Standing up again, she had to lean forward for balance. It was an awkward posture but once she got used to it, not as difficult as she'd thought at first.

"Are you okay?" asked the Mother, opening the door.

The girl grunted. "Uh huh. I can do it."

While her mother locked the door, the girl stared amazed at the street. Outside, people crowded the sidewalks, hurrying in the same direction. They carried suitcases, bookbags and even simple paper bags. Some merely held a pile of clothes in outstretched arms—whatever they could carry. The commotion was frightening, almost infectious; she felt her own fear rising. But when Mother held the girl's hand that made it a little better.

"Where are we going?" the girl asked.

"There's a building on Daddy's base," Mother explained. "It's underground. We'll be safe there."

"Why?"

Mother hesitated. "There's a...there's a storm coming. Everyone has to stay inside until it passes."

"We never had to before."

"Honey, this storm is different. It's very bad. But don't worry. We'll be okay."

"Will Daddy be there?"

Mother shook her head. "No, not right away. His ship had to leave port. But he'll be okay, too. And when the ship comes back, he'll meet us there."

The girl looked to the east. A vast dark cloud like none she had ever seen before clung low to the horizon. Not white, nor storm-tossed, nor a solid gray wall like the typhoon that had swept across the open ocean the year before and given her such a scare. This one was a black, billowing thing and indeed looked much worse than any storm she had ever known.

Although she believed it when Mother said they would be safe, one thing worried the girl: where the cloud rose its thickest, roiling with a reddish-orange colour, the city—Tokyo it was called—was in that direction. The skyline that had stretched so high and wide it blocked the view of the solitary snow-capped mountain in the distance had simply disappeared. Where had the city gone?

There was no time to ask her Mother. A mini-bus pulled to the curb and they got inside. The driver was dressed like the girl's Daddy in a dark blue uniform with the funny white hat. Most of the seats were taken already by other Mothers with their children. Two in back were still empty, and as they walked down the aisle, she saw a boy her age crying. His mommy wasn't holding his hand.

The mini-bus pulled from the curb and wound through the tight, crowded streets. The driver honked the horn and sometimes said bad words like Daddy said when she wasn't supposed to hear. They passed more people than the girl had ever seen in her life, even more than crowded the streets at the shrine-carrying festival a few months before. It seemed the whole city was moving and the girl thought it must be a very bad storm coming.

With the streets so congested, it took longer than usual to reach the base where the big gray ships were anchored. Eventually they came to the main gate and passed inside. A lot of people dressed like Daddy were there, but some wore all white uniforms and some all tan and as the mini-bus drove through the wide streets she saw all the different types, walking alone or standing in big neat groups like blue farm rows.

She didn't like the base where Daddy worked. It was kind of ugly with hardly any trees or grass to play on. There were a lot of buildings and hangers that looked the same—a little plain, a little grimy. And the big cannons on wheels: she especially didn't like those. As the mini-bus drove past, some men in blue were inspecting the cannons like on holidays. She hoped they wouldn't be firing them; they hurt her ears.

From the window seat, she spotted a few classmates and tried waving at them. No one saw her, though. Most were in too much of a hurry to look, and in the eyes of those who did she saw only fear. She'd held back her own until then, but reached for Mother's hand now, and felt a reassuring squeeze in return.

"You're being a very good girl," the mother said. "I'm very proud of you."

"Mommy, I'm a little scared," the girl admitted.

Mother kissed her forehead. "Honey, it's all right to be a little scared. Stay close, do what I say, and if it makes you feel better, squeeze my hand like you just did."

They stopped outside a low curved building of unpainted metal with a line of people waiting to get in. The girl and her Mother went to stand at the end and slowly made their way forward. Two men flanked the double doors. They weren't dressed like Daddy but in green camouflage uniforms, with shiny black rifles held across their broad chests. She didn't like how they stared straight ahead at nothing and still looked angry at everything. She kept her head down when they went by.

At first, she wondered how everyone could fit; the building seemed so small from the outside. But a stairwell led down four flights underground and at the bottom waited another set of doors, these metal and studded with rivets. They passed inside into an immense room with long rows of evenly spaced columns. A man dressed in a blue uniform holding a light stick waved them off to the side.

Mother found an empty place against the wall. She dropped the suitcase and shrugged off her coat, which she then draped on the bare concrete floor for them to sit on. The girl let go the heavy book bag with a relieved sigh and started to do the same with her coat until Mother stopped her.

"No, honey, keep it on. It's cold in here."

"But won't you get cold?"

"Come here!" She held out her arms. "You can keep me warm."

The girl snuggled up and watched with great interest as more and more people entered and found spots to sit down. An older man walking with a cane and a striped tablecloth knapsack slung on his shoulder approached and asked in Japanese if the place next to them was taken.

Mother shook her head and said, "*Dozo.*"

"*Domo arigato*," he replied, sitting with a tired sigh.

In an hour, the two were hemmed in on both sides, with row upon row between them and the door. It was very crowded, though oddly quiet. When people spoke, it was in whispers like in a library. Whether out of politeness, fear, or both, the girl couldn't tell.

When there was no more room, the metal doors were closed with a loud booming sound whose echo resonated through the space. Only then did the girl's fear slip free and get the better of her. She squeezed Mother's hand very hard.

"Mommy?"

"Shhh, it's okay, honey. Don't worry. I'm here. We're safe. Are you hungry? Do you want something to nibble on?"

"Not hungry. Sleepy."

"Why don't you get some rest? When you wake up, Daddy will probably be back from his ship and we'll able to leave together."

"Promise?" said the girl.

"I promise," said the Mother.

The girl nodded, sank into her Mother's shoulder and closed her eyes. In a few moments, she was asleep.

When she opened her eyes, it was impossible to say how much time had passed. There were no clocks anywhere on the walls and in the rush to leave home she'd forgotten her watch. Her Mother lay asleep with her purse for a pillow and the girl didn't want to wake her.

The big room was even quieter than before and the ceiling lights were dimmed, making it difficult to see anything. Almost everyone was sleeping, it seemed. Some read books by flashlight or listened to music on earphones. Hiding beneath a jacket, the furtive glow of a cigarette illuminated a young man's face, while a couple of rows over a baby gurgled happily. Only the two uniformed men from outside were standing, almost invisible in their camouflage at the shadowy far end of the room.

The girl closed her eyes but she couldn't sleep. She had to pee. No signs pointed to the bathroom and no one around was awake to ask, but she was a big girl now and she decided to find it herself. Keeping low so the mean-looking soldiers wouldn't see her, she crawled down the aisle towards the entrance, the only doors she had seen, pausing breathless and scared at the head of each row to make sure no one was looking.

The doors were big and studded with metal rivets. How to get them open was a little worrisome at first, but when she tried to pull on one it wasn't nearly as heavy as it seemed. She got the left side cracked open just enough to scuttle through.

The landing was bare. There were no bathrooms, only the stairs leading to the top. Thinking she remembered seeing a door on the first floor, she started up. At home, she always climbed steps using her hands and Daddy would laugh, calling her "Monkey Girl." But the concrete steps were very cold to the touch and when her fingers began to burn, she switched to the rail.

There were four flights leading up. At the next landing, she thought she heard something outside. She listened, but the sound was muffled by distance. It might have been an explosion or it might have been something else entirely. For a brief moment, she thought of going back down, but her need was growing urgent and so she continued.

At each successive landing, the strange sounds outside grew louder and more distinct. They were explosions, big ones. But that wasn't what worried her the most. As she climbed, she began to feel the stairs shaking under her. Like the earthquakes and aftershocks that occurred almost weekly—only not, because those didn't start and stop every five seconds. It had to be something else.

She peeked over the last step at the top. The doors were shut now but an odd orange light glowed around the edges and through the rectangular window slots. The keyhole cast a shape on the floor inches from her face, like a circle of sunlight through a magnifying glass.

In the burning outline of the door, the bathroom and everything below was suddenly forgotten. She got up and walked slowly forward. The doorknob looked hot to the touch. Afraid of getting hurt, she felt it with the tip of a finger. It was cold and she pulled the door open.

Many hours had passed and night had fallen outside. The base was dark, the streetlights unlit, but she had no trouble seeing. The strange orange glow illuminated everything like the nightlight in her bedroom. She stepped outside and felt a prickly warmth on her face and arms, not unpleasant but as odd as the light in its own way. The heat didn't envelop her body the way summer did, but grew more intense when she faced a certain direction. She grinned and spun around in a circle, wanting to feel it all over.

And stopped.

The horizon was burning, a curtain of fire stretching far as she could see. The huge flames leaped halfway up the sky, roiling clouds of black smoke rising even further, concealing the moon and the stars.

She heard the muffled explosions again and looked up in time to see streaks of light arcing across the sky above her. She turned to seaward just as multiple cannon-fire briefly lit the gray silhouettes of battleships far out in the ocean. The sound of the big guns—poompoom poom…poom—hit her a few seconds later as she traced the trajectory until they disappeared into the black smoke. Huge explosions followed, more flames and smoke.

The sound, far away but still too close, broke the spell of the warm midnight day. She shouldn't be outside. She turned back to the door when one of the strange earthquakes almost threw her to the ground. Only the door handle stopped her fall. She grabbed it, swinging around and slamming her back against the metal. Dazed but not hurt, she stared out at the city of flame.

And then she saw it.

It strode forth from a cloud of blackest smoke, a living creature taller than the flames, the oily vapour clinging momentarily to its scaly hide. Like a walking storm. It roared thunder at the ships, its mouth suddenly spitting a beam of yellow lightning; and when its enormous body swung around, a spiked tail ripped through the air, creating a gale of wind that struck her face hard enough to draw tears...

"Mommy?"

*

...And then the thunder came as a low rumble in the distance, fading quickly. Soon there was only the soft sound of gentle rain. The worst was passed.

"Mommy?"

"What is it?" the Mother asked.

"I wish there were never any storms," the girl said.

"Well, I don't know if you would really like that," Mother said softly. "My mother once told me that everything in this world has a reason for being. A reason for you and for me and even for the rain. You like flowers, yes? Well, rain makes the flowers grow."

The girl's eyes opened wider. "And storms make rain."

Mother nodded. "If there were no storms, there would be no rain to make flowers. Would you want to live in a world without flowers?"

The only place the girl knew that had no flowers was the desert. She tried to imagine living in one, all hot and dry with sand stretching in all directions.

"I don't think I'd like it much," she said. She yawned and snuggled deeper into Mother's warmth, her eyes growing heavy. "When's Daddy coming home?"

"He's waiting out the storm. He'll be home later."

"Promise?"

Mother's breath hitched and she suddenly squeezed tighter than before. The girl didn't know why, only that it felt good, and she hugged back just as firmly.

"Yes, I promise," Mother said.

For a long time, the girl clung quietly, content to listen to her Mother's heartbeat and the patter of rain. She started to get sleepy, but she didn't want it to end just yet.

"Mommy, what was it made you scared that time?"

Mother took a deep breath. "It was a...storm, honey. Just a storm. Like this one. It went away in time."

"And how did Gramma make you not afraid?"

"Oh, she sang an old song I liked."

"Do you still remember it?" the girl asked. "Would you sing it for me?"

"Sure." Mother began to hum a slow pleasant melody, and then softly sang words she'd learned long ago in some far away place:

"Torrianse, torrianse
koko wa doko no hosomichi jya
tenjin-sama no hosomichi jya
chotto toshite kudashanse
goyo no nai mono toshasenu
kono ko no nanatsu no iwai ni
ofuda o osame ni mairimasu
iki wa yoi yoi, kaeri wa kowai
kowainagara
torrianse, torrianse ..."

The girl knew some Japanese, but not these words. It didn't matter. It still sounded nice, whatever it was. She closed her eyes, her breath soon steady and deep.

"Good night, Mommy," she whispered and drifted off into a pleasant sleep.

Pulling the covers around them, Mother kissed her forehead. "Good night."

Another streak of lightning lit the sky. Mother looked up, unafraid. She stroked the girl's hair, covered her ears, and waited quietly for the thunder to break.

English translation of the traditional Japanese folksong used in this story:

Go down the path, go down the path
What narrow path is this?
This is the shrine god's path
go ahead down the path
if you have no errand, don't go
I come to pray in celebration for
this child's seventh birthday
going is easy, coming back is scary
even though it's scary,
go down the path, go down the path

Running

MARTIN LIVINGS

The three of us sit on the beach, keeping a keen watch over the Indian Ocean; the waters are grey, of course, reflecting the grey skies above. I've seen photos of Mauritius before, with clear azure skies and crystalline oceans, the sand a brilliant white beneath a blazing sun, but I'm assured that those days aren't as common as the advertising would lead you to believe, even when there isn't a major storm brewing off the coast. The gusting winds and occasional smatterings of rain are deceptively subtle reminders that Tropical Cyclone Katrina is on its way, sweeping in low across the ocean, a wall of foul weather rising from the sea to the clouds. But it isn't the cyclone we're waiting for, watching for, rather something which is travelling with it, behind it, inside it. Something far more destructive, and far more attractive.

I glance over to my left, where Belinda sits with her long legs stretched out on the pale sand. She's a statuesque woman in her mid-thirties or so, judging by her background at least. We must look a little like reflections in a funhouse mirror; her hair is cropped short the same as mine, and we're dressed in similar clothes—black motorcycle leathers with boots and gauntlets. Mine are brand new though, virgin-smooth, untested, while hers show signs of previous use, previous runs: patches repairing tears, edges frayed, the leather as rough as sun-aged skin. I know what to wear from reading about it, seeing videos; she's simply wearing what she's always worn. That thought alone makes me feel very humble.

I look away from Belinda, to my right. Ryuichi is there, sitting cross-legged, eyes closed, wearing only a tank top and shorts, his feet dirty and bare. He looks very old to my eyes, though I know he's only in his sixties; his bare limbs are wrinkled and sunken, but wiry and muscled beneath the sagging skin. His worn face is placid; he barely seems to be breathing, as if meditating. I wonder if he's asleep. Sitting here next to Ryuichi makes me feel like a baby in the presence of a god; he's a genuine legend in the field, arguably the first runner, and easily the oldest still participating. When I'd heard he was heading here, I knew I had to come as well. It was probably the only chance I'd have to meet the great man. If the next run didn't kill him, old age eventually would.

As if he feels my gaze, he opens an eye and looks at me. A

smile flitters across his lips like a blown leaf. I blush and looked away, further to my right, behind us. There's a grassy area back there, set up with umbrellas and chairs for those who simply wanted to enjoy the views of the ocean without getting their feet sandy, lined with palm trees that are swaying quite violently in the growing wind. A Japanese film crew is there, frantically setting up cameras and barking incomprehensible orders to one another. They are understandably excited, of course. In their own way, they're as eager as we are, perhaps even more so. Beyond them, framed against the dramatic green-coated mountains that jut out at random points throughout the island, the seaside town of Flic en Flac is hunkered down, low and spread out, almost as if it knows what's coming. Its inhabitants certainly do; most have fled into the ocean in rough fishing vessels, or travelled by any means available into the centre of the island, hoping to avoid the worst of the damage. And not from the cyclone; they'd withstood hundreds of those over the years. No, they're running from something else entirely.

Running from, running to, running with. One way or another, we all run, sooner or later.

I'd been incredibly lucky to get a flight here earlier in the day, an eight-hour stint from Melbourne, arriving at Sir Seewoosagur Ramgoolam International Airport just shy of noon. The plane had been virtually empty, only the flight staff and myself. It was the first time I'd ever flown, and in other circumstances I might have enjoyed the experience. But I never even looked out of my window, instead using the hours of bumpy flight to re-read everything I'd brought with me in my carry-on luggage, the books that covered sixty-odd years of history, theory and practice. I didn't even notice that we'd landed; the stewardess had to call me three times before I looked up from my studies. We'd disembarked pretty quickly, heading into the airport, whisked through customs, then I'd walked calmly through the doors that open into the main airport proper, into chaos. Hundreds of people trying desperately to get seats on flights out of the country, screaming children, natives shouting in French and Creole, angry and frightened. I'd never seen anything like it. Luckily Belinda had been there to meet me, holding a sign high over her head with my name on it. She'd freed me from the jostling crowd, and taken me to the deserted town, the quiet beach. To the man who would lead us in our run.

"How long?" Belinda asks, her voice barely louder than the wind around us. I turn to her reflexively, ready to answer that I don't know, but realise a moment later that she isn't addressing me, of course she isn't. Why would she? How could I possibly know?

"Soon," Ryuichi replies calmly.

"Can you see it?" I ask, nerves making my voice crack a little. "Where?"

The old man smiles slightly. "Right there," he says, pointing to the shore, not twenty metres from our feet.

I look, but don't see anything, just water licking the sand like a cat drinking. I hear Belinda take a surprised breath, so I know she's figured it out. I feel stupid and young. Again.

"The tide," she whispers, and I see it. The waters are receding visibly, pulling away from the beach, leaving seaweed and tiny panicked sand crabs exposed to the open air. I see this happening, and in my mind I picture the implications, extending into the ocean, towards the horizon. A dip here means that there's a bulge out there somewhere, a bulge that's headed our way at a rate of knots. The thought both thrills and terrifies me.

Soon, Ryuichi had said, and he knows about these things. Soon, then. The waiting is nearly over. It's almost time to run.

I get to my feet and stretch, my leathers cracking along with my joints, both stiff from disuse. Belinda does the same, almost a foot taller than me. She catches my eye and winks, grinning.

"Ready, kid?"

I nod, trying to smile back, though my guts are telling me fairly forcefully that I'm not ready, not by a long shot. I need more time. Minutes, hours, days. Years. I won't admit it though, not in this company. This is the opportunity of a lifetime, and I'm not going to let it escape me, no matter how scared I might be. I've prepared as well as I possibly can, given the circumstances; I've worked out religiously for years to increase my fitness to its optimum, studied hundreds of videos and written accounts of previous runs, even learnt to surf to get a feel for the general dynamics, though nothing can really simulate the real thing with any degree of accuracy. If I'm not ready now, I never will be. I nod again, more forcefully this time, mainly to myself.

Belinda speaks again to Ryuichi, who's limberly getting to his feet, showing no sign of discomfort or difficulty. I hope I'll be as fit as he is when I'm his age. Hell, I wish I was that fit now. "Where should we start?" she asks, almost reverentially.

The old man thinks for a moment, rubbing his stubbled chin with his fingers. Then he turns and points behind us, past the picnic area where the film crew are still frenetically preparing their equipment, active and noisy as a bag of popcorn in a microwave. "On the street, back there. By the shops." He seems to be visualising it in his head, seeing the patterns of possibility, imagining the unimaginable. "Yes, right there should be fine. Yes." His Japanese accent is faint, eroded by decades of globetrotting, but still there. I guess you never really lose your heritage, even if you lose pretty much everything else.

Belinda nods. "Okay, let's do it."

We walk up the beach, Belinda and I leaving deep imprints of our boots in the sands, Ryuichi barely leaving a trace of his passing. As we reach the grass, Ryuichi veers away from us for a moment, crossing to the film crew. They all fall silent as he approaches them, looking at him with a peculiar mixture of pity and awe. Mainly awe, I like to think. He says a few words softly in Japanese, and the crew members look out towards the ocean suddenly. Ryuichi turns away from them, and the film crew's chaotic bustle returns and redoubles, as they grab their equipment and begin to retreat with an air of relaxed panic. I look out to the ocean as well; it's a reflex, I can't stop myself, any more than I could stop myself from flinching if someone faked a punch at my nose.

Is part of the horizon raised now? I can't tell, not really, but I suspect it is. The other half of the wave is approaching, the peak that matches the dip that's pulling the ocean back behind us. I turn away, concentrate on putting one foot in front of the other. Focus on the moment, that's the advice Ryuichi himself had written in his book, *Life on the Run*, a combination autobiography and instruction manual. I've read it at least a dozen times. I'm always amazed by how he could talk about his life with such candour, especially about his childhood, about the loss of his family and his first run. *The* first run.

"There," Belinda says, pointing back, excitement making her voice tremble a little. "Here it comes."

I look back over my shoulder again and look at the ocean. Yes, it's definitely there, cresting the waves. My stomach lurches at the sight of it, even though I'd already seen it in news reports as helicopters followed its path through the shallower waters a few days earlier. It's faint and blurred, seen through a curtain of distant rain, but it's there alright. Somehow the sight of it makes it abruptly real, makes everything real. My heart pounds so hard it hurts, and the breath is sucked out of me like I've been sucker-punched in the stomach.

They say that everything looks smaller on television, somehow, even with other objects to offer some helpful perspective. I've never really paid much attention to that until now. The thing is *huge*, rising from the waters, still only visible from its massive shoulders up. Even through the distant rains offshore, I can see the long, curved spines that run along the length of its head, from its snout up its face and beyond, looking incongruously like a mohawk haircut. Its eyes are shaded by a heavy brow, but I can make out a faint red glow there, like a campfire deep in a cave. Its mouth is closed for the moment, a fact for which I'm profoundly grateful. Its neck is almost nonexistent, its head joining straight up to a barrel chest, only a little of which is visible yet. Its skin is rough, covered with oddly shaped scales that fit together like a three-dimensional jigsaw puzzle. Each one must be the size of a car, and I can already see dozens, hundreds of them. At the point where it emerges from the sea, the water is bubbling and roiling like an overexcited jacuzzi. It must be doing forty, fifty nautical miles an hour, pushing up massive amounts of water as it goes. Pushing it towards us.

I'm frozen in my tracks, a pillar of salt in the shape of a man who foolishly looked back.

Belinda's gloved hand touches my shoulder. "C'mon!" she hisses, and I'm restored to life in a heartbeat, my limbs suddenly obeying my commands again. I turn away from the ocean once more, concentrate on moving. Belinda and Ryuichi are still walking calmly, and I attempt to do the same. *Dead man walking*, I find myself thinking, imagining myself on death row in prison, heading for my own execution. But it's not that at all. Not dead man walking. Live man running.

I watch Ryuichi's back, remembering the story in his book about his experience in Nagasaki. It was a matter of days after America had dropped the second atomic bomb on the city, setting a tiny sun ablaze over its streets, levelling it in a matter of moments. Some of his family had lived there, an uncle and aunt, and his parents had gone looking for them amongst the rubble, blissfully ignorant of the dangers of radiation. They'd brought their child with them, only three years old, holding his hand tightly and trying not to let him see the twisted figures amongst the debris, arms curled by the intense heat, fists raised. The pugilist stance, it was called, a classic indicator of death by burning. Ryuichi had broken free of his parents and went to play, the ruined landscape a gigantic playground in his three-year-old eyes.

Then it had appeared, the first one seen in modern history. Until that day, we'd believed them to be legends, dragons and wyrms of myth. Figments of superstitious imaginations, primitive fears manifesting in exaggerated tales of giants beasts. We'd been comfortable in our modern, clinical, rational world. Safe from monsters.

Until that day, when the first *daikaiju* appeared, a hundred metres tall, crashing through what was left of Nagasaki, flattening what remained. It resembled a gigantic lizard raised on its hind legs, though its face was more ape-like in shape, and it had jagged plates lining its back like a stegosaurus. Later on, they would give it a name that became legend, a combination of the Japanese words for "gorilla" and "whale", in an effort to describe something that was, in essence, indescribable. But on that day, in Nagasaki, nobody thought about what it was, or what to call it. They were too busy. Busy running. Busy dying.

Ryuichi saw his parents crushed beneath one enormous foot, mercifully vanishing into its shadow an instant before the impact. It was headed towards him, as unmindful of the child as we are of the insects we crush as we walk here and there. Moving with deceptive slowness, each step like walking through water, but crossing twenty or thirty metres each time. It approached like an avalanche, like a tidal wave.

The boy turned and ran.

We step off the grassed area, the hard leather soles of my boots clumping on the rough black bitumen. The road here is uneven and crude, but better than many of the roads we'd driven on earlier in the day to get here. One had been barely more than gravel, a long stretch of straight but hilly road, blocked off at one end with a gate that probably would have been manned any other day. Today it had been deserted, and we'd opened the gate ourselves, granted ourselves access.

On this day, the island of Mauritius virtually belongs to us. At least for the moment. But in a few minutes, I suspect that ownership will be transferred to the gargantuan creature ploughing towards us through the Pacific. Another glimpse over my shoulder reveals more details, as it grows nearer; its shoulders are clear of the waters now, and instead of arms there are maybe half a dozen enormous tentacles on each side, whipping around in slow motion. They must be as long as the creature is high, at least a hundred metres, possibly more. And it continues to rise from the sea, as it pushes a wall of water in our direction. I hope Ryuichi has calculated this correctly; otherwise our run could be over before it's even begun.

After the first appearance of the *daikaiju* at Nagasaki, encounters grew more and more common. At first only one would appear at a time, then two or three, coming together as if drawn to one another, battling amongst the cities and towns of men. The devastation was staggering; thousands killed in a matter of minutes, then they would retreat once more, into the mountains and valleys, oceans and lakes, and not be seen again. Expeditions were sent after them, armed with everything from prayers to nukes, but there was no trace of them. They appeared when they chose, and disappeared just as readily. And on those occasions when we had the chance to organise a military response while they were still there, we found that weapons had little or no effect on them, apart from enraging them even further. Slowly but surely, mankind began to adapt: setting up early detection systems, preparing evacuation plans and drills, organising shelters. Humans are pretty flexible, really. We just learned to run. Mostly away, but not entirely. To begin with, a few film studios realised the amazing potential in these giant monsters, and risked life and limb to capture their rampages on celluloid. These *daikaiju* films found instant popularity in their home country of Japan, and over the decades they gained a cult following overseas as well. It was the thrill of the danger, without the actual danger accompanying it.

But for some, that wasn't enough. Some wanted the real thing.

We walk a little while longer, passing a few touristy shops on either side of us, until we reach an intersection. Here the road joins a larger road, on one corner of which is a decent-sized grocery store, not dissimilar to the ones back home, apart from the unfamiliar name, "Cora". Beyond this road, the area becomes more residential, ramshackle houses mingling with newer tourist villas. A lot of the older buildings look like they've been added to repeatedly over the years, mixing styles and materials, never quite finished. I read once that the native Mauritians often extended their houses piecemeal as the money was available, resulting in an architectural style I'd categorise as "hodgepodge". Here, at this intersection, Ryuichi stops.

He nods. "This will do." He looks back over his shoulder, and I do the same. The film crew has vanished, presumably retreating to a safe distance, safer than ours at any rate. All I can see is the beach, and the ocean, and the monster. It's almost clear of the water now, its hindquarters splitting into four enormous legs, like roman columns covered in barnacles, and I realise that it looks a little like a centaur at this point. I can hear its passage, a dull roar like an airplane heard from a distance, and something else below that—a deep hum that I can't identify. The wind is picking up, but I don't think it's the cyclone yet, just the rush of air that the creature is pushing in front of itself.

Then the wave at its feet hits the beach and explodes, spraying water high into the air, and for a moment I can't see it anymore. My heart feels like it's trying to smash its way through my ribs, as the deep guttural crashing of water fills my ears. I'm certain we're going to be engulfed, swept away by the agitated sea, crushed against the rough walls of some Mauritian house before getting sucked back across the grass and sand and towed out to sea, pulled underwater to a tropical ocean grave. I can see it in my mind, clear as a photograph, clear as a premonition.

It doesn't happen, of course. The wave gurgles across the grassed area, foaming like detergent, and then washes weakly around our feet. It barely passes our ankles. I look over at Belinda, recognise a hint of the same fear that I'd just experienced, though she covers it up with a thin, tight smile. Ryuichi, on the other hand, looks as relaxed as a yogi.

"Get ready," he murmurs.

Then there is the first tremor, a minor earthquake, and I know without looking that the creature has reached the land. The sand on the beach is muffling its massive footfalls for the moment, but that won't last long. Soon it will hit solid earth, not that far behind us. Soon we'll start to run. My first run. I've dreamt of this almost my entire life, and now that it's actually happening, I'm having trouble believing it's real.

The road beneath my feet lurches, almost tipping me over, and I yelp once, surprised. It's real alright. "Be ready!" Ryuichi calls, bending his knees and touching his spread fingers against the rough bitumen. I do likewise, though it's harder to bend in these damn leather pants. I'm starting to think Ryuichi had the right idea. After all, if something goes wrong, I might as well be naked for all the protection these leathers will offer me. I close my eyes, feeling the vibrations in the street beneath me, trying to see what is happening in my mind. See the centaurine behemoth galloping towards me, each step covering hundreds of metres, each footstep crashing into the ground, sending plumes of dust into the air, and pushing dirt forward, forward, until ...

"Now!" Ryuichi cries, but I'm already moving, as the ground beneath me rises sharply. It feels like being in an elevator, my weight suddenly increasing. I spring up and begin to run.

We all run, one way or another.

Ryuichi was the first. In his late teens, a little younger than I am, he travelled to the site of a *daikaiju* encounter. It was an enormous pig, but with a mane like a lion and tusks the size of city buses, and it was ravaging a small city in the south of Japan. He sought it out, while everyone else was fleeing. He remembered the sensations as a small child, his experiences then, and somewhere inside those terrifying memories he found something wonderful. Watching footage of subsequent monster attacks over the years that followed, he barely saw the creatures themselves, majestic and huge, towering above the buildings like gods. No, what he saw was the ground that supported them, and what it did beneath their weight, their power. How it reacted. How it *flowed*.

That day, that young man did the unthinkable, the unbelievable. And since then, a small group of crazed enthusiasts have followed, quite literally, in his footsteps, seeking adventure or adrenaline or even some kind of enlightenment at the pounding feet of these monsters. Most everyone else ran away from them, and the maniacal film crews ran to them. But we don't run away, or run to.

We run *with* them.

This is the most bizarre feeling I've ever experienced, a surreal dislocation. It's a little like riding on an escalator, being pushed upwards and forwards, but the speed of the journey varies quite wildly. It's considerably less smooth than surfing, but the sensation isn't completely dissimilar to that nonetheless. As I run, the road begins to fracture and break beneath my feet, pulling off in different directions. I don't have time to think; I step hurriedly from the chunk of bitumen I'm riding onto another in front of me, then another, each one falling by the wayside as I pass it. Somewhere behind me, I can hear the creature, its breath hot and wet on the back of my neck like a tropical breeze. Droplets of water splatter on my shoulders, and I hope it's the cyclone catching up with us, rather than monster slobber. That would be kind of disgusting.

I catch sight of Belinda on my left. She's running like Hermes himself, winged heels masked by knee-high leather boots. I'm momentarily hypnotised by the fluidity of her run, moving from platelet to platelet like a gymnast, never pausing, never faltering. Never stopping. When you're running, as the old saying goes, he who hesitates is lost. I can't see Ryuichi; I don't know whether he's behind or in front of us. I hope he's okay.

The piece of road I'm riding lurches suddenly to one side, and my balance begins to falter. A burst of cold fear splashes up my back, and I react without thinking, quickly shifting my weight and leaping forward, leaving the crumbling bitumen behind me. I hear it collapse, crashing into a thousand pieces of rubble, and I realise how close I was to joining it. I have to concentrate, stay focused. Live man running, or dead man falling. It's up to me and God to decide which one I am. And the monster, of course.

To my right, I can see the town begin to fade, or what's left of it at any rate. Flic en Flac has been shaken, flipped upwards on a wave of rock, and then dropped back down in its wake. What remains looks more like a rubbish dump than a seaside tourist town, wreckage and debris spread surprisingly evenly across the ground. Beyond the town, we begin to enter more rural surroundings, huge expanses of sugarcane stretching for miles ahead of us. I hope that the creature sticks to the roads, where the solid ground will help us keep our footing, stay ahead of it, like riding a stormfront. But I know I can't rely on that. I've seen footage of runners getting caught in a tidal wave of soft earth, feet stuck in the sucking mud, dragging like ploughs, until they're finally pulled beneath the monster's feet and crushed into the dirt, just messy smears left in its wake. This is an extreme sport, often a death sport. But I feel I have to do it anyway, despite the risks. After all, you're never as alive as when you're close to death.

The rock I'm running on begins to list to one side, the left, and I realise that the creature is turning slightly. I don't need to see it to know this; I can picture the shockwave of earth, imagine its alignment. I know that the front of the wave will always be angled away from the direction it's moving, whilst it veers off to the sides the further around you go. I'm still travelling forward, but I'm leaning left, so my position on the wave is too far to the left of the *daikaiju*'s path. I'll have to sidestep in order to continue running. Of course, I could always allow myself to slip off the wave on this side, ride the ever-decreasing ripples of rock back down to ground level, and end the run here and now. It's a tricky manoeuvre, but hardly impossible.

Ah, the hell with that. I didn't wait this long and come this far to wimp out now.

I start stepping across, my legs pumping, my breath burning my lungs. I'm starting to tire, I have to admit, and it's only been a matter of minutes. Running is incredibly demanding both physically and mentally, and it's starting to take its toll. I ignore the fatigue though, ignore the pain, and continue to run, cutting across the creature's path. This is where it could go horribly wrong; a miscalculation, a misstep, and I could end up beneath the feet of the beast, monster toe-jam. I can see it to my right now, from the corner of my eye, its breath steaming in the air around its maw, tentacles flailing like an underwater anemone. Its legs swinging back and forth, so slowly, so deadly. The ground is rising higher and higher beneath my feet the closer I get to it. Alarm bells start to ring in my head.

Turn.

Turn.

Turn!

I turn left and redouble my efforts, trying to get some distance between myself and the monster. My legs are steel springs, my arms pistons in a perfect engine, my brain a supercomputer. I focus utterly on what's in front of me, striding from rock to rock. I am a legend, a superman, a godling. Invulnerable. Invincible.

A noise to my left catches my attention. I glance across and see Belinda stumble, crying out as she rolls from her platform, head-sized chunks of rock and soil tumbling with her as she vanishes, her yelps of pain cut off suddenly. I watch the spot for a moment longer, horrified. Frozen.

I'm just a man. Barely more than a boy. Flesh and blood, same as Belinda. Less. Vulnerable.

I'm going to die here.

"Go!" a voice behind me screams, and without thinking I obey. My legs work independently, pushing me forward, and after a few stumbling staccato seconds I find my rhythm again. The ground underneath my feet is softening, long broken stalks of sugarcane whipping past me like slalom flags, and I have to dodge left and right to avoid being hit in the face. But it's still solid enough to support my weight, thank heaven.

"Thought we lost you for a second there," the voice calls out again, and I glance to my right. Ryuichi is there, further back, closer to the creature, but running almost casually, not a worry in the world. I can't understand his attitude to the monster at his heels, despite reading his memoirs. If my family had been killed by a monster, I'd hate them, fear them, keep the hell away from them. Instead, Ryuichi seeks them out, not to try to hurt or kill them, but to share an experience with them. To run with them. It makes no sense to me.

"Belinda?" I call back to him, legs moving automatically, boots slapping the mud beneath them fast and loud enough to sound like a drum beat, or a heart beat. Life signs.

He nods in an exaggerated fashion, almost theatrically. "She'll be fine," he yells, barely audible over the rumble and roar of the beast's rough progress.

I relax a little, relieved both for her and for myself by proxy. I've seen videos of runners doing what she'd done; it's similar to a surfer's ignominious exit from a particularly large wave, painful and dangerous but not often fatal. She'll be battered and bruised, perhaps even a little broken, but she'll live. I hope that's the truth, at any rate. We believe what we need to believe, in order to keep going.

The wind whistles through my buzz-cut hair, my eyes watering a little. I'm keeping a close eye on the ground just in front of my feet now, stepping left and right, back and forward, depending on where the heaving earth is carrying me. And always I'm acutely aware of the massive presence behind me driving me on, and the smaller one to my side sharing the experience. I wonder for the thousandth time why Ryuichi does this. In his book, he spoke of his reasons, but they were masked by rhetorical questions, so there were no easy answers. The one that's always puzzled me was simple—six ordinary words—but the old Japanese man seemed to find something more in them, a philosophy that I didn't understand.

His question was, *Why are there no daikaiju fossils?*

Ryuichi is waving to me, grinning. I wave back with a smile. He continues to wave, more animatedly than before, and with sudden dread I realise that he's not smiling, he's grimacing. And he's not waving, he's gesturing. Gesturing ahead at something. I raise my eyes from the undulating soil at my feet, knowing it is dangerous to do so, but suspecting that it would be even more dangerous not to.

I'm right. Worse luck.

We're headed directly for a mountain. Mauritian mountains aren't like the gentle slopes back home, where you can often barely notice the incline as you climb one. No, they are acute lumps of stone, easily taller than they are wide, jutting defiantly at the sky. The one in front of us looks suspiciously like a pudgy finger carved in rock, covered by a thick blanket of dark green vegetation. It must be four or five hundred metres high, dwarfing even the behemoth at our heels. For a moment I'm caught in its majesty, its beauty, its grandeur. Then I snap out of it, and see it for what it really is.

A wall. A huge stone wall. And we're hurtling towards it.

I look left and right, hoping for a way off the earthwave before we hit, but both Ryuichi and I have been too skilful in our placement; we're right at the tip of the arrowhead, which is aimed directly for the centre of the mountain. Even if we skipped to the sides, we'd still be smashed against it. I look to Ryuichi for some kind of comfort, some hope, but his posture doesn't offer much of either. He's almost back-pedalling, as close to panic as I've ever seen him, in all the years of watching the movies of him running. Between us, we've had a deadly combination of inexperience and overconfidence. *He who hesitates is lost*, they say, but they also say *look before you leap*. And *pride cometh before the fall*.

I look back over my shoulder, fear falling away from me as if caught in the slipstream. The creature continues to advance, not slowing at all, perhaps not even noticing the mountain. I still can't see its eyes, just the dull red glow from beneath its brow, but I suspect that even if I could, I'd see nothing there, no intelligence, no will. Looking at it this close, it's somehow less monstrous, less bestial than from afar, or on a television screen for that matter, stripped of dramatic music and editing.

... no fossils ...

Turning back, I see Ryuichi signaling me again. I'm not certain what he's trying to tell me, so rather than attempting to interpret his motions, I pay attention to his actions. He's allowing himself to fall back, closer to the creature, and this time he appears to be doing it on purpose. I blink a few times, trying to both clear my eyes of tears and to comprehend what he's doing.

Then the penny drops. The closer we are to the creature's feet, the more force will be behind us when it hits the mountain. Too far forward and we'll be dashed against the rock. Too far back and we'll be caught between it and the monster. But if we get it just right ...

Goldilocks never played for such high stakes.

I slow the pace of my run, feeling the earth under my boots start to jerk and wobble more violently as I do so. We're closer to this moving epicentre now, and the Brownian motion of the ground is become more pronounced and chaotic.

I just hope we have time before ...

The outskirts of the wave ahead of us crash into the mountain, sending a wall of dirt into the sky. Like a wave breaking on rocks, the soil is scattered into a million directions, raining down on us in large sodden clumps. I have to dodge desperately in order to keep my footing on the ground, which is starting to tilt upwards, rising ominously. I look over at Ryuichi one last time. He gives me a thumbs up signal. I return it, though I wish I were as confident as he is. I hear the monster behind us bellow, just once, as if thwarted by this gigantic rocky finger in its way. I can sympathise.

Then we hit, and I'm flying.

At first the ground is still beneath my feet, pressing them hard as it accelerates into the sky carrying me along with it, rising on a column of soil and sugarcane. Then it falls away, and I'm running in thin air. The gap between me and my footing widens, ten metres, twenty, fifty. In front of me, the vegetation cloaking the mountain speeds past my eyes. It's impossible to judge how close I am to it. Too close, I'd wager. Any moment now, it'll slap me hard in the face, and then I'll be scraped along it like an insect hitting a sloped windscreen, leaving a long smear behind me as I'm sanded into oblivion on the rough shrubs.

Suddenly, the mountain is gone, and all I can see is grey cloudy sky, and distant vistas of fields and roads below me. I realise I was right about how useless my leathers really are.

My stomach turns over, and I realise I've stopped ascending, gravity finally taking a firm grip on my ankles. And slowly, almost reluctantly, I begin to free fall. I don't even think to scream; the sensation is both exhilarating and terrifying, and between the two emotions I'm struck completely dumb. My muscles have gone dead, arms and legs flapping in the wind like a paper doll's. I look down and see the mountain again, the finger pointing up at me. Now it doesn't look defiant. It looks accusing. *You*, it's saying, *you human, you proud, stupid human. This is what happens. Icarus flies too high, Pandora opens the box. Now reap what you have sown.*

Then there's an impact, a tumbling, and everything goes green, then grey, then black.

I'm not certain how long I'm out for. It can't be long, maybe a few seconds. Still, for a short time I'm floating in the dark, warm and safe and numb. It's bliss. Then there's water splashing on my face, and I come to. I'm sprawled in the bushes on my back, bent in an uncomfortable position, a warm barrage of huge raindrops splattering on my forehead and cheeks, running into my nose and mouth, choking me a little. I try to sit up, but a sharp pain in my back persuades me to stay put for the moment. Instead, I raise my head and look down myself.

It's nowhere near as bad as it could have been, I have to admit. My leathers are looking pretty torn and tattered, and there's a reasonable amount of blood coming from a dozen or so minor wounds that I can make out, but I seem to be pretty intact, no obviously broken bones. I turn my head painfully to the side, and see that the shrubs I've landed on cushioned my fall quite effectively, still green and springy despite the sunless skies. All in all, it could have gone much worse for me. I'm alive.

"Ryuichi," I croak, then again, louder this time. "Ryuichi?"

There's no answer. I try to sit up again, this time ignoring the sharp recommendations of my bruised coccyx, and manage to reach a sitting position without fainting, though my head is spinning like the clouds above me. They catch my eye for a moment, and I look upwards. We're in the midst of the cyclone now, though I've landed in a shallow depression in the peak of the mountain so I'm shielded from the worst of the winds. But over my head, I can see Katrina venting her fury, the clouds streaming in enormous circles across the sky. It looks like we're almost in the storm's eye.

"Ryuichi?" I call again, and look around carefully for the old Japanese man, my idol, my hero, my teacher *in absentia*.

I see him, maybe ten or fifteen metres away from my position. He's landed in the vegetation as well, though he landed face down. Unfortunately, the tree hasn't saved him; it's bare of leaves, a jagged lightning bolt of wood standing upright on the top of the mountain. He isn't moving, and I know he never will again, not of his own volition. The branch he's impaled on, through the chest and out of his back, is a darker shade than the rest of the tree, and I realise it's Ryuichi's blood staining it almost black. Blood also streams from the old man's mouth, pooling on the ground beneath him. He has that posture, that near-indefinable body language that speaks of death; I've seen pictures of corpses, and of unconscious people, and there's something about the dead that silently screams out, tells you that the person, perhaps the soul if it exists, is no longer present. Something has departed.

Ryuichi's life has ended, his long and tumultuous life. I feel tears begin to burn the corners of my eyes, but I blink them away, determined not to cry. This was exactly how he always said he wanted to die, in books and interviews. You really are never as alive as when you're close to death. And before he died, he truly lived.

I feel a burst of hot, moist air against my back, through the rips and tears in my leathers, and I turn my head and look up. And up. And up.

I almost forgot about the *daikaiju*. How strange is that?

I'm not afraid, not anymore. If I die here, then this is where I die. I'll be proud to share a grave with the grand master. But somehow I don't think that's going to happen; the monster isn't even looking in my direction. It's raised up, its tentacles stretched to the skies, like a footballer about to take a mark, or an evangelist beseeching the Almighty. And it's so *still*—just a slight waving of its serpentine arms in the gale force winds that must be whipping around them. It's as if it's waiting for something. I look up as well, follow its gaze.

And then I see it. Right above the mountain, hovering like a halo. At the centre of the storm, the point around which the angry grey clouds are rotating, I can see it, just barely through the rain that's pouring into my face.

The eye of the cyclone. It's the purest blue I've ever seen.

A tiny hole in the clouds has formed there, opened up by the tremendous forces unleashed by the storm. It's fragile, and fleeting, but it's there. Then the eye blinks, once, twice, then closes for good. I'm blinking back tears and raindrops, wiping my own eyes desperately, hoping to catch sight of it again. But it's gone. It takes me a while to accept this. Once I do, I lower my eyes again.

The creature is gone as well.

I clamber to my feet, my knees trembling violently under my own weight. I stagger to the edge of the mountain, where the *daikaiju* had been just moments before, and look over, but there's no sign of it, apart from the enormous trail of destruction it has left in its wake. I see that now, from high above, and find it hard to believe that I'd been riding that wave. Running with the monster.

Why are there no monster fossils? There must be a thousand answers to that one, from biodegradable skeletons to ancient animals predating the fossil record. But standing here on shaky legs, hundreds of metres above the torn fields, I can only think of one that seems plausible to me, and I suspect it's what Ryuichi believed as well.

These creatures, these *daikaiju*, leave no fossils because they're not animals, not even alive as such. They're forces of nature, like the cyclone that still roars around me, or an avalanche that swallows a dozen daring skiers whole. Ryuichi couldn't hate the monster for killing his parents, any more than he could hate a flood or a drought. Some people might, but not him. All he could do was try to understand it, get close to it. Run with it.

Down below, picking its way through the torn earth, I can see a figure limping, tiny as an insect. I can make out black clothing and short hair. It's Belinda, making her way painfully towards me. Behind her, driving up in the distance in some kind of open-topped four-wheel drive, comes the film crew, cameras still pointed my way despite the lack of a *kaiju* to film, *dai* or otherwise. Belinda waves to me, and I wave back tiredly, leaning on the rocks on the edge of the mountain, ignoring the wind and rain. We'll do this again, her and I, and perhaps others will join us, new blood to replace the old that's been spilled.

I smile at this thought, finally understanding Ryuichi's attitude, his serenity. I don't know if I'll ever be as sanguine as he was, but at least I'm on the path now. To be a part of something like this, something so magnificent, that was enough, and it will continue to be enough.

We all run, one way or another.

THE TRANSFORMER OF WORLDS

STEPHEN MARK RAINEY

"So, Mr Black, which world is this?" Ryuhebi asked, his segmented underside tightening nervously around my left arm. "Doesn't look like any place I've ever been."

"I don't know," I said, gazing curiously at the uniformly purple sky, the quicksilver sun hovering above the eastern horizon, the coal-black lake at the base of a rocky decline, and the sea of gray-green, metallic-looking trees that marched away to the west. "I don't think I've ever been here either. But *he* has. Looky there."

The crystal sculpture sprouted from a boulder-strewn hillside like a twisted pillar of ice, its style unmistakably Luserke's. Upon closer inspection, I fancied that the sparkling, thirty-foot-tall construct resembled a monstrous strand of DNA, its double-helix-shaped trunk bristling with thorn-like barbs and creeping tendrils. It was an evil-looking thing, commensurate with its purpose. As I slowly approached it, I detected an erratic, warbling hum, disturbingly human in tone, like a chorus of mad Buddhist monks whose tongues had been cut out. This meant it was active and that danger almost certainly lurked nearby.

I started towards it, but Ryuhebi squeezed my arm and said, "I'll check it out. It's more likely to defend itself against something your size than mine."

Ryuhebi slipped to the ground, faded, and slithered towards the sculpture, leaving only shallow, S-shaped grooves in the charcoal-like soil as evidence of his passing. For a sometimes-invisible, frequently cranky, and positively outspoken Japanese coral snake, Ryuhebi could exhibit remarkably selfless behaviour. I had first encountered him in a dreamworld called Daigoramu, where he had accosted me and demanded that I pay a tribute of two delectable baby Chiko rats before he would allow me to pass unbitten. The catch, of course, was that Chiko rats did not exist in Daigoramu. However, being anything but the average, half-disoriented, neophyte dream explorer he undoubtedly expected, I knew of a kingdom or two where such creatures thrived and managed to procure a pair in relatively short order. Ryuhebi, impressed almost beyond words with my offering, then and there appointed himself my inseparable traveling companion. It was a serendipitous meeting, for he and I shared similar objectives; he no more desired to see his world devastated by Ivan Luserke than

I did mine.

Few who had met him or even glimpsed his work would deny that Luserke was a profoundly gifted artist; far fewer, though, would recognise him as one of the most dangerous men ever to walk the earth. But they knew of him in Kadath, where he wove his dreams into fantastic constructs of clay, stone, glass, or pigment, the results of which, possessed of their own malignant intelligence, became the brutal masters of all in their domains. So it was in Cathuria, and in Ulthar, and on the far island of Oriab, and in all the lands that lay at the bottom of the 700 stairs to the realms of deepest slumber.

The artist did not create the horrors to which he gave shape; they had long existed in distant, shadowy dimensions, beyond the conception of even the most horrifically inspired lunatic mind. No, Luserke was merely a medium, a craftsman who provided a means for the incorporeal to assume shape. His brain, transformed beyond all human limitations by his not-infrequent communing with these horrors, became the architect of gateways, his works the portals by which they passed from one space to another, leaving terror, destruction, and despair in their wakes. These eldritch powers were the very dross of creation, hurled in the beginning to inescapable corners of the universe, seething and howling in insane fury, endlessly seeking to destroy the barriers that contained them.

In dreams, certain sensitive individuals could sometimes perceive their existence—and some unfortunate souls not only became aware of them but connected with them, like receivers tuned to some esoteric radio broadcast. Inevitably, the dreamers' madness resulted, their minds expanded but permanently tainted by the powers they both revered and dreaded. And Ivan Luserke, whose twisted meditations drove him to build artistic bridges to those chaotic spheres, used his talents to offer the dross of creation a foothold into any world that caught his fancy.

Ryuhebi had encountered the artist himself on more than one occasion, but had never managed to get close enough to deliver the fatal bite. Luserke's unique ability to traverse astral barriers in the blink of an eye was legendary, and his omnipresent retinue included at least two drokwights who could see Ryuhebi even when he was camouflaged; in a nutshell, barring a successful surprise attack, the artist was virtually untouchable.

"Something's forming in the west, Mr Black," came Ryuhebi's voice. After nearly ten years, he still called me "Mr Black," rather than "Gregory" or even "Greg." His voice sounded more or less like a human male tenor with a fine grasp of English, sans any trace of difficulty with *S*s and *L*s, despite his forked tongue. "If you can't destroy this priceless *objet* in about the next thirty seconds, we might as well hang it up."

I took a quick inventory of my armaments, already knowing I possessed nothing that could bring down the sculpture in time to stop whatever it was summoning. The .45 Colt was useless, and neither grenades nor plastique would detonate in these remote dreamworlds. As fragile as the helix-thing appeared, one could not simply knock it over; well, maybe with a bulldozer, but I didn't see a handy one lying about just then. I might mention here that things had not always been so difficult; in the early days, I had shattered many of Luserke's best-laid plans with a ballpeen hammer. However, over the years, his placement of protective force-fields had grown more sophisticated, his concealment of key pieces ever more devious.

"It's not looking good," I said. "I'm afraid this may have been a wasted trip."

"Maybe not," Ryuhebi said. "We've learned at least this much—the things he's attempting to call down are more powerful than ever before. This is the most intense work of his I've ever tasted."

"I feel so much better."

A new, serpentine trail appeared in the dark earth, heading my way, and a moment later, Ryuhebi materialised at my feet and slithered up my left leg. He had just settled back in his customary place around my wrist when a heavy *boom* shook the ground, a shadow fell over the land, and a foul-smelling wind began to rush in from the west, nearly making me gag. The crystal sculpture appeared to waver, as if surrounded by a heat haze, and then the very air began to boil. Bubbles erupted from its tendril tips, dancing like enraged dervishes before swelling and bursting, releasing thick clouds of sulfurous gas. Then, at the western horizon, beyond the onyx lake, a portion of the sky fell away, and from the resulting black chasm, something gigantic emerged: a hulking, lumbering silhouette that at first resembled a giant, horned man wrapped in a leathery cloak. But then the cloak unfurled and became a pair of mammoth bat wings, hundreds of feet across, the beating of which made a sound like a tornado. Its golden eyes ignited like a pair of blazing lamps and began to rove to and fro as the beast surveyed its new environs.

In all my travels, a more malevolent-looking thing I had never seen.

"That, if I'm not mistaken, is Pachacutec," Ryuhebi said with obvious distaste. "Ghastly fellow."

"Pachacutec?"

"On your world, it's an Incan name that means *Transformer of Worlds*. The thing's actual name cannot be pronounced by your tongue or mine."

The behemoth took a thundering step forward, into the illumination of the silver sun. I now saw that its head resembled a crocodile's, with a pair of bony, goat-like horns above its brows, and a sharp, curving spike atop its tapered snout. Its chest and belly were segmented, almost like Ryuhebi's, but its scales glittered like metal, refracting the purple sky into rainbow hues that shimmered over its body. Its upper limbs resembled a muscular man's arms but ended in birdlike talons, which appeared capable of both grasping and shredding. Behind it whipped a lithe, serpentine tail, easily as long as the body was tall—some 200 feet or more, if I had to guess.

And though it must have been over a mile away, the creature turned to regard us as if it knew exactly where to look—or so I thought, until I realised its actual focus was Luserke's sculpture; regardless, the end result was the same. It dropped its jaw and bellowed, its voice a legion of foghorns, and then it began to move. With every step of its elephantine legs, the ground shuddered, threatening to collapse beneath my feet. Nearly swooning, I took a faltering step back, overcome by the sheer majesty of this gigantic, alien intruder.

"Consider waking up soon," Ryuhebi said. "In fact, *now* couldn't hurt. Catch you next go-round. You know where to find me."

The pressure around my wrist subsided, and the coiled snake vanished with a little *pop,* as air rushed to fill the void he had left.

I quickly willed myself to return to consciousness, which ordinarily posed little problem—though too hasty an emergence could result in a case of astral whiplash (usually manifesting itself as a brief but splitting headache). The customary vertigo and sense of dislocation that occurs just before the transition came over me, but control of my body seemed to be slipping. My eyes refused to turn from those distant blazing embers; I couldn't even close them for longer than it took to blink.

Suddenly, the far-off eyes began to rise higher and higher; the beast had left the ground and was now gliding over the surface of the black lake, its wings spread wide but stationary, its mammoth body supported by some non-aerodynamic force—probably an energy field generated by Luserke's sculpture. There was no time to ponder the phenomenon; I had thirty seconds at most to shatter the hypnosis or meet a most ignoble end.

As I watched, the water began to swirl, forming a roaring whirlpool beneath the monster, and a dark, spreading bruise marred the violet canopy directly above it. The metallic-looking trees on the banks began to bend away from the airborne horror, and I realised that it was somehow warping the space around it—to what end I really didn't care to guess. That it portended a hastening of my own demise I had no doubt; so, digging deep into my last reserves, I channeled all my energy to my eyes in a desperate attempt to sever the connection I had unwittingly opened between us. Astral whiplash or not, I had to—

"Greg?"

The room was dark, though a few droplets of city light trickled through the slits in the Venetian blinds. Sure enough, a white-hot spike had driven itself into my forehead, just above my eyes, but after the nightmare I had just escaped, the pain was a small price to pay. Turning my head stiffly, I saw Cayce standing next to the bed, her emerald eyes alight with concern.

"What happened? Where were you?"

"Nowhere familiar. Luserke had been there, though. Unfortunately, I was too late to do anything about his handiwork. It had already opened the way for ... something."

"Are you going back?"

"Now that it's loose, there's little point."

"You look a fright. It must have been a bad one."

"Very," I said. "Ryuhebi called it 'Pachacutec'. I shall have to look it up. What time is it, anyway?"

"Almost five."

"Thanks for watching over me."

"Happy to do it." Cayce's little smile brightened the room more than the Gold Coast lights outside the window, and I sighed somewhat wistfully. I had threatened to propose to her at least 365 times during the past year, but something always held me back—probably the knowledge that my little avocation was singularly hazardous, and while she understood the reasons for my endeavours, she lacked the ability to participate in them as she believed she desired.

I had mastered traveling to the dreamworlds when I was very young, initially via the "traditional" means of descending the 700 stairs after entering sleep, then by the more direct method of rending veils, which allowed an experienced dreamer to move from place to place by sheer force of will. This particular shortcut, however, exposed the dream explorer to the unique danger of becoming entangled in what might be termed "astral perdition"; if he strayed into the wrong realm, or literally fell *between* them, he might end up lost forever, his unconscious physical body doomed to eventual failure.

My advanced ability resulted directly from being the son of an inhabitant of the dreamworlds; my mother's spirit had come from an astral kingdom called Janduro. She had little love for the physical earth, but she cared deeply for my father, an ordinary man of the waking world who also enjoyed the ability to wander in the shadowlands. (In his youth, he had been tutored by various dream sages, including the renowned Randolph Carter.) Sadly, Dad had been lost when I was a teenager. His earthly body had died after years in a coma, and none of the explorers I knew had ever found a trace of his spirit, even in the most obscure of the attainable provinces.

His death had not been an accident. He died because he befriended the wrong man.

Like Luserke, Dad was an artist, and he had naturally gravitated to someone who ostensibly drew inspiration from the scenes of his own out-of-body sojourns. Outwardly, Luserke appeared to be anything but dangerous, and his instructive techniques were sound. However, his actual intention, as I eventually learned, was to use my father to get to my mother and initiate her into his perverse little cabal, whose aim was nothing less than releasing the powers of chaos. When Dad learned the truth about his mentor, he immediately sought to expose and then kill Luserke; sadly, though, this had been his undoing. Grieving, and beyond all hope of ever finding him again, Mom had returned to Janduro, never to return. Her mortal remains lay beside Dad's in Lakeview Cemetery in Wrigleyville.

I had followed my father in my choice of profession. But unlike Dad, I had no illusions regarding Luserke's nature. I hoped to succeed where he had failed, but even I had to admit that his murderer held too many high cards for my comfort.

An hour or so remained until dawn, but Cayce went to the kitchen and started a pot of coffee rather than catch a few winks to make up for her long night watching over me. As soon as it was ready, I poured myself a super-sized mug and threw back a handful of *ibuprofen* to help the whiplash; thankfully, the pain had already receded to a dull throb behind my right eye. I had downed half the mug when the phone rang. It was too odd an hour for a mundane caller, so I felt a little rush of anxiety when I picked up the receiver.

"Good morning, Greg," came a thin, rather reedy voice through a weird, warbling hiss.

"Hello, Ivan."

"What did you think of Pachacutec?"

"Ghastly thing."

"Quite. I'm calling to invite you to join me for drinks this evening. I can safely say it would be in your best interest to accept."

"So, you're in town?"

"For a very brief time."

I barely suppressed a shudder, for I knew what that meant. "Where?"

"Studio Zeta. You know it."

"Yes."

"Seven o' clock sharp. Don't be late."

The line went dead, and I stood dumbly holding the receiver for a minute. I had no idea where he had called from, but it certainly wasn't a local area code. His ability to transmit his words, even his thoughts, from distant dreamlands still mystified me. I was years behind him in innovation, if fairly matched in raw talent. I sometimes wondered why he hadn't already killed me; my guess was that he actually felt guilty about murdering my father. Luserke was a man of strange passions and shifting moods, and although warped by powers beyond imagination, he was still human. At his core, I believe he was simply lonely.

The phone call was his way of either getting me where he wanted me or warning me to be far, far away at the appointed hour.

"Was that who I think it was?" came Cayce's soft voice.

I turned to her and nodded. "All Hell's going to break loose just after sunset. I want you to leave town. Right now."

She scowled in her own inimitable way. "Think again, please."

I eyed her reprovingly, but from long experience, knew better than to argue. "Then get hold of the mayor. The media. Anyone who will listen, no matter how crazy it all sounds. Anything to get as many people as possible out of the city before nightfall."

Her attractive features clouded. "No small task, Greg. What's going to happen?"

"If my guess is right, Luserke's already been at work here. Somewhere in the city, he's got at least one active sculpture."

"Any chance of finding it in time?"

"If there was, he wouldn't have forewarned me. But I'm sure he expects me to go looking because he knows I'm sensitive to their vibrations—at least in the dreamworlds. It's different here. But don't worry, I'm not going on a wild goose chase. I have...other ideas."

She raised a concerned eyebrow. "What are you planning to do?"

"When I'm finished, you and I will both know."

*

Studio Zeta occupied the 88th floor—the penthouse—of the Wabash Tower Center, Chicago's newest and most celebrated lakefront skyscraper, situated just off Columbus Drive between the Tribune Tower and Navy Pier. The building housed mainly offices, but the lower floors contained shops, banks, restaurants, apartments, and convention facilities. The penthouse art gallery was the city's most exclusive, catering to the eclectic tastes that only the ridiculously affluent could afford or appreciate. The cylindrical tower offered visitors a spectacular 360-degree view from an altitude of 900 feet—only slightly lower than the observation decks of the nearby Hancock Center and Sears Tower. The monthly soirées for Artists of Uncommon Repute generally drew about 60 guests and ran till all hours; most evenings, the place was empty and closed by 9:00 pm.

For Ivan Luserke, however, the gallery stayed open as long as he wanted it to.

At the tower's entrance, armed security guards thoroughly searched both Cayce and I, less intent on finding conventional weapons than drawings, paintings, sculptures, or other tools for manipulating astral forces. And the moment we stepped out of the elevator into the gallery foyer, I knew we were far from alone; I could feel the oppressive energy around me, lurking, coiling, breathing. Amid the shadows of the faux-Corinthian columns at the gallery entrance, two drokwights skulked, unseen, as insidious as black widows and many times more lethal. Something I could not identify, masquerading as a streak of light on the floor near the columns, studied me with a gaze as cool and calculating as a tiger's, probably hoping Luserke would give it leave to have its way with me. I will confess that, just then, I felt more fear than I had ever known in the darkest dreamworlds.

"Good evening, Greg," came a soft, rather nasal voice. Luserke, whose strangely long, twig-like limbs lent him the appearance of a walking stick insect, stepped into a soft golden puddle cast by dim overhead fixtures and eyed us coolly from behind ludicrously thick, horn-rimmed glasses. He had no chin; just a slight knob in the pouch of flesh that sagged from his lower lip to his collarbone. In contrast to our semi-formal attire, he wore his ubiquitous black-and-beige-checkered button-down shirt; dark, wrinkled slacks; and scuffed leather loafers. He finally acknowledged Cayce with a nod. "Ms Coder. I'm glad you came."

"So, Ivan, how is it we rate an invitation to your private sanctuary?" I asked.

"You know that's not what this is," he whined with the petulance of an insulted child. "You've exhibited here as well, and quite successfully."

"You can't deny you had a hand in engineering this place."

"For the benefit of the public."

"A very selective slice of it. And unless I miss my guess, after tonight, your 'public' won't be quite what it used to be."

His bloodless lips curled into a sneer. "It's merely time to replace one with another. A far more interesting one, at that. Now, I'm sure you've had a busy day. Any luck?"

"If I'd had any luck, I wouldn't be here now."

"The art of concealment is one *you* forced me to learn, Greg." Then he added, "Not to diminish your father's efforts, of course. But I've always been a quick study. And your resources are somewhat more limited than mine. Still, I admire your tenacity."

"Did you call us here to prattle, or do you have some sort of proposition?"

"I didn't call 'you' plural, I called 'you' singular. Don't get me wrong, I don't begrudge Ms Coder's presence. She is welcome to stay. But for you, Greg, I have affection; I hoped you would come to witness my next great work of art. Apart from a few isolated instances in remote areas—test runs, you might call them—this will be the great unveiling of chaos in the waking world. It's only fitting that you have a grandstand view. Your mother would have approved, don't you think?"

I resisted the urge to strike him, knowing that doing so would bring down the wrath of his guardians. "It would have made her sick," I said, infusing as much loathing as possible into my voice.

"You didn't know your mother as well as you think. Janduro is no friend of Earth's. I'm surprised she tolerated life here as long as she did."

"And you have no more use for Janduro than you do for this place. As I recall, you unleashed a few of your nightmares there as well."

He appeared to ponder the remark and then smirked. "Have you ever known me to do anything halfway?" With a glance at his wristwatch, he beckoned us to follow him through the columned portal into the gallery proper. The right-hand wall was decorated almost exclusively with lurid, abstract canvases, mosaics, and figurines, none of which came from his hand. (I had long since ruled out the gallery as the site of an active sculpture; apart from being too obvious, it stood to be damaged in the event of an attack.) To the left, beyond the curved wall of glass, the lights of Chicago blazed like a manmade galaxy against the purple twilight backdrop, traffic flowing like luminous rivers in the gulfs between buildings. The view faced southwest, towards the Loop. I felt a jab in the hollow of my gut; despite her influential contacts, her untarnished credibility as an editor for the *Tribune*, Cayce had hardly succeeded in warning the populace.

Directly before me, across the Chicago River, the windows of the columnar Aon Center building peered incuriously back at me, and far beyond it, the glittering, cubistic shaft and twin antennae of the Sears Tower dominated the skyline: a glass-and-steel monarch surveying its kingdom. To the right, the massive, sprawling bulk of the Merchandise Mart dwarfed its neighbours along the river, even those whose pinnacles surpassed its own. Everywhere, light flared from buildings, broadcast towers, traffic signals, streetlamps, signs, cars, trucks, boats. Blinking red-and-green flashes dotted the sky as airliners dropped out of the void above and drifted slowly towards O'Hare—a mass of white-and-blue light on the far western horizon. I had lived here most of my life, but the incredible energy, the *life* that coursed through the vast metropolis never ceased to enthrall me.

"Ivan," I said softly. "What can I do to change your mind about doing this?"

The stick figure shook his head slowly. "Nothing, Greg. Not a single thing."

Cayce gave me a worried, questioning glance, and her hand fiddled nervously with the sash around the waist of her black, ankle-length wraparound dress. I put a steadying arm around her shoulders, but then froze, for something in the room seemed to change. Behind me, a soft, oddly modulated sussurus rose, followed by the distinctive clinking of glass and ceramic. Turning, I found that, though I was still obviously in the gallery at the top of the Wabash Tower Center, certain fundamental alterations had just taken place. Most notably, all the works of art had been replaced by numerous tall, wooden tables, around which dozens of shadowy, wraithlike figures sat, some quaffing mugs of a dark, frothy brew, others leaning close to each other and whispering. Their faces hid in the shadows of heavy black cloaks, which concealed their features. But a short, gray-bearded man dressed in a tatty brown-and-white suit came shuffling towards us with a tray of drinks in hand.

I recognised him at once. His name was Bland Mason, and he ran a tavern in Arthagia, a remote but not inhospitable dreamworld. His wrinkled face split into a smile when he saw me, and he cheerfully handed me one of his special dark ales. "Evenin', Mr Black. So pleased to see you. Have one on the house."

This unlikely transposing of familiar but disparate realities rattled me only briefly. I thanked him and accepted the mug, but Cayce's face had lost all its colour and her eyes bulged disbelievingly behind her narrow wire-rimmed glasses.

"And for you, missy," Bland Mason said, presenting her with a snifter of cognac—her favourite drink.

She looked at me blankly, so far beyond shock that I had to take the glass for her and place it in her hand. Bland Mason then went to Luserke, paying him special deference, so I leaned close to Cayce and said, "Stay calm. Ivan is manipulating our surroundings somehow. We're actually safer this way. Try not to be afraid."

"It's a little late for that," she whispered, her drink quivering violently.

Luserke eyed Cayce with amusement. Then he said to me, "It's a little trick I learned a while back. Perhaps one day I'll teach it to you." He pointed out the window. "Now, just relax and watch. Enjoy your drink."

For the moment, I had little alternative. The ghoulish shades behind me were every bit as dangerous as the drokwights, and there were still certain entities present whose nature I could not even determine. Though his heightened security complicated matters, I had to give Luserke credit for fully appreciating the danger my presence posed to him.

To the south, above and beyond the illuminated, foreshortened rectangle of Meigs Field, a dark blotch appeared in the sky, a black bruise in the navy velvet backdrop, which slowly expanded to become a swirling mass of onyx—like a drill bit bursting through a sheet of luminous fabric. Then, as in the dreamworld I had visited, that portion of sky collapsed, leaving a wide chasm above the horizon that seemed to open directly to outer space. And finally, within the gaping mouth, emptiness gave way to the suggestion of movement.

Unaware of the phenomenon occurring in the southern sky, the city pulsed blithely on, its remaining seconds of normal, familiar reality ticking rapidly towards zero. Now the black hole in the sky abruptly dilated, and a gigantic silhouette emerged on outstretched wings, soaring over the placid Lake Michigan and generating a shock wave that split the water into two separate, roiling bodies. I barely felt Cayce's hand squeezing mine like a vise.

Time seemed to stop.

And Pachacutec fell upon the city.

I actually felt the heavy vibration as the thing touched down on south Lakeshore Drive, just beyond McCormick Place. As it landed, its muscular legs compressed like shock absorbers, and for a block each side of it, all the lights winked out. A cloud of dust billowed around it like smoke from a volcano, and a portion of the long, flat roof of the McCormick Center building caved in. The reptilian giant reared back, opened its jaws, and bellowed, and even through the glass, from two miles away, I could hear the thunderous, foghorn-like roar as it wended its way up the teeming channels between the dense walls of skyscrapers.

I saw it happening all around the city: vehicles screeching to a stop, windows of buildings opening, tiny figures freezing in their tracks and peering to the heavens. As yet, only a scant few in the city would have seen what had arrived on Earth, but within a five-mile radius of the beast's landing site, not a single soul could doubt that *something* dreadful was happening. As if carried by an ethereal wind, the angry blaring of car horns crept to my ears— the sound of traffic congealing on all roads south of the Congress Parkway. As awareness spread through the city with an almost tangible rippling effect, the monster took a single step forward.

More lights went out, and now, as far north as the river, people began to run, gripped by sheer blind panic, for at street level, none could yet see the source of the incredible sounds.

Pachacutec, its steely scales gleaming in the city lights, lumbered onto Lakeshore Drive and smashed through the 23rd Street Bridge. The eruption of dust and debris briefly obscured it from view, but then, behind the cloud, a pair of immense batwings unfurled and beat together, quickly dispersing the filthy veil. A number of vehicles on the lakefront expressway tried to break free of the gridlock, only to careen off the road or slam into one another, and a series of tiny, golden flashes sprang up as cars exploded or caught fire.

Cayce teetered against me, remaining on her feet only by clinging to my arm. Her cognac glass slipped to the floor and shattered, unnoticed by Luserke, who gazed at the unfolding spectacle with an expression of unbridled delight. Like an adrenaline-charged adolescent, his hands trembled with ecstasy, so he set his own drink onto a nearby tabletop to keep from sloshing it all over himself. So absorbed by the monster's rampage, he seemed completely oblivious of Cayce or me. Her fearful eyes shifted towards mine, and I heard her whisper, "Now?"

I glanced back and saw that the cloaked figures at their tables still seemed to be regarding us, radiating suspicion. I shook my head. "Not yet. You'll know when."

"I don't know if I can do this."

"You'll be fine."

She nodded reluctantly, her hand still fiddling nervously with her sash. I was just as terrified as she, but neither of us could allow fear to cloud our judgment, our timing. Now that her voice had diverted my attention, I became aware of a slight tingling at the back of my neck; very soon, the first phase of my own design would commence. Would it work as I had planned? If it did not, I could be responsible for even greater devastation than Luserke ...

Now, sirens began to wail throughout the Loop as the nature of their predicament gradually dawned on city authorities. Meanwhile, the creature continued its advance. The pedestrian bridge at 18th Street fell across Lakeshore Drive and the adjacent railroad tracks, smashing countless cars. As the towering figure approached Soldier Field, a pair of helicopters appeared out of the west, bearing rapidly down on the monster and circling its head like buzzing gnats: news choppers, anxious to get the first live pictures for their respective networks.

Pachacutec, as I had feared and anticipated, now decided to draw upon its massive, internal energies. Its glittering, metallic-looking body seemed to waver insubstantially for a few moments; then a purplish, bubble-like sphere formed around the beast, distorting the figure like a convex lens. Nearby buildings began to sway and lean, as if a terrific, invisible force were pushing against them. Then the bubble rapidly expanded and burst with a horrendous *boom,* which shook the floor and rattled the gallery windows.

For a quarter-mile radius around the monster, everything—including Soldier Field and the Field Museum of Natural History—had simply vanished. Beneath the monster's feet, the ground had been flattened, marblised, and now oozed rivers of steam. The pair of helicopters orbiting its head had simply ceased to exist.

Pachacutec was warping space, turning matter inside out. Transforming order to chaos. And Ivan Luserke was giggling like a love-struck girl.

The tingling at the base of my skull intensified. Although I had trained extensively for a moment such as this, I had never before accomplished the feat in the waking world. Suppressing my own rising doubts took an immense act of will.

Pachacutec turned to its left and smashed its way through Grant Park, across Columbus Drive, and onto Michigan Avenue. The tall, roughly H-shaped structure of the Chicago Hilton shuddered and fell to rubble, sending up another cloud of dust that obscured the beast. A large portion of the southern end of the city went dark as power lines fell apart and circuits overloaded. Flames erupted amid the billowing plume of dust and ash, but as if by Moses' command, the roiling column parted and the towering behemoth stepped through.

The next block of structures along Michigan Avenue trembled and collapsed, including the Columbia College building, and I felt a sickening, knifelike jab to my chest. These were not just anonymous, meaningless buildings being razed, but places I knew and cared about. I had attended Columbia in my youth, been intimately acquainted with its halls, met many friends there. Who could count the human lives at this very moment being snuffed out—innocent victims of an extradimensional horror brought here for little more than the amusement of a madman? Here I stood, helpless, afraid to act on my own, unable to speed up the events I had set in motion that *might* halt the destruction and murder.

Then, in the west, beyond the Sears Tower, something new began to happen in the sky. Just above the burnished copper horizon, a pinprick of light appeared and slowly expanded—like a negative image of the black hole that had admitted Pachacutec into the world. The swirling, miniature sun flared so brightly I had to shield my eyes, and behind me, Luserke's cloaked shades hissed like angry vipers in surprise.

From the seething fireball, a fantastic figure now emerged: a flying serpent with vast, bronze-coloured eagle wings, its body banded with black, crimson, and gold, its limbless body easily as long as the raging Pachacutec's. It soared eastward, in the direction of the growling, amok giant, opening its jaws to expose a row of long, serrated teeth.

Luserke fired an accusing look at me, his fists clenching in shock and fury. A more livid face I had never seen, all the more remarkable because it belonged to the homely, chinless Ivan Luserke. "Impossible," was all he managed to utter. "This is far beyond your capability."

"What do you think I've been doing while you've been playing with chaos?" I asked. "Having sweet dreams?"

For months, using all my skill, all the arcane knowledge I possessed—with Ryuhebi's cooperation—I had been working on a sculpture to rival Luserke's most intricate device, praying all the time that his hypersensitive faculties would never detect what I was doing. I had always known that a moment such as this was inevitable; now I would learn whether my preparations had been adequate, my talents sufficiently developed—and whether Ryuhebi's expedition into the remotest dreamlands, the dwelling place of his most distant ancestors, had been successful.

In the loft of an unpretentious, rented warehouse in Melrose Park, west of the city, a crystal and ivory tower—not dissimilar to Luserke's own masterpiece—had for hours been actively transmitting its own vibrations into the astral realms. That portal had finally opened.

Now this new, gigantic incarnation of Ryuhebi soared straight towards Pachacutec, screeching like a gargantuan hawk. He slammed into the behemoth, which spun in anger and smashed into the globe-crowned Straus Building, which fell to dust with a terrific rumble at the monster's feet. Ryuhebi soared upward and hovered above his adversary, just beyond the reach of its talons, lashing its head with his tail. Then, as if propelled by a catapult, Pachacutec soared into the air, lowered its head, and gouged the dragon-snake's segmented belly with its bony horns. Ryuhebi cried out again, this time in pain; but rather than pull away, he coiled his tail around Pachacutec's upper body, twisted violently, and sent the winged giant toppling to the earth.

Buildings from Michigan Avenue to State Street collapsed in ruin, throwing up so much dust that I could no longer see either of the fallen beasts. More helicopters appeared out of the west, this time staying well back from the scene of raging battle. Ryuhebi reappeared above the column of dust, beat his wings dramatically, and soared westward towards the Sears Tower. Then, ascending, he banked northward—directly towards our vantage point high above the city.

I drew back involuntarily, but Luserke simply smiled, confident that the astral barrier he had erected around Studio

Zeta was impenetrable. The winged snake hovered just outside the windows, peering in with immense, glistening black eyes. Gradually, the eyes changed to fiery gold, sweeping over us like glaring searchlights, and Luserke unwaveringly met their gaze, egotistically believing that the new creature had come to challenge him directly.

This, as I had foreseen, was his crucial mistake.

Beside me, unnoticed by the mad artist, Cayce had released her sash, allowing her silken dress to slip over her shoulders; now it fell to the floor, leaving her standing naked and exposed to all present, human or otherwise, and as the glare from Ryuhebi's eyes struck the intricate designs that covered every inch of her skin, rendered by my hand over the course of the day, her figure took on a luminous, golden sheen. She stood there erect, eyes closed, a living work of art, activated and working to counter the barrier force that Luserke had so carefully constructed.

This was the moment I feared most. If I had made a single mistake, or if one of Luserke's guardians were able to get through to her before the spatial alteration was completed, our deaths would be neither quick nor painless.

Brilliant light flared around me, blinding me for several seconds. I heard a hideous shrieking sound, then a gut-wrenching *thump;* when the light faded and I could see again, the art gallery had reverted to its everyday state—the paintings, sculptures, and mosaics all in their rightful places. The ghouls, the drokwights, Bland Mason, and all other alien presences had vanished. Cayce's painted body, however, continued to glow, highlighting Luserke's features with a ghostly, golden light. He made a menacing move towards her, his twig-like arms raised as if to throttle her, but with one step I placed myself directly between them. Physically, he was not even close to a match for me, and he had just lost his primary means of defense.

"Think you've won?" he hissed in a thin little voice. "This was just one of many options I've devised. You will never be able to stop me."

"You'll never have a chance to activate them," I said softly. "It ends here, Ivan."

Suddenly, the building shook as if buffeted by a tornado, and over Luserke's shoulder, I saw Ryuhebi spin around to face westward. Beyond him, Pachacutec appeared, airborne, bearing down on him with wings trailing smoke. The devil crashed into him with astounding force, but Ryuhebi somehow held fast, preventing a deadly collision with our building. But the shock wave shattered the gallery windows, and I found myself in the grip of a terrible wind, which threatened to drag me into the void. Cayce staggered drunkenly, and the light surrounding her body quickly faded; I lurched towards her, grabbed her arms, and pulled her roughly to the floor, just in time to save her from a falling light fixture, which shattered a scant few feet from our heads.

Her copper hair hung in her eyes, which blinked bewilderedly several times before focusing on me. "What's happening?" she whispered.

"We've got to get out of here. Ivan's barrier has collapsed."

Ryuhebi absorbed another blow as Pachacutec went berserk above the city. The evil giant plummeted suddenly, smashing into the Wrigley Building, sending its gothic spire toppling to earth in ruin. Directly adjacent to our building—much too close for comfort—the tall Equitable Building split in half vertically and collapsed, the dust from the implosion billowing as high as our windows. The air became thick and gritty, torturing my lungs, but I managed to pull myself to my feet and help Cayce to a standing position. I saw Luserke clutching one of the vertical struts of the shattered windows, his hand oozing blood from a protruding shard of glass, his eyes locked on the battle raging just outside, too absorbed to bother considering his own safety. But I knew he was too quick-witted to remain oblivious for long; in a moment, if he felt himself threatened, he would simply cross dimensions and conceal himself until he could devise something even more horrendous. Knowing I had to act immediately, I released Cayce and launched myself towards him, caring little whether my own momentum might propel me straight to my death.

My body slammed into his with such force that he only had time to utter a brief "peep" as he pitched into space. I fell heavily to the floor, inches from going over the edge, stopping myself only by grabbing the same post he had held. A chunk of glass bit deeply into my palm, but I felt only the slightest pain; an end to the horror that Luserke had wrought was all that concerned me now. His writhing figure shrank rapidly as it plummeted towards the earth, soon to be swallowed by the billowing dust below.

Then a vast, black shadow fell over me, diverting my attention upward. The hideous visage of Pachacutec loomed only a few feet away, and I could feel the furnace-like heat radiating from its body. Its piercing, blood-red eyes locked with mine, and then—just as when I had encountered it in the dreamworld—they captured my very essence, preventing me from looking away or even blinking. Its jaws slowly parted, and in that foul cavern, I saw not a throat of living flesh and blood but a gaping portal to distant, black, chaotic realms, within which lay only the promise of eternal torment. The monster inhaled, and I felt my grip on the glass-encrusted strut loosening as a malignant, ethereal hand seized my body.

Then a gold, crimson, and black whip quickly encircled Pachacutec's throat, and the ghastly, reptilian face disappeared like an image on a television screen suddenly switched off. Ryuhebi's screeching voice rose above the subsequent, thunderous *boom,* and the tower shook so violently that I feared its end was imminent. Now Cayce was the one to haul me to my feet, adrenaline blazing like magma in her veins. She tugged me towards the foyer entrance but had the presence of mind to pause and grab her discarded dress. Then we were in the elevator car, panting and gazing at each other in shock and wonder.

"Should we take the stairs instead?" she asked, her voice hoarse from the dust.

"The building's still standing, but probably not for long," I said. "We either get out fast or not at all. We have little to lose going this way."

Cayce pressed the button labeled "L." And our stomachs lurched as the floor seemed to fall out from under us.

We obviously survived, or I would not be here to relate this tale. By the time we reached street level, Pachacutec had mysteriously vanished, and Ryuhebi had taken to the air, defensively circling the battered but still intact Wabash Center Tower as Cayce and I made our escape. Before returning to his rightful world, our benefactor's eagle-like wings blew away the dust and smoke, clearing the air so we could relieve our agonised lungs. The wreckage of the nearby Equitable Building so choked the plaza that it took us nearly an hour to make our way to Michigan Avenue. There, police officers, firemen, and paramedics tried to cajole us into ambulances, since both of us were coated with soot, grime, and blood, but we beat a hasty retreat and, supporting each other as necessary, proceeded on foot back to my Gold Coast flat, since my car was now buried beneath the rubble of the Wabash Center parking garage.

Of Ivan Luserke, no trace was ever found. He may indeed be dead, but my personal belief is that he somehow survived his fall by working his inscrutable magic and escaping to some distant dreamworld. But his exit from physical reality severed the astral connection that allowed Pachacutec to remain corporeal, and thus the monster was drawn back to its native dimension; similarly, at the moment of Luserke's passing, the active sculpture that held open the door between worlds, wherever it was, went instantly inert, though I have yet to discover its hiding place. Despite my success in bringing an altered projection of Ryuhebi's essence from his own remote kingdom, I still am unable to comprehend, much less reproduce, Luserke's methods of merging astral and physical realms by will alone. As I have previously said, his abilities exceed mine by a tad; only by exploiting his all-too-human weaknesses was I able to overcome him.

Still, my own success represented a significant personal breakthrough, and if Luserke yet lives, he will be doubly wary of the threat that I now pose to him. Unfortunately, the inevitable result of this victory is that he will devise yet more innovative and artful ways to become the instrument of universal devastation, which he sees as his destiny.

In the weeks following Pachacutec's rampage, certain alterations to the Chicago cityscape have occurred that have baffled even the most open-minded and imaginative government authorities: in the devastation left in the creature's wake, great forests of strange flora have sprung up in a shockingly short time—forests that are impervious to cutting, burning, or any other method of elimination. And they appear to be spreading. I have seen such forbidding woodlands in the outermost dreamworlds, and even the inhabitants of those realms avoid their shadowy depths, for none who enter ever return alive. That *something* exists in these new Chicago wilderlands is indisputable, for the sounds that pour out of them at night are often shocking to human ears. But as to what sort of horrors might actually emerge from those outposts of chaos, well... only time will tell.

I have redoubled my efforts to learn as many more dreamworld secrets as I possibly can before Ivan Luserke again shows his hand, as I have little doubt he will. Ryuhebi, having reverted to his rightful, considerably diminished stature, is still my frequent traveling companion; I often bring him delectable baby Chiko rats to keep him in a tolerable humour.

For what it's worth, in the waking world, the everlasting love of my life, Ms Cayce Coder, has consented to become Mrs Gregory Black.

We are registered at numerous surviving Chicago department stores.

BIG DAY

CHRIS BARNES

Harry hadn't slept well for years, but sleep was especially elusive on the eve of Big Day. The slightest noise woke him—the cat pattering down the wooden hallway, a passing car, the distant beat of patrolling helicopters. Anticipation of the day ahead kept him restless.

He snapped awake yet again. The clock showed 4 am, as far as he could tell without his glasses on.

A faint, familiar sound hung in the air, like the last reverberations of a fading drumbeat, and the air was silent again. He looked at the glass of water next to the pill bottle on the bedside table. Was that a faint ripple on the surface of the water? Ah. The city wouldn't be silent for long, he guessed.

He sat up in bed, slowly. His back twinged and he groaned. The cat stirred from her position at Harry's side and regarded him with calm, wide eyes. She knew what had woken him. She waited for him to speak.

"He's arrived early," Harry said. The cat stretched and yawned. Her disdain was magnificent.

"Well," Harry said, lowering his feet to the floor. "May as well get up. Get us some breakfast."

Through the window, he saw lights coming on in houses along the street. Others had also been roused from sleep by the tremor of distant footfall.

The floor vibrated a little. He heard the noise clearly this time—though it was still very distant—like the solid thud of a felled tree, but magnified a thousandfold and heard from a hundred miles away. A dog howled, and immediately the neighbourhood came alive with the noise of frightened dogs. They'd sensed the approach of Big Day much earlier than their masters, and now that one of the pack had snapped, all were crying their fear into the night.

Harry dressed, then he and the cat went to the kitchen. They tried to ignore the howling, but even the cat's poise was now a little disturbed. Her instincts ran deep, too. "It's all right, Puss," soothed Harry. He poured milk into her saucer and she lapped at it. He went and opened the front door. There was still no hint of dawn in the sky. Noises carried far on the cold air. He could hear the Bensons next door, packing their mini-van. Food for the journey to the mountains, and whatever last-minute keepsakes they'd forgotten to send to the caves. And their dog. Harry heard his own name mentioned. He went out onto the front porch and waited for Daryl Benson to lean over the fence.

"Hey, Harry. Hard to sleep, eh?"

"Reckon." Harry liked the Bensons. Polite. Kept to themselves, mostly. Good neighbours.

"You sure you won't ride with us this time?"

"I'm sure. I always take the Army bus. With the other veterans, you know. Old buddies. Thanks anyway." Harry smiled and nodded. "Safe trip, Daryl. Give my regards to Mary and the boys."

"Will do. See you in a day or two," said Daryl. He didn't add: hope our houses are still here. He turned away, and shortly Harry watched their mini-van drive away. Harry regretted lying, but he couldn't possibly tell Daryl the truth about today.

Other cars were appearing on the streets now, too, all travelling according to their allotted time.

Harry went back inside. His stomach knotted with sudden hot pain, as if a huge electric hand were squeezing his guts into mush. He had to grab the door frame for support. The pain slowly faded, and he sighed. The cat was watching. "Better take my pill, Puss," he said, heading to the bedroom. "Have to be in top shape for Big Day."

The Bensons had gone, thinking he'd be following in an Army bus. The Army took his phone call last night and thought he'd be going with the Bensons. No one would know any different until the checkpoint in the mountains. And no one would bother by then to come looking for old Harry. Not during the excitement of Big Day.

Harry turned his transistor radio on and went around his house listening to the news. He closed shutters and locked windows, turned off appliances, tied cupboard doors shut so that the crockery would not be shaken loose onto the floor. He turned the water heater down low. He shook his head at this pointless routine, but old habits were insistent.

When everything was ready he sat at his desk and looked at the photos lined up on it. A parade of memories. Jeanie and himself on the wedding day—by golly she was a stunner back then. Always was, right up until her own illness took her. Harry and the boys in uniform, off to the war. And back from the war again, fewer of them in that photo. Then the dwindled gang from the final reunion a few years back. And here I am, he thought, the last one of the gang.

He took a copy of his will from the top drawer and read over it once more, though he knew it mostly by heart. He pinned it to the desktop just in case his solicitor's office downtown was destroyed today. A third copy had been deposited in the public record storage facility in the mountains. Harry had always been a belt-and-braces man.

But not today, he thought. Today he would do something wild, something dangerous and reckless. And he had carefully planned just how he would do it.

On the radio, a breathless announcer gave up-to-the-minute reports on the Big Fella's progress. He was well clear of the water now and was making his customary relentless city-bound march. Veering a fraction further north than usual, said the announcer excitedly, but still well within his usual route, the so-called Monster Alley.

She sounds young, thought Harry, everyone does, lately.

A panel of learned voices dissected the Big Fella's apparent direction, predicting which suburbs would be crushed this time, which monuments destroyed. Harry smiled. They sounded curiously like earnest schoolboys talking about sex, trying to sound wise, unaware their ignorance was brutally obvious. They even called him by his official name. *Suprafaunum singularis*, indeed! Well, the scientists had to find some sort of label, otherwise they'd have to admit they know bugger all about him, wouldn't they?

Scientists and doctors, they didn't know anything. They couldn't even fix my old guts, thought Harry. That Doctor Lee, always on at me to try some new drug or other. Stuff him. He's as useless as the rest of the experts.

Another footfall sent a shudder through the house. Harry wondered if that one felt fainter than the last. Was the Big Fella moving away? For a moment, Harry felt his plans slipping into ruin, but then he pulled himself together. It was time to go.

He made sure the catflap was unlocked. The cat twined herself around his ankles and he stopped to give her a final caress. "You're a good puss," he said. "You'll be all right." She rubbed her head against his hand, then squatted by the door, watching him. He sighed and locked the door behind him. Then he picked up the box of cat food and other sundries he packed last night, and carried it next door to the Benson's front doorstep. There was a note in the box, too. The Bensons'd take care of the cat. Harry looked around at the street and all its familiar sights.

Another bolt of pain seared through his gut. Harry gritted his teeth and set off to meet the Big Fella.

Kyra woke at oh-three-fifty-eight. Her watch was expensive, chunky, made for Special Forces and explorers, but it couldn't beat her subconscious, her lizard-brain instinct that the Day had come early. She was up and fed and dressed by oh-four-fifteen.

Her stuff was laid out and ready, triple-checked the night before. She put on her radio and clipped in the earpiece. The newsreader murmured updates into Kyra's ear, confirming what she had already guessed. The Monster was coming. She knelt before her neatly arrayed gear, checked it all again: the gleaming carabiners, nylon cords, the crampons, the vivid Kevlar jumpsuit.

These she packed swiftly and precisely into her backpack, her movements economical from practice.

Her gaze fell on the other black nylon satchel. She opened it and looked at the collection of steel pieces waiting to be assembled. She took them out, clicking each one into place as she went—grip, barrel, cable reel. The last piece, the lustrous grey metal arrow, slid home into the barrel, click-clack. Then she rose, hefted the gun to her shoulder, flipped down the sight, took aim at the wall. Tracked slowly to the ceiling, aiming the jutting barbed projectile at the light. She squeezed the trigger. Click.

"Bang," she said. If she had powered up the gun, there would have been a gaping hole in the ceiling, and matching holes in the floors and ceilings of at least two levels above hers. The rocket-propelled titanium harpoon was her own design.

What effect it would have when the time came to really fire it, she didn't know. Nothing had ever hurt *Suprafaunum singularis* in the past. Bullets he ignored, bombs did more harm to the city than to him, gas and flame were mere annoyances. The prevailing wisdom for the past twenty-one years had been to just leave him be. "Not me," she said to the gun. "Me and you, we're gonna make history today."

Harry paused for a breather in the shelter of a railway underpass. The long walk was more difficult than he'd expected. He'd walked it only a couple of weeks ago, checking the timing, marking out places to hide from the patrols. He'd managed okay then. It must be lack of sleep that had him tuckered out today. A man can't sleep a few fitful hours and expect to be in top form the next day, not at my age, thought Harry. And my guts are on fire again.

"You're going downhill fast, old son," he said quietly.

Just like everything else. Look at the graffiti on these walls. Bloody kids. *Tha Monsta rockz,* indeed. Can't even spell properly. No respect for anything.

A vehicle roared along a nearby street. It faded into the distance and he exhaled, relieved. Probably a police patrol. The cops wouldn't hurt an old man like him, but it'd be "Come on, Grandpa, got lost, eh?" while whisking him off to safety. And later to a dementia ward, probably.

He popped another pill and pushed on. No point saving any energy for later.

"I'm not going to slowly die in one of those bloody nursing homes," Harry said to the city as he marched towards Monster Alley. "Not going to slowly die anywhere!"

Kyra stopped in the shadows of a laneway. Another helicopter was thudding overhead, olive-drab and sleek. Martial law was in force. "From first footfall to last": that was when the Army ruled, though the City Monster Act was rather more precise and considerably more long-winded about it. She squatted beside a dumpster and waited. The shadow of the chopper flickered darkly across the pavement, then the beat of the rotors Doppler-shifted and melted into the background rumble of the distant Monster.

Don't wanna get mistaken for a looter now, she thought. Though not many people were game to try looting anymore, not since the Army got serious about martial law back in the sixties.

More likely they'd mark her as one of the usual religious nutters, trying to break through to commune with her God. The cults had lots of names for the Monster: Leviathan, Tiamat, Shiva, The World Serpent, Gaia and more. She liked the City's unofficial moniker best: the Big Fella. A friendly sort of name for their own gigantic prodigal son.

A few leaflets lay nearby, spilled from the dumpster: the usual trash handed out by assorted loonies on street corners in the weeks before Big Day. *Bow Before The Great Dragon. The Lamb, Not The Monster—Return to Christ.* And Kyra's personal favourite: *The Apocalypse Comes, This Time For Sure.*

But still, if the Army spotted her...the snipers on those choppers rarely got to prove their skill. One twitch of a nervous trigger finger, and bang. Game over.

She adjusted her backpack and radio earpiece, and waited for another minute, counting the seconds, until she was sure the chopper wasn't coming back, or being tailed by another. She moved on. Time and the Monster waited for no man...or woman.

The radio tracked the Big Fella's progress. He was taking his usual route through the eastern suburbs, Georgetown, Oakville, Hinch Park. The announcer skilfully managed a tone of excited solemnity, somehow sounding sympathetic yet amused that the famous North Hill Baptist Church had been trampled into rubble yet again. Every Big Day, no matter what the Big Fella's path, that building always ended in ruin. Crushed by taloned foot, swept by spiked tail, caught up in fire; one year the church escaped the Big Fella completely, only to have a malfunctioning TV helicopter crash through its roof. "The Lord moves in mysterious ways," said the North Hill pastor to a radio reporter. Kyra smiled. What was it with these people? Any sane congregation should have taken the Almighty's repeated hints by now.

But the people of this city were legendary for their stubbornness. It was a point of pride to them, to not let the Monster's three-yearly visitation drive them from their town. In another alley, a message had been chalked onto a brick wall: *We Await Yore Coming Our Migty One.* Kyra snorted. No literacy tests for joining a cult, it seemed.

She reached her first target—a stormwater tunnel mouth, in a drainage canal near the Central Park. She checked her map to be sure, though she'd scouted this route for weeks, including the subterranean network of concrete stormwater and sewerage tunnels. These would get her to the Monster's path unseen by patrolling helicopters. They were solid, these tunnels, rebuilt again and again until finally they'd become so deep and massive they routinely survived the Monster's passing.

She made sure the area was clear, then quickly climbed the cyclone wire fence and clambered down the rusted ladder into the tunnel. She stood there, silent, listening. Just the faint ghosting of air and the amplified tremors of another footfall, sounding much closer than it really was.

Another chopper began to approach, and Kyra slipped into the dark tunnel. Down there, the echoes of the Monster's footsteps drowned out her own.

*

"**I made it,**" murmured Harry.

There was a constant hum in the air here, as the buildings vibrated between each jarring tremor. It permeated Harry's body, too, an uncomfortable buzz that sent little knives through his stomach. He swallowed the last of his painkillers.

His heart was pounding, and not just from the long brisk walk, ducking from shelter to shelter. I shouldn't have made it this far, he thought. Not with those Army helicopters and all. They mustn't be looking too hard. Gotten lazy over the years, they have. He looked disapprovingly at the sky. Wouldn't have got away with that slackness in his day. Better discipline, back then. Times had changed. "And not for the better," he said.

There was one thing that hadn't changed, though. The Big Fella. Same day every three years. Same route—more or less— each time. He rose out of the sea, marched along with the same measured stride, through the city and down into the sea again on the other side of the peninsula, going about his own mysterious business. Paid no heed to no one. Harry respected that. He couldn't think of a better way to go than the instant crushing oblivion of shaking hands with the Big Fella.

He drew in his breath and walked out onto the main road. There in the distance was the Big Fella himself, towering above the buildings, stomping thunderously forward to meet Harry.

Kyra climbed up through the manhole onto the street, the shuddering street that danced and crackled under the rolling thunder of giant feet. Her harpoon gun was locked and loaded. She'd donned her crash helmet and goggles, and scarlet jumpsuit and harness, bright colours against the dark bitumen, a defiance to the helicopters that circled far above. She wondered if they'd seen her; wondered (as the earth jumped again beneath her, sending flickering ripples up walls, cracking windows and sending shattered glass earthward like fistfuls of jagged hail) what the hell she was doing, tried to orient herself, turned around and around, but her plan had fled her mind in sudden panic. Was she mad? For fuck's sake, Kyra, what are you...

turning around and around she saw the Monster

vast

impossible

green as a mountain

a bipedal tower of muscle and armour

his shadow fell across her
his mighty head was crowned by the Sun.
His foot crashed down only one block away.

Kyra moved, Godstruck no longer, snapped back by the
renewed din of cracking bricks and clattering debris. She sprinted
down a sidestreet at right angles to his approach, turned and
knelt, unslung the gun. Then the Monster strode into view, framed
by buildings, presenting his flank like a mountainside to her.

Bam! A brief blast of white smoke blurred Kyra's view. Then
she was yanked forward and dragged along the road until she
regained her feet and began to run. The harpoon had held! The
thin silvery cable stretched up, up, to wherever the harpoon had
lodged itself between the Monster's scales. Kyra wanted to whoop
with glee, but couldn't spare the breath, not yet. She sprinted
hard, gaining some slack in the cable. Hooked the gun into her
harness clips, and released the catch on the cable reel.

She soared up, flying to meet the side of the Monster, and
only then gave her elation a voice. She screamed her exhilaration
to the world.

Hard reality thumped the thrill from her as she slammed
against the Monster's side. She gasped for breath. Got to keep
moving, she thought, before that thump hurts too bad. Her hands
and feet scrabbled against his lamellar skin, which was hard and
slippery as ice. Each scale was the size of a table top. He smelled
like seaweed and brine, earth and heat.

The cable reel on her gun kept slowly winching, pulling in
the slender steel rope that held her entire weight. She spotted the
harpoon above. By some miracle, it had found a chink between
two scales and hooked itself in deep. The Monster seemed not to
have noticed this tiny thorn in his side.

Where there was one chink there must be more, she hoped.
Months of planning had got her to this point, but now she was
making it up as she went along. She had reached the frontier of
her knowledge and training; now, a hundred metres above the
ground, anything could happen.

She reached the harpoon. Easy ride's over, she thought; it's all
muscle work now. She found a handhold, wrestled the crampons
from her belt pouch and clipped them one-handed to her boots.
Hanging free, she let her body feel the sway of the Monster, his
stride rhythm, one mighty leg swing, crash of footfall, the other
leg, and on and on, unstopping, unstoppable.

Ignoring the ache from her bruised arms and chest, Kyra
grinned and hauled herself upward, a methodical, brilliant bug
against the dark sheen of her host.

Harry stumbled as the road shook again. He considered sitting
down to avoid being thrown off his feet, but decided against it.
He'd rather meet his end standing up. He felt quite calm, almost
peaceful. His stomach pains had even eased up a bit.

The helicopters must have spotted him by now, but they were

too late. They didn't dare come this close to the Big Fella, not after he'd snapped up a couple that buzzed him, seven visits ago.

The Big Fella was very close now. A few hundred metres away maybe, but that was close for a creature thirty storeys tall.

Harry hoped he'd estimated the Big Fella's pace correctly. He hoped he was standing in the right spot. It was hard to be sure, being short-sighted as he was. But as the Big Fella got closer, he could adjust his position. He took off his glasses and cleaned them with his handkerchief, then put them back on and blinked the world back into focus.

Here he came. Magnificent creature, simply magnificent. Harry felt a strange affection for the Big Fella. How could anyone call such magnificence a Monster?

Wait a moment. There was something different. What's that bright red thing on the Big Fella's head? It…it was *waving*.

Was that a *person* up there?

Kyra stood atop the Monster's head, clipped to a cable she'd slung around one of his lesser horns. No one had ever done what she'd done today. All the months of preparation, research, training, designing equipment—and she'd done it! She was riding the Monster!

Helicopters and aircraft swarmed and circled at a distance. She gave them a cheerful wave, knowing there must be dozens of zoom lenses focused on her. She wished she could hear the newscasts, but her radio had been crushed when she slammed against the Monster's side. Her ribs pulsed with pain at the memory. But it didn't matter, there'd be plenty of time to watch the replays later. They'd be playing the footage for weeks. For Kyra, there'd be TV interviews, magazine articles, book deals. On the downside, the City would probably try to lay charges against her for violating the Monster Act. Let them. She'd fight that battle when it came.

She pulled up her goggles for a moment to wipe away tears with the back of her hand. "I did it!" she said. "I did it!" Her words flew away in the wind, unheard, except maybe by the Monster himself.

Kyra couldn't tell if he'd even noticed her presence yet. She was just another gnat to him, she guessed. She couldn't help wondering what slow reptilian thoughts were passing beneath her feet. She squatted and put a hand on the broad smooth scales of his head. "What are you thinking, old leviathan?" she whispered.

There was no reply. Only the continued rhythmic sway of his lumbering stride, and a periodic tiny tilt of his mighty head that suggested he was keeping a casual eye on those buzzing mechanical pests in the distance. He could have swatted her off with his forelimbs, or just brushed his head against a building; but he had not. They continued on together, the Monster and his tiny partner. It was an astonishing sense of power, looking down on the world from atop her colossal mount.

But she didn't want to tempt fate—or the Big Fella—too much. She'd planned her exit. She didn't want to make her escape once he'd reached open country and begun his descent to the sea. That ground was too open, no cover if he decided to come after her. Best to get off here in the city, now, while they were clear of the tall towers, but with plenty of sewer entries she could hole up in if she had to.

She unclipped her cable from his horn and stowed it in her pack. She squatted for a few seconds longer, feeling reluctant to leave. After so much preparation, the ride was so brief. Well, that's how it had to be, she told herself.

And later, when people asked why she did it, what would she say? The adventurer's answer, which only other adventurers ever really understood. *Because he was there.*

"Thanks for the ride, Big Fella," Kyra shouted. "So long!" And she took a running leap, off the side of his head, caught a brief glimpse of herself reflected in the huge black bowl of his eye, then released her chute, snap-crack, and steered herself down through the buildings. She thumped onto the road.

The impact sent a jarring stab up through her aching body, but she picked herself up and shrugged off the chute harness. She hobbled away, before realising that something felt different. She glanced over her shoulder.

The Monster had stopped walking. He stood still, head cocked, looking down, unmistakeably at Kyra.

She willed herself to move, to get somehow out of sight, but for once her body failed her. She was rooted to the road, mesmerised by that huge, distant, unreadable eye. The air closed around her, hot and still. Sweat trickled down her back. The longest seconds of her life ticked glacially past.

Then the huge head tilted away, and she was released from scrutiny. The Monster raised himself up, opened his mouth—so many teeth!—and let out a long, vast bellow, laden with majesty. In that cry Kyra heard the mystery and solitude of the deep places of the world.

And having given voice, the Big Fella lifted a foot and strode on, again making his steady, unknowable journey back to the sea.

Kyra remained in the middle of the deserted street, ignoring the helicopters that were already descending to meet her. She wondered about the Big Fella's cry, and if it was directed at her, and what she could ever say in return.

Harry waited before the Big Fella, as both of them watched the red-suited parachutist float down between the buildings. The gaudy parachute soon disappeared from Harry's sight.

He looked up and saw that the Big Fella was standing with head cocked, apparently still watching the parachutist. Harry wondered what the Big Fella thought it was. An insect? A bird? A piece of dust? Or maybe he was a lot smarter than that, and knew exactly what it was.

What did the Big Fella make of all this, the city, the humans and their buildings and helicopters and all their crazy ways? Are we just ants to him, thought Harry, vaguely interesting, occasionally annoying, but basically irrelevant?

The Big Fella lifted his head and roared, a terrifying and melancholy noise that seemed to carry the weight of lonely eons. The sound rolled across the city, shaking windows and souls alike. If the world itself had split open and cried its sorrow, it could not have been louder or more filled with anguish than that roar. Harry found himself blinking away tears.

Then the Big Fella raised his foot. Harry was cast into shadow as it loomed overhead—and came to ground behind him. Harry sank in confusion to the road as the Big Fella passed overhead and tramped on, down the road, heading back to the cold deep sanctuary of the sea.

"But..." Harry said eventually. "You were supposed to..." He stopped, realising he was actually happy to still be alive. He picked himself up from the road, and stood with a hand on his stomach, watching the receding back of the Big Fella.

"Did you mean to spare me?" he asked, but there was no reply.

Well, at least my stomach doesn't feel too bad, he thought. Maybe the excitement did me some good! He looked around at the cracked pavements, spangled with glittering fragments of broken window. He bent down and picked a fragment out of the gutter, and held it up. It sparkled in the sunlight. "He leaves jewels in his wake," Harry murmured, then snorted. "I sound bloody daft!" He turned the fragment again, watching the light refract into little rainbows inside, and slipped it into his pocket.

He walked around the corner where the parachutist had descended. The red-suited figure still stood there. Climbing the Big Fella! What a crazy idea! Harry shook his head in reluctant admiration.

A wild idea began to form in his mind. Riding the Big Fella...No, I'm too old for a stunt like that! But still...wouldn't mind another chance to meet him. The poor old Big Fella had sounded so alone.

But I'd have to wait another three years to do that, Harry thought. I might give Doctor Lee another go after all.

Harry suddenly wanted nothing more than to make it to another Big Day.

FOOTFALL

TERRY DARTNALL

Bricks were crushed into powder. Stone crumbled and broke. Pine sleepers fractured and flew at the first footfall. We used oak beams, rough and irregular, ten inches of seasoned timber. We laid them on rubble and bedded them in with heavy engines. The earth heaved. There were gunshots as the beams splintered and snapped like matchwood.

The huge foot retracted and withdrew.

Jorg eyed me from the recesses of his hood.

"We need girders," he said.

We dragged girders into place with dray horses, laid them on top of the beams and welded them together. They formed a steel corridor to the bottom of the steps.

There was a creak and hiss of hydraulics as the god lifted its foot and lurched forward, lowering itself onto the walkway. The girders bent and sang under the strain. But they held.

And there the god rested, with one leg on the steel corridor.

We burned the pine sleepers that night. The snow around our fires melted into small rivers in the ice that gleamed and glinted in the firelight. Wisps of smoke from the green wood drifted amongst us like strangers. It was a cold night waiting for the god to move and we were thankful for the fires.

The sun rose over the edge of the world and silhouetted the huge leg against a skyline sprinkled with stars. Was the god resting or did time move differently in its world? Was it deep in thought, performing calculations, wondering how to proceed? Was it having second thoughts? Was it afraid? Could a god be afraid? I tried to imagine what it would be like to walk into another dimension. Would it be like putting your foot into a pool of very strange water—water that might do anything to you? Was that what the god was thinking? "Should I get into the pool?" Perhaps it was savouring the experience, putting its leg into a special place and—

"It's moving!" said Jorg.

A beast lurched into our world and blocked out the light. One moment there was only the leg. Then we were invaded by a creature too terrible to imagine.

We turned and fled towards the caves. When we were halfway

there we looked back.

The monster was still emerging from whatever hell it came from.

"It's huge!" said Jorg.

The full bulk of the creature appeared, teetering uncertainly on the steel corridor. It moved slowly, as if it were concentrating on every step.

"And mad," Jorg added.

I looked into the dawn sky and saw eagles wheeling and circling around the huge head.

"Eagles!" I shouted, pointing up. "Eagles!"

Jorg grabbed me by the arm and dragged me forward. The eagles knew. The eagles always knew.

I felt it first in my feet—a low rumbling vibration.

We almost didn't make it. The ground began to move, sliding under our feet in the direction of the god, as if a huge carpet was being pulled towards it. Jorg held me and forced himself forward. The earth was moving faster now. Trees swayed and slid downward. We stumbled and fell, but we got to the caves.

The god was sinking into the ground, slowly at first, then faster and faster. It flailed its arms and kept upright, but its vast bulk was falling. Then the steel walkway whipped up and struck it like a severed cable, clamping itself to the god's body as it disappeared into the ground, accompanied by the snap and crack of splintering timbers. The god sank to its waist and I was reminded of a deer I had seen once drowning in a quagmire, its eyes full of terror.

Then the monster was gone, dragged down by its own arrogant weight.

The eagles were wheeling over the abyss. One by one they broke off and drifted towards the sun.

We ran to the back of the caves and came out with the ladders. When we got to the chasm where the creature had fallen we laid them on the ground so that they protruded beyond the edge. Some of us stood on them whilst the rest crawled out over the abyss and looked down.

The god had fallen through the thin lamina of the world and was turning over and over against a backdrop of stars, the walkway snaking and bending beside it.

"How many have fallen?" said Jorg.

"Many," I said.

"How many?" said Jorg.

"Ten in my lifetime. Twenty in my father's. Twenty-three in my grandfather's. But," I said, "I think it has been going on forever."

"How long is forever?" said Jorg. "How many have fallen?"

"Many," I said.

"Why do they come?"

"To climb the steps. You know that."

"They fail."

"They always fail."

"Will they ever succeed?"

"There's nothing there. They're following an ancient instinct. But there's nothing there. Nothing at the top of the steps."

The god was dwindling into the distance. It would soon be out of sight, gone with the other fallen gods. Could they see us as they turned over and over in their long, slow fall? Could they see our little life-raft world, with the steps on it: a piece of flotsam floating in the void, a fragment, a memory, an aspiration? Could they see what they wanted the most, to which they were drawn by ancient instinct—the Steps of the Gods, that once led to the Great Hall of Valhalla?

daihaiku

SEAN WILLIAMS

(1)

daybreak in Tokyo:
people screaming, earth shaking;
scaly head rises

(2)

where are the dragons?
nature abhors a vacuum;
Gojira provides

(3)

take, under clawed foot,
grim comfort from the knowledge:
nature bounces back

Seven Dates That Were Ruined by Giant Monsters

OR

Why I Really Need to Get Out of This City

ADAM FORD

1. Katie Chambers—Saturday 27th July, 1988

I was fifteen years old, standing outside the cinema, waiting for Katie Chambers to show up. I'd just been dropped off by my parents and was nervously watching the family car drive away after managing somehow to fend off an uninvited PDA from my mother. I knew that I'd cop it when I got home that night with the "What's the matter, are you too much of an *adult* for me to kiss you goodbye anymore?" routine, but I didn't care. For the week that had passed since I had got the guts up to ask Katie Chambers—Katie *Chambers*, mind you—to the Saturday Matinee at the Odeon, I had been coasting on pure adrenaline and nothing, absolutely nothing, could touch me, except maybe the nagging fear that Katie wasn't going to show. The fear grew exponentially with each minute that passed, each nervous glance at my watch, but she finally turned up, only three and three-quarter minutes later than we'd arranged. There she was, stepping out of the passenger seat of a parental-looking station wagon that had pulled up across the road. Things were starting to look okay. The adrenaline was back and I had a great opening conversational gambit along the lines of *parents, what the hell are they good for, hey?*

All of a sudden it got dark, like a cloud was passing across the sun. I looked up and Gigantadon was swooping down out of the sky and everyone was screaming and running inside the theatre except for me. I just stood there and watched as two hundred tonnes of giant radioactive pterodactyl reached out one claw and picked up Katie's parents' station wagon and flew off. Katie started running down the middle of the road screaming, *Give me back my mum, my mum, give her back!* I waited for another half an hour for her to come back, but by then the previews were definitely over and the movie had started for sure. I could hear helicopters in the distance, and guns, and that weird high-pitched screaming sound Gigantadon's sonic-wing-attack makes, so I walked to the phone booth on the corner and called mum and asked her to come pick me up.

2. Megan Lan—Thursday 18th October, 1991

I used to see Mee almost every day at uni, wandering across campus in that purposeful kind of way, striding confidently across the quadrangle on one of her various extracurricular missions. She was heavily involved in student union stuff. After six months of watching her walk past, noticing the clothes that she wore, the people she was with and the way she hooked stray loops of hair behind her ears with her pinkie finger, I decided that it was time to meet the legendary Megan Lan face-to-face.

One afternoon I saw her putting up posters, attaching them with a giant roll of masking tape to the bollards that were scattered around campus. She had dropped a pile of the posters on the ground beside her, and just as she was tearing a strip of tape with her teeth a punk on a skateboard shot past and the jet stream from his board sent the unstuck posters flying. I took the opportunity and ran over to the bollard, frantically snatching at every poster I could get my hands on. With most of them recovered, I turned to Mee and smiled what I hoped was my most self-effacing-yet-fascinating smile as I handed them back to her. She smiled back as she took them from me and tucked a stray loop of hair behind one ear. I took a deep breath and to stop myself from staring I checked out the poster she'd just stuck up. It was advertising a public lecture by Professor Jane Damage on the interface between contemporary urban planning strategies and philosophical interpretations of the role of kaiju in long-term social development. Professor Damage was Mee's honours supervisor, and she was helping out with promotion of the event to try and score some brownie points from the Prof. I offered to help Mee out with the rest of the posters, and she took me up on the offer, splitting the pile in two and arranging to meet me back at the Student Activities Office in an hour.

We had coffee that afternoon and arranged to meet at the lecture that Thursday, and then go out to get something to eat afterwards. Though it was great to be hanging out with Mee, I didn't enjoy the lecture very much. Professor Damage's theories were a little old-fashioned, which is something that often happens with tenured academics—they tend to carve out their niche at their institution and dig in, ignoring any developments in their field that post-date their appointment. The Prof. was just about to demonstrate one of her theories when the containment unit short-circuited and the three juvenile Carnivopteryxes that had been held in short-term nanostasis broke out. Within ten minutes they were big enough to fill the auditorium, and ten minutes after that they had burst through the ceiling, growing bigger and bigger as they slashed at each other with their talons and screeched telepathic war cries, shooting golden death rays at every building taller than three storeys. Mee and I were crushed up against the back wall of the auditorium in the rush to escape. When the second monster knocked over a support beam with its tail, I caught a chunk of masonry in the small of my back and a rafter came down on my right arm. Apart from some bruises and scratches, Mee was okay. Luckily, I'd fallen on top of her and most of the debris landed on me instead of her. She came to visit me in hospital a couple of times. A few weeks before I was released she started going out with a mutual friend from my botany tutorials. I hate to admit it, but they made a really cute couple.

3. Lucy Darnell—Friday 9th August, 1993

Lucy worked in the office where I was doing a three-day-a-week internship. She was always helpful when I wasn't sure who I was supposed to deliver which forms to. Her kindness made her stand out from the rest of the arseholes in the company who mainly saw me as their personal courier-slash-mailroom slave. Lucy wasn't like that at all, maybe because she was a lot younger than most of her co-workers. She had got the job out of an internship she'd done there herself a couple of years earlier. I think she sympathised with me having to put up with all the crap I had to put up with from my superiors, which was pretty much everyone in the building, including Lucy. I would bitch to her about them when we would go to lunch at this sleazy café that served bad "modern Australian" food but made good coffee. We got close, like you do when you're having lunch together almost every day, talking about your lives and ambitions and that sort of junk.

I don't normally go out with people that I work with, but this was an internship, not a full-time job, and it was only a six-month position so I figured if it went really badly I would only have to hang in there a little while and then I'd never have to see her again. That was the worst-case scenario, though, and didn't seem too likely because we got along really well and had a lot in common. One day I asked Lucy if she wanted to go out after work some time. She smiled a coy little smile and told me she had been wondering how long it would take before I asked. We organised to go out that Friday night—she'd ditch end-of-week drinks and I'd come by after classes and we'd wander down to Little Vietnam and pick a place that looked good.

I left classes early that Friday so I could go home and change. I caught the bus to the office only to find that the whole building had been pounded into rubble, along with everything else within a seven-block radius, during a fight between Robosaurus and some weird bee-headed creature nobody had ever seen before. I hung around and tried to talk to some of the emergency guys, but they were pretty busy so I headed back home and started calling hospitals. Lucy wasn't in any of the hospitals that I called, and no one from the office knew where she was. She never came back to work at the relocated office, either. I couldn't call her at home because we'd never swapped numbers—we always saw each other at work. Someone told me that the bee-monster thing had been using some kind of hypno-pollen to turn bystanders into an army of zombie bee-drones, so I figured that that was probably what had happened to Lucy.

A few years later I bumped into her at a garage sale. She was there with her husband—she was married by then, to a really nice guy who worked in landscape gardening. She said she'd followed the bee monster for a couple of months until the hypno-pollen had worn off and she had come to her senses in Ulan Bator. She'd had to stow away on a Cathay Pacific flight to Townsville, and then hitch-hike back down from there. We swapped email addresses, but I never heard from her and to be honest I never sent her anything myself.

4. Serina Coustas—Sunday 26th January, 1997

I had met Serina at a party of a friend of a friend, and we'd struck up a conversation that had lasted until 4 am, when we'd exchanged numbers and caught separate taxis. We arranged to meet in the botanical gardens on Australia Day, which was coming up, to check out the open-air concert that was happening that day. Serina knew someone in the headlining band, and I was just keen to tag along. We brought picnic stuff, and when it started raining we moved in under the fig trees along with everyone else who hadn't thought to bring an umbrella. The bands were pretty good. Serina's friends' band had named themselves after Doctor Malevolent, whose talk show was popular at the time among people who liked to think that their superior sense of irony made that kind of pop-culture trash actually worth watching.

Two songs into their set a scruffy, bearded, barefoot guy who had been wandering among the crowd came up to us and handed us an invitation to a march that was coming up to protest against the government's recent military action against Krigga and other offshore daikaiju. I made some offhand comment about nobody caring about giant monsters and Serina got upset. She didn't think that the government had been justified in their pre-emptive strikes, but I told her that I thought that they had done the right thing. Our conversation soon devolved into an argument, and from there it became a series of personal attacks, each of us caricaturing the other as warmongering nationalistic speciesists and naïve bleeding heart hippies, respectively. Serina got up in a huff, packed away the food she had brought and pulled her blanket out from under me before storming off into the easing-off rain, leaving me sitting by myself on the wet grass next to a soggy half-eaten baguette, with the rally invitation still crumpled into a ball in my left hand.

*

5. Tracy Evans—Friday 20th February, 2000

My housemate Tran set me up with Tracy. He was sick to death of hearing me whinge about my recently unsuccessful love life. I met her at one of those "hidden" bars in the CBD that everybody knows the name of, stepping over the vomit puddles and syringes that littered the obscure back-alley laneway which led to the seemingly barricaded entrance. Tracy was sitting at a corner table by herself, sipping a gin and tonic. I introduced myself and she stood up to shake my hand. Our voices were only just audible over the DJ's choice of up-to-the-minute noise. I excused myself for a moment and grabbed an overpriced beer from the bar before rejoining her. Conversation was slow-going, especially with the omnipresent beats, but she seemed nice enough.

We were both shy, and a little nonplussed about being out on a blind date, but we made an effort to entertain each other anyway. After a couple of drinks I suggested that we grab some dinner somewhere, and pretty soon we were in a cute little yakuza-run Japanese restaurant sharing bowls of agedashi tofu and nasu dengaku. I excused myself to go to the toilet and when I got back she was talking to the guy sitting at the table behind ours. Turned out he was an old friend of hers from high school who'd gone on to join the city's damage-control unit. He was charming the pants off Tracy, bragging about his close encounters with Nerodon and King Zenah, showing off in high-resolution detail about rescuing grandmothers from the claws of Batroxigon and finding children still alive in the collapsed basements of buildings destroyed by Gaijantizu and her Twelve Twin Sisters.

I took my seat after being introduced and watched Tracy's eyes sparkle and heard her make quiet thrilled noises at the back of her throat as Mister Damage Control went on and on about himself. After ten minutes I got up, paid the bill and left without either of them noticing me. On the way home the train was diverted to avoid a battle between the Neutrazilla Posse and Harmonadon. Everyone in the carriage rushed to the window to get a better look, but I pretended to be absorbed by the torn copy of *MetNews* on the seat beside me.

6. Lainie Goldberg—Thursday 8th October, 2002

It took weeks before Lainie would agree to go out with me. I'm not usually so persistent with women, but there was something about Lainie that made me decide to take each of her excuses at face value and keep trying to find a night of the week that she wasn't already doing something. Hearing about the things she would be doing instead of going out with me just made her seem more interesting: theatre, dance recitals, Vipassaña retreats, looking after guest artists from the innumerable festivals that the city hosted, gigs with her band…I'd gone along to a couple of her shows, but Lainie had always been surrounded by a gaggle of

cool-looking hangers-on and groupies at the end of the night and
I'd caught the last tram home rather than bothering to try to catch
her attention.

I'm not sure what it was that changed her mind. Maybe she
genuinely was free that night. I was just happy to be finally on a
date with Lainie Goldberg, drummer from Retort Stand and the
friendliest bartender at the Stars and Garters Hotel. We were
meeting at the steps under the clocks at Central Station, so I
walked the few blocks to my local station and jumped a train into
the city. We were approaching the major inter-city station when a
voice came over the PA system. It was an incomprehensible jumble
of vowels and consonants, like all railway announcements, but
among the garble one word could be heard clearly: Zillasaurus.
The train slowed to a halt and the emergency lighting came on.
The buzz of nervous conversation filled the cabin as people tried
to work out what was going on. A guy with a walkman radio
tuned into a news channel and relayed the news to us all over the
continual, indecipherable chatter coming from the PA. Apparently
the so-called "defender of children across the world" was being
mind-controlled by his old enemy Power Outage and forced to cut
the city off from outside help by destroying all major transport
centres.

It took an hour before the CyberSamurai arrived with their
Z-Bot Restrainivore so that they could hold Zillasaurus down
long enough to deprogram the mind-control device, and another
three hours before external power was restored to the trains
and the doors of the carriage could be opened. I caught a taxi to
Central Station, unable to help rubbernecking at all the flattened
buildings and stomped-on cars. The taxi driver gave me his own
personal spin on the attack, a conspiracy theory that made John
Pilger and Chris Carter seem like suburban right-wingers by
comparison. I paid the fare and took the steps two at a time, but I
hadn't really expected Lainie to wait.

Her shifts at the pub changed soon afterwards and I didn't
see much of her after that. I sort of lost interest, to be honest.
The prospect of hounding a girl at least five years younger than
me into giving me another chance seemed less than appealing all
of a sudden. The last time I saw her was about six months ago in
a Retorts clip on *Rage* late one Saturday night. She looked good.
But then she always looked good.

7. Nancy Kiyanfar—Monday 12th April, 2004

I hadn't seen Nancy since uni. We had had a couple of the same
history lectures, and had been part of the same study group. I'd
always enjoyed her sense of humour and her insightful, intelligent
way of looking at the world. At the time she had had a long-term
boyfriend whose name was Jaived or Javed or something like
that. I bumped into her in my local newsagency a few years later.
She'd split up with the boyfriend about a year after graduating

and moved out of the city to work as an environmental consultant for rural councils. She was back in town, visiting cousins who coincidentally lived at the end of my street, and was thinking about moving back permanently. We arranged to have dinner that night. Being Monday, most restaurants were shut, so I invited her to my place and promised to cook her my special vegetarian carbonara. At seven-thirty she rang my doorbell and I opened the door to the sight of Nancy dressed in a gorgeous burgundy dress, which wordlessly confirmed my hopes that the late-teenaged flirting I fondly remembered had not been purely the product of nostalgic self-delusion.

Dinner was delicious and the conversation was comfortable and continuous. We filled each other in on what we'd been doing for the last five years, which of our classmates we'd stayed in touch with, and joked about how we were dealing with the terrifying prospect of entering our early thirties. I cleared the dishes away and poured us both another glass of wine. I was just about to get dessert ready when I noticed that she was looking a little pale. I asked her what was wrong and she waved her hand dismissively. Just a bit of a headache, she said, frowning. She pushed her chair back from the table and began massaging her temples. I offered to grab her some painkillers and went to the bathroom to dig out some ibuprofen. When I came back into the kitchen, Nancy wasn't there. I could hear the sound of her voice coming from the back yard. I assumed that she was talking to someone on her mobile, but when I followed her outside I realised that she wasn't alone.

Standing in front of Nancy, dwarfing the pair of fully grown ghost gums that grew on the back fenceline, was Cygnatora, all two hundred feet of her. She had curved her snake-like neck downwards so that her head was only five feet from the ground, and was looking straight at Nancy, her jagged-toothed beak only inches from Nancy's face. As I stood there in the doorway, Cygnatora turned her massive head slightly and stared at me with her deep-red, smouldering eyes. I froze. Nancy turned around and saw me standing there, then turned back to Cygnatora. The two of them kept talking for a while, the giant creature making weird subsonic groans that I could feel in the pit of my stomach as it spoke. Nancy came over to me and explained that she had had a psychic link with Cygnatora since she was a little girl, and that she was going to have to go off and help out with a battle that was taking place on the other side of the Moon. She apologised for not mentioning it earlier, thanked me for dinner and told me how nice it had been to see me again. She stepped onto the monster's beak and climbed up to sit directly behind her head. She waved as Cygnatora spread her enormous wings and took off into the sky, leaving me with a flattened back shed, a pair of footprints in my back yard each the size of an above-ground swimming pool, and an entire black cherry cake with cream-cheese icing to eat by myself.

Aspect Hunter

ANTHONY FORDHAM

And so the yak and I rode out of the deep past to save the world from ice. Again.

As usual, we Associated deep among the glaciers, high up in the accumulation area of a new icefield. On distant ridges snow fell thick and fast as the glacial *anima* called down more ice to its banner. They were preparing for war. It was, after all, why the yak and I had been called.

We sat on an abandoned railway platform all hung with icicles, the tarmac slippery with frost. It was clear and crisp here, even as blizzards raged to the north and south, the snow held back by residual energies from the Association. Phosphorescent lines of force still curled around the cast-iron legs of the benches ranged along the platform. Overhead, the sky was the peculiar pearl colour that belied ice high in the wind. A sign half-buried in a snowdrift said ATOOMB. It seemed appropriate, despite the dyslexia.

The yak slumped on one of the benches and sighed as I paced up and down. The tracks were deserted in both directions. This mountain town was frozen, dead. The telegraph wires were forearm-thick with a coating of rime. Windows in abandoned shops glittered as a cracked pedestrian crossing sign dangled from a cord slung across the street. The sign carried its own little burden of snow.

It would be ironic indeed if, in order to help those who had summonsed us, we had to fight our way through miles of ice and white-demons just to get to the muster point, only to turn around and fight our way back up the hill. I stood on the edge of the platform and looked out to the north east. A line of dark ice lay there, beyond the reach of the early morning sun, drowning the old landscape.

"Lokboksfrost, apparently," I said to the yak, glancing over my shoulder. The yak grunted and chewed the cud. Its arms were folded under its massive shaggy chest, the killing talons hidden beneath great curls and snarls of wool. But I knew it was always alert; woe betide any white-demon that should choose to jump out at us now.

Lokboksfrost. I rolled the name around in my mouth. He had nicknames, of course: the Widowmaker, the Great Darkness, the Big L. All cliché. But I could hardly blame the folk who named him, the folk he'd chased out of these mountains. How were they supposed to respond to thrice ten million tonnes of malevolent ice? Poetry? Was it fair of me to expect great lyricism of these people, as their homes were crushed under his blister-drop and his white-demons slaughtered their loved ones?

He was a new glacier, was Lokboksfrost, and angry for it. He had much to prove to the Rebel Princes and the Glaciation Front. Word had it that the Fenris Wolf in Europe wouldn't even receive Lokboksfrost's emissaries. And great Kuf of the Canadian Shield thought of him as nothing more than a frozen puddle, a piddling little glacier barely three hundred kilometres long. As for Long Lambert and the Antarchs, it was true they took at least a passing interest, since Lokboksfrost was the first to breach the great dry continent—Australia—and bring ice to its warm hills. But it was a condescending and patronising interest. Antarctic ice didn't think the Widowmaker had the will to march on any human holding. He lay poised on the edge of one of humanity's most important cities, which stretched glittering across the plain of Albion only a hundred kilometres to the east, but still the Cold Husband and the Cold Wife thought him too weak to make any move.

They were very wrong.

The USGS saw it. They had their headquarters in Greater Sydney now, ever since so much of North America had been buried under the Laurentide ice sheet and the Cordilleran marched southward towards their western cities. In Greater Sydney, a small USGS detachment on Kent Street had quickly grown into a regional office, then a regional headquarters, and now word had it that all USGS operations were launched from the sixth floor of Veritas Tower, and that the goldwire nexus itself was quartered there.

I touched the goldwire threaded through my right ear and listened for the whispers of the USGS. The goldwire was silent, any cogent energy dampened and drained by the massive power of Lokboksfrost's *anima* and the lingering backwash of the Association.

The yak and I were immune to both, of course. The yak, because it had been designed for these conditions and me because...well, that was the mystery. And that was why the USGS had so much use for me.

A great curtain of icicles shivered on the morning breeze and then fell from the station eaves to smash on the rails with a sound like a yak in a china shop.

The animal in question pricked its ears and looked east. There was nothing yet, but the rails began to sing, shedding frost and rime as whatever approached sent vibrations shrieking towards the station. More icicles fell, but we ignored them; they were just dead ice, after all.

A curve obscured the tracks to the east, but shortly an armoured train came barreling around the bend, white-demons clinging to the roof and trying to drive killing spikes of self-assembled ice through the roof and into the brains of whoever had come to fetch me. The train flashed its fog light and sounded its horn. I could see generators throwing a static field around the squat, gunmetal locomotive and the single carriage, designed to counter the confounding effects of Lokboksfrost's fright-lights and *anima*.

A chainsaw blade, specially reinforced, snarled through a slot in the side of the carriage and sliced one white-demon neatly through the waist. The creature fell away, then deftly leapt up onto its hands and skittered across to where its legs lay spasming in the snow. It reached out, held its pelvis to its waist and was whole again, just like that. And *that* was the problem with these damn things.

The train sounded its horn again. I must confess, the yak and I were surprised by its sudden appearance, and stood there slack-jawed. It was so unlike the USGS to use something like this. Attack choppers and tanks were more their style.

A flamethrower on the front of the locomotive belched, and a clinging white-demon melted like snowflakes on a summer breeze. The tiny mind-prism fell away, pulsing blue, into a snowdrift. Seconds later, the white-demon reassembled itself by fusing the snow into new blades and limbs, and leapt back into the fray.

"Come on," I said to the yak. We leapt, too, with our own blades akimbo.

The train dropped the brakes and came shrieking to a halt on the platform in a shower of sparks. More white-demons came charging up from the east, but they took one look at the yak and me whirling into combat and abandoned their...well, *companions* is the wrong word, but it'll have to do here. They fled back into the mist. Six white-demons remained, focused on peeling the sheet metal from the carriage walls like someone opening a can of sardines. The howling was constant, and terrible.

The first one I reached seemed surprised to see me. It raised a bladed limb and I shattered it with a well-placed strike from my right-hand ice pick, and used my left-hand pick to spike the creature squarely in what passed for its face and gouge out the tiny mind-prism from between its ghostly blue eyes. With a practiced flip I dropped the pick and let it dangle from its wrist-strap, snatching the mind-prism before it could fall. As I crushed the tiny black-blue crystal, the white-demon froze—pardon the pun—, turned to snow, and scattered to powder on the light morning breeze.

In the meantime, the yak had engaged two of the larger specimens and led them in a cruel dance across the platform, parrying, jabbing, always seeming to fall back. Triumphant, the white-demons pressed what they saw as their advantage, only to have the yak gore one to pieces and shatter the other with a double palm strike from those terrible talons. Hooves flashed out, crushing the mind-prisms before the white-demons could reassemble.

The train's flamethrower took care of two of the remaining monstrosities, and I was quick to trample the mind-prisms before they could cause any more mischief. The last white-demon stood atop the carriage, hauling on some kind of vent covering, only to explode into shards and fragments as the yak somersaulted into it. A click of flat, ruminant teeth and a gulp, and the mind-prism began its long and painful journey through the yak's complicated set of stomachs.

There was a curious silence. Ice spun in the wind, outraged. The glacier, never far away, grumbled and shuddered, no doubt throwing more white-demons over the edge of the escarpment to run us down and skewer us. Time, I thought, to head out.

From the side of the carriage came the sound of bolts being drawn, and then a door slid back, revealing the bruised and bloody face of my old adversary John Quick, of the USGS.

"Oh great," I muttered. The yak peered over the top of the carriage and rolled its eyes.

"This train is express to the city," said John Quick with an insufferable grin. "And given today's travel conditions, we do mean *express.*"

Then the heat island from my recent Association collapsed, and the blizzard hit us like a jackhammer. Fat barbed snowflakes beat at my head, trying to suck the lifeforce from me, collecting on my beard, singing me to lay down in the snow and sleep, sleep forever. I easily shrugged off the effects of the *anima*, and cocked an unimpressed eyebrow at the flaring fright-lights racing through the streets of the town to engulf the abandoned station in great curls of glowing red and green and ghostly blue.

"Welcome to 1986," said John Quick as the yak and I clambered awkwardly onto the train. "Coffee?"

"You've just Dissociated from 11,000 BC?" asked John Quick, as the train finished a complicated shunting procedure to turn itself around. Now we clattered eastward towards the lowlands and the city, static field running at full strength now and bouncing white-demons off into snowdrifts even as they leapt on us from the embankments. We were, to all intents and purposes, immune. Still, the carriage rocked alarmingly.

"That's right," I said, as a mighty gorge filled with ice flashed by to the north. I could see the tiny figures of white-demons clustered around crevasses below the equilibrium line. There were thousands of them. Perhaps tens of thousands. Lokboksfrost had been busy in my absence.

"What's happening back then? I forget," said Quick, sipping at his coffee.

"Megafloods," I said, by way of explanation. My mind filled with a brief but intense image of the yak and I clinging to the side of an uprooted Californian redwood as it barrelled towards a set of falls a thousand metres high. "Wild days."

"I can imagine," Quick replied. He let the steam from his mug work at his frostbite. "How long since you've been back here?"

I shrugged, my own coffee mug empty on the tray table in front of me. "Seven years real time, three years subjective."

The yak sat across the aisle, filling both seats. It was oiling my ice picks, making sure the clips and carabiners that attached the stout titanium handles to the triple-weave nylon wrist straps were free of ice and rust. Since the yak needed no weapons of its own, it always volunteered to clean mine.

I sighed. "So what's the deal, Johnno? I mean, it guess it's obvious why I got the call, given the state of the landscape, but why did they send you? Last time you saw me I recall you gave a speech along the lines of the USGS being able to fight its own battles. Freelancers, you said, were surplus to requirements."

Quick held out his hands and shrugged.

"That was ten years ago. Things change. You know how it works. Maybe back then I didn't show the right degree of respect for the mighty Aspect Hunter—" he said it with just the wrong amount of barely concealed disdain, "—but the situation is different now. All this you see around you is less than a decade old. He's done all this in just eight years."

I looked out at the frozen landscape around us. We flashed along the lines, the flamethrowers melting ice as we went, the great metal cow-catcher on the front of the locomotive scattering the boulders that some of the more enterprising white-demons had rolled onto the tracks. We were unstoppable, but we felt small and vulnerable as we passed through town after abandoned town. Dead places with names like Hazelbrook and Faulconbridge, Warrimoo and Lapstone. Mountain towns where cheery little cottages had once filled the air with the safe smell of woodsmoke and children had built snowmen on street corners. All silent now, frozen under tonnes of ice, the ruins picked over by white-demons and the occasional wandering glacial champion. Oh yes, there were seracs abroad in those silent streets, and I had a feeling the yak and I would cross paths with one soon enough.

"So first you reject my help," I said thoughtfully, "and now I get the call, because you've lost control. You've failed to keep your house in order, Johnno, is that it?"

Quick was playing a game. I could tell from the way his watery green eyes narrowed imperceptibly at this barb. This was all for show. He no more had a newfound approval of me than I had a newfound respect for him. This was a man who favoured the toys and tricks of USGS science over the old, tried and tested ways of fighting ice. So far, every one of his marvellous devices had failed him, and taken more than a few good field researchers down into dark crevasses besides. He was pompous, ridiculous and dangerous.

"Good coffee though," I said, tapping my empty mug.

Quick clicked his fingers and a terrified research assistant ran down from the far end of the carriage with an urn wobbling on the end of her shaking arm. She tried to keep one eye on the bulky mass of the yak as she poured me another cup.

"Oh, don't worry about that thing," I said. "It's harmless."

The yak bared its flat teeth and then gave a complicated cough as it spat up the cud and resumed chewing. The research assistant fled back to the train's galley.

"Who was that?" I asked.

"Never learnt her name," Quick replied, which was typical.

"Look," I leaned forward. "How about we drop the charade? I can only imagine that you agreed to collect me as some part of some condition of some plot you've hatched in your continuing quest for glory. But that's not important to me. Thanks for picking us up and all that—you've saved us a long and unpleasant walk. But I'm not here to take a supporting role in some power play you've set up. I'm the Aspect Hunter. That's what I do. I hunt glaciers and the yak hunts with me. We don't play politics."

Quick raised his eyebrows.

"Well then," he said. And that seemed to be it. But then he went on. "All right, since you're so fond of plain speaking, I'll say that my coming to get you wasn't a condition or a punishment from the steering committee. I came of my own accord. I wanted to see you first, to explain. I want you to give me a chance to use my new weapon against the ice."

I rolled my eyes; I just couldn't help it.

"This time it's different!" hissed Quick.

"It's *always* different," I moaned. "And it always turns to crap the moment you deploy your cockamamie doohickey against a real glacier. Remember the napalm bombs? Remember the thermal inversion field generator? Remember, dare I say it, *the yak?*"

The yak looked up from its knitting and nodded. It remembered.

"This *is* different," insisted Quick.

"Oh really?" I asked. "What is it?"

By the time we rolled into Central towards mid-morning, John Quick and I were no longer speaking. As the train lurched to a halt in front of a platform of USGS dignitaries who regarded its scarred and pitted armour plating with expressions of horror, the yak and I threw down our cards and leapt from the train.

It was oppressively hot here deep among the lofty towers of Greater Sydney, almost six degrees above zero. I peeled off my overjacket as I shouldered my way through the crowd.

"Where's Lawler? Take me to Lawler!" I demanded.

The USGS director stepped out from behind a local government nobody and extended his hand.

"Aspect Hunter," he said, "I'm so glad you could—"

"What's this crap about letting Quick fool around with the weather?" I cried.

Director Phil Lawler had just managed a good look at the remains of the train. "What the devil happened to the—?"

Quick popped up like some kind of scrawny jack-in-the-box.

"Director, you really must explain to this time-skipping meddler that—"

"Oh, don't give me that!" I spluttered. "Of all your schemes, Quick, this one really takes the big biscuit. The possibility of disaster and the potential scale of that disaster is—"

"I hardly think you're in a position to make any comment on a system *you've* never even—"

"Gentlemen, please!" spluttered Lawler. "Look at that gouge in the side of the locomotive there! Are either of you hurt?"

"Excuse me?" I asked.

"Ah, yes, well. John, are you hurt?"

"Just my pride, Director, just my pride. If I could explain, this oaf has already—"

"I'll give you oaf!" I cried, and went to punch him in the mouth. The yak, with animal wisdom, gently stayed my hand. The whole exchange had caused some consternation among the crowd, but naturally none of them wanted to get too close. Most probably hadn't realised that putting a goldwire call through to me also meant calling the yak. Most of them probably hadn't realised a creature like the yak even existed. It was an enigma, that was for sure. A battle beast from the old wars, so the pamphlet said, with a six-foot horn span and terrible talons where the hooves should have been. Some wild-eyed geneticist had cooked it up in an embattled Canadian lab at Quick's mad request, and now here it was. Once, it had been barely bigger than a pony. Now it was massive, bulked up by an impressively intense gym routine to make it more than a match for any white-demon, and a serious threat even unto the seracs, those mightiest warriors of ice.

Quick glowered at me. I glowered at him.

"Why don't we retire to my office?" Lawler suggested, with typical diplomacy.

"But Director," hissed a flunky, "what about the antipasto?" He waved to where some kind of reception brunch or morning tea had been assembled beneath a hastily strung up length of bunting.

"The devil take your light finger food and your internationally acclaimed string quartet, too!" cried Lawler. "We have a war to fight, gentlemen, and now our most potent weapon has arrived, we must plan our attack!"

"Second most potent," corrected Quick.

"That remains to be seen."

"But Phil!" I spluttered, secure in the knowledge that only I, of all the people who crawled across the face of this rapidly freezing little ball of slush we called a planet, could get away with calling him that. "Messing with the weather! It's a recipe for absolute disaster."

"Or absolute victory," insisted Quick. "The REALBOW is a sophisticated piece of software, Aspect Hunter. Not a blunt instrument." He looked pointedly at the yak. The yak looked pointedly at him.

"Bring the car!" Lawler growled to the flunky. We marched as a loose but loudly arguing gaggle through the vaulted grand concourse of the station. Other trains—steam and diesel now that Lokboksfrost had frozen the power stations in the mountains— shunted and hissed on other platforms, disgorging passengers who were trying to get on with what passed for normal lives even as ice crowded in the hills to their east and the days got colder and colder.

Outside the station, a line of black cars waited in the street, exhaust billowing in the cold air. Lawler's car had a couple of little flags on the bonnet, the crossed rock hammers of the United States Geological Survey. The USGS was the supreme power now, bigger than governments, bigger than the military. Of all organisations, only they understood ice. And of all the USGS, only I *really* understood ice. The goldwire in my ear tingled as it mated itself to the local network. I was online now, able to instantly requisition any field equipment I needed: snowploughs, dog teams, corers, GPS pings and last-ditch napalm strikes on high concentrations of white-demons. A thousand gallons of jellied petroleum would slow even the biggest attack force. Only for a while, sure, but five minutes is an eternity when you're crawling along the dark moraine of some cruel glacier of evil name.

Inside, the car was plush and warm. The convoy spooled through the city streets in the chilly shadow of the great towers. Beyond, small, mindless icebergs clustered in the harbour, butting up against the pylons of the bridge. Icicles dangled from the sails of the Opera House and pack ice choked the little bays and inlets where once people had eaten fresh salmon at seafood restaurants. Weddell seals honked on the rocks around the promontory at Mrs Macquarie's Chair.

It was funny, I thought, the hairs that humans would split to convince themselves they hadn't already lost the war against ice. Sure, their summer city was groaning under its eight-hundredth consecutive day of frost, but as long as no actual glacial ice covered the wide boulevards and heaters still burned in the lofty towers, the war was still being hotly contested.

Hot. Now there was a word that didn't get much use nowadays.

Eventually, the convoy pulled into the lee of the looming bulk of Veritas Tower. The charming little café at street level was closed now, frost heavy on the folded umbrellas and the tables slippery with ice. But lights burned brightly on all levels as telecommunications companies and PR agencies and insurance brokers and, of course, the USGS worked day and night to redefine the meaning of stoicism and determination, keeping up appearances, getting on with life.

Still squabbling like children, we hauled ourselves out of the cars, into the lift, up to level six and into Phil Lawler's spotless office. Pride of place on the wall behind his desk was an enormous photograph of the last human team ever to survive a winter in

Antarctica. The expressions on the faces of those six men and four women were something to behold.

"Right!" said Lawler, sitting in his chair and motioning Quick and me to take a seat. The various flunkies and hangers-on found themselves quietly but firmly ushered back out into the corridor by the yak. It stood at the door, arms folded, chewing the cud.

"Let's start from the beginning," said Lawler.

Quick and I both opened our mouths.

"*I'll* start from the beginning," said Lawler. "Aspect Hunter, we've called you here to ask for your help in a final assault on the glacier that now threatens the city. His name, as you will have been briefed, is Lokboksfrost. He's a conglomerate of new glaciers that have formed in the Gross, Megalong, Jameson and Hawkesbury valleys. You will have seen on your maps that he seems to have chosen to invade the Albion plain from out of the Hawkesbury. For a while we thought he would come through the Warragamba dam, but, ironically enough, by freezing our main water supply he has created a vast plug of mindless ice directly in his path. So Hawkesbury it is."

I expected some kind of cool animated map to unfurl from a hidden compartment in the ceiling, but Lawler just went on, assuming correctly that I could picture the landscape in my mind, or call it up on the goldwire if I became disoriented.

"We have two courses of action open to us," Lawler continued. "Either we do what we have always done—send a force to the equilibrium line, where you and the yak will smash your way down to the mind-prism and destroy it—or we use Professor Quick's new weather control program."

I made a small whimpering noise in the back of my throat.

"Now, John, I think it is an appropriate time for you to brief us properly on this new device."

"It's not a device," said Quick. "It's software. The really big weather algorithm, which someone on my team abbreviated to REALBOW..."

I tried to figure this one out in my head, but couldn't.

"I don't get it," I said.

"No, it's one of those acronyms that don't really stand for...that's to say...well, REBWA wasn't considered very...oh look, it doesn't matter! The important point is that with the REALBOW we can generate very powerful, localised hot-weather events by channeling lines of quantum flux within the atmosphere to bend isobars, change air pressures and focus intense sunlight on an area as small as fifty metres across."

"Sounds like bullshit to me, Johnny," I quipped.

"Now now," warned Lawler.

"But what does he mean 'bend isobars'? They're just lines drawn on a chart!"

"It's a *metaphor*, you prehistoric putz!"

"Gentlemen, sit down!" screamed Lawler. We subsided.

"The obvious advantage to the REALBOW," Quick continued

smoothly, "is that we can burn the mind-prism from five hundred feet up, safe in a helicopter. No field personnel need risk their lives climbing all over icefalls and white-demon lairs. And can I remind you of the rumours of seracs coming down out of the high hills to spread terror and mayhem? Wouldn't it be fine to avoid all of that?"

"Oh, it'd be *fine* indeed, Johnny," I snarled. "But it's a fantasy! Think this through: you say this REALBOW is just an algorithm. Remember, if you will, what ice did to the US military's fledgling post-war global information system, the so-called interweb. Ice can control information, Quick, and it can control this REALBOW of yours. Can you imagine the kind of destruction a glacier like Lokboksfrost could unleash if he could control the freaking *weather*? Even considering this is insane."

"But—"

"I know you and the USGS have only had thirty years of subjective experience with ice in its current manifestation. I know that the International Geophysical Year in '56 and '57 was the first time you realised glaciers were alive and full of menace. But remember this: I have been hunting these things for thousands of years. I am old, Quick, and I am wise. I have seen cultures rise and fall on the tide of ice and I have seen every crazed, wild, and ill-considered human plot to defeat the glaciers ever conceived."

"Even a system to control the weather?"

"Let me tell you about this one night in medieval Florence. Da Vinci said to me—"

"Gentlemen, please," Lawler interrupted. "This is getting us nowhere—and anyway," he steepled his fingers on the top of his desk, "the goldwire informs me that question of the REALBOW has just become moot. The steering committee has voted against its deployment. I'm sorry, John."

Quick's mouth made a line like a tiny fissure in a thirty-metre wall of white ice.

"That's disappointing," he said.

I tuned my own goldwire into the final moments of the committee meeting. They were all congratulating themselves on a job well done, a decision well made. For once, I thought they'd made the right one.

"Look," I said to Quick, letting a conciliatory note creep into my voice, "full marks for trying, okay, John? No one blames you for wanting to reduce the risk and figure out some definitive way of beating the ice. But take it from me: there just isn't one."

His eyes were narrowed so far it was a wonder the man could still see.

"Quite," he bit off. "If you gentlemen would excuse me."

"Of course," said Lawler, and, yeah, he was pretty damn patronising. "Go and prep your field team, John. We ride out in just a few hours."

Quick nodded tersely and stalked from the room, almost bumping into the yak as it leapt aside from the doors. The various sub-directors and committee chiefs clustered in the corridor listening at the keyhole reeled back in surprise. Then the yak shut the doors again. I took a deep breath.

"Okay," I said. "So, let's plan this attack, huh? And could we make it snappy? I'd kind of like a few minutes with Ellen before we ride out."

My relationship with Ellen had always been awkward because, on the one hand, she was Phil Lawler's daughter and, on the other hand, I knew that in the high future she would rule an interstellar matriarchy called Auntish and thrice three-score billion people would call her their leader. And ten billion more would call her conqueror.

Her fiery obsession with liberating the homeworld from the persistent grip of ice was renowned up there in the future, so it was always odd to find her here, oblivious of her eventual fate, calmly handing out field kits from the USGS storeroom, known, of course, as the Q.

"How do?" I said with a smile, leaning nonchalantly against the doorframe. She turned around, all pretty and dark-haired, in the middle of cleaning an ice-proof compass. Her eyes were green like John Quick's, but bright.

"Hello," she said in the kind of tone that sent a shiver up my spine. "Dad 'warned' me you were in town. How's the yak?"

It grunted that it was indeed fine. She walked over and ran a hand through its coarse pelt. To my knowledge, she was the only other person in the universe the yak let touch it. She favoured me with another smile. I had last seen her eight or nine months ago, subjective, when she had been seconded to a USGS detachment rolling out sensor arrays in the Upper Palaeolithic, and now here she was again, back in the present.

"Bad business, this glacier," I tipped my chin in the direction I thought Lokboksfrost lay.

"Well, you know ice. Dad's especially worked up over this one. I'll assume he told you all about the REALBOW, at length."

"You got it. So did Quick."

"And I assume instead of using the REALBOW, Dad's having you go up there by yourself, to challenge the ice, as usual?"

"Two for two."

We stood in silence for a moment.

"And I guess you won't take any of the new weapons I've invented?"

I sighed. This was an age-old argument. I could hardly blame her; she was human after all. It was ever in their nature to tinker and create, to make new things, to think up new ways of tackling problems and challenges. And I could never properly explain to them why ice was immune to all trickery. A bold declaration of war and two stout picks, that was all ice could understand, and thus that was all to which ice was vulnerable. Over the years I had replaced iron with steel, then steel with aluminium and titanium, sure, but the design remained the same, the essential weapon unchanged. As for new toys, a million microwave scatterguns and napalm slingers couldn't help me.

Ellen looked sadly at the rack full of gleaming new devices she'd spent hours building from scraps around the workshop. Field packs were lined up on a table near the door, but they too were useless to me.

"Okay," she said sadly. "But I'll still keep building them, right? I'll still keep inventing for you. Maybe one day you'll try some of them out."

"It's the thought that counts," I smiled.

"Look, maybe just for me you'd take one thing? It's just a little thing, it won't get in the way. It goes on one of your picks." She reached into her pocket and pulled out some kind of metal box with a stout brace on it. I was intrigued, despite myself.

"What's all this then?" I asked.

"It goes on your pick," she motioned for my left-hand pick, my dominant hand. I unclipped the carabiner and handed it over. The yak had cleaned it well; the titanium gleamed under the fluorescent lighting in the Q.

Ellen slipped the brace over the handle and slid it up until it rested against the point where the blade of the pick was bolted to the titanium handle. Then she flipped out an electric screwdriver and tightened the brace against the handle. She swung the pick a couple of times and then handed it back to me.

"It hardly changes the balance at all," she said.

"What does it do?" I asked, looking closer. There was a button, easily reached by my thumb if I held the pick high up the handle, as I did when delivering a shattering blow.

"There's a powerpack in the box, rigged to pump several hundred amps of juice into the blade when you press the button. The blade will superheat in about half a second, while an insulator on the brace prevents the handle from getting too hot. At four hundred degrees, it should slice through pretty much anything."

"Actually, that is a neat idea," I said, giving the pick a couple of experimental swings to confirm the box didn't tip the balance. It was fine. I clipped it back onto my harness, and adjusted the straps across my hips, from habit.

"It's a one-time thing, though," she said. "Once you've set it off, the blade will stay hot for a few minutes, less if you happen to plunge it into the frigid heart of a mind-prism. But after that you need to bring it back here for recharging. Sorry I don't have a second one for you. I only thought up the idea last night."

"It's awesome," I said, genuinely touched. It was still a curious feeling, having the future ruler of the known galaxy, Aunty Ellen herself, lovingly build instruments of death for me in the wee hours.

"Tell me about my future again," she asked quietly.

I sighed. "You've told *me* on more than one occasion not to tell you anything," I admonished.

"Not yet I haven't," she pointed out.

"Yes, but you *will*," I insisted. "No, we have to focus on the ice. I can smell that bastard planning something big. He's going to surge on the city, I know it. And I have to stop him."

Ellen regarded me as though she maybe wanted to throw her arms around me and kiss me full on the mouth, but was held back by the curious way I always regarded her: part brotherly love, part fierce all-consuming passion, part abject gibbering terror. Whenever I looked at her, sure I saw Ellen Lawler, green-eyed and dark-haired and sweet and true, but I also saw Aunty Ellen, howling imperatrix of the western spiral arm, sweeping down out of Scorpio with her hair burning like a thousand supernovas and worlds crumbling to ash in her wake. It was, as I've said, a hell of a relationship.

I was her champion on this slush-ball of a planet. And whenever a glacier fell beneath my blade, another would spring up half a world away and I would thread my way through time and space to face it, too. Over and over, on and on.

"When you fight the ice," Ellen asked after a while, "do you ever feel like you're one of those circus guys spinning plates on poles, except that whenever you move to set a plate spinning, another plate on the far side of the stage falls with a terrible crash and the audience boos you?"

"All the time," I said.

Before an assault, I always tried to give myself a precious five minutes in the USGS coffee room, nursing an espresso, my mind a studied blank. The yak would stand or slump in the corner, picking its nails, bored and irritable and ready to fight, but I would ignore it. It had travelled with me for the better part of ten thousand years, and I had long grown desensitised to any attempt at emotional blackmail. But make no mistake: it had my measure as well.

So there I sat in a low chair, head slung back, looking at without seeing the corporate-issue foam ceiling tiles and sprinkler outlets that had never been tested, when Lawler burst into the room with such violence that even the yak jumped.

"It's Quick," he spluttered. "That no good underhanded filibustering lie-mongering son-of-a-bitch has taken his team, two choppers and the REALBOW deployment pods, and has gone to launch against the glacier."

"Oh, for the love of fine weather!" I cried. The yak bellowed its mighty battle cry in consternation. Bits of foam fell off the ceiling and the sprinkler system activated.

As we stood there covered in black gunk from the untested pipes, I thought unkind thoughts about John Quick and his precious science project. He would doom us all, nothing surer.

"What a freaking idiot!" I managed.

"That cold water feels rather good," said Lawler, lifting his face into the spray.

"All right!" I snapped out of it. "Sign off on two teams! We'll chase this bastard down and format his tape drive. Which direction did he go?"

"Somewhere over the REALBOW," muttered Lawler.

"Cute but unhelpful," I replied. "Forget Quick then—we'll strike against the glacier now, smash him before Quick can do any damage. I'm off to the helipad. Since the sprinklers will have shut down the lifts, I'll be five minutes getting to the roof. Make sure there's something waiting by the time I get there."

I nodded to the yak, or at least the great mass of wet hair and horns that must have been the yak, and we ran for the stairwell. Five minutes and sixteen flights of stairs later we erupted into a light sleet that was marginally worse than standing under the sprinkler system, but only marginally. A bright orange USGS Bell 212 sat on the pad, rotors spinning. The pilot gave me an almost comical thumbs-up through the plexiglass window.

The yak and I jumped in the back where two field agents sat hunched in extreme weather gear, field packs at their feet.

"Hey, no pets!" yelled the stupid one, and then screamed as the yak swatted him easily out the other side of the chopper. It liked to ride a-port, facing forward. Groaning, the kid picked himself up and clambered back inside, rubbing his ribs. He resentfully buckled himself into the rear-facing starboard seat, and reached forward to slide the door closed.

"What's your name, kid?" I yelled as the chopper spun up and lifted off the top of Veritas Tower to swing away to the west.

"Steve," he replied, "and that's Alan."

"Hi, Al," I yelled.

"Alan!" insisted Alan.

"Whatever!" I yelled. "So what are you guys, glaciologists?"

"I am," said Steve. "Al is my research assistant! And by the way, I'm thirty-six."

"Yeah, that's why I called you 'kid'."

I became aware of the pilot waving at me from the cockpit, indicating by use of signs that there were radio headsets hung on pegs near our seats, so we wouldn't have to shout.

"Welcome aboard, sir," he said as I plugged in. "I'm sorry, but they didn't brief us when we scrambled. We're heading for the glacier, right?"

"You got it," I replied. "We *were* going to chase down a rogue field agent, but the glacier has shifted our priorities. I'm expecting it to surge at any moment. We're gonna make a bold assault on the mind-prism, so head for the ELA."

"The...?"

"Equilibrium line altitude, where the accumulation area gives way to the ablation area. The ice is still and silent there, and the mind-prism lies deep in the fluted caverns below. These eggheads here should be able to patch their T-maps through to your autopilot. Is that right, guys?"

"You got it!" said Steve brightly, fiddling with a veritable medusa's-head of wires.

We flew out across the CBD and the inner suburbs, rotors settling into a steady whine.

"So what's your doctorate on?" I asked Alan.

"Effects of human-emitted greenhouse gasses on global temperatures," he muttered. A shy one, then, behind those thick geeky glasses.

"Eh?"

Steve leaned forward.

"Al has this crazy idea that CO_2 and other gasses prevent long-wave radiation from escaping back into space. Like in a greenhouse, right? Generate enough of these gasses and the planet should heat up by several degrees. It'd be the ultimate weapon against ice."

I thought it over.

"Crazy idea," I said after a while. "You really think it might work?"

Alan shrugged. "It's just a theory."

"He calls it Global Warming. Pretty funny, huh?"

I had it admit, it was a good one.

"Sir?" said the pilot. "Something's happening up ahead. Some kind of weather phenomenon."

Which of course was the kind of expression I had been dreading to hear ever since we took off. I unbuckled and slung myself into the co-pilot's seat. We flew across the city through open air with a little sleet, kept clean and more-or-less clear by the heat island generated by all that human industry in the streets below. But up ahead, far closer than it should have been, the solid grey wall of a massive blizzard was chewing its way across the western suburbs.

"What is it?" breathed the pilot.

"It's the icedamned REALBOW," I grimaced. The heat island was clearly collapsing, borne down under the weight of all that snow and ice. Something had augmented Lokboksfrost's *anima* and I had a pretty good idea exactly what was going on. I slung myself back into the passenger compartment.

"You guys know Professor Quick?" I asked.

"Sure," said Steve. "He's a great guy. Industrious, you know? Always working late hours, always trying to increase the body of scientific..." The chopper gave a fearful lurch as we plunged into the blizzard. Darkness enveloped us, and the rotors howled against the buffeting winds. The chopper thrashed like a cat in a bag, outraged at its loss of liberty and clear air.

"Pilot!" I shrieked.

"No worries, sir, she should hold up. For a while anyway!"

I nodded at the yak. It closed its eyes. Born of ice and sworn to destroy it, the yak's not-unimpressive *anima* forced a tiny bubble of clear air around the chopper and we flew on smoothly, like a borer through an expensive antique sideboard. Or an encysting parasite through the gullet of some gigantic beast. Steve goggled at the yak.

"How long can he keep that up?"

"*It* can keep it up all day if it has to," I said mildly, inspecting my nails.

"The T-map is uploaded," said Alan, who seemed completely unperturbed by the whole experience. The pilot shouted something vaguely affirmative but otherwise incoherent, and the chopper swung to a more southerly heading. Lokboksfrost was in our sights now—that frigid bastard—and I would slice and dice him soon.

Alan had his hand to his goldwire. I tuned in myself, to find most of the USGS shouting at once about the collapse of the heat island over Greater Sydney and the sudden inrush of foul weather. Quick had screwed the pooch most definitively this time. I could guess the series of events: REALBOW gets deployed by an idiot who doesn't understand how the glacial *anima* works. Glacier absorbs energy from REALBOW that Quick assumed would change the weather. *Anima* suddenly becomes bloated with power. Glacier surges. Heat island collapses. Millions die. My job was to prevent that final step.

"Clear the goldwire!" I howled. "This is the glacial assault force and we're inbound to the ELA! I need weather updates and data for my eggheads here—and where the hell is my second team?"

The cacophony died down a little as the lesser field agents were shunted off the wire by the demonically efficient switchboard girls back at the nexus. Lawler spoke, his voice tinny and twisted by the impossible technologies from the future that powered the goldwire.

"The second team is en-route. We delayed it to load on an ice drill."

"I don't *need* an icedamned drill, I need GPS specialists to track the surge, Phillip, and I need them five minutes ago!" I screamed.

"I can hear you perfectly well. You don't need to shout."

I glanced across to where Steve was smirking, hand to his ear. He went deadpan with remarkable speed.

"When will you understand that your toys *will not work against ice*!" I shrieked. "A bold declaration of war—"

"And two stout picks, yes yes, we've heard it all before," snapped Lawler, probably sitting in his office staring at the terrible faces in that photo from Antarctica. "But just in case, Aspect Hunter. Do it for me. Or do it for Ellen."

"Oh, leave her out of it, for your own sake!" I cried.

Suddenly the yak's *anima* faltered, and the chopper was thrown violently about the sky. We clung to what frequent flyers called the 'Jesus handles' until the yak regained control.

"What? What?" I demanded. "Is it the surge? Has the surge started?"

The yak just sat there, eyes shut. Had its brow not been covered in thick shaggy hair, I'm sure it would have been sweating.

"LANDSAT update," said Alan quietly over the goldwire. We had priority at the nexus now, so we didn't need to use the chopper's intercom anymore. "Lokboksfrost has begun his surge. The terminus is moving east-nor'east at forty-eight point two klicks."

"Forty-eight point two," I muttered. Top speed. He was charging the city. The Widowmaker meant to finish it here, this afternoon. I glanced at my watch, for what it was worth. As far as humans were concerned, it was about three o'clock. Three hours of sunlight remained. After that, when night fell, we would all be as good as dead. "How far is he from the CBD?" I asked.

"Seventy-four klicks," Alan replied. Less than two hours. Well, that was alright then. It would all be over one way or the other by nightfall.

"John Quick!" I yelled across the goldwire, "Can you hear me!"

A brief burst of static and then the nexus cut in. "We've no header on his signal, sir," said a pleasant female voice. "We should assume his node is offline."

"Hell and low mercury," I cursed. Then I composed myself. "This is a general broadcast. Is there anybody out there who knows anything about the REALBOW?"

"Yes," came a small voice, male and reedy. Classic nerd.

"Who the hell is that?"

"My name's Angelo."

"And who are you, mate?"

"I'm on the REALBOW team. I refused to go with Quick. He was angry, he said things about the Director. And about you, sir. I didn't like to—"

"Your loyalty is admirable, but you can kiss my arse later. Do you have control of the REALBOW at this time?"

"No," said Angelo in an even smaller voice.

"Brain farts!" I screamed. "Can you *regain* control of it? Does it work like that?"

"Maybe," said Angelo.

"WEATHERSAT reports the Greater Sydney heat island has completely collapsed," Alan looked up from his dials and readouts for the first time. "We're wide open."

I nodded. "Okay, okay, it's all good. Ladies, I want you to give Angelo complete mainframe access at his location, unrestricted. I want every last flop of processor power diverted to his station—he *must* regain control of the REALBOW, now." The switchboard ladies voiced their acknowledgement and the quality of data from the goldwire flickered for a moment, as if titanic energies were being redirected.

"Wow," said Angelo, wherever he was.

"Less awe, more saw," I said as the chopper thundered onward. Was I scared? For myself, not at all. If it all went pear-shaped, the yak and I could simply Dissociate to the deep past, or the high future, safe and secure and beyond the reach of ice. But if we left now, Greater Sydney would fall. These brave boys in the chopper would be flung from the sky and diced by white-demons. And the families in their tidy suburban bungalows would all be turned into middle-class popsicles, grinning insanely into a frozen future. I had to stop it.

"I think..." said Angelo, and stopped.

"Think what, think what?" I demanded, well, screamed really.

"I think I have control. Limited control, but control. I can... I can give it orders. It's back online. The extra power did it, I'm sure, but..."

"Do it!" I screamed. "Push the big red button, blast this icy bastard with everything you've got!" The chopped thumped and lurched in the storm. The yak began grinding its teeth.

"Okay!" bleated Angelo. "Attempting a full temperature inversion! Now!"

Nothing happened. Alan put his hand to his ear.

"You have to press ESC to execute the command," he said quietly. "It's weird, I know, but the mainframe's kind of old and the guys who designed it were—"

Suddenly, the blizzard stopped. Just like that. The thick snow clouds seemed to freeze in place and then break up into dazzling crystals of ice. The air was alive with it, singing with it, and slowly the ice spun apart and melted. We flew onward, through clear air, under a blue sky. The yak let out an enormous breath and slumped in its seat.

"Nice work," I said absently as I stared out around us. Quick's damned toy had really done it, dissipated the blizzard, the work of a moment. "Incredible!"

"Sir, Director Lawler is requesting goldwire resources be reconnected to the steering committee," a switchboard girl said.

"Hell!" I blurted. "Angelo! Amazing, mate, truly amazing. You'll get the OAM for this, don't you worry about it. Awesome job! Keep it up down there and don't go home yet. We might need another shot."

Angelo made some kind of stunned noise, and then his connection was redirected back to the boardroom.

"The glacier!" Lawler was screaming as we swept lower towards the mountains, "Where is the glacier?"

Then I saw him.

*

Lokboksfrost had surged, that was for sure, down out of the wide, U-shaped valley towards the suburbs. He was clearly bent for the CBD. From this altitude he looked like a worm, a great beast of legend, curled and menacing. Yet, he was no stranger here. He looked like part of the land. Along his moraine, where ancient sandstone cliffs shattered and trembled at his passing, he seemed extruded from the very rock. He was massive. He looked like a great weight on the Earth, his *anima* so bloated with energies it caused the clear air to ripple.

He was angry, I knew this. He was furious that his blizzard had been defeated and his armies ran naked under the harsh sun. I could see white-demons swarming from crevasses and spreading out across the frost-stung suburbs, breaking into houses and killing everyone they found. It was a massacre, but it was my job to stop it turning into a genocide.

"This is a big surge," I muttered. The yak grunted in agreement.

"Too big," Steve offered, leaning forward so he could see out our side of the chopper. "I know you'll tell me if I'm wrong, but doesn't this amount of speed and movement suggest that he's brought the mind-prism down much closer to the terminus—sorry—blister-drop?"

He was right, of course.

"Pilot! Swing back to the east, we're gonna land on the head of this damn thing!" I called. The pilot nodded, bless his mirrored shades. We all hung onto the Jesus handles again as he hauled on the stick. Now we rode up behind Lokboksfrost, pointed towards the frigid ocean, dropping lower towards his broad flank.

"Can you see it?" I asked the yak. It stared down as crevasses and screaming white-demons flashed below us, but it shook its head. I looked, too, looked for the tell-tale curdle in the almost-invisible *anima*, the gyre that swung and swung around Lokboksfrost's great mind-prism.

Then we saw it, a little to the side, beneath a smooth unbroken icefield. The humans couldn't know what we were looking for, of course, but they followed our orders. They knew we were the only viable weapon. The REALBOW had shot its load, so to speak, and had nearly killed everyone besides.

I looked at the yak. Now it nodded. We were in agreement—we would make our stand on that icefield.

"Bring it down to fifty metres!" I yelled to the pilot, checking my picks and harness. "No lower. Without us down there to protect you, the *anima* will fry your brains!"

Steve and Alan were already looking put upon as Lokbokfrost tried to get inside their heads and whisper to them that it was all pointless, that they should lie down, sleep, let it all flow across them. Ice, said the Widowmaker, was the great answer. Believe in ice, and all the pain and confusion and fighting would stop. Silence would reign. Silence and cold.

"That's it!" yelled the pilot. The yak and I jumped...

...and four seconds later I hit the ice and rolled. It was cold down there, and the *anima* raged. The yak landed behind me with an almighty woollen thud and when I turned to look, it was squatting, supporting itself with one terrible hand and grinning. We had landed in the centre of the gyre, directly over the mind-prism. This was going to be easy.

I deftly flipped my pick from my harness into my hand and made a firm, definite first strike on the ice.

It was like striking diamond.

"Hmn," I thought, and struck again, harder. The pick just bounced off. Finally, I swung at the ice without grace, without method—I just put my whole weight behind the blow. The pick bounced back so violently it hit me in the centre of the forehead.

I reeled, swearing. Gripping my pounding head, I turned to look at the yak again. It screamed at the ice, stamped at it, gouged at it, without success. We were locked out. Deep beneath us, the glacier rumbled.

"Is he...is he *laughing* at us?" I screamed. To the north and south, I could see the suburbs passing us by as Lokboksfrost ploughed inexorably on towards the CBD, the USGS goldwire nexus, and ultimate victory.

"What is going *on?*" I demanded. Then it hit me. The REALBOW. The icedamned REALBOW had, in raising the temperature so quickly and dampening the blizzard so precipitously, somehow channelled that energy into fusing the surface of the glacier. "We'll need a bloody drill to get through it!" I bawled.

"Sorry, what was that?" asked Lawler, over the goldwire.

I stood there, picks dangling, and fumed. He'd been right. The cagey old bastard had been right. So, on the one hand I could give in to him and admit my blinkered short-sightedness, or on the other hand, millions could die on the whim of my ego.

"Send 'em in," I said, deadpan.

"They were right behind you all the time," Lawler replied, a little smugly.

A huge blue helicopter of obscure Russian design swept low across the glacier and thumped awkwardly onto a complicated set of skis. It slid towards us, sideways. The yak and I stood our ground. The chopper kept sliding. We stood. The chopper slid. I glanced at the yak, noted the dangerous glint in its eye, and took a casual step to the left to avoid some kind of protruding radio mast thing as the chopper spun through a half circle to a complete stop. The rotors whined, slowed, and cut out. The unearthly silence of the glacier returned, thrown into sharp relief by the forty-eight-point-two-kilometre-an-hour slipstream created by Lokboksfrost's continuing charge.

Through the plexiglass canopy, the pilot's face was ashen.

"Dude!" screamed a USGS field agent in a patched snowsuit as he jumped wildly from the chopper's side door. "Dude, you nearly got totalled! Oh, dude!" Behind him, three other men were dragging a coring rig out of the cargo compartment.

"Hello," I said. "Who are you?"

"Dude, I'm totally Dave," said Dave. "Your drill sergeant, geddit? Drill sergeant?" He looked at me and stopped grinning. "We'll set up over here."

He trudged away and started giving orders. I turned to make some quip to the yak, but it was looking the other way and pointing. Across the distant sastrugi, white-demons were charging us. About fifty of the damn things.

I swung my picks into my hands and took a battle stance.

The yak stood beside me. Behind us, I could hear the drill team swearing as the motor stuttered, caught and then howled as the bit struck the unusually solid ice. All the yak and I had to do was hold off the onslaught long enough for the team to punch through into the fluted caverns of the mind-prism chamber.

The white-demons charged, and then, at less than fifteen metres, the front rank just peeled away and ran off. I blinked.

For a second, I didn't see the serac. For a second, I thought it was part of the glacier itself, a great boulder of ice, jagged and impossible. Then it reared up and thumped a blade nearly a metre long into the ice right near my left foot. And then it roared.

The yak and I stared up at it, this ultimate manifestation of Lokboksfrost's will, an enormous, semi-autonomous, self-assembling juggernaut of destruction. Half-a-dozen rusted ice picks were embedded in its blocky flanks. It was kind of a like a bear, if you asked a completely crazy person to draw a bear and then made it out of ice.

The next swipe came from the right, and the yak managed a nimble backflip to avoid getting disembowelled. I was less fortunate—the creature clipped me and sent me spinning into a snowdrift. I looked up to see a white-demon leaping for my throat, but all it got was an ice pick in its own as I rolled out of the way. I struck again with my right hand and the mind-prism seemed to leap from the creature's skull. To my amazement, it evaporated in the late afternoon sunshine.

"Oi!" I yelled to the yak, where it was sizing up the serac. "The REALBOW is still running! Knock the prism out and it's as good as dead!" The yak nodded: message received.

Two more white-demons fell to my picks as I swung and slashed my way back towards the serac. There was a sort of arena of awe formed around the yak and the beast, the lesser white-demons watching the serac strike again and again. The ice beneath us cracked but held, curse it, and always the yak danced away.

I flung myself at the serac's flank, but it just shifted its weight and I bounced off inelegantly. I looked up to see the drill team staring at the battle.

"Drill, damn you!" I screamed.

"Dude!" Dave howled, but went back to work.

"Keep it away from the drill team!" I yelled at the yak. "And watch your back!"

The animal looked over its shoulder to see half-a-dozen white-demons leaping at once. The yak ducked and the serac's next strike shattered them all as they glided in an unstoppable trajectory towards its terrible blades. Mind-prisms puffed into vapour under the REALBOW's glare.

But the serac knew the drill was the real risk. It knew the yak and I were eternal and unstoppable, but by some quirk of fate it couldn't hope to understand, we needed these puny humans to strike at its master. It shouldered the yak aside again and lumbered towards the drill team. They were staring again, even as the drill whined and bit at the ice, they stared at death charging them.

The yak leapt high and landed on the serac's back. The animal raised one shaggy arm, talons gleaming, and struck hard at the beast's shoulder. The serac's right arm came away in a clean fracture, shards dancing, and there was John Quick, frozen in the serac's heart, a grotesque trophy. He looked shocked, but defiant. I staggered backward at the sight of him. He had the REALBOW actuator clutched in one frozen hand.

The serac tumbled heavily onto its side. Screaming in anger, it lurched onto its hind legs, grabbed the yak with its remaining hand and flung my friend and silent travelling companion in a flat trajectory into the drill rig.

Men and machinery went in all directions. The vital drill bit, the vital, essential drill bit, went sailing off and disappeared down a crevasse.

Dave sat up in the snow, dazed, and said "Dude?"

"Go!" I screamed. "Flee!" He scrabbled to his fleet and ran back towards the chopper, which was spinning up its rotors for a quick getaway, already leaving the ground. The pilot's face was still ashen.

Howling with rage, I charged the serac, swung my picks deep into its back and hauled myself up towards the misshapen chunk of ice it called a head. It moved, fast and powerful, trying to throw me, but the picks bit hard and I hung on. The yak was only a dozen metres away, rising to its feet, groggy and stunned.

The serac focused its attack; it saw the yak was vulnerable now, this one time, this one remarkable time. It could score a mighty victory for its master, for all ice, by felling the yak that had harried them all for so long. It raised its remaining fist and swung, meaning to crush the yak and end its endless journey at last.

Then the whole icefield collapsed.

We fell. We fell through ice. The yak, the serac and I, tumbling through fluted caverns, through delicate sculpted halls, past the honeycomb iceforms where white-demons are born, through the fissures, into the deep blue heart of the glacier.

We landed, inelegantly, among shards of ice, on a great scalloped ledge. It was terribly beautiful. The air was still. All around us we heard the groans and splinterings of a surging glacier. We could feel the movement, sense it in our bones, but there were no visual cues. It was a cathedral of ice.

And there, flanked by great columns, was the prize. Pulsing white and blue and green and casting great flickering waves of the *anima*, there stood the source of all Lokboksfrost's malevolent energy—the mind-prism.

It was about the height of a man, six-sided, irregular but possessed of some strange symmetry that was both alien and terribly familiar. It was alive, intelligent. It saw us, here in its sacred temple. It was outraged. It directed more energy into the broken form of the serac lying near the yak on the precipice. I peered over the edge—it was easily two hundred metres straight down into blackness. Not even I could survive that fall.

I hefted my left-hand pick, taking the handle deep into my palm and fingering the button on the device Ellen had fitted. I saw it all stretched out before me—heat the blade, plunge it into the mind-prism, kill the glacier, end the assault, save the city. It was clear, like the air on a day after snow. I took a step forward, and another. The *anima* would not slow me. If a white-demon leapt, I would strike it down. I was unstoppable. I was the Aspect Hunter.

The yak screamed.

I spun around, to see the serac holding the animal out over all that nothingness, held there by the throat. I didn't even stop to think or consider what it would mean, I just pressed the button on Ellen's device and charged.

The superheated blade of the ice pick sank easily through the serac's ice-armoured forehead and with my other hand I snatched out the fist-sized mind-prism. Instantly, the creature was dead, mere dumb ice, and the yak was dangling from just another spar, like ten thousand spars it had dangled from before.

It whinnied, the first time I had ever heard it make such a sound. It grabbed at the spar with its talons, swung awkwardly around where it was held by the throat until it straddled what had once been the serac's arm, and hacked itself free.

Moments later we stood before the mind-prism, scratching our heads.

We hit it with ice pick and talon, but it wouldn't crack. We kicked it, beat it, even breathed on it, without result. Lokboksfrost, too, tried everything. He tried pulsing us with the full fury of his *anima*, he tried his fright-lights, he tried icy blasts from the great crevasse behind us. We stood through it all. It was, as they say, an impasse.

"Angelo?" I asked, over the goldwire.

"Er, hello? So you're still alive then?" he replied.

I grinned at the yak.

"More or less, mate. Look, we're standing in front of this mind-prism, trying to work out how to smash it into a million bits, and I recall that madman John Quick saying something about a focused strike from the REALBOW. Can you still do that? On my location?"

"Um..." said Angelo.

"Remember you have to press ESC," I added, nodding at the yak.

There was a pause and then the prism chamber seemed to grow brighter, as if a cloud had passed from in front of the sun. Then it got brighter still. Then uncomfortably bright. Then dazzling. Then blinding. All of John Quick's misguided will was beamed down that shaft from high above, and it would melt

Lokboksfrost like snow on a summer's breeze ...

... except that the glacier, damn him, was holding it back. With sharp focus of his own, Lokboksfrost held the heat and light at bay, by directing the full force of his *anima* upward, outward.

"This is ridiculous," I muttered. Then I felt the serac's mind-prism twitch in my hand. I looked down. It was jumping, eager to find new ice and reassemble, draw power from its master and rejoin the fight.

Draw power from its master ...

I swung around and plunged the serac's mind-prism into the wall of Lokbokfrost's inner sanctum.

Instantly, the wall shattered, then bulged, twisted, created shapes, legs, arms, blades. The serac howled to be reborn, sucking at the glacial *anima*, taking vital power from Lokboksfrost's battle with the REALBOW.

And then the light was all around us, and the great mind-prism cracked, slumped, and shattered into snowflakes. The walls of ice became snow. The serac, without a body, became snow. The scalloped balcony, nothing more than snow. And the light was all around us.

Later, back on the surface after a hard climb and much boasting of who had been the more bruised and battered by the serac, the yak and I met a chopper full of USGS personnel. The one in the green parka looked kind of familiar.

"Come on," said Ellen. "I'll buy you a beer, and you can tell me about my future."

I cocked an eye at her. She was quite pretty, all done up in her snowsuit, the crossed hammers of the USGS proud on her chest.

"Your future?" I asked. "Well, at least now we know you've got one."

We swung away into the sunset, while beneath us, a great line of snowploughs crawled along the Great Western Highway. While we partied, they'd be working all night.

But in the morning, it would be spring.

Notes Concerning Events at the Ray Harryhausen Memorial Home for Retired Actors

ANDREW SULLIVAN

Chess is a game of strategy, skill and patience. It requires considerable forethought and knowledge of the rules. My opponent, however, had none of these attributes and, to be frank, probably thought that full-body contact would add a certain dimension to the game.

"What's the matter, Ken?" asked Giro, my aging Nipponese opponent, after moving a pawn. His false teeth turned all his 'esses' into sibilant 'sshhhses'. "Can't take the heat? Then get out of the kitchen." He laughed at his own joke, the way he does, and slapped the table with one clawed hand, making all the pieces jump. The spines that ran down his back waggled like latex prosthetics.

"It's only the fifth move, Giro," I said, grinding my well-worn molars. "Keep your colostomy bag on."

Giro stopped laughing and his red eyes narrowed. "Just what are you implying, you over-sized monkey?"

I bristled at the slur but decided not to react. "I'm not implying anything, you old fart. Just play the game." I moved one of my advance pawns forward.

The old lizard stared at the chessboard in bewilderment, as he always did at this point. Generally, he would either get in a huff, smash the board to the floor and stomp off in a rage, or he would sit and stew until Matron Medusa came and dragged him off for a sponge bath. This time, however, was different. He reached out, moved his own knight and took my pawn. He tipped his head back and yowled his triumph. Oh, brother.

The others in the common room looked up at the ruckus. Stan the Cyclops, Merv the CFTBL, MF (the giant moth whom we affectionately called MothraF*cker or MF for short), the Kraken, and Cerbie the huge three-headed dog who was suffering badly from fleas of late. The dogs barked, MF fluttered and the Kraken went thump—his sign that he was hungry again. Stan just smiled and I knew the old codger had been coaching Giro. I winked at him and the single great eye in the middle of Stan's forehead blinked back in return in what I assumed was a one-eyed wink.

Giro was still chuckling in glee. I reached out and moved my own knight and took his. Giro's smile disappeared and his red eyes began to glow like burning embers. He opened his great jaws, which could fit around a semi-trailer, took a deep breath to let loose an enormous howl of frustration—and his false teeth promptly fell out and clattered on the floor. His eyes dowsed and he dropped to all fours to look for his chompers. I began laughing so hard and loud that I lost control.

You know how it is when you're getting on a bit and things aren't as tight as they used to be, and once or twice, here and there, you sort of let go when you shouldn't? This was one of those times. Honestly. Incontinence pants help but they ride up so uncomfortably and I wasn't wearing any at that moment. As it turned out, Giro was ferreting under my chair and ended up with a bucketful of the yellow stuff all over his head.

I stopped laughing and there was a moment in which the only sound was my water dribbling onto Giro's snout. There was another moment of nothing while Giro's pea-brain worked out what was happening, then all hell broke loose. Him screaming and me laughing.

The chessboard went flying. So too did the table and some chairs. Giro was royally pissed off and he let everyone in the Home know it. He stretched to his full sixty-foot height and let rip with a deafening but toothless roar. "You lousy frickin' ape," he thaid through thlick and thlimy jawth, spraying half of us with lizard saliva. "I'm gonna rip your frickin' arms off." He came at me and I leapt away. I may be old and incontinent but when it comes down to it, I'm still an ape and still have it where it counts. I dropped into a four-hand crouch and scooted around the big lumbering oaf.

Giro's tail was his main mode of attack against a smaller foe, as I'd learned over the years, but with his sciatica he didn't like to use it that much. Generally, he relied on his roar, which, even with his teeth in place, was much worse than his bite.

We skirted around each other. Our growing audience probably thought we were sizing each other up. In reality I was trying to think of a way out of the situation without getting hurt or losing face. Before anything came to mind Matron Medusa arrived.

"Just what in the name of Zeus is going on in here?" she boomed. "I can hear you lot from other side of the hospital."

The sound of a flight of jet fighters taking off is barely audible compared to Matron at full volume. She stood in the common-room doorway, hands on hips and headful of snakes all hissy, staring at the two of us standing toe-to-toe and towering above her. "I've warned you two before. There shall be no fighting. All games privileges are revoked. And that means for *everyone.*"

The assembled group moaned as one and Matron went ballistic. "Right. That's it. If you want to complain, no custard for the next two weeks." The group shut up. "Everyone back to their wards. NOW!"

We all shuffled off.

"Not you two." Matron indicated Giro and me. "You two will clean this mess up. And for Kronos' sake, put some pants on, Ken Kong."

*

The Ray Harryhausen Memorial Home for Retired Actors is not as bad as some old folks' homes. The staff are friendly and the facilities are second to none and each of us residents has each of his or her unique needs looked after.

Apart from Matron and a particularly beefy green male nurse named David something-or-other, the staff are regular people. By that I mean they weren't in the industry. Acting, that is. Matron had had her share of the limelight back in the fifties and sixties before following her calling into nursing. And nursing's gain is acting's loss, believe me.

Most of the residents had had a fleeting moment of success at some point in their careers but, unlike Matron, had persisted beyond the point of common decency and been left high-and-dry by producers, directors, writers, the movie-going public and, finally, agents. The Home is the final resting place for a lot of stars of yesteryear. It seems that the world has turned and we've been left behind by the wonders of computer-generated images. But such is life. There are always other things to do.

When I was first discovered by Merian C. Cooper and Ernest B. Schoedsack back in 1932, I had no idea that it would turn into a movie career lasting decades. My big break was *King Kong* alongside Fay Wray—the best co-star an actor could wish for. When it was released, I was literally on top of the world. Next was *The Son of Kong*, which flopped, and then followed a string of box-office bombs. In 1949 came *Mighty Joe Young* and my career revived for a while, but subsequently I was B-grade fodder and my career went into decline. It wasn't until Dino de Laurentis discovered me sweeping dung from horse stables that my career hit one final high point. It took him a good dozen years to convince the Hollywood movie moguls to remake the 1933 classic, but he did eventually and in 1976 I achieved movie history by reprising my award-winning role as King Kong, this time alongside Jessica Lange. I was getting on in age by then, and not as nimble as I used to be, so Mr de Laurentis had to use considerable special effects on some shots, but the majority of it was me, especially my love scenes with Jessica. Memories I will hold close to my heart forever.

Bath-time at the Home is generally a time of great coordination, timing and grace—not unlike ballet. The nursing staff find it extremely difficult, even when the old flesh they're trying to bathe is willing. When the flesh isn't willing, the itty-bitty fellas have to bring in the block-and-tackle and literally hoist us big'uns into the tub and scrub us down, wash off the piss and shit, and then reverse the process to get us out and dried. It's not the most dignified of procedures and the flesh tries to be willing as much as possible to avoid it. The humans mean well and try hard to make it as painless as possible.

That was why, when they brought the new fella in, I was saddened to see him hurting the little ones. He was not a happy camper. From my window, I saw the truck pull up and all the nursing staff on duty rush down to help. They brought him out trussed up like a roast. He looked to be some sort of giant lizard—like Giro—only bigger, perhaps as tall as seventy or eighty feet. His snout was clamped and his front claws crossed and tied. He was thrashing about from side-to-side and trying to roar through the muzzle. Doc O'Brien shot him up with sedative using his high-powered syringe, but it didn't seem to have much effect. The newcomer batted young Marcel Delgado away like he was a fly (which wasn't that far from reality, given the differences in their sizes). Even Matron had to move quickly to avoid being stomped to a pancake by the guy's huge webbed feet.

"What's happening out there?" Giro asked from his bed.

"New fella coming in," I replied. "Big one, too."

MF pushed back his covers and fluttered over to look out the window over my shoulder. "Oh no," he said. "Not another giant lizard."

Giro leaped out of bed the way giant geriatric lizards do (i.e. slowly) and joined us. "He's not that big," he said finally. "Never seen him before, though. Aggressive, isn't he?" he added when the newcomer thrashed loose of the binding the two nurses' aides were putting on his legs. It was then that the sedative Doc O'Brien had given him began to work and he finally became manageable. They put him into the big front-end loader and brought him inside.

For about half an hour, MF, Giro and I sat on our beds discussing who this guy might be. No one had seen him before— certainly not a big box-office attraction. MF thought he might be a transfer from one of the other homes—the Storemen and Packers or Waterside Workers. But I didn't think so.

"I reckon he's one of those new fangled Nipponese anime-type creatures. His uncouth behaviour certainly suggests it."

"I beg your pardon?" Giro said.

"I meant the animes are uncouth, not the Nipponese."

Giro harrumphed but seemed satisfied. "I still say he's not that big."

"He's bigger than you, Giro," MF said.

Giro harrumphed again.

"Well, maybe we'll see him tomorrow at morning tea," I said. But we didn't have to wait that long. Matron came bustling into our ward a moment later.

"Okay, boys," she said. "You have a new roomie."

MF looked at me, I looked at Giro, Giro looked at MF. We all looked at the bed that had recently been vacated by old Harold Hydra who had gone to five-headed beastie heaven. Uh oh.

Two nurses' aides pushed the comatose newcomer into our ward and used the block-and-tackle located above every bed to manoeuvre the huge SOB onto his. They then buckled him into the restraints. Matron checked on him and turned to us. "I want you three to keep an eye on your new roommate. He's a little excitable so I want you to make him feel welcome when he wakes up, which shouldn't be for another ten or so hours." She then turned and left.

The three of us looked at our new roommate. "What's his name?" I called after Matron.

She stopped in the doorway and referred to her clipboard. A snake looked at me and hissed in irritation. "Zy-zor," Matron said and left.

We did the three-way look-around again. Zy-zor snored and tried to roll over but the restraints stopped him.

"He's not so tough," said Giro critically.

"Look at those claws," MF said in quiet awe. Anything with a solid skeleton impressed MF. "They'd rip a decent hole in your pudgy belly if you got too close, Giro."

"I don't intend on getting that close," Giro said. "I'm going to speak to Matron and see if he can't be put in another ward."

I looked at Giro. "You have to give the guy the benefit of the doubt, Giro."

"I don't have to give the guy a frickin' thing. Harold's not even gone a week and already they're putting someone else in his bed."

"It's not his fault he's in Harold's bed," MF said. "Besides, someone has to move into it eventually."

Giro looked sulky but satisfied. I turned to look at Zy-zor and blinked in surprise when I found Zy-zor looking back at me.

"Zy-zor," said Zy-zor sleepily.

"Ken Kong," I said, trying to ignore the fact that they had pumped enough dope in him to put a whale into a coma. "Giant ape actor, retired. Starred in the *King Kong* movies. What were you in?"

"Zy-zor," he said again, this time with a little more gusto. I looked to Giro and he looked back at me.

"Maybe he's had a stroke or something," said MF.

"Yeah," agreed Giro, "and the only thing he can say is his name."

I shrugged. I wasn't so sure. I began to get that bad feeling in the pit of my stomach, just like back in the seventies when my agent handed me the script of some European thing called "Queen Kong".

"ZY-ZOR!" Zy-zor roared with great ferocity and pulled at his restraints. Built by the same company that makes anchor chains for supertankers, Zy-zor wasn't going anywhere in a hurry. Despite this knowledge, all three of us took a step backward.

"Someone call Matron," MF said, now beginning to flutter nervously beside me.

No one moved. Instead, we watched as Zy-zor raised his manacled hands and stared at the restraints. Suddenly, two beams of light shot out of his eyes. One struck the manacle and vaporised it. The other struck the air-conditioning unit and blew it into next year. He then did the same to the other manacle, melting my bed into slag in the process.

"Holy crap," Giro said. He turned and ran into MF who was turning and running into Giro. Zy-zor ignored both of them and leapt out of bed. He turned his deadly gaze to me and I leapt behind Giro's bed. You've never seen an old bugger move so fast. Nothing happened, though. I poked my head up in time to see Zy-zor striding from the ward. A moment later there were screams of distress and general mayhem as Zy-zor looked for a way out. I was about to get up and make my own way out when I heard the ominous thump-thump of a Zy-zor-sized creature coming back down the corridor into our ward. I ducked behind the bed just as Zy-zor stomped backed in, picked up MF's bed and threw it through the window on the other side of the room. Glass shattered and the wind whipped in.

MF and Giro happened to be under that bed. They looked up like startled slaters. Zy-zor ignored them and climbed up onto the windowsill.

"Hey," I called out.

"Shhh," Giro hissed. "Don't piss him off any more than he already is."

I ignored him. "Hey, Zy-zor!" This time Zy-zor turned and looked at me. Steam rose from his great black nostrils and his eyes glowed that deadly red—but, mercifully, there were no beams of light. "Calm down, fella," I said. "You don't want to go running off so soon. You've only just got here. Give the place a chance before you go making any hasty judgements."

Zy-zor looked at me uncomprehendingly. I thought for a moment he was going to blast me with his stare of death. And then he did. Or at least he tried. Two beams left his eyes and two beams struck the wall behind me, leaving a hole big enough for both Rocky and Rocco (the two heads of the resident Roc) to poke their heads through. I watched in horrified fascination as the beams crossed in front of me and realised old Zy-zor was cross-eyed. Didn't stop me from weeing myself again, though.

Zy-zor roared in frustration and leaped from the window to the ground, two storeys below. The building shook when he landed. MF, Giro and I rushed to the broken window in time to see him shoulder-charge the main gates and head toward the city, twenty miles away.

"Uh oh," MF said. "Not again."

"What the Hades is going on in here?" Matron demanded as she entered the ward. She took one look at the hole in the wall, my melted bed, and the vacant spot where the window used to be and said, "Oh, crap." She reached into her pocket and pressed the remote emergency button. A klaxon began to sound. She then looked at us. "Right. You three come with me." She walked out, leaving us three to do the one-two-three look around again.

We followed the tiny form of Matron downstairs and into the open quadrangle formed by the four wings of the Home. Here the massed force of the nursing and aide staff were gathering—all eight of them since the last budget cuts.

"We have a runaway," Matron said, getting straight to the point. "His name is Zy-zor and he's a genetically modified Kaiju about 30-metres tall—hard to miss. We believe he suffers from Alzheimer's and has acute visual impairment, being short-sighted and cross-eyed. It is vitally important that we find him and bring him back before the military catch him. These three here—" She pointed to me, MF and Giro, "—have volunteered to help. As far as we can tell, Zy-zor only has one main mode of attack, that being stomping on things."

I put my hand up. "Uh, Matron, I think that he has las—" My voice was suddenly drowned out by the arrival of a huge military helicopter—one about the size of my wiener.

The chopper landed in the centre of the quadrangle, sending staff scattering in all directions, and a very important-looking man dressed in a razor-blade sharp army uniform complete with bright sparkling medals strode directly for Matron.

"You have gone too far this time, Matron," he thundered. "One of your abominable creatures has just reduced the international rollerball rink to a smoking ruin, and it's on its way to the National Filking Centre as we speak. And by God, there is nothing I will not do to stop it destroying that."

The Matron tried her best to placate the General. "You're such a wanker, Doug. But I love you all the same. Just leave him to us and we'll bring him back without any further harm to anyone or anything."

Doug the General went apoplectic and sputtered and fumed for a few minutes. "Right," he said finally. "That's it. I've had enough of these monstrosities running amok in the city. I'm recommending the use of extreme force to bring down each and every creature I find wandering outside these gates." He pointed at the iron gates that Zy-zor had turned into steel wool on his way out, and then double-timed it back to his chopper. Matron watched him go and then said, to no one in particular, "That man needs to get laid more often."

It wasn't hard to find Zy-zor. He left the proverbial trail of destruction wherever he went. He seemed to have an extreme dislike of sports stadia and Mitsubishi Magnas. Many examples of both were flattened all over the city. But the trail led inexorably toward the harbour.

But between Zy-zor and the harbour were the 4th, 6th and 9th

Armies, four squadrons of tactical fighter aircraft, two divisions of mechanised infantry and a battalion of anti-aircraft units. Zy-zor turned them all into molten or pressed scrap metal. Despite his visual impairment, he managed to hit most things with the beam from one eye or the other.

Then he stomped off the battlefield towards the city that stood between himself and the harbour. MF, Giro, and I stood up from where we had been cowering behind a group of apartment blocks and followed him. We hadn't taken two steps before General Doug choppered into view right in front of us in his pretty helicopter.

"There's some right there," he shouted into his radio, loud enough for us to hear him. "Kill them where they stand!"

I was about to say something witty to Giro about the fact that General Doug was commanding an army that no longer existed when I felt a flea bite in my arse. Then another, and another. I turned to see that, despite the fact Zy-zor had left the 4th, 6th and 9th Armies in smoking ruins, there were still plenty of other armed forces around to do Doug's bidding. What looked like the 2nd Army, complete with infantry and mechanised divisions and air-defence units, was presently deploying along the edge of the river. One or two of the more aggressive foot soldiers were taking pot-shots at us with their rifles. Nothing major, but enough to be annoying.

"Don't they understand we're on their side?" complained MF.

"Maybe it's just a case of mistaken identity," Giro replied. "Besides, their little popguns can't hurt us."

"No," I said, pointing to the horizon, "but I think those bigger popguns can." The flight of attack helicopters banked towards us and there were sudden screams of dismay from below as my bladder let go again.

"What do we do?" MF asked, fluttering nervously.

"Beat the crap out of them," Giro said, rubbing his front claws together in eager anticipation.

"No," I said. "They *are* on our side and Matron told us to try not to hurt anybody."

Giro pawed the ground and swished his tail. "Oh, trust me, I'll try."

"Behave, Giro!" I growled.

He pouted. "Okay," he said. He reached into a pocket and pulled out a pair of spectacles and put them on. He then bent down and roared at the troops arrayed before us. He waited a moment for them to flee then turned and used his tail to sweep their vehicles and weapons into the river, providing us with respite.

We watched as the helicopters closed in. I saw the pilots lower their attack visors. Hovering off to the left, Doug sat in his helicopter watching everything closely through binoculars. The helicopters fired their missiles, the exhaust trails spiraling in towards us.

MF suddenly fluttered forward then turned to face us. He

spread his wings as the missiles arrived and shielded us as they impacted on his back—great blossoms of light, heat and noise. MF grimaced but bore the pain surprisingly well. Then a second volley of missiles was fired.

"That," said MF as he fluttered to the ground, supporting his back with one hand, "hurt like a son of a bitch."

"Get up, MF!" Giro said. "Here comes some more."

"I can't. Once is one time too many."

I dodged quickly to my left, leaped high and reached out my long arm (don't get smart, they're both the same length) and grabbed Doug's chopper right out of the sky before his crew could react. I managed to avoid both the main rotor and the tail rotor as I grabbed the fuselage. With the engine screaming and the rotors spinning madly, it was like holding onto a rabid canary. I held my breath and stuck my right hand into the main rotor disc and stopped it spinning. It hurt but I wasn't going to let them know that. The engine and gearbox whined like a scorned wife and then something went bang and there was a bit of smoke and it went silent. I could hear the shouts and screams of the occupants. Bugger 'em, I thought. I returned to my place in front of the fast-approaching missiles and lifted the now quiet chopper up so they could see our mutual doom.

"Stop the missiles!" I said to Doug.

Doug looked out his window and saw the dozen missiles heading for him. He started yelling into his radio for the missiles to be aborted. A moment later all the missiles exploded—thankfully well short of us. I put Doug's helicopter down gently, ignoring the bleatings of its occupants, and we continued on our way after Zy-zor.

Zy-zor had disappeared into the vast warren that was the city. Street after street, block after block of tall skyscrapers that towered over even us. I could hear his rage-filled bellows of "Zy-zor" and the terrified screams of the city's citizens, but the sounds echoed and re-echoed off the buildings, making it impossible to pinpoint the source.

MF fluttered up above the buildings and acted as our scout. "Left, right, straight ahead," he called as he guided us between the buildings towards where he could see Zy-zor. Giro had trouble keeping his long tail from smashing into buildings but he was doing his best to minimise the damage. That didn't stop concerned citizens from hurling abuse and rubbish at us. I felt compelled to urinate through their windows, but alas, my bladder was empty.

I was certain that MF had no idea where Zy-zor was and was just leading us around in circles for his own moth amusement—I swear I passed the same foul-mouthed loser in the same thirtieth-floor window at least four times—but eventually Giro and I filed out into the central park. At the other end of the great green expanse, just entering from another street, was Zy-zor. MF, exhausted, settled on the roof of a building and promptly fell asleep.

"ZY-ZOR!" said Zy-zor.

"Howdy," I said.

Zy-zor bared his teeth and roared his inane roar. To add effect he reached out and smashed the tops off the buildings to either side of him.

"I know what his problem is," said Giro quietly.

"What?" I asked, eager for any clue.

"I felt exactly the same way myself when I was suffering from it. Irritable, cranky, needing to tear the tops of buildings."

"I don't have all day, Giro. What's his problem?"

"Constipation."

Oh, brother. As though in response, Zy-zor roared and smashed another building flat with his tail.

"Do something, Ken. He's getting angry."

"What do you want me to do?" I asked.

"I don't know. Talk to him."

As if I needed a prompt, Giro then shoved me in the back and sent me stumbling forward, squashing a carousel and a hotdog stand in the process. Zy-zor looked at me with his red eyes as though I had compared his mother to a nasty fungal infection and then let loose another round of "Zy-zors" and associated roars. He took a dozen steps into the park and stood opposite me like a dance partner waiting for the music to start.

I didn't wait. "Take this, you son of a bitch!" I said and gave him the old one-two to his stomach. It was like punching a frozen side of whale wrapped around a sizeable cast-iron anvil. With both hands stinging, I took a step back. Zy-zor now looked even more pissed off than usual.

"Uh, Zy-zor, mate, pal," I said. "I hope I wasn't too out of line with that crack about—"

Zy-zor smacked me backhanded over a stand of trees and into the ornamental lake, the water of which ended up flooding the whole westside of the park and the buildings bordering it.

"Holy crap!" I heard Giro say. I tried to move but found my not-inconsiderable backside stuck in the lake mud. "Your turn," I said to Giro.

Zy-zor took a step toward Giro.

"Not on your life," Giro said. "Count me out!" And with that the self-proclaimed king of the monsters took off in the opposite direction. Zy-zor waited a moment then turned and continued on his way to the harbour.

But Doug wasn't through just yet. While I was trying to get myself out of the lake and Giro was trying to find a rock big enough to hide under, Doug and his troops had regrouped at the docklands surrounding the harbour. By the time I scraped the mud off my arse, found Giro and got to the area, Doug and his troops were bunkered in and had managed to force Zy-zor to take refuge behind a huge shipping container warehouse. They had given up on the small arms fire and were firing rocket-propelled grenades, missiles and rockets to keep him at bay.

Zy-zor had taken a few serious hits. He was bleeding profusely on his face, chest and legs. He was now truly pissed off and had given up the yelling of his name to concentrate on trying to laserblast the soldiers. But his aim was woeful and all he succeeded in doing was to turn the docklands into a smoking mess.

As we watched, a flight of fighter aircraft swooped into the battle zone and began peppering Zy-zor with cannon fire. Bastards. He tried to lash out at them but they were too quick and their rounds hurt too much. I saw one fighter plane stitch holes across his eyebrow and another rip a piece out his cheek.

Off to one side I saw Doug. He was getting right into it, standing in his command vehicle, binoculars to his eyes, urging his troops on to even more destruction.

I couldn't take any more. I had to do something. I headed forward to see what I could do.

"Where are you going?" Giro asked.

"I'm going to help him."

"Why? Doug's doing all right without us."

"Not Doug, you idiot. Zy-zor."

"Zy-zor? What on Earth for? His days are numbered anyway. Deserves everything he gets in my opinion."

"Not if I can help it," I said and went to help the beseiged behemoth.

I hadn't taken a dozen steps before Doug saw me and sicked his army onto me. I ducked one missile, dodged another and caught an arseful of large-calibre machine-gun bullets for my trouble. Zy-zor looked at me with his red laser eyes and I couldn't tell whether he was happy to see me or he was going to zap me into a pile of scorched hair and skin. Just as I assumed the former and was about to say something about us being in this thing together, he pulled back his head and let loose with two sizzling laser beams, one of which parted the hair on my head right down the middle.

"Holy shit!" I yelled as I dropped to all fours. The crazy old bastard wants to kill everyone, I thought frantically, even those who want to help him. Then I heard the shouts and screams from the men in the helicopter that had taken the second beam and was now spiraling out of control into the ground behind me. I looked up at Zy-zor and for the first time there was the merest hint of acknowledgement. I winked at him and he growled in response.

A mobile rocket launcher pulled up and began to deploy. I let loose my best roar but they ignored me. I pouted but that didn't work either. Zy-zor tried to blast them but they were too close and both beams went astray. The annoying little shits then began firing at us. One caught me in the arm. Zy-zor copped a few in the legs and stomach. They finally ran out of missiles.

"Giro!" I yelled.

"What?" he replied from his hiding place.

"Give Zy-zor your glasses!"

"What?"

"I said—"

"I heard you, you deaf coot. I'm not giving that thing my glasses. You know how much these cost?"

"Zy-zor," I said loudly. "Blast the crap out of Giro!"

"No!" Giro yelled. "Here, take them! I'm going home." He threw his glasses at us and took off in the opposite direction. I picked them up and handed them to Zy-zor. He looked at them as though they were made of cow dung. I could see Doug's army advancing and we didn't have a lot of time before the missile launcher reloaded. I reached up and put them on Zy-zor's snout before he could react.

The missile launcher crew finished reloading and prepared to fire again. Zy-zor was caught between wanting to tear the glasses off his face and doing something to the missile launcher. In the end, he let out a loud roar and gave the launcher the old laser one–two. But this time his two beams focused on the launcher and the weapon disappeared in a smoking flash of energy. *Holy crap!* was my only thought. Must have been Doug's thought, too, as his army halted its advance.

Zy-zor grinned as he straightened up to his full height and surveyed the battlefield—suddenly one sensed that the tide of the battle had swung very definitely to our advantage. But Doug was not to be so easily deterred from his objective. He rallied his men and arrayed the full force of his mechanised divisions before us, their cannon and missile launchers pointed at Zy-zor and me.

Zy-zor then began to systematically vaporise Doug's weapons. But for every one Zy-zor turned to molten metal, another would fire its payload at us. It was like a game of chess writ large: pieces moved and fired then were wiped from the board.

I noticed a train of oil cars parked at a railway siding beside us. I then noticed that many of the shipping containers in the warehouse yard were marked with the logo of a fertiliser company. The seed of an idea sprouted.

We fell back under General Doug's onslaught until I was within arm's reach of the train. As Zy-zor blasted battery after battery of missile launchers, I grabbed the lead carriage and hoisted it into the air. Most of its sibling carriages came with it, only a few at the other end decoupled and fell off. I then threw the train with all my might into the stack of shipping containers. Several cars fell short but more than a few crashed into the containers, rupturing both oil cars and containers.

I waited but nothing happened. Fuel oil from the oil cars flowed into the spilled ammonium nitrate from the fertiliser containers but nothing happened.

Damn, I thought. And then I remembered. One last ingredient.

"Zy-zor! Blast the shipping containers!"

Zy-zor looked at me as though I'd gone completely bananas—
but he was rapidly being overwhelmed by superior forces.

"The containers," I gestured. "Make go boom!"

He shrugged then idly zapped a ruptured container in the
middle of the mess I'd made.

Well, let me tell you, I didn't expect it to be *that* big a deal. I'd
never actually seen an ANFO explosion, though I'd read about
them. This one was actually about a hundred times bigger than
anything previous—on a par with a medium-yield tactical nuke.
The blast knocked both Zy-zor and me off our feet and sent a
mushroom cloud up ten thousand feet. It flattened the docklands
and left nothing taller than a bee's dick standing upright for miles
around, including General Doug and his army.

"Holy shit!" I said once more as I climbed back to my feet.
Zy-zor grunted. I looked around and saw our chance. Before
the smoke cleared and anyone else had an opportunity to do
more than consider the idea of thinking about the possibility of
contemplating the notion of maybe doing something more than
cleaning the debris out of their ears, I grabbed Zy-zor's hand and
we tipped-toed away to the harbour before anyone noticed.

"Well," I said. "Here we are. What are you going to do now?"

Zy-zor turned to look at me but remained silent, as usual. He
pointed out into the harbour and, God help me, there was another
one just like him rising out of the water. Clinging to this one's
chest were two miniature versions of Zy-zor.

"Ha-zars!" the newcomer called.

"Zy-zor!" Zy-zor replied. Except he wasn't Zy-zor at all, was
he? His name was Ha-zars and he had been calling Zy-zor the
whole time. I shook my head in amazement. And then the two kids
leapt off the real Zy-zor and swam towards the old Zy-zor. And
they were yelling at the top of their voices: "Ammah! Ammah!"

I'd heard the words before, though for the life of me I couldn't
remember where. While making one of those off-shore el-cheapo
flicks I'd been forced into in the eighties perhaps? At any rate, I
suddenly realised we'd been wrong about the Monster-Formerly-
Known-As-Zy-zor in ways other than the name.

Mummy, mummy!

Kaiju-sexing has always been more an art than a science.

I stood flabbergasted as the two kids climbed up onto Ha-zars
and she hugged them back. Ha-zars turned to me and for the first
time since I had known him…her…she smiled at me. She took
Giro's glasses off and handed them to me.

"*Ungal uthavihalukku mikka nanri,*" she said in some foreign
language. "*Avarkal ennudaiya peychchai kertka maartaarhal.
Aththudan ennudaiya veetitku thirumbi poy kudumbaththudan
ceruvathaiyey naan seiyya ninaiththane.*"

I smiled back, even though I only understood a word here and
there—but the sentiment of apology was clear in her manner.

She smiled and slipped into the water, the two little tackers clinging to her back. She swam to her husband, offered me one final wave then disappeared beneath the water.

I waved in return, heaved a big sigh and turned to trudge back to the Home. It struck me how often people's perceptions of old folks' homes—and old folks in those homes—are coloured by what they expect to see, rather than what is there to be seen. Monsters grow older, not old.

I passed the smoking remains of the docklands and Doug's army. Soldiers were picking themselves up and dusting themselves off. No one seemed to care that Zy-zor was gone, or even that I was still there. I saw General Doug being helped up by Matron M. who looked very stern—the snakes were doing the hula and looked very excited to be out and about. She was giving him an earful and I could hear it clear on the other side of the battlefield.

"Douglas Myron Hornibrooke," she said. "You are a very naughty boy. But I still love you."

Matron grabbed him in a lover's embrace and planted a big fat smacking kiss on his lips. Doug melted in her arms and that was the end of him. She dragged him from the field and he deserved everything he got.

I shook my head and continued home. I found Giro lounging beside the rapidly clearing battlefield.

"Hello, Giro," I said. "Fancy meeting you here."

"Ken," he nodded. "Do you realise that no one actually cares what we do at this very moment?"

I looked around us at the soldiers limping back to their barracks and understood what he meant. In their misery, they were ignoring us. "So?"

"We could make a break for it. Give society the finger and live for ourselves."

"Where would we go?"

"I've heard there's an enclave of Kaiju up in the mountains who live life the way it is meant to be for us big'uns."

I raised an eyebrow and looked to the horizon as I considered the possibility. It certainly sounded tempting. To live and breathe without regard for the humans…To free the beast within…

"What day is it?" I asked.

"Thursday," Giro said. "Why?"

"Bangers and mash night at the Home," I mused.

Giro looked at the horizon for a moment then at me. He smiled. "Ahh, Ken, I was only joshing. How could I give up bangers and mash night?" He put an arm around me and we began walking back.

"What happened to Zy-zor, by the way?" he asked.

"She—he got away. In all the smoke, I didn't see where he went."

"Right," Giro said. He looked at me sideways. "You never were much of an actor, Ken."

"Mr de Laurentis said I was the best he'd ever worked with."

"Mr de Laurentis worked with idiots. Did you ever see that

Austrian guy in those barbarian flicks? Idiot."

"I heard they're doing another remake of *King Kong.* That Kiwi who did the Tolkien movies."

Giro's eyes narrowed. "They haven't rung you, have they?"

"No. They've gone for more computer-generated crap."

"Tell me about it," Giro mumbled. "The remake the yanks did of *Godzilla* sucked the proverbial big one. There's just no soul in a movie like that without a real actor of calibre playing the part."

"Such as yourself," I said.

The way he grinned made his false teeth stick out weirdly. "Who else?"

WATCHING THE TITANS

CHRIS DICKINSON

July 26th, 1999—night

Today I flew so close to Old Finback's face I could feel his hot breath in the downdraft of the rotor blade. I've been slowly flying closer to him each day for a fortnight now, and he seems to be quite accustomed to my presence. My little 'gyro doesn't seem to bother him at all. It's proven to be the perfect observing tool. Of course, to Finback, I'm about the size of a mosquito, so I'm hardly a threat. But the most exciting thing about the fly-by was that I saw his eyes following me. He was aware of my presence! A gaze both serenely unconcerned and yet terrifying. But his attention was brief. As soon as I moved away he turned back to the meal in front of him.

I am writing this in my shack on Peak 5. It is dark, and I have closed the shutters on the window to write by the light of a kerosene lamp. There is little danger that my small light would excite the Titans, but it's best to be careful. These camouflaged shacks are my lifeline here on the Island. With them dotted across the landscape, each well stocked with supplies, I can rest and relax no matter where I end up after the day's observations. If I do nothing to attract attention to myself, I should be able to keep the shacks intact indefinitely.

My sponsors at the Leakey Institute emailed me today. The National Geographic Society have purchased exclusive rights to my pictures, which will meet the cost of the project. After their coverage of the expeditions of Jane Goodall to study wild chimpanzees and Diane Fossey to learn about the mountain gorillas, they felt my project was a natural for them. Goodall stopped by to wish me luck before I left. If I can be as successful as her, I will be well-pleased with myself. But my subjects are more of a challenge than hers.

My family thought I was mad, volunteering for this. But the Titans have fascinated me from the first time I saw Old Finback towering over the buildings of Tokyo. I was just a little girl then, watching the news reports on TV and barely comprehending what I was seeing. It was before the migration channels had been cut into the city, and the mighty creature was smashing its way through the buildings like a child stomping a sand castle. I remember asking mother if it was enjoying itself, and being told to stop being silly, this was a national disaster. Well of *course* it was a disaster. Over a thousand people lost their lives! I knew that. But that didn't make the Titan less interesting.

In later years, when the migration channels had been completed, I would rush to the viewing platforms to see the giants pass on their migration to the peak of Mt Fuji. The channels ran like huge concrete culverts through the city, enabling the Titans to go about their business without disrupting the daily lives of the populace. As a clerk in the Bank of Japan, I would see their great heads passing by my building every day, only a few hundred metres away. People began to take them for granted, but I never tired of the sight of their marching silhouettes in the Tokyo smog, surreal against the angular architecture. No two forms were alike, and insects, reptiles, even the occasional mammalian shape marched between the skyscrapers, like a May Day parade by Hieronymus Bosch.

The great Titanologist, Ishiro Tsuburaya, was the first to realise that the creatures always used the same paths to Fuji, and ordered the building of the channels, thus saving countless lives. He also engineered Kaiju Island, luring them here with tempting shipments of radioactive waste, so that they do not roam destructively between migrations. He was doubtful about my project at first, but I think he's getting used to the idea of a slightly built girl on an autogyro buzzing around his precious island. In fact, I suspect he may be getting infatuated, the dirty old man! He's not my only fan either. Since the tabloid press published my photo under the headline "Ekio Shimura, Monster Girl", I've been deluged with mail. After the first few, I stopped reading them.

July 28th

Over the two months I've been on the project so far, I have built up a sizable body of observations. Goodall and Fossey gave names to the animals they studied to help get to know them as individuals. I don't need to do that; mine have already been given names by the press. Old Finback was the first of the Titans to climb out of the sea and menace Japan's cities. The Shell, which resembles a giant turtle with long horns on its carapace, was the second. Over the years, more have arrived: The Bat, Spikey, and Mister Fluffy were soon named by the populace. The insect-like member of the herd took a little longer to get a nickname, until the press settled on *Tombo*, "dragonfly".

Despite having such varied anatomy, the creatures seem to recognise each other as members of one species, and exhibit herd behaviour. Finback is clearly the dominant male, although The Shell tries to usurp him every now and then. Tombo often seems to step in to calm things down when there is a confrontation. I'm not sure why. All the Titans eat the same thing, enriched uranium or plutonium. They might be a useful way of disposing of nuclear waste, but before that can happen governments and insurance companies need more data on their behaviour. That's where researchers like me come in. I'm not doing it for financial gain, so it's weird to think that my notes may someday make some multinational corporation huge amounts of money.

August 2nd

Damn that Heinz! His blasted "internal probe" got launched today, and promptly caused some trouble, just as I had expected. Heinz is the other PhD student here on the island, but his research is into what makes the Titans tick. Their insides, that is. He has designed a probe that he says will be able to survive the heat, acid and radiation in the stomachs of the beasts. It's like a metre-long lozenge, with sensors and cameras in a transparent bubble on one end. The idea is to launch it by air cannon into Old Finback's mouth and hope he swallows it. The crazy thing is supposed to take pictures and measurements of Finback's insides as it wends through his digestive system, then be expelled with the rest of the waste when he takes a dump.

Sounds simple, but then Finback notices these humans pointing the cannon in his direction. He's seen artillery before, and he just goes wild when they shoot the probe into his mouth. Soon there's people running for their lives and the cannon is a flat pretzel of metal at the bottom of a footprint. Thing is, Old Finback decides to go on a rampage, wrecking anything that looks artificial. The ultrasonic sirens were supposed to keep the Fin and his friends at a distance, but he was so mad he just ignored them. They stopped irritating his ears when he stomped on them. Heinz's little experiment has cost the Kaiju Island authorities about two million dollars in wrecked buildings, including two of my shacks. I'll kill Heinz when I see him next! To top it all off, Finback was too agitated for me to make my usual fly-by today. I'm trying to study his social interaction with the other Titans, their herd behaviour, not how he stomps things. We know all about *that*.

August 3rd

I think my ankle is broken. Moving it is agony, and I've bound it tightly with my scarf. But I can't do more for it at the moment. I'm trapped!

The island authorities had delivered a fresh container of tasty plutonium and The Shell tried to make off with it, directly challenging Old Finback's dominance. There was going to be a battle. The two Titans were circling one another warily, their warning cries deafening even over the noise of my engine. It was time I got to a safe distance. But before I could go far, The Shell charged and Old Fin dodged to the side. I flew right into him.

I was lucky to survive the crash, but now how am I to get away?

No one in their right mind would land a rescue chopper here! I'm sitting high up on his back, about level with his shoulders. On either side of me, I can see the huge radiator fins that run in four rows down his spine, like giant cacti. He was exerting his whole strength in the battle with The Shell, and the radiators glowed with heat from his internal fires. I had to hide in a cleft in his rough hide or I'd have been baked alive! Not to mention irradiated. My radiation badge says the dose isn't dangerous yet, but I can't stay up here long, that's for sure.

My 'gyro is not too badly damaged, but with the control rod of the main rotor snapped, there's no way to fly it. My only hope is that Old Finback will decide to rest for long enough to let me climb off. But *that* is a slim hope. It will take all day to climb down his back, injured as I am, and he never rests that long. And when he is in motion, he's moving too fast to climb down safely. I have to remain up here, where I can maintain a firm grip. There is no way off!

August 4ᵗʰ

I don't know if anyone will ever find my notebook and camera, but I may as well keep up my observations. I have been exploring as far as I dare. No one has ever examined the skin of a Titan this close before. The pics will be impressive, if anyone ever gets to see them.

Close up, Old Finback's skin is like a landscape of jagged rocks. There are large knobbly boulders, and deep clefts. Water runs down the clefts, forming streams and pools. Here and there, some hardy lichen or algae manages to flourish in this strange environment. Old Finback's skin is not really organic, seen up close. It's more like some kind of mineral. I spot a small piece that seems to have been worn loose, and put it in my knapsack. You never know, I may yet get to take it back to the lab and examine it.

The most interesting and disturbing thing I found came when I looked into the deep clefts in the skin. There are objects trapped down there, some pushed far down into the epidermal folds, others apparently forced beneath the surface at some distant time and only now coming to light as the outer layers slowly weather away. There are stones, of course, but also pieces of metal, some recognisable as parts of cars or appliances, things he has picked up when crashing through buildings or stomping along freeways. Most disturbing are the human remains—bleached bones now, shattered and crushed. How long have some of them been here, I wonder? I found what looked like a crumpled Samurai helmet near one. Had Old Finback walked abroad in ancient times?

Perhaps I have a new dicipline here, *Kaijuarchaeology*: the study of detritus caught in the skin of the Titans. Despite the seriousness of my predicament, I have to smile at that.

August 6ᵗʰ

Perhaps all is not lost! I've found a long length of metal wedged deep in one of the clefts of skin. A part of a bicycle, I think. I had to fight off an archaeonid to get it. These are small crustacean-like animals that thrive on Old Finback's skin, eating organic matter that accumulates there. They seem to need his background radiation to survive. They have often been found scattered on the ground in his wake, shaken off his hide like fleas, but they never live long away from him. If they clean his skin, they may have a symbiotic relationship with their large host. Anyhow, I reached down into the cleft to retrieve the metal bar, and this bug shot out and tried to bite my arm. I was only saved from serious injury by my thick leather flying jacket. After a brief battle, I managed to shake it off and seized my prize.

August 6ᵗʰ—later.

There! I have fitted the bar to the autogyro. I take a few moments to write in my journal and savor my small victory. It took a bit of bending, and I hope the rusty wire I fastened it with will hold, but it should do the job. I have a new control lever for the prop. Now, all I need is the right chance to take off. That won't be easy. I usually need a few feet to build up speed. But how am I going to get that here? I realise now that there is only one way. I have to chance it. I'm going to jump, and hope to hell I get up to flight speed before I hit something hard.

August 7ᵗʰ

My ankle hurts so much I can hardly move. It was broken in my crash five days ago, and now I've had to climb up the mountain to get to this shack. I am resting on the bunk as I write this, with my foot raised on a pile of pillows. It dulls the pain to a throbbing ache. That's good. I need a clear head to take in what happened today.

I launched myself off Old Finback as soon as the sun rose this morning. From that point on, it's all a bit of a blur. I remember bouncing down the rough skin on his back, then the 'gyro falling through the air. The rotor was spinning, but I couldn't build enough speed to get any lift. I remember seeing the ground rushing up at me, then an impact—and coming to to find myself on one of Finback's outstretched paws. He was looking down at me, perhaps wondering what this tiny, fragile thing was that had leaped from his back. Did he recognise me as that little creature that had been buzzing around his head for the last few weeks? As he stared right into my eyes, I think he did. Not very scientific of me, but it's what I believe. Because then he put me down, as gently as a 300-metre-tall lizard can. I tumbled off his paw onto the dirt. The 'gyro was trashed, but I was all right. I just stood there as Old Finback walked away, his tail dragging behind him like a freight train, cutting a deep trench through the soil. I wished there was some way I could thank him.

I made my way back to this cabin, hobbling all the way on my injured ankle. The climb up the sloping mountainside was agony, and I'll have to radio the Island Rangers to come pick me up as soon as it's dark. At least I still have my photographs and journals. *National Geographic* will be glad to get them, I'm sure.

Postscript— August 9th

God, lying around in hospital while doctors check you for radiation effects is *boring*! The tests are all coming back negative, thank heaven. The exposure wasn't long enough to be a problem. Meanwhile, I'm reading in the papers that Heinz's internal probe has been recovered intact, and the press is making him into a hero! The photos are blurry, but there seem to be lifeforms inside there, things that live within the Titan's stomach. Now Heinz is talking of a second probe—a *manned* one this time. The press thinks I'm a natural for the crew. I don't know—the method of exit is so undignified. Not exactly the triumphant return of the brave explorer! Still, I wanted to get an intimate knowledge of the Titans, and it can't get more intimate than that...

Prologue

Somewhere out amongst the infinite *lay a strange, nameless realm—a realm where once-verdant groves of pomegranate, peach and citron rolled gracefully beneath a sky of midnight blue, luxuriant in the light of countless distant nebulae; a realm encircled by a contiguous, mystic river that mortals might call the Tao. This was the realm of the Nine Wind Dragons—a realm that would soon be dead.*

From their number, an emissary was chosen to journey back to the worlds of their origin, back to the worlds of Man—there to gather the spiritual energy needed to sustain their singular existence. With their very reality losing cohesion around them, the Dragon Gods knew such a journey was their last and only hope.

Provisions were gathered and the yarrow stalks were cast, naming the venturer and pointing the way back to the universe they had left so long ago. And so it was that the Nine stood before the great crystalline delta that marked the mouth of the mystic river, and sent the child called Varanox out across its dark and storm-tossed waters, alone.

REQUIEM FOR A WILD GOD

GEORGE THOMAS

One

Kobe, Japan

Charles Chi strode with cautious confidence through the crowded streets of the commercial district. People from across the world had come to set up shop here, transforming the community back into the semblance of a small city. It was a transformation almost as amazing as the terrible earthquakes that had decimated the region only a few years before—the quakes that had claimed his parents' lives.

For Charles, today had been another long work day piloting the enormous H3 Leveler: a one-hundred-plus-ton metal monster built to pulverise debris and pound it flat, clearing the way for new housing developments slated for construction in the residential sector. The job was good karma and better pay than any other he had found, which of course made no impression whatsoever on his disapproving uncle Yao.

Yao Ziang Chi, or "Uncle Joe" as he had come to be called, was of Chinese descent, as was all of Charles' family, making them a most distinct minority in the islands of Japan. This was a circumstance Charles had listened to his uncle lament tirelessly ever since he arrived in the country. Though Charles loved and respected his father's elder brother, the mistrust and prejudice the man espoused could at times become intolerable, and invariably led to conflict—this day had begun with just such an argument. Charles found himself growing increasingly reluctant to return to the old storefront that was their home.

Slowly, Charles became aware of emergency lights strobing somewhere down the road, framed by thick black clouds massing on the horizon. His nagging reluctance became a too-familiar dread as he realised that the phalanx of police cars coming into view was converging upon his own family's shop.

Kunlun mountains, ancient China

A great rush of water swept suddenly across one of the many lakes strewn about the region, hurling an old fisherman from his tiny boat. Cast upon the shore, the man regained his bearings only to find that an enormous shadow had darkened the foreshores. When he looked up, he saw a monstrous black-winged tortoise, his net in its mouth, rising from the lake and striding off into the fields.

Varanox wondered at his strange new surroundings. A single sun shone brightly overhead, the scents of grass and honey sweetened the air. Whatever realm this might be, the great beast decided that he liked it.

A dim memory came, flitting just beyond his full cognition. The giant raised a foreleg, and there found a silken pack. Varanox unstrapped the burden with the tip of his bony beak, spilling its contents onto the ground.

He recognised the fruits and foodstuffs first. A collection of olives, fu-sang and pomegranates lay atop a bed of shining stones. These are river gems, he thought, catching his own reflection in the jumbled, multifaceted mass. Varanox was surprised at the animalistic image staring back at him from the stones, and could not help but wonder if his form and appearance had always been so.

Movement caught the great beast's eye; a group of creatures strange and small were gathering at the edge of the fields. There were what appeared to be males bearing weapons, and females with full breasts and bottoms and their young close by. So familiar they seem, the creature thought, raising its head with a greeting call.

It struck him then that there was something important he had forgotten, that his mind held few memories beyond his own name. One thing was clear: he was newly born to this realm, and so could not reason why the tiny mortals around him seemed so frustratingly familiar...

Kobe, Japan

The Autumn sun had just begun to set as Charles made his way through the crowd of neighbours, gawkers and reporters vying for position around the Dynasty Apothecary. There, as he had hoped, he found the familiar face of his friend Police Officer Yoshio Shimura.

"Yoshio!" Charles shouted, catching the cop's attention. His heart skipped a beat as an ambulance arrived, running sirens off. Shimura guided the medics quickly into the shop, then waved for Charles to join him.

"Yoshio, what has happened?" Charles asked with frantic concern.

"The shop has been robbed, your uncle gravely injured," Shimura explained plainly. " I am sorry, Charles."

"Stand clear!" came a shout as the medics hurried a casualty-laden stretcher out of the shop.

"Uncle!" Charles raced to his uncle's side. "You're going to be all right, uncle Joe. I will stay with you. I—"

"Charles! Charles, he took it..." Joe forced the words past shattered ribs. "He took the Dragonstone."

"The old crystal?" Charles frowned. "Uncle, who did this?"

"That lunatic friend of yours—Tomita, the gangster's son." The man's eyes began to flutter, rolling up towards the back of his head. "Charles, you must listen to me now. You must get the crystal back, or the Dragon God will return to smite Japan—"

"Uncle, I..." Charles began, then realised his uncle could no longer hear him. The sky grew dark and overcast as the ambulance raced away, leaving Charles shuddering at the possibility of losing his last living relative and angered at the thought of the sadistic madman who had succeeded in victimising him yet again.

Ancient China

Varanox gazed at the tiny creatures and a memory slowly clarified in his fragmented mind, a memory of beings known collectively as "Man."

Around him, the minuscule mortals bowed in supplication. His mind riddled with curiosity and questions, the Godbeast size-shifted to a less intimidating scale, closer to that of a large house than a small mountain. The men drew nearer, and Varanox nosed some of the fruit from his pack towards them, then backed slightly away.

An elder approached and cautiously reached for the offering. He took up an olive and held it forth to the crowd, then took up a pomegranate so they could see that as well. He marveled at the quantity of jewels and the fine silken pack from which they spilled. The man ate the olive and, with a collective gasp from his fellows, again bowed low before their strange new benefactor.

"We thank thee, most gentle and generous Spirit," the man called, the meaning of his words becoming clearer to the giant as he spoke. "We thank thee, most noble host!"

"You...are welcome," Varanox responded, manifesting a sudden curious command of the man's language. "But it is you who are host to me, as my Spirit is but newly born to this plane."

The crowd stood shocked at the creature's words. "As is so, kind lord," the elder cautiously replied. "Though your arrival here has blessed us nonetheless. To be in the presence of such a great and mighty being is too grand for such humble folk as we."

"Then, mortal, I believe there may be matters which, upon our further conference, we would both be enlightened to discuss." The people smiled at the voice of the beast, for he spake as many gems sifting in a gentle tide. "For now, I bid you tell me and please do confirm, that there is a grove close by where the silkworms spin? A grove of mulberry where perhaps I may dwell?"

"Not only is there such a grove, but an old and wondrous shrine that shall be made your own," the mortal replied.

"You have already given me both acceptance and counsel. I desire no shrine, elder—only to dwell in the grove itself shall suit me."

The man excused himself to confer with his fellows. It took but a moment for the group to address the giant and bow in acquiescence to his request.

Varanox smiled at his success. His mind was lost in a maze of questions and doubt. The barest recollections of some great journey and even greater purpose eluded him. A mighty fatigue came over the lost child of the Dragon Gods, and he followed the tribe of mortals wearily as they beckoned him towards the lovely grove.

Kobe—the Apothecary

Charles sat on the counter in the darkened, ransacked shop alone, the thrum of falling rain the only sound. The investigators were gone, leaving Charles to deal with cleaning up. He did not relish the thought of working demolition all day to find more rubble to be cleared at home, and could not yet bring himself to begin the laborious task.

Outside, a police cruiser pulled up to the storefront. It was Yoshio, checking in as he said he would.

"Dozo," Charles welcomed his friend. "You'll have to pardon the mess. It's tempting to take the Leveler to it and be done with it."

"This little shop has survived far worse, Chi San. So has your uncle, who has yet to regain consciousness, I am sorry to report." Yoshio shook the rain from his coat. "Not to sound indelicate, but his injuries were more extensive than we thought. More than a few broken bones. Serious head trauma. I doubt his assailant escaped unscathed either. From the look of it that old man fought like a tiger."

Charles responded with a tight-lipped grin. "Yeah, he's plenty tough. Stubborn, too, especially when it comes to stuff like that stupid crystal."

"Everyone knows this shop was more than just an Apothecary, Charles," Yoshio said. "That was strictly your mother's vocation. Your father was an infamous collector of historic objects and was known to broker trades between our countries. He may have kept some rare or even priceless relic here."

"You're right," Charles concurred. "But it wasn't value that concerned Uncle Joe. This crystal's got a curse on it, and he insists I pursue its recovery with all due haste." Charles hopped down from the counter and approached his friend. "I'm hoping I can count on your help with that."

"That's my job," Yoshio smiled. "An APB has already been issued to apprehend the suspect."

"Yeah, our old friend Tomo," Charles mused, his anger rising at the thought of the sadistic punk.

Tomoyuki Tomita was a kid with issues. Major issues. The kind of kid who tortured animals, who liked watching things suffer. The deranged delinquent had harassed, beaten, bullied and intimidated Charles throughout their years in school. Only Yoshio stood by the awkward boy from China, taking more than a few lumps of his own in the process. Such childhood conflicts went mostly forgotten as Tomo sank deeper into an inexplicable dementia, finding himself disowned by his family and finally committed to an asylum. An asylum from which he had recently escaped.

Yoshio could see his friend's discomfort and decided he could be considerate enough to change the subject. "What more can you tell me about this relic, or its supposed curse?"

"Some legend about a Dragon God or something," Charles replied. "I never paid much attention when the family went on about that kind of stuff."

"Great!" Yoshio rolled his eyes. "Maybe we can track down some of your father's former colleagues or contacts to see if they know anything?"

Charles' eyes widened at the suggestion. "There is one man in particular whose name comes to mind: Wing Lee, the multinational importer based in Osaka."

"Your father had dealings with Lee?" Yoshio's eyes narrowed suspiciously. "His company remains under close scrutiny due to suspected ties with the black market." A grim glance passed between them, leaving a grimmer implication unspoken. "Such a man may have more answers for us than you'd thought."

Ancient China

The seasons passed as the Godbeast dwelt in the mulberry grove. The men repaired the ancient shrine and it became a gathering place for them to praise the Dragon God. With their prayers, Varanox's powers grew.

Varanox gave what recompense he could, fertilising their fields with his dung and clearing the land to plant new groves for them with the seeds of his own fruits. His affection for the land and its people grew strong. He sensed they played an integral part in his elusive mission, and wished to do more to earn the prayers they so freely offered.

And so it was that Varanox began to manipulate the natural environment. He controlled the wind and rain to improve their harvests, he sheltered them from fire and storm. The Godbeast's influence over Nature grew, and he began to explore, venturing ever farther from his grove.

With his absences increasing, the giant felt compelled to leave his people a totem that might continue to keep him connected to the spiritual energy their worship supplied. He took one of his larger crystals and placed it in the shrine, giving them a focal point for their ceremonial praise. Great tributes of fish were prepared upon his increasingly infrequent returns, and each New Year the giant could be seen cutting the clear night skies with brilliant trails of elemental fire that circled the world.

Time passed, and more people came to worship him, and they called him Great Lord, Light Giver, and Fire God...and Varanox was pleased.

Then came a time of war between men. Conflicts raged across the globe as the mortals fought amongst themselves, sometimes for resources and riches, sometimes from jealousy and fear. Sometimes, Varanox observed, they even fought in the name of their Gods.

He returned to his mountains then, and found his own home fallen to the work of some violent invader. The groves had been torched, the village plundered, the shrine razed to the ground. Even the crystal his people kept sacred was gone. A terrible anger was born that day, born of the energy of Man's own violence that flowed through the stolen crystal to strike deep into the Dragon God's heart.

Enraged, Varanox followed the crystal's trail of now negative energy to an island nation not far from the mainland. The people there rallied their armies to drive him away, but the monstrous creature would not be dealt with so easily. The Godbeast took his revenge then, toppling their towns with earthquakes, burning their fields with volcanic eruptions and rending their harbours with powerful storms. Before long, their leaders surrendered and relinquished the sacred crystal. The Dragon God warned them, then, that should they harass the crystal or its keepers again, he would return and destroy their land entirely.

Varanox retreated to the shore of his lake, a pall of deep remorse and unfulfilled purpose heavy upon his reptilian soul. Something in those waters called to him, something far away, like a ghost that refused to rest until some long forgotten mission should be accomplished. It was useless, he knew, to seek the answers in this world, as mankind themselves had so pointedly proven. His quiet grove was gone, his temple destroyed. Most of his people had left as well, cursing him in the end for the savage scorn of the invaders he had brought upon them.

What happened next, no one truly knows. Some say Varanox left Earth to seek his forgotten mission on other worlds. Others claim he re-entered the lake to search for the path from whence he came, and searches for it still. Some say the mighty Godbeast died of despair that day, and some that he simply ceased to exist. Whatever the Dragon God's final fate, his mystic crystal remained, kept by those few surviving descendants of the Kunlun villagers who chose not to forsake the creature's tragic memory, nor the kindness he had shown them.

Two

The offices of Lee Imports, Osaka, Japan

Charles and Yoshi felt very much out of place as they entered the forty-storey glass-and-steel monolith that served as corporate headquarters for the most notorious antiquities broker in Asia. It was not every day the cop and the hardhat found themselves among such elite, the kind who could afford what others deem priceless. Yoshi was sure most of them were either wanted by Interpol or under investigation. Charles could not help imagining the impressive edifice reduced to a mountain of rubble, and pounding it flat with his rig.

"Officer Shimura, Mr Chi," a cute, business-suited hostess greeted them in the lobby. "Mr Lee is expecting you. This way, please."

A private express elevator shot them skyward until the level indicator read '39'. The doors opened, but not upon some plush office, rather an elaborate gallery or trophy hall. The hostess bade them enter, then disappeared as the lift's doors closed behind them.

Charles and Yoshi trod slowly down a long central corridor flanked by the most eclectic and unusual collection of relics, memorabilia and objets d'art in the hemisphere. There were strange suits of battle armour from civilisations so ancient they could no longer be named; all manner of tools, tomes and exotic musical instruments; the remains of animals long extinct preserved for display and scattered throughout the exhibit. A marsupial wolf stalked a dwarf mammoth from behind a large urn; a Didus Ineptus watched lazily nearby. Some unnameable species of small, furry anthropoid crouched atop a display case filled with shrunken heads. The thing appeared half human, and they could only conjecture as to its origins.

"Fascinating, is he not?" A voice called from nowhere. With that, overhead lights slowly brightened upon a far wall to reveal an exquisitely furnished conference area, and the man they had come to meet. "A juvenile male from a race of proto-hominid cave dwellers discovered in the Japanese Alps. All driven to quick extinction, of course, poor bastards." The old man stepped forth, revealing himself to be garbed in most unconventional attire: ceremonial robes of red, black and white. "Take a good look, gentlemen!" the eccentric-looking figure declared. "This collection will be packed and on its way back to China by the morrow."

"It is truly marvelous, Mr Lee," Yoshi remarked sincerely. "Thank you for agreeing to consult with us so quickly."

"Of course, officer Shimura. Charles," Lee addressed his countryman in Cantonese. "Your father and I were colleagues and friends once. I am sorry to hear of your family's current misfortunes, and I will not hesitate to grant whatever boon you may ask."

Charles considered the man's words, unable to decide whether such disarming cooperation made him more or less suspicious. He took a cue from his friend and played it straight and cool. "Thank you, Mr Lee. We need whatever information you can give us about a relic called the Dragonstone, and any clue you may have as to its current whereabouts."

"There are few men on Earth who know that crystal even exists, let alone where it came from," Lee responded. "Lucky for you that I am among them.

"The crystal is about a quarter metre long, clear, spiky, and as big around as your fist. It was a gift to the villagers of the Kunlun mountains of China from a wandering Dragon God they called Varanox. The village was raided by invaders from Japan who coveted the gem for themselves. The Dragon God intervened, recovering the crystal and returning it to its appointed place. Sickened by the barbarism he had witnessed, Varanox took his leave of Earth, but vowed vengeance should the crystal be compromised by violence or treachery again, which it seems has just come to pass."

"Still," Yoshi interjected. "It is just a big gem after all, despite the mythology. Looking out for angry dragons is our least concern regarding the relic's theft, and I'll bet the thief feels the same way."

"Not dragons, Officer Shimura. A Dragon God. A very big, very angry one." Lee's face was grim. "The legend describes a gigantic being resembling a tortoise, with the power to control Nature. I'm sure you've both noticed what a lovely turn the weather has taken since the relic's theft."

"I am wondering," Charles asked, "what made the crystal so important to Varanox?"

"No one knows," Lee replied. "Though your father thought it served as a conduit for spiritual energy."

"A power source?" Charles hypothesised.

"Possibly. Your father also insisted the crystal was psychosensitive: able to manifest its keeper's mental and emotional states in their environment. I won't argue the myth's validity, but neither will I remain in this gathering tempest to test it," Lee frowned grimly. "As you see, I have even dusted off my good robes, in case of company."

"There's still the matter of the crystal's location," said Yoshi. "You've been most gracious and informative, Lee sama. However, I am a policeman, and you do have intimate knowledge and a personal interest in the relic."

"Of course," Lee agreed. "I would return the crystal to the mainland if I had it. Something I tried to convince Charles' father to do for years. He insisted that here in Japan the relic was at its most potentially dangerous, and therefore least likely to be harassed." Lee stepped closer to the men as though to speak in confidence. "I do not have the crystal, nor do I know what savages took it. My own investigators are working on that now. I will instruct them to keep you informed, if you'd like."

"That would be most helpful," Yoshi bowed.

"Charles, you are welcome to accompany me back to the mainland," Lee offered.

"I promised uncle Joe I would recover the crystal." Charles acknowledged the man's generosity with a nod. "Thank you, but I must stay."

"Well then..." Lee forced a smile and, as if on cue, the elevator doors opened and the hostess stepped in, waiting to escort the men from the building. "May fate find us all in the Dragon God's favour this day."

Kobe—The House of Tomita

Whatever else might be said of the man, Takeshi Tomita was slick. A consummate businessman and diplomat, a master of subtlety and stealth. His family knew it was only their patriarch's immutable practice of keeping their less-than-legitimate activities quiet, covert and untraceable that kept them all from prosecution. Discretion was Tomita's first rule of business, a rule he knew he could count on his estranged son Tomoyuki to break.

Takeshi was also known to be fond of his saké, and could be found sharing many a Saturday with a bottle in his study. It was just such a day when a familiar silhouette appeared on the rice paper panels of the study's sliding doors. Takeshi bade his wayward son enter. "Dozo, Tomoyuki."

Tomo stepped in, dripping wet from the rainstorm outside. "Father," the young man spoke but did not bow, a point not lost on Takeshi.

"There has been some trouble in town, Tomoyuki. A violent beating and theft at the Chinese Apothecary." Takeshi downed the last glass of wine, the heat of it bringing goosebumps to his flesh. "Your current unscheduled leave of absence from the asylum has led the police to suspect you. Tell me now, what was it that made you defy me yet again by taking such a risk?"

An involuntary smile flashed across Tomo's bruised and swollen face. A mistake, he knew, as he watched the anger rising below the surface of his father's stern countenance. "We suspected for years that there were valuables secreted there by those Chinese dogs, and we were right. The mainland scum were insulting us, keeping a treasure hidden in plain sight."

"A matter we have discussed more than once," Takeshi seethed. "A matter I thought you knew enough to let go. You disappoint me greatly, Tomoyuki. Your bigotry, disobedience and lack of clear judgement continue to bring dishonour to this house and unwanted scrutiny upon this family."

"This family is Yakuza, father." Tomo allowed his own anger to rise, sparked by the familiar sting of his father's disapproval. "Whatever wealth and status you enjoy has always been gained at the expense of others."

"I do not beat old men to get what I want, Tomoyuki," Takeshi barked.

"But you beat me," Tomo glared in rage. "You never once hesitated to beat me, father." Tears spilled from the young man's eyes as he spoke, mixing with the rain that dripped from his long, tousled hair.

"You insolent little prick," the half-inebriated Takeshi spat as he lurched to his feet. "I gave you everything you wanted, taught you everything I know, and to this day not a word of it has gotten through to you. Not one stinking word of it!"

"K-keep away from me!" Tomo stammered as he drew a strange shining object from his coat.

Takeshi blinked, flash-blinded by a brilliant glare. Then he saw it; Tomo was clutching what appeared to be a thick crystal spike. "Oh no!" Takeshi gasped, realising what it was that his son had taken from the apothecary. "Tomoyuki, no..."

The look of rage on Tomo's rain- and tear-slicked face melted into madness, lit by the glare of the mythic crystal. He seized upon the strange rush that came over him when he grasped the weighty spike, and advanced menacingly upon his father...

It is said that on that day the skies turned black above Honshu, assaulted by increasingly vicious weather forming over the Akashi Strait. An intense low-pressure system moved inexorably inland, pushing a massive rotating stormfront of rain and ice ahead of it. A fierce wind rose, tearing at the shoreline and buffeting the neighbouring cities of Kobe and Osaka, onward to Nagoya and Kyoto. The driving rain intensified, becoming a torrent, then a deluge. Conditions for flash flood and mudslide quickly reached critical levels. Local authorities went on alert and began evacuating all low-lying and coastal areas in an effort to minimise casualties.

Lightning flashed, brilliant beams of power erupting from the storm's black core and arcing into the sky. Peels of thunder shook the clouds, and the earth responded with rumbling tremors of its own. Climatologists across the globe watched in horror as an enormous Force Six typhoon broke spontaneously over the mainland of Japan, pounding at the island like some Wild God gone mad.

It is said that within the storm's dark and mystic eye there formed a kind of haven, an area of clear sky and dead calm where not a blade of grass bent nor fallen leaf stirred. Even the surface of the sea fell still and flat, becoming a featureless mirror-like sheet.

An eerie silence filled the cold motionless air at the centre of this great storm as the water's surface parted, and something monstrous rose ghostlike from the sea...

Three

"This is getting serious," Charles remarked, indicating the near-complete lack of visibility on the road. Highway traffic had slowed to a crawl, the tail lights of the cars ahead of them were their only guide. Some drivers began to pull over, stopping to wait out the storm. More than a few had lost control, and the increasing number of fender benders they passed threatened to become some major pileups.

"We're almost home now," said Yoshio. "We'll check in on your uncle before deciding our next move."

"Aren't we going after Tomita?" Charles inquired anxiously.

"We've got half the police force on the lookout for him now. It won't be long before he's caught," Yoshio assured his friend.

"We may not have much time," Charles observed. "I've never seen a storm like this, not even the worst of typhoons. I can't help thinking it could be the work of a Dragon God."

Yoshio acknowledged that with a firm nod. "I know." It did indeed seem as though the atmosphere were bending to some malevolent will. Sheet lightning danced across the roiling clouds, bringing blasts of thunder and light. The intense flashes illuminated the landscape, allowing brief glimpses of the damage the weather had begun to inflict. The sky itself fairly churned, thick with billowing, spinning thunderheads charged with incalculable electrical force. "Ha-ta," Yoshio gasped as he spotted a massive funnel snaking its way to earth. "Charles, look!"

Lightning arced around the cloud as it struck ground just east of Kobe proper, sending plumes of debris flying into the sky. Another flash, and Charles thought he saw something else, something moving within the twister. Something big.

"Yoshio, is it just me, or...?" Charles began shakily.

"I see it," Yoshi replied, watching the cyclone advance like some enormous shadowy beast. "It's heading straight for the heart of town. We've got to find the crystal before that thing demolishes the city!"

"You go on," Charles advised his friend. "Find Tomita. If he has the crystal, then just get it the hell away from him. We'll figure something out from there. The construction site is close by now, right on the outskirts of the residential district. I want you to drop me off there."

"What exactly do you have in mind?" Yoshi inquired.

"Something that may buy you enough time to find the crystal, before that thing out there destroys us all."

Tomoyuki Tomita sat motionlessly in his father's favourite chair, staring at the corpse sprawled upon the tapestried floor. The crystal spike he held dripped with the blood of two families, two nations, their histories stained as red as his hands. A mad banshee wind howled outside, echoing the maelstrom inside his head.

Slowly, Tomo got up and staggered across the room to the well-stocked bar. He clumsily emptied his pockets onto its smooth black surface. Dozens of tiny pill bottles spilled from his hands, prescriptions taken from the stockpile kept by his former Doctor Mizuno. Tomo opened one of the green-capped containers, shook out a handful of tablets and swallowed them whole. He reached for a bottle of wine and gulped from it, washing the unpronounceable pharmaceuticals down. Firelight cast his reflection in the clear shining glass, an image frighteningly similar to that of his father. He gasped at the unwelcome sight, and hurled the bottle into the burning hearth.

"Just like him," a voice echoed hauntingly through the room.

The young man panicked at the sound and drew his gun. "Who's there? Show yourself!" Tomo's gaze darted desperately about, settling upon a single silhouette cast among the shadows. He steeled himself against a dread he could not name, and turned to face its source.

There beside the hearth stood the old Chinaman. *"Just like your father,"* the spectre spoke again.

Tomo screamed and fired his weapon. His eyes blinked involuntarily as the gun discharged, then refocused to find the vision gone. "Bloody meds!" he groaned, snatching a yellow-capped bottle from the bar and swallowing its contents, shaking his head violently to force the capsules down. The deafening drumbeat of his heart receded, growing softer and slower, until Tomo thought that if he wished it, it would stop.

A terrible howling noise filled the air, shaking the foundation of the house. Tomo's spine tightened in the grip of electric fear, shaking him as well. "Bloody storm!" he hissed through trembling lips and moved to the window to peer outside. His eyes widened in terror then, and he quickly turned away. Tomo had seen more than his share of adversity and death over the years, but nothing compared to the enormous, unnameable horror making its way towards his home. "My God!" he cried at the sight. It was as if the devastation that twisted and marred his own spirit for so long was being inflicted upon an entire city. His grasp tightened around the Dragonstone, and with his mind lost in a drug-induced mania, Tomoyuki Tomita smiled.

Charles clawed his way along the remnants of the shaking chain-link fencing surrounding the Kaibishi Corporation construction site, fighting the savage winds to reach the battered hulk of the main office. The door had been blown off its hinges, and he quickly pulled himself inside, thankful for the small respite the remaining walls provided.

The place was in chaos, its contents scattered and strewn as if run through a deranged blender. After just a few minutes outside, Charles felt much the same way. He clambered a path through the wreckage to a far wall where a cracked plexiglass case that held the keys to all the company's vehicles still hung. He forced his fingers into the seam where the case's cover had split, and broke it free.

An involuntary laugh escaped the young hardhat then, as though his mind had finally acknowledged the madness of his mission. Charles took a moment to regulate his breathing and steady his nerves, then with the keys to his rig in hand, made his way back out into the storm.

The storm advanced through the streets of Kobe, roadways crumbling as though crushed beneath gigantic bone-sheathed hooves. Wild elemental powers churned the atmosphere into a miasmic matterstorm, pummeling the structures and sending vehicles flying through the streets. Fires spread throughout the city, marking the phenomenon's cyclonic wake.

Water, power and phone service had all been destroyed, even radio waves could find no purchase on the static-charged air. Evacuation was impossible. Police, Fire and Defense Forces were rendered immobile, faced with the fury of Nature gone mad. The massive stormfront reached from Fujiyama south to Hiroshima, and threatened to tear Nihon itself apart. The fragile façade of Man's power was crumbling just as it had so long ago, revealing a far truer, darker nature. That darkness shone like a beacon now, pointing the way to the sacred gemstone that had again been defiled by the treacherous mortals of this world. This time, the power of the Dragon God would leave the contemptuous island nation a desolate, lifeless rock.

Four

Yoshio fought to maintain control of his vehicle, but the little Suzuki Swift was no match for the relentless storm. The cop floored the accelerator, relying on momentum to carry him the last length of straightway down the thickly forested road that led to the Tomita Estate. He could feel the wheels leave the ground as he struck the main gate, and smashed through. He hit the brakes, skidding to a stop mercifully close to an open doorway. A savage wind snatched the car door from his hand and swept it into the sky. Yoshio hit the muddy ground as the car itself began to slide away behind him. He dug in, and clawed a quick and desperate path into the house.

"Tomita sama?" he screamed above the thunderous gale. "Tomoyuki san?" he called again, his words lost to the deafening tempest. Slowly, he rose to his feet, shivering, soaked and sheathed in a layer of mud and twigs from his frantic crawl from the car. He found an inner door unlocked and quickly entered to escape the icy wind, trailing muck into the luxuriant home.

The dim glow of embers cast the barest luminance into the room. Yoshio was surprised to find the walls and windows still intact. Most likely constructed of reinforced materials, probably even bulletproof, he surmised. He drew his pistol. "Tomita sama? Tomoyuki? Is anyone here?" The boom of thunder was the only response. He moved carefully through the darkened study, then his foot struck some indistinct obstruction on the floor. Another blast of thunder rumbled through the walls, accompanied by the flash of lightning close by. The brilliant flashes illuminated the room, revealing the nature of the crumpled mass lying at his feet. "Tomita sama!"

Thunder struck again, and with it, a searing pain tore through Yoshio's left thigh. The leg gave way as the force of impact registered, and he knew he had been shot. "Tomoyuki!" Yoshi growled into the darkness. The sharp, distinct snap of an ammunition clip being loaded caught his ear, and he fired his weapon at the sound. The shot was answered by a moaning cry, and he fired again. Another groan, and his assailant stepped shakily from the shadows.

Tomoyuki's head and arms hung limply, as though from exhaustion; in one hand he clutched a gun, in the other an object like a knife. Blood ran from twin bullet wounds in his abdomen, the dark stains quickly spreading to saturate his clothes. He clamped one arm across his gut, then painfully raised his head to face the cop, his face a twisted, grinning mask of malevolence.

Yoshio flinched as Tomo squeezed off a wild shot. "Tomoyuki, you bastard!" Yoshio fired again and again. The first bullet tore through the man's arm, the next blew the gun out of his hand.

Still Tomo advanced, blood dripping from the tip of the large crystalline spike clutched in his other hand. "Don't need...a gun...to finish you, Shimura..." he snarled, taking another stumbling step. As weak as he was, he laughed then, a sound that barely reached Yoshio's ears yet seemed to resonate with the rumbling of magmatic tremors deep within the earth. Those tremors grew, shaking the walls with an intensifying vibration, until at once both men realised it was not the earth that was shaking—rather, something was shaking the earth.

Harnessed and helmeted, Charles hit the ignition and fired up his mammoth rig, following the trail of destruction leading straight to the Tomita Estate. The fancy to cut the wheel and roll off across the few remaining acres of countryside like this had struck Charles more than once before; he couldn't help thinking how he had imagined it being a sunnier day when he did.

The Kaibishi H3 Leveler was a unique piece of equipment, and Charles knew its specs by heart. One of a pair of experimental prototypes designed for sub-sea construction, it had been converted to serve a more conventional role when cost overruns made further production prohibitive.

A trio of ten-ton scraping blades fed debris to an array of omni-positional augers, flanked by a single set of tyres six storeys high. The control cabin was isolated from the main body, floating on a platform of shock-absorbing gel, the same substance that powered the hydraulics. The enormous engine module was tread-mounted and capped with a wide drag-plate designed to channel the engine's vibrational energy, pulverising, flattening and compacting all matter beneath it. It was the kind of gigantic earthmover that little kids loved, and Charles had yet to find anyone who saw her that was immune to that same thrill. The sense of invulnerability and power when at the controls of such a juggernaut was intoxicating. Now, Charles knew the time had come to test that power in a way the rig's makers never intended; he would ride the immense machine into battle.

Outside, the Spiritstorm raged impotently against the pressurised, soundproof blister of the Leveler's control cabin. The near-complete sensory isolation made the horrific tableau around Charles seem unreal, allowing doubt to creep into his thoughts. What exactly was it he now raced to confront? Could what he glimpsed moving within the storm be some trick of the mind, born of the power of suggestion? Or had some angry, elemental Godbeast indeed returned to wreak its vengeance upon Japan? Either way it would be folly to stand against it. Yet he knew he had no other choice.

The massive funnel cloud loomed close now, a whirling vortex expanding and contracting in a primal dance of destruction. Charles stared into the cyclone, peered deep into the storm's black heart, and again there came a vision. Something vague and indistinct, kept obscured by the chaos of the winds. Something almost insubstantial, ephemeral, yet enough for him to know that there within that spinning maelstrom a giant walked.

His course now set, Charles raced full throttle to intercept the beast.

The cyclone had just reached the perimeter of the Tomita estate as the Leveler burst through the tree line. Charles hit the air horns, blasting a mechanical battle cry. The massive machine came alive at his command, activating an array of powerful spotlights, sirens and strobes. The whirlwind seemed to pause, then turned to face its challenger with a thunderous war cry of its own.

Charles watched in horror as the shadowy, illusory beast moved within the storm, the details of its gigantic form slowly clarifying as it approached. This was not the image of some classic Asian dragon; instead he faced what appeared to be a strange, anthropomorphic tortoise standing roughly sixty metres high. Wide panels of armour overlapped in layers across its shoulders and back, forming a V-shaped shell. Bands of similar scaly shielding covered its long forearms. The hind legs were stunted and curved like a dog's, sporting massive single-toed hooves. The head was wide and flat with tiny red eyes and broad bony beak. Spiky growths of horn jutted from its face, back and arms, framed by tufts of leathery plumage. Glider membranes stretched from its wrists to its waist, and a short vestigial tail hung beneath the lowermost layers of its shell.

Charles shut his eyes fiercely for a moment, clearing the incredible image from his mind. Quickly, he thumbed a switch, reconfiguring the rig's triple scoops to overlap, forming a single enormous shield. "The moment of truth," he thought aloud as he raised the massive blade high, and rammed it edge-on into the cloud.

The control cabin rocked violently as metal struck monster, the impact setting off every warning light in the cockpit. The storm-beast howled as lightning sparked wildly from the open wound in its leg. Charles pressed the attack, twisting the blades deeper, then retracting them for a second go. The cyclone retreated, backing off a pace. Charles gunned the engine and rammed the cloud again.

Suddenly, the Leveler stopped. The raging winds intensified around the rig, forcing the enormous machine back. Charles could hear the metal of the blade extensors groan and crack as though caught in the grip of powerful claws. The massive drive wheels spun in vain as the Leveler lifted off the ground, twisted, then toppled over completely and smashed to earth.

The Dragon God howled in triumph then, lightning dancing around its gargantuan form. The creature closed upon the fallen machine, raising a huge hoof high to deliver its final crushing blow...

"Tomoyuki," Yoshio seethed. "One more step and you are done. Do you understand?"

The young Yakuza laughed, and took a single deliberate step. Yoshio shot the man's right foot out from under him. Tomoyuki loosed a shriek of pain and leapt for his opponent. Yoshio fired again, grazing Tomoyuki's head. Tomo fell on the cop, knocking him out with a roundhouse strike across the face with the crystal.

"I got you, Shimura!" Tomo whispered between ragged gasps of air, then smashed the cop again. "I got you!" Another blow and Tomo could feel the man's thick skull begin to crack. "Got you!" The psychopath raised the relic high for a final blow.

"Just the same as your father," a spectral voice intoned.

Tomoyuki froze at the sound, then forced his gaze towards its source. "You!" he growled, once more confronted by the image of Yao Ziang Chi. "You can't stop me, old man."

"That's right, Tomoyuki. Hate me. Just as your father always did," the vision replied.

"I'm not like him," Tomoyuki screamed. "I am nothing like him!"

"Look around you, Tomoyuki. See the terrible suffering you have caused," the spectre leaned close to the madman. *"Is it not the same as your father did to you?"*

For a moment, a look approaching lucidity flashed across Tomoyuki's features, as though some long-awaited realisation had finally been uncovered. The mask of rage left his face, replaced by grim resignation as he gazed first at the Chinaman, then down at the beaten form of Yoshio.

"No!" he spat, letting the bloodstained crystal slip from his grasp. Shakily, he reached for Yoshio's gun. "I don't want to be like him." With the last of his strength, Tomoyuki raised the barrel of the gun to the side of his head. "I don't want to be like him anymore," he cried.

Then Tomoyuki Tomita pulled the trigger.

It is said that on that day there came a moment when the great storm ceased, vanishing as suddenly as it came. The winds disappeared, the seas grew calm, the rain stopped as though cut off by a switch. A final roll of thunder lingered like a gunshot in the air, accompanied by the subtlest of aftershocks as the shifting continental plates ground once more to a halt. Over several hours the deadly tempest had laid waste to Japan, turning its mountains and forests into frozen, glaciated wastelands, and leaving its cities and towns ablaze. Then in a single moment, it was gone.

Slowly, the survivors emerged from whatever shelter they had managed to find, pulling themselves up from the cradle of carnage their world had become, and stepping forth into a new and fearsome reality—a reality shaped by a history of prejudice and a legacy of power, where the depth of pain in one man's tortured soul had been released to ravage a nation.

And so the realm of the Wind Dragons was finally lost, unable to sustain itself either apart from or as part of the universe of Man. It was that universe that had spawned them, then cast them out when their power grew too great. It took the sacrifice of two children for them to finally learn that they could never go back. Now, only their memory remains; that and a single shining crystal culled from the banks of the river Tao.

Epilogue

Yoshio bolted awake, his arms flailing wildly as though to fend off some unseen attack. "T…Tomo…Tomoyuki!" he cried, then the terrible pounding in his head knocked him flat.

"Yoshio," came a familiar, far away voice. "It's alright, Yoshio. It's me, it's Charles."

"Chi san," Yoshio struggled past his pain to speak. "Tomita, the Storm…?"

"The storm has passed, my friend, and Tomoyuki is dead. For a while it seemed you weren't far behind him, though it looks like that rock head of yours saved you." Charles smiled.

"Right. Where are we?" Yoshio inquired, unable to recognise his surroundings.

"My shop, though it's more emergency medical centre now than apothecary, like most of the buildings left standing. That storm, that...monster, very nearly destroyed Japan, Yoshio. Medical supplies and relief workers are coming from all over the world to help." Charles fought back tears as he spoke, consumed by the emotion of the moment. "You know how it is. It takes a tragedy like this to bring mankind together, otherwise we kill and abuse each other all too easily."

"I know, my friend." Yoshio reached out a shaky hand, and Charles grasped it tight. "Tell me now, did you recover the crystal?"

Charles hesitated a moment. "No," he finally admitted. "I did not."

"But Tomoyuki had it, Charles, just as your uncle said."

"Yoshio, my uncle Joe died even before our return from Osaka. Tomo may have had the crystal as you say, but by the time I escaped the wreckage of my rig, it was gone."

Yoshio considered their failure with disbelief. "Then what the hell happened to it? It couldn't have just ceased to exist or something weird like that, could it?"

"I wouldn't rule it out," Charles responded. "But I think there may be a more mundane explanation this time." Charles reached into his jacket and withdrew a small piece of paper, a business card. "When I found you, this was sticking out of your shirt pocket."

Yoshio took the card, the print coming slowly into focus. "Lee Imports," he whispered. "But I didn't take a business card from them—I never take business cards."

"I know," said Charles. "I know."

Five Bells

Trent Jamieson

Bell the First

(i)

She cut herself not because it felt good, but because each cut was
a mirror, or a portal, and she did not care if it hurt. She deserved
the pain, because that mirror or portal was her.

I am a ball, she would think, dense as a black hole, lacking
a miracle singularity within—only nothing, endless horrible
nothing. And she craved that nothing as much as she feared it.

(ii)

Harold Holt boiled out of the water at Portsea, forty-four years
dead and four hundred metres tall.

Revenant Prime Minister transformed, mutated, his bathers
had rotted away to a mere whisp of fabric. His penis hung limp
and barnacled like some massive pendulum of the ocean, a great
white shark caught in the folds of his foreskin, two tonnes of
muscle thrashing uselessly.

He crashed and raved all up the coast, striking Melbourne,
swatting down the few fighter jets mobilised to take him on.

His arrival was by no means the first. The secret was to put
on a show of defence, but not to commit too greatly militarily.
They had made that mistake with Monroe—troops and nukes
and stealth bombers—and she had sucked it all in; destroyed LA
more thoroughly than the 2006 Earthquake. Princess Diana had
blitzed Paris. Lincoln and the Kennedy Boys were left to sort it out
amongst themselves in the Arizona desert.

You buzzed and made noises and you tried to get the people
out, before you engaged the big guns.

Bell the Second

(i)

There was a building in the city. Reasonably tall, though not tall
enough that anyone paid it much notice. Its outer surface was
constructed of sheets of mirrored glass, so that at night, when the
lights were on, it gave up its secrets.

Except, at night, if you were to watch from outside—perhaps
peering in from a nearby block of units with a telescope—all you

were likely to see was a man, or a woman—though mostly it was a man—in overalls, trundling a vacuum cleaner backwards and forwards, backwards and forwards, in one room then the next and so on. The lights blinking on with each entrance and blinking off with each exit.

Not a secret at all, that ceaseless industry; and by week's end, with the rooms done, it was time to begin again.

But deeper still, secrets pulsed and crackled.

(ii)

Sometimes she would find the night and that it denied her rest, because all she could think about was that any seventeen-year-old could come in and do her job any time they decided to make a few cuts, because, let's face it, staff wages are an easy thing to cut back on and seventeen-year-olds earned two-thirds of her income, so there was five thousand dollars a year, straight up.

So every time a slim young thing, all smiles and obvious go-getting qualities came out of the manager's office she knew she would find the night and it would deny her rest.

Precarious.

That was how she described her existence.

At least when she ran the razor over her leg she was in control. At least she was constructing metaphors. Externalising internal chaos.

Bell the Third
(i)

The phone rang, but nobody answered it.

"We don't answer our phones around here," his new boss said. "We make the calls, remember that."

Slessor nodded. There were lots of phones around here.

Another phone started ringing and Slessor ignored it.

"You're learning, kiddo," his boss said.

(ii)

"The Japanese are years ahead of us," he said. "Conventional weapons don't work, but even the most ridiculous shit is effective if you assign it to a team consisting of bubble-gum chewing girls, angst-ridden handsome young men and an old professor with a pituitary condition. You gotta give it a kooky name, too, or it doesn't work. We lost the first three because we didn't take it seriously enough.

"This whole shit is as ritualised as a Noh Play. *Super Rampage Contrawise Hero Force* is our best weapon yet.

"But the truth is, the rules change every time. I dread the day when nothing makes sense."

Bell the Fourth
(i)

It felt like a movie. Disjointed, overly significant. As though her existence had become a sequence of pyrotechnic events, none of which actually related to any of the other scenes, but by the tenuous thread of her own presence—and the swift dance of the blade against her skin—were forced into something called Bernadette's life.

(ii)

Holt had never known such power, and it was ringing in his ears, and it was a madding pulse, like a booming heartbeat, like a blinding slashing fire. He had been a fit man. Well, admittedly not as fit as he'd like to believe. Thought of himself as a bit of a James Bond. Though he'd never wielded his Prime Ministership as well as he'd liked. Damn Americans. All the way with LBJ. He'd crush the little fucker now. He batted at the stinging bursts from the planes. He remembered the cold, and the blinding pain in his skull. Then the scolding tone of Menzies. Time for a little more of the old 'Holt's Jolt'. Time to get the big feet walking.

(iii)

"Not on my watch," Glory G Hatori shrieked. "Go *Super Rampage Contrawise Hero Force!*"

Their podules launched into the sky, described wide loops and collided with a burst of Capricious Melancholy Energy, transforming into the multi-limbed battle beast *Hope Engages Fire 4*. *Hope Engages Fire 4* let out a shrill cry then hurtled towards the Holt monster.

"Time for a dismissal, Mr Prime Minister," Jackie Achebone hissed, launching a scattering of powerbursts at the monster.

"His mouth is opening."

"I don't like the look of this," said the Kid, whose name no one could ever remember.

(iv)

She slid the razor over her knee. Swift and reverential. The skin puckered and wept.

The ground shook.

(v)

Hope Engages Fire 4 disintegrated.

And Holt let fly with another burst of sonic destruction. High rises toppled.

Slessor watched it on the direct video link-up, vomit bubbling in his throat.

The phone rang, his hand hovered over the handpiece.

"Don't you answer that fucking phone," his boss snarled.

"It's her," he said, reaching for another phone. "We have to ring her, now."

Bell the Fifth

(i)

I'm calling it, she thought. I'm calling it. Every swipe of the razor, every downward strike. It's drawn to the siren-song of my misery.

She felt its rumbling approach.

Closer. Each mighty step shook her house, until it seemed

the whole building was going to go down. Books tumbled from their shelves, the microwave crashed from the top of the fridge. Windows imploded.

I am the author and the architect of my destruction.

She scurried to the shattered window and watched as the giant foot swept overhead—overhead and kept on going.

The beast did not even pause and soon was gone, less than a shiver to mark its distant passage. A glass—should she have had a single unbroken one—filled with water would not so much as ripple. A vast pupil would not dilate, then shrink to junkie pinprick, outside the window.

All along the street car alarms sang their dreadful song.

The universe didn't give a shit about her at all.

She dropped the razor and wept, her tears mingling insipidly with the blood on her knee.

The phone rang, its machine-tolls urgent; she stumbled towards it. Five rings before she reached it.

"Hello."

There was no answer.

(ii)

Slessor put down the phone. "We won't need to call that number again," he said. "Wrong number."

His boss nodded, brushed at the flakes of dandruff on his crumpled suit shoulders and crossed her name out of the phone book. "We make the calls, Joe. We ring the bell and we find the answers."

"What if there is no answer?"

"Then we laugh into the darkness until it laughs back."

(iii)

Holt reached Canberra, the city long ago evacuated, devoid of populace as much as policy. He tore open old Parliament house and found it empty. With a dreadful roar, the beast went into permanent recess.

(iv)

The razor went in the bin. Razors, scissor blades, pen knives, sharpened plastic lids: objects that cut were easy to find.

She picked up the phone and obtained the number that had called her, which was odd because she had expected it to be a pay phone or a silent number.

Then she called the number, until it rang out. Then she called it again and it rang out once more.

Then she called it again.

(v)

Slessor looked at all those ringing phones. Through that door, the next, and the next were rooms crammed with them: phones and their tintinnabulations.

"How many lines do we have here?" he asked.

"How many unhappy people are there in the world, Joe?" his boss said. "Now you stop thinking about those damn phones."

Once Giants Roamed the Earth

ROSALEEN LOVE

The sea murmurs on the rocks. Last night, there was no murmur. There were no rocks. The thing was out there, lying there, and when it stirred, the waters moved up and over and under, and the thing was there, underneath, near the surface. It's gone today.

If Kai goes to the jetty and jumps in the water, he'll be in way over his head. The thing that came yesterday has gone away today.

It will come back.

Kai knows. He's heard this story before. It's a story from the old people.

They're here today, the government people, to talk to the old people about sea rights, and land rights, but their talk is just hot air. Kai knows better. That mob, they own this land, from here to the horizon. Sea, land, doesn't matter. What's under the water, in the bay, it's land, right? Happens, for now, to be covered by sea.

For the moment.

Wasn't always like that, in the time before this time, and the time to come. What is sea was once land, what is now land was once sea.

The gods walked on the earth. They came to a place they liked, and there they settled. They turned into land, the gods, and look, you can see them, there; how across the bay, that island, a god lay down, and stretched out and there you can see the curve of his back, and in those rocks you can see where he set down his fishing net, and that's his canoe. Must've got wrecked, like, just a bit, and he said, No worries. I like it here, the bay, the sea grasses, the mangroves. It's a good place. It's home.

Sea rights. That's what it's about. From these shores to the horizon, who owns what.

Last night, Kai stepped out. He walked out on the water. He's not going to tell them today, that mob from the government. They wouldn't know how to listen, so hung up on their rights are they, on their legal rights. Who owns what, from the shore to the horizon, and the land that's there, under the water? They reckon, no one. Others know better.

Last night, when Kai walked on the water, the sea sloshed round his ankles. His feet gripped what lay beneath, firm enough to give him rubbery passage, though his toes had to dig down deep.

Kai was there, when the sea rose, and flooded the jetty and swept the men away, and their dog.

It was the dog that saved the fishermen, that's for sure— Chippie, the old red mongrel who came to after the flood, and found himself standing on top of the ocean, far from shore, far enough, in a different enough place, to make an old dog yelp himself silly. They came to, the men, Kurt and Eddie, with Chippie howling, and lights from shore beaming out, and the rescue party turning up, their boats refusing to launch on the rubbery sea, until they, too, the rescuers, learned not to fear, but to step out on sea as on land, in the knowledge that what was under the water would sustain them for the duration. The rescuers came in the moonlight, over the sea, to where the three men flopped around on top of the water, there to save them—three Jonahs from the belly of the deep.

Old Wally was in a bad way, but Kurt and Eddie, they were big men, and they came to and gave Wally the kiss of life, that's what brought him back, as Chippie barked his head off, and Wally woke to curse his rescuers, but he's not too sorry, not today.

They took Wally off to the hospital, just to be sure. At the time, his story made no sense.

The government man is back today, with something he wants the old people to look at. He's brought the drum from the museum, and the museum people, with their video cameras. They want the old people to tell the old stories. The old people are happy to oblige. They like the old stories, but better still, they like to turn the old stories into new stories.

The people gathered under the trees and passed the drum around, carefully, whispering. On the rim of the drum they traced here the marks of the sun as it shimmers on calm noon water, there the glimmer of the full moon on the place where salt water meets fresh. The story is told in the marks. The story is told in the music. The story is told in the dance. Today there is no music, no dance. The story will be told, but not fully.

Kai's there, at the meeting place, with the old people, to help fill in the silence with words, to make the museum guys feel good about their meeting.

'You bang that drum', they murmured, the old people, one to another, 'Trouble comes looking for you. Big time.'

Kai was there, the go-between, interpreter, to tell the museum guy that the drum was played on special occasions, to summon the creatures of the deep. Maika, they said, it's her drum, and Maika is from the old times. Maika, she travelled south with her mate, and as she travelled, she created all the land along the coast, and all the people, all the families, all the creatures of the shore.

Someone's given that drum a bash, they reckon, the old people. They whisper their agreement. That's what happened yesterday. Those fellas in the museum, they packed the drum to bring it up here, and some smart-arse played the fool, and thumped it, and that's why it happened. The fishermen, and Chippie. That's the drum of Maika who travelled down this coast and created the bays, the rocks, the headlands, the islands. She travelled south and now she's on the move again. She's come here, and she's mad. That storm, her breath made the clouds. That flood tide, her spirit frothed the salt spray. That land under the sea, it's her resting place, a place for which they have a name, and the government lot do not.

Maika is moving now. She's moving because she's heard about them fellas, she's heard about the new laws that say sea places are owned by everyone and no one. Maika doesn't like that, so that is what she is saying, that is what all this means. Them fellas on the jetty last night, who were swept away into the water, they could have drowned. But they were saved, that time. Maika, she did that.

Not like she'll change her ways, not for the government people, and their laws that are not her laws. Their laws will wash away in the salt and the spray.

The old folks, they knew. That night, last night, they weren't down by the sea, not like those men who got swept away. The old people stayed up high, on the cliffs, and made their fire. They looked out over the sea, and the islands, and inland to the place where the fresh water comes down from the hills, and swirls into the salt of the sea.

In the museum, they take good care of the drum. They smear it with oil and turn up the air-conditioning. The old people used to make a new drum when the old one fell apart. This drum is the last drum, and must be kept away from the coast, away from the shacks of the old people, which do not have climate-control and adjustable lighting. Fair enough. The drum can stay where it is. The old people stay where they are.

Maika came that night, then went away again. She swept the men on the jetty into the sea, and then she gave them back again. That was Maika's will.

So much has happened since, but as to cause and effect, questions still hang in the air. Maika came back, and this time she stayed.

Maika returned, and filled the whole bay. She settled, and as she came to rest, she threw fish high out of the sea and they rained down far inland. Maika lay down in this place, like a god, and look, you can see her eight arms, how they plug up the rivers that used to flow down to the sea. Shells lie where they fell, pushed into high mounds, heaped in waves on the former shore. The sea now pounds on reefs far, far away.

Maika settled and stayed. Where once the rocks were exposed at high tide, now Maika covers them with her white, translucent flesh. Her body stretches to the distant headland. The jetty stands, uprooted, across the giant's back.

Each day the flesh becomes firmer and darker, until you can

walk across to the other side of the bay. The children bounce over, boiing boiing boiing, but the old people are more respectful, and watch where they put their feet. Some places are slippery, where water still lies, and salt encrusts the high plateaux.

Maika is changing from one state of being into another, from god to land. At night, she glows with phosphorescent light. If you climb the cliffs, you can see the new night-lights, stretching west far inland along ancient river beds, glowing east from here to the horizon.

Ant, spider, crab and starfish find new habitats. The turtles that once swam to graze the sea grass meadows must give this place a miss, now the sea meadows are history.

The jetty juts out over land. Its foundations are not firm.

Maika roamed the seas. She came to a place she liked, and lay down, and became land.

The old sea markers are gone, but that is the way of the sea. Once there were roads in the sea, and the old people slipped their canoes along tidal currents through mangrove flats.

The sky signs remain but the sea signs are gone. Headlands become hills, beaches lie stranded far from the sea, swamps are born anew in the places where Maika stretched out her arms, as fresh water forces new paths.

The smell of the sea has left this place.

Soon the real estate fellas will come. Maika has changed from god to land, and back to god again, in their way of looking at it, at their gods of what is bought, and what is sold. What was once sea has become land, and public rights to the sea will not prevail. Their mob still owns this, from the ancient shore to the horizon. Land, sea, doesn't matter. Now they know it, the government mob and their lawyers. Now they come north with papers to be signed.

Sea rights become land rights, and land rights may be sold. See these papers, note their promise of great riches. Sign here, at this place.

The old people say they never learned the ways of signing papers. Sorry.

The matter of sovereignty will be solved. One day, a new city will be built.

They will drill canals through to the distant sea, and beside the canals, the land will be carved into lots. Mansions will rise, each with its personal jetty, though the foundations must be drilled deep, and piles pushed into the bedrock far beneath. New roads will lead to the city. Development will bring its own rewards.

Maika came, and stayed, but only for the duration. Her time here will pass, and one day, she will arise and move on somewhere else. They will call it earthquake and tsunami. The mansions will crumble to dust, and the canals yield up their niche inhabitants, the crocodiles and bull-nose sharks, to lie in the air, surprised, and, for the moment, lost for evolutionary inspiration.

Maika will rise and slide out of the bay, just as once she

entered it. Her arms will curl in to her belly, drawn from the buried beds of fossil rivers. Her eyes will open, and her gaze will be fixed on the ocean depths, where the fumaroles smoke, and the hydrothermal trenches guard the magma sheath beneath.

One day, Maika will have had enough. She will call to the deep, to her mother, and her mother will call to her, "Come". What is sea will once more become land, what is land will become sea. Maika will say, our time has come, my mother, my sisters. The gods will walk over the waters, but where they make their home anew, they will choose to change it to suit themselves, and the oceans will rise, and rise, and the land will build up, but this time, beneath the sea, and no one will own the sea, from here to the horizon. No one will own the land.

All will be sea, and the gods will, once more, come rightly into their own.

CRUNCH TIME

MICHELLE MARQUARDT

Smoke shifted, catching a hint of red from the flames. Sirens oscillated on the breeze somewhere far away.

Eric squinted in the failing light. "It's a dog... Over there... It's pissing. See its leg? Damn, they've shifted again. But it was a dog, like that one back on the roof in San Francisco. You paying that?"

Cecil frowned. "Didn't look like any kind of animal to me—but maybe I saw some legs, just for a second there. Changes so damn fast though, hard to tell for sure."

"That's the beauty of it." Eric moved a little to the left in an effort to get a better view. "I'll take half points on that one. Your turn. You've got ten, starting now."

Cecil stared hard. It was so damn difficult when things changed so quickly. Perhaps it had been a mistake to come here. It had been easier down by the lake; not so many trees obscuring the view and not so much smoke in the air. Less cluttered.

Patterns shifted before his eyes but it was only random movement, swirling tides of colour and sound.

"Five," said Eric, tone suggesting he'd already won. "Four, three, two—"

"Elephant." Cecil pointed. "There. By that bunch of trees."

Eric swung his head in that direction. "Where? Don't see it."

"There. It's moving its legs. Quick. No, its trunk's dissolving. Wait a moment..."

He lifted a foot and brought it down hard. The ground trembled with the impact, trees shaking and thrashing. "Ground's pretty soft, should still be there." He carefully lifted the foot again.

A few motionless bodies clung for a moment to the fine scales on the underside of his toes, then dropped back to the ground. They had comprised the tip of the elephant's trunk, he saw sadly. Now they lay as a scattered tumble of tiny arms and legs, their colourful clothing darkened by mud.

But the rest had stayed in their places, at least a hundred of them, neatly pressed into the green of the grass. There were the ears, the tail. Even the four legs had been perfectly preserved.

"Elephant," Cecil said.

Eric swished his giant tail in annoyance, its spiked end taking out the last of the buildings nearby. The tide of noise from the panicked, fleeing crowd below swelled on the evening air. "Alright, you win. Next bridge is yours. But there's a big glass dome over on the east side. Now we're playing for that."

CALIBOS

PAUL FINCH

It came ashore at Port Isaac on Britain's north Cornish coast.

The terrain was difficult—steep, rocky, heavily wooded—but that in itself didn't present an insurmountable problem. The invader had ranged far and wide across the many and varied landscapes of the abyssal floor; its articulated, titanium legs and multi-jointed feet were specifically designed to handle every conceivable geological obstacle. For a brief time, though, it paused there, perched over the quiet coastal road, sea water raining down from it, its frontal antennae twitching as their ultra-sophisticated sensors ran myriad checks in all directions. At length, it opted to go north by north-east, and set off in its curious 'sideways' gait, the ground shaking under the colossal impacts of its eight gigantic feet and crumbling beneath the onslaught of its thirty-thousand tons.

"How did you people ever get permission to build this damn thing in the first place?" the general demanded.

All around him in the Ops Room, there were blank, helpless expressions.

Professor Karis slumped in his swivel chair. His thin, bearded face was sickly white.

"General," came a cool, clipped voice. It belonged to Miss Lewis, the professor's PA and official 'Number Two'—a handsome, very elegantly dressed young black woman seated at the control console beside her supervisor. "Professor Karis didn't build the device. He was involved in the design-and-development team as part the British government's commitment to the CALIBOS project. The device itself was constructed in Japan, mostly with American money. I think it's a bit harsh to keep on blaming *him*."

"Someone's got to take the blame, haven't they!" the general retorted. "Or does that not happen in this age of political correctness? I mean Jesus H. Christ…it happens to be us—the British—that the damn, wretched thing's attacking!"

"General!" the professor snapped. He'd paled even more, if that were possible. "It's not *attacking* anyone or anything. CALIBOS has no aggressive or belligerent directives whatsoever—"

"Then what the hell's it doing here?" the general snapped.

They glanced at the row of screens across the console. On the two central ones, the images were being beamed back from a Bell-Jet helicopter currently tracking the mechanised monster as it ploughed its way across the vast grassy wilderness that was Bodmin Moor. The picture quality was poor, but the crater-like footprints that the giant left in its wake were quite evident. When it barged through a line of power cables, the seventy-foot pylons, which it simply dwarfed, came down like a row of skittles.

The professor hung his head. "I'm sorry, I don't know."

"The device isn't responding to any outside signal at all," Miss Lewis answered for him.

"Why?" the general demanded.

She remained calm, unruffled; she indicated an open 'instant-messaging' link beside her. "We're still waiting for data on that. There's an unobstructed line between here and Tampa. Every technician we've got is working on it, as we speak."

The general's breath hissed out through tightly clenched teeth. He was a big, bullish man, at least fifty years old, but, despite his close-cropped hair and thick grey moustache, strongly built and trim around the belly. He fitted his battle-fatigues snugly, wore the revolver at his hip with the air of a man well-used to confronting his country's enemies. On this occasion, of course, that enemy was rather out of his league; hence his rounding on the pair of scientists, who presented an easier and more convenient target.

"You two are typical, aren't you," he sneered. "Bloody university eggheads. Ivory tower people... always think you're right and always end up being wrong—though, of course, *you're* not to blame. It cost the bloody Earth to build this thing, and six months later it's completely out of control—"

"A technical glitch, nothing more," Professor Karis interrupted.

"Technical glitch! Have you seen the damage it's doing!"

And now, at last, the general's own second-in-command stepped in. Colonel Carson, while not General Buttering's regular assistant, had been specially seconded to his outfit for the duration of this crisis. Though he looked young—he couldn't have been much over forty—he already had a long and distinguished career in counter-insurgency. Despite his refined, almost scholarly manner, there was a hint of steel in his cool, blue eyes. Only those in the inner sanctum of the Ops Room would know that he'd been brought in from the elite Special Air Service, or, as it was better known, the SAS.

"Sir," he said quietly, "I think we should let the scientists deal with their end of the problem, while we deal with ours."

"Usually I'd agree," the general barked, "if we had any bloody room to manoeuvre." He shook his head again, hating the fact that he was deprived of at least half his normal offensive capability. "When I think of the precision air-strikes we could call against this goddamn thing, and be done with it in one fell swoop!"

They glanced back at the screens. The device—or CALIBOS,

as everyone was now referring to it—was making swift progress over the bare, flattish countryside. The shadow of the helicopter, a bee-like object in comparison, was vaguely visible on the sun-drenched grassland next to it, but was having to fly at full belt just to keep up.

When CALIBOS came to a clutch of pine trees, it simply strode through them, smashing them to matchwood.

"How fast can the damn thing move?" Buttering asked.

The professor ran trembling fingers over his wrinkled brow. "The top speed ever recorded under the sea was around forty knots. But that was in a highly pressurised environment, pushing against deep ocean currents. On land, in the open air, who knows?"

The general gazed back at the scientist with renewed contempt. "Who knows? That says it all!"

"General," Colonel Carson put in.

"I know, I know." The general straightened up. "Let them deal with their problems, we'll deal with ours." He glanced at the younger officer. "I sincerely hope this team you've put together knows what it's doing."

"It's our specialised Aerial Assault Unit, sir," Carson explained. "They're the best in the regiment at what they do. Which, if you don't mind my saying, sir, means they're the best in the world."

Captain Howling first saw the object of his mission from the gun-deck of a Chinook helicopter as he and his men sped over the wild, undulating moors of central Cornwall.

In appearance, it was like a crustacean, a titanic crab in fact, maybe three-hundred metres across, equipped with eight gigantic legs, each one correctly hinged and articulated the way they would be on the real-life creature. It also had two immense claws at its front: massive bulky objects, razor-toothed on their inner grips so that when down in the sea it might carve its way through reef and rock and mountainous stands of coral, or, if necessary, grapple with the more ferocious denizens of the depths, such as the sperm whale or the giant squid. Its casing, however—or perhaps the correct term should be its 'hull'—was its most impressively mollusc-like feature. With a sheet-steel base, but covered all over with polyethylene fibre-coat, and on top of that several layers of inch-thick bitumen-rubber to protect against salt-erosion, it gave off a glittering aqua-purple sheen. In addition, it had a rounded, almost moulded finish and was at least as smoothly contoured as the armoured shell of a real-life blue crab. At first glance, one could be forgiven for assuming that this wasn't a synthetic creature at all, but was in fact a product of Heaven—or maybe Hell—but certainly not Earth. As they bore towards it, however, changing their angle of attack to come in low, Captain Howling and his men could hear the cacophonous echoes of its progress: the grinding and crashing of steel, the ground-shaking impacts of its footfalls. Great strands of kelp still hung from its lower extremities, though as the team closed in, they could also see that, from many points on its underside and around the rim of its upper carapace, numerous additional if smaller appendages were visible, most of them retractable cables with vicious-looking hooks on the end.

CALIBOS, the captain thought. A dramatic-sounding name—there was no denying that—especially when screamed from the newspaper billboards:

FISHING-BOAT SUNK, CALIBOS BLAMED!
CALIBOS RISING!
CALIBOS LEAVES TRAIL OF TERROR!

CALIBOS—Cartographic Abyssal Laboratory Intended for Biological Oceanic Survey.

Howling was a soldier by trade, and had never been anything else, so the only information he had about the incredible thing they were fast encroaching upon he'd gleaned from a quick, last-minute briefing. Apparently, the device was unmanned and entirely automated, an immense but mobile and totally self-contained research station, designed to scour the deepest, most little-known tracts of the ocean trenches, to root out and catalogue as many previously undiscovered organisms as possible. Howling remembered reading somewhere that since investigations into the abyss, or 'inner space' as it was now fashionably known, had seriously begun in the mid-1970s, new species had been discovered at a rate of roughly one every ten minutes for the duration of each exploration. It wasn't hard therefore to understand the value to science of a device like CALIBOS—which would never get bored or jaded or weary, would never need to rest, or to come up for air, or to be re-pressurised, which would never run out of fuel, or need medical assistance, or seek to be reunited with its family, or require to be re-stocked with supplies of food and water, and which, theoretically at least, would never break down or malfunction even under the harshest conditions. For not only was it reinforced to withstand the crushing weight of billions of tons of seawater, but it was thermally protected as well. Its delicate innards were thickly shielded against temperatures that might range in a matter of moments from the chill sub-zeros of those deepest, blackest regions, to outflows from volcanic vents where the brine could be superheated to fifty times the temperature of a boiling kettle and still, owing to the incalculable pressure, remain in a liquid state.

CALIBOS.

It was an awesome opponent—though, according to data, it wouldn't regard itself as such. Though highly computerised, its mainframe based on those developed for the NASA Mars probes and thus one of the most advanced on Earth, it didn't think like a human or even like an animal. CALIBOS didn't have friends or enemies. It was purely and simply a machine.

"Why can't we just bomb the shit out of it?" Private Matthias asked. He was chewing hard on a piece of gum, his broad Welsh face florid and sweaty.

"Because its propulsion drives are powered by heat generated in a pressurised water reactor," Captain Howling replied. "Even if we did manage to breach the outer hull, which is armoured to withstand the extreme pressures of the deep sea, we'd likely cause damage to the fusion systems—a contingency that could very well lead to a thermonuclear explosion. That means no missiles, no heavy artillery, period."

"So instead," Matthias said wryly, "we have to switch it off."

Captain Howling nodded. "That's *all* we have to do."

"And are we qualified to do that, sir?" Sergeant Spears wondered.

By his tone, even Spears was shaky—and that would be a first. The teak-tough Geordie was shaped like a gorilla and as sturdy as granite. What was more, he had nearly twenty years' service, most of it spent on active duty. It was a sobering situation indeed when a trooper like Spears was visibly unnerved. All the more reason for Howling to radiate his usual aura of calm professionalism. "We just need to get on board," he reminded them. "We'll be guided from there."

Almost as an afterthought, he reached up to check that the camera lens in the left shoulder-pad of his Kevlar bodyplate wasn't obstructed, then adjusted his helmet mike. It wasn't a new experience for them go into battle with each man hooked up to Ops via combined video and audio links. They'd pioneered it in December 2001, when fighting their way through the Tora Bora cave system in eastern Afghanistan. But at thirty-five Howling was an SAS veteran, and had cut his teeth on covert operations where the most they'd taken with them behind enemy lines was a map, a compass, a spare ammo-belt and a water bottle. This hi-tech rig still took some getting used to.

"It's moving at a hell of a speed," Private Gavin observed.

"The sooner we get cracking the better then," Lieutenant Briggs replied sharply.

Howling glanced at his subaltern. Briggs was a good man—immensely strong for his relatively slim stature, and highly athletic—but on this occasion his presence wasn't ideal. His home was in Bristol, which was over a hundred miles away...but directly in the path of the rampaging monster. What was more, his wife and child were still there. The team was ready to go; they ought to be edgy, tense...but even by those standards there was an odd, icy glaze to Lieutenant Brigg's pale green eyes.

Its motion-detectors brought it to a brief halt.

A profusion of life was suddenly swarming around it—warm-blooded, according to its sensors, but bearing away in all directions at an unusually sluggish speed.

Immediately, it began to gather and collate.

In the Ops Room, the two scientists watched their screens agog as CALIBOS, crouching down, now employed its numberless array of hooks and snares to pick up the many sheep that were trying to scamper away from it. Invariably, despite their frantic struggles, those animals it caught were drawn inside the mechanoid via the countless ports and hatchways through which the snares had originally issued. But, where necessary, the device also utilised its two great pincers, with which it scooped up even more of the terrified creatures, often six or seven at a time, and then—almost delicately—fitted them through the great letterbox-shaped opening that was its maw. There they were deposited on a swift, backwards-rolling conveyor belt, from which CALIBOS's many lab-assistants could claim them.

"Dear God," whispered Miss Lewis, "it's collecting samples."

"What?" General Buttering growled.

"I said it's—"

"I know what you said! What do you mean?"

The woman could barely speak. She pointed a shaking finger at the nearest screen, on which CALIBOS could now be seen to have targeted a small herd of ponies. But even these—stronger, bigger and far, far swifter than the sheep—were proving no match for it. As they scattered, it moved back and forth among them with spider-like agility, leaping as well as scuttling, every shock of its landing setting off a minor earthquake, which hurled the hysterical animals from their feet.

The general swore. "I thought you said this damn thing had no hostile directives!"

"It doesn't," Miss Lewis replied in a disbelieving voice. "It's just doing what it was programmed to. As far as CALIBOS is concerned, this is nothing more than ongoing scientific analysis. Only on dry land instead of the ocean floor."

"But ..." the military man was almost lost for words, "but...those creatures are going to die in there, yes?"

The two scientists exchanged harrowed looks. The answer to the general's question was painfully obvious.

"So," Buttering's voice rose to a bass roar, "does this mean it could start gathering up people?"

Once again they didn't reply, because the answer to that one was just as clear.

"You realise it's only five miles from Launceston!" he yelled. "There are over seven-thousand *samples* living there!"

Professor Karis seemed incapable of responding, though Miss Lewis made an effort to regain her composure. She turned urgently and efficiently to her superior. "What did Professor Tracker say in his last communiqué?"

General Buttering listened intently. As far as he knew, Professor Tracker was the top man over at Tampa, the project director. If anyone could stop this juggernaut, surely he could.

Karis only shrugged, however. "He can't affect a manual override. He just can't. He's tried."

"But that's impossible." Miss Lewis's voice almost broke, as though the true meaning of this disaster was finally coming home to her.

Karis gave another of his helpless and infuriatingly familiar gestures.

Buttering turned to Colonel Carson. "Get your men in there now!" he said. "Forget ministerial protocol...they're green-lit. I'll take full responsibility."

Carson only hesitated for a second. The cabinet were in session right at this moment, debating the pros and cons of the special-forces option. Apparently, the cash value of the mechanised monstrosity was so extraordinarily huge—one explanation he'd heard was that "an ordinary grunt like him wouldn't even be able to comprehend it"—that even the idea of inflicting relatively minor damage on the thing had divided the government down the middle.

But lives were now clearly at stake. British lives. And he and General Buttering were British soldiers, and just for once to goddamned hell with soulless, money-grubbing accountants!

Carson sat at his console, put his own headset on and promptly began to give orders.

Buttering, meanwhile, turned back to the two scientists. He was in 'shouting and bawling' mode, but there was enough of the senior manager left in him to realise that only steady and rational thought would see them through this. "I thought you people said this wretched thing had broken from its original programming?"

"It has to have done," Miss Lewis replied, "just to have come to the surface."

"So tell me, why is it suddenly carrying out preordained tasks?"

Professor Karis shook his head. "It's a malfunction I can't account for."

"Unless ..." Miss Lewis glanced up at the soldier, her eyes suddenly wide. "Unless...oh, but that's ridiculous."

"What is?"

She swallowed. "Unless it's not actually broken from its original programming. Unless it's been *re*-programmed. I mean...by someone else."

The seven-man team made a rapid descent. In fact, they plunged down their abseil lines so quickly they were almost in freefall.

This, of course, was what they were trained for and had practised countless times in genuine combat situations, though this particular exercise had more than its fair share of unique complications. To begin with, the chopper overhead was having to travel at high speed just to keep level with the monster. Secondly, they had to descend from a distance of over two-hundred feet, as that was the maximum reach of the snatch nets on CALIBOS's upper carapace.

It was these snatch-nets that brought the SAS team their

first casualties. The objects sprang seemingly from nowhere, shooting up from their trapdoor hatches with rocket propulsion, unravelling in midair and engulfing their targets in blankets of fine steel mesh, which would then magnetically seal themselves around the enclosed prey and quickly be hauled back in.

Private Gavin was snared first. This was one of the reasons they were rappelling down so quickly, but Gavin hit a snag in his fall line and for a moment was suspended there—and that was all it took. The next thing he knew, he'd been netted, swathed in steel webbing. Before he could respond, the net's clamps had adhered to each other and then it was tugging him downwards. His desperate squawks were lost; the swirling blades overhead chopped the air at deafening volume, while the clanking and crashing of the steel leviathan below was thunderous on the ear. Gavin kicked and threshed like a madman. He drew his knife and slashed to left and right, but it made no impression. And all the while, the retraction-motors pulled with ever greater force and the cable connected to his net went taut. His abseil line began to drag downwards on the Chinook. It was only a matter of seconds before the copter crew took the option of cutting it loose. Not that this proved necessary, for a moment later Gavin's belt clip—strained to breaking point—finally gave, and then he really was in freefall.

CALIBOS's snatch-nets were designed to capture creatures that were swimming past it—creatures that would in fact continue to swim all the time it hauled them down. Private Gavin, of course, couldn't do that, so the apprehension-systems were taken by surprise when he plummeted the remaining eighty-five feet, finally crashing onto the giant crustacean's back and breaking every bone in his body. They recovered smartly, though, and hurriedly drew the gurgling, twitching bundle that had once been a man towards the yawning trapdoor, a gory trail smeared behind him.

With forty feet still to go, Private Martindale went the same way. On this occasion, his dilemma was spotted by Lieutenant Briggs, who immediately drew his Kurtz and tried to cut across the snatch-net's cable with a stream of gunfire, but the target was too slender. None of the slugs struck home, and Martindale was also plucked from his tether and went howling to his death. Briggs shrieked in rage, but then barely managed to avoid ensnarement himself. A net came tumbling up towards him, blossoming as it went—a metallic flower of death—and he had to swing himself bodily around his fall-line, so that the net bounced harmlessly backwards.

Even when the rest of the men made it to the bottom, additional problems awaited.

The top of CALIBOS's shell—its back, for want of a better term—while level enough if the thing was stationary, was now in perpetual, frenzied motion. The giant mechanoid was proceeding at an awkward gait, its upper surface bucking continually, or tilting from side-to-side like the deck of a ship in the worst storm imaginable. The team had prepared for this. They had ice-cleats fixed to their boots, which they could sink into the bitumen-rubber skin, though this only gave them a tentative grip. They were also equipped with pin-guns of the type mountaineers use; the moment each man alighted, he freed himself from his abseil harness, drew his gun and shot-fired a steel peg into the floor near his feet. The peg would not penetrate the polyethylene fibre underneath, but would lodge beneath the rubber and afford additional security. Before discharge, each peg was primed with a high-tensile line, which ran back to a specially prepared reel on the trooper's belt. It was like a fishing line—the idea was that it would pay out as he progressed, but lock if any especially violent movement threatened to hurl him around, thus providing an anchor.

Only this way were they able to forge a steady path across the upper carapace, frequently needing to cut their lines, hook up new pegs and shoot them into the bitumen. Howling was already receiving instructions from Colonel Carson. They'd landed close to the mechanoid's rear, which unfortunately meant they'd now have to trek two-hundred metres to get to its front right-hand shoulder—the weakest portion of the hull. This point had already been marked out for them. A military fire-fighting plane had deluged the area with bright yellow paint, but it was astonishing, now that they were here, how little they could actually see. On all sides, the mottled, purple-green surface ebbed away to indefinite horizons. With its constant upwards and downwards motion, with its endless pitch and roll, it was an utterly alien environment. A strong stink of salt hung over everything, and much of the time the men were stumbling through clusters of barnacles or sliding on greasy masses of weed that had actually taken root in the rubber. They tried to move in classic 'stick' formation, but continually caromed into each other, or were knocked to their knees. They cursed and sweated. Despite their hyper-fitness, such difficulties took a savage toll on their joints and by the time they'd reached the yellow zone they were bruised and exhausted.

If nothing else, though, this was a better position from which to see beyond CALIBOS. In all directions, the men could now view splendid panoramas of sun-drenched countryside: moors, fields, woods, a thread-work of country lanes. Directly ahead, a summer haze concealed much of the conurbation that was Launceston, but to the north-west, the sea, even though it was twelve miles away, made a glittering navy-blue mantle that seemed to stretch into infinity. Of course, there was no time to admire such scenery.

Captain Howling had them form an immediate perimeter, perhaps twenty yards in diameter. Sergeant Spears and Private Pershing hooked themselves down again, then set up the two GPMGs—heavy 7.62mm rapid-fire canons, effective to nearly two-thousand metres—Spears covering the north and east quadrants, Pershing the south and west. The rest, who had also anchored themselves, now took spikes, knives and crowbars from their equipment packs and began to rip and tear at the yellow-stained bitumen, within seconds exposing the pristine polyethylene below. Private Matthias then lowered his Perspex visor, fired up his oxyacetylene torch and, with a slow but practised hand, began to burn a line across the shiny metallic surface.

According to the plans, directly below their feet there now lay an intricate tangle of coolant pipes instead of the usual hardware that packed the underside of the mechanoid's hull. If they could cut a manageable hole in the surface, they could worm their way inside without too much difficulty. Though they knew things were never as simple as they sounded.

"Spooks topside!" Briggs shouted.

Every man looked up.

Though they'd all been expecting it, it was still a shock to see thirty or forty miniature versions of CALIBOS come scuttling into view on every side. The majority of them were advancing in squad-like formations across the monster's back, but several individuals emerged from below, as though, insect-like, they'd defied gravity to scale the mechanoid's precipitous flanks. As one—as though some telepathic signal had warned them that they'd been spotted—they now came to an abrupt halt. They were, each one, about the size of a large dog, and coated claw-to-claw with gleaming white enamel. In the middle of each of their faces, if they could be said to have such a thing, two reddish, glowing pinpoints marked the location of their visual-sensors. Above these, their antennae twitched feverishly.

"It's alright," Miss Lewis said hurriedly. "Maintenance-technicians, that's all."

"They're not designed to fight?" General Buttering asked.

The woman shook her head. "No, to repair damage. But that's what they're here for now. They'll need to be held at bay."

"This thing's a walking nightmare," Colonel Carson said under his breath.

"Wait until your men get inside it, Colonel," Professor Karis mumbled; despite his renowned intellect, the great scientist was becoming less and less coherent as the crisis dragged on. "Then they'll have the lab-assistants to deal with. You can tell which ones those are because they're red. Blood-red."

Carson made no reply. He'd known all this in advance, from the pre-deployment briefing. General Buttering, however, had been too busy to attend, and he was now bewildered to learn they could be facing yet more problems.

"Lab-assistants?" he asked.

"Yes," Karis said. "They'll try to incorporate your men into the analysis programme. As specimens."

"Jesus Christ!"

"But that's not the worst of it, I'm afraid."

"You mean it can actually get worse?"

The professor nodded, white-faced. "Oh yes, general. A

lot worse. When the team penetrate the inner works—start to encroach on either the reactor or the brain-cortex—they'll have to contend with antibodies."

"Antibodies? That's got to be a joke!"

Miss Lewis shook her head. "You won't think so when you see them, general."

"Covering fire!" Howling shouted, and the two GPMGs started up simultaneously.

The maintenance-technicians had begun to advance again, at a slow, menacing creep, but they were now hit by a storm of lead, which wrought chaos among them. The heavy barrels of the GPMGs swung back and forth, the shells ripping home with spectacular force. There was a relentless crashing, like the beating of a million hammers on tin. Enamel casings buckled and exploded, limbs and severed antennae went twirling through the air. Briggs and Howling drew their Kurtz submachine guns and joined in the fray. With the constant swaying and tilting of the hull, it was difficult to pinpoint targets, but for the moment there were so many of them that it was practically impossible to miss.

Between them, the four troopers drove blazing fusillades in every direction. But the enemy, of which there were now even more appearing—hundreds more—simply refused to retreat. It wasn't fearlessness on their part—not as such. It was programming. There were various degrees of damage that the technicians were primed to respond to, and threats to the integrity of the hull rated as the most urgent. Thus they came on...and on, and on.

Belt after belt went through the GPMGs. Clip after clip was snapped into the submachine-guns. The thunderous shooting echoed in all the troopers' ears, their trigger-fingers were soon aching, but they continued to fire, strewing CALIBOS's upper surface with the broken, mangled wreckage of its innumerable children. And still the maintenance crews refused to withdraw. They did try to avoid the gunfire, darting from side to side, but even when they were severely hit—gutted or de-limbed—they did everything in their power to advance, clawing their way forward, sometimes on a single leg.

In the middle of the perimeter, meanwhile, Private Matthias worked steadily with his oxyacetylene kit, the sweat dripping from his broad, red face.

"How you doing, Ron?" Howling shouted over to him.

"Nearly there, sir."

The high-tech armour plate was intensely durable, but the big Welshman had now almost completed a glowing red square at least four feet in width.

Still the technicians advanced, though they were hampered by the vast numbers of smashed and sliding carcasses they had to haul out of the way to get past. They were closing in to a horrible proximity, however, and though Howling knew they wouldn't attack the men, their overriding instinct would be to start repairing the hole, whether his team had gone in through it or not, or even whether they were actually in the process of going through.

"Keep 'em back lads," he shouted. "We're almost there!"

The hail of bullets continued to rain on the technicians, bashing in their shells, smashing their sensors, tearing out long intestinal strands of circuit and wiring.

"Millions of quid already gone up in smoke here, boss!" Sergeant Spears laughed.

"Don't worry, Jamie, the insurance'll cover it," replied Howling.

The Geordie guffawed all the more, and then Private Matthias's melodious Welsh voice called over to them: "We're through!"

Howling turned. Matthias had already cast down his torch and was unbuckling the fuel-canisters from his back.

"Jamie, you and Nigel hold position." The captain scrambled along his line into the centre of the perimeter. "The rest of you, to me!"

When he reached Matthias, the Welshman had already jammed a pry-bar into the red-hot crack and was levering the piece of armour plate up and out. Howling joined him. A moment later, Briggs did the same. Part of the secret of polyethylene fibre was that it wasn't heavy, and it took them only seconds and a few singed fingers—even through their thick, flame-proof gloves—to manhandle the freshly cut panel out of the way. Below it, as they'd hoped, lay a dense lattice-work of plastic tubes, fluids visibly pulsing through them.

"Marcus, you first," Howling said, turning to Briggs.

The lieutenant nodded, slotted his Kurtz back into his webbing and, taking care to step over the glowing edge of the hull, worked his boot through the upper layers of pipes, made space for himself, then climbed down into them properly. He rapidly descended from view, like an ape through a tangle of branches. Private Matthias went next.

"Jamie!" Howling shouted.

On the edge of the perimeter, Sergeant Spears abandoned his GPMG, turned and came clambering towards them, at which point the mechanoid began to negotiate especially awkward terrain. If they'd looked, they'd have seen that it was entering the outskirts of Launceston, shops and bungalows collapsing beneath its feet like houses of cards. As such, it began to tilt and sway more alarmingly than before; the sergeant fell several times as he worked his way in, but made it and dived headlong through the hatchway. Out on the perimeter, Private Pershing was still keeping up a terrific rate of fire, but he now had to cover all quadrants, and in addition to that, because of the increased jolting, more and more of his rounds were going wide. Captain Howling could see that they were about to be overrun.

"Nigel!" he shouted. "Over here, now!"

Pershing abandoned the heavy machine gun, swung around

and went blundering towards his senior officer. It was only a short distance, and he fancied he could make it without anchoring himself. But he'd not gone five yards when the giant mechanoid reared up and then down again. The floor beneath Pershing simply dropped away. The private found himself in mid-air, the way one does in the cabin of an aeroplane when it suddenly loses altitude. But less than a second later, the casing swung back up to meet him...from a distance of sixty feet or more. The private was slammed upwards like a human shuttlecock.

Howling could do nothing but watch as the young soldier arched three-hundred feet through the air, before finally dropping from sight.

In the Ops Room, they watched Pershing's descent to earth through his own shoulder-cam, staring dumbly, unable to look away as a stretch of rubble-strewn roadway surged towards them at terrifying speed. There was no sound, only a prolonged hiss of static. At the point of impact, the screen blanked out.

There was a momentary stunned silence. Nearly everyone was thinking the same thing: three men down already, half the team, and penetration of the hull not yet complete. The exception was Miss Lewis, who was numbed with shock at the loss of yet another young life.

In front of her, meanwhile, on the screen connected to Sergeant Spears' shoulder-cam, she could now see Captain Howling climbing down through the squarish aperture. She'd only caught glimpses of him thus far, but had been impressed by what she'd seen. He was square-jawed and fair-haired, with clean-cut good looks—the way a World War Two flying ace, like Guy Gibson or Douglas Bader, ought to have looked.

"Captain Howling seems very capable," she said slowly.

Colonel Carson nodded stoically. "John Howling's the best. If he can't pull this off, no one can."

The evacuation from Launceston had failed to materialise to any serious degree, chiefly because people found the whole idea too improbable. A colossal, mechanised sea creature on a rampage through the countryside! How could such a thing be possible?

Yet they asked themselves this in the full knowledge of what that giant mechanoid was—despite having watched the newsreels with rapt attention when CALIBOS had first been painstakingly designed and constructed, despite having shared the worldwide excitement on the eve of its launch, and despite having read in the newspapers about its progress as it combed the ocean floor. Even with such knowledge, the current threat was a disaster that—as far as they were concerned—simply wasn't going to happen, an accident that couldn't possibly befall them. It was media hype—and all too unreal to be worried about.

CALIBOS, meanwhile, was again beset with teeming lifeforms; as it was encoded to do, it began to collect. It had no feelings, no sympathies, no concept of guilt. Those multitudes it squashed beneath its feet, or buried in rubble as it knocked down their dwellings, were the inevitable flotsam of scientific progress. Those it crushed and tore as it kicked its way through the log-jammed road networks, or even incinerated when the news helicopters that had defiantly breached the no-fly restrictions were yanked down and slung as fireballs into the midst of the fleeing, hysterical mobs...all these were fall-out, debris, the waste-product of discovery.

In truth, of course, it didn't have thoughts even on this level. If it had, even CALIBOS—heartless, soulless CALBIOS—might have balked at the vast numbers of samples that it now fed into its analytical systems, where intensive biological evaluation and then methodic chemical break-down were only the primary-stage procedures.

General Buttering was handed a clipboard, and what was on it stopped him in his tracks. His neck went stiff, the eyes almost popped from his skull.

"Known fatalities...four hundred," he said, in a hoarse whisper. "Injuries already top two thousand. Missing...ninety-five and counting."

Miss Lewis rose to her feet, a manicured hand clasped to her mouth.

Colonel Carson looked around in astonishment.

Professor Karis began to shake—violently, as though he was undergoing convulsions—then slumped forward, his eyeballs rolled white. His head banged hard on the map-table, and a stream of saliva issued from the side of his puckering mouth. The Ops Room staff ran amok around him. Not only did they need to get him medical help, but with Professor Karis unavailable, who would advise the mission?

On the console screens, the firefights continued.

The SAS had been equipped with respirators in case they encountered toxic fumes generated by the interior's many industrial processes. There had never been a high possibility of this as the giant creature was riddled with vents and ducts designed to allow a constant flow of seawater through certain sections of its innards. This had been partially to aid with buoyancy, but also to bolster its infrastructure against the terrible weight of the ocean. Now, on land, fresh air penetrated the system instead, so from the moment the team had entered and begun to work their way down through a multi-levelled maze of pipes, conduits and vast arrays of complex, oily instrumentation, they'd had no difficulty breathing.

Which was a good thing, because almost straight away they had other far more serious problems to contend with.

A steel serviceway ran like a catwalk through the heart

of the throbbing machinery, most internal areas of CALIBOS having been designed to be accessible to human beings, in case a major overhaul ever became necessary. Once the intruders reached it, the so-called lab-assistants appeared. These crab-like mechanisms, gleaming a brilliant scarlet in the light of the troopers' belt flashlights, were designed to tackle even the most aggressive forms of marine life; they were bulkier, sturdier and generally larger than the maintenance-techs. They closed in on the team from all directions. No sooner had the men hit the catwalk than the nightmare things came scuttling out of the darkness...two advancing along the catwalk from its eastern end, others descending ladders of pipework, their steel-tipped feet bonging like bells.

The men opened fire, their blazing weapons filling the dimly-lit interior with staccato flashes of lightning. Even in that first panic-stricken moment everyone hit his chosen target, but the lab-assistants withstood the leaden hail with horrifying ease. Dents appeared in their armour-plating, panels cracked or buckled, pieces flew off, but the damage was less significant than that inflicted on the maintenance-techs. Sergeant Spears managed to blow the feet off one of them as it crouched directly overhead, sending it spinning into the darkness below, but, all in all, their successes were few.

"Grenades!" Howling shouted.

Though they'd not been equipped with substantial battlefield ordinance, the team had been allowed to bring hand-grenades along, even if they were under orders to use them sparingly. Lieutenant Briggs rolled two together along the catwalk. They detonated under the belly of the nearest lab-assistant, catapulting it into the chasm below.

"Captain Howling!" came a female voice in Howling's ear. "Captain Howling—"

"Copy!" he shouted, now pouring fire at another red shape as it reached the catwalk with a single bound. "Who is this?"

"This is Miss Lewis, Professor Karis's PA," she said urgently. "Colonel Carson asked me to speak to you. To direct you out of there. You're currently in the recycling zone and making no progress at all..."

Howling lobbed a grenade at the latest assailant, the subsequent explosion showering him with fragments of searing-hot technology. "Well, we're a bit tied up at present with—"

"Captain Howling," the woman interrupted, "CALIBOS is now in Launceston itself, and killing hundreds of people. You must try and move on."

Right on cue, the last of the lab-assistants—for the moment at least—disappeared off its overhead perch, Matthias and Spears knocking its feet from under it with concentrated volleys.

Howling pushed the mike closer to his mouth. "Talk to me, Miss Lewis—"

*

The woman was surrounded by charts and diagrams. On her laptop she'd also called up a 3D display that detailed every level of the mechanoid's interior structures. A single lock of lush black hair fell over her brow, which in its turn was damp with perspiration.

"I should inform you, Captain Howling," she said nervously. "Professor Karis has been taken ill, so I'm going to have to fill in for him."

"You're doing alright so far," came the response.

"I'm sure I can get you to the brain case without any hitches."

"You'd better hope you can," General Buttering growled over her shoulder. "Your job depends on it."

Studiously, she tried to ignore him. "That's…er, that's what we call the area where the cortex is located. The cortex is the mechanism you'll need to disconnect."

There was no reply to this, just a harsh, heavy breathing. Miss Lewis detected annoyance in the captain's silence. She'd been present at the briefing, where the team had had it forcibly impressed on them that they mustn't damage the brain-cortex in any way. Not because, like the water reactor, it could cause an atomic blast—it couldn't—but because several billions of dollars had been sunk into the cortex alone. Though physically small, it was regarded as a marvel of modern micro-engineering and thus invaluable. Destroying it was totally unacceptable. The infiltration team were therefore under strict orders to switch it off—and to exert great care when they did so.

"Captain Howling?" she asked worriedly. "Are you receiving me?"

"Go ahead, Miss Lewis."

"Right…er, the first thing you need to do is backtrack along that gangway, until you reach a pressure door. On the other side of that, there's a service chute. This will lead you down into the water-duct system."

CALIBOS clambered back and forth through what remained of the historic town centre in order to ensure that it hadn't missed a single specimen. Huge numbers had already been swept up, either by claw, clamp or snatch-net, but its remit was thoroughness, and when excessive numbers of the same species were encountered swarming in one particular sector, a more intensive enquiry than usual was to be launched.

It had never been the mechanoid's intent to flatten so many fine buildings: to crush the Norman castle to powered rubble, to implode Lawrence House like a thing of plywood, to topple the Georgian frontage of the White Hart Hotel; or, for that matter, to leave chaotic trails of shattered, burning car-wrecks, not to mention heaps of charred and twisted corpses, along Launceston's main roads. Even after all this, though, the job was far from complete. Already, its sensors were picking up huge concentrations of lifeforms to the south and east.

CALIBOS didn't realise, of course, that a wholesale stampede was now in progress; that every highway leading out from Launceston was clogged with running, screaming, shouting, shoving people; that cars were shunting together; that buses were being overturned as hordes of refugees packed into them.

It proceeded in their wake at a calm and measured pace.

The infiltration team was now negotiating a labyrinth of cylindrical steel shafts, most so tightly enclosed that the men were forced to crawl along them on their hands and knees, lugging what equipment they had left behind them.

This was part of the water-ducting system. As such, the passages were bright and clean, and minus obstructions. They constantly made right-angled turns, however, not just to the left and right but occasionally up and down. There were numerous junctions where the men had to pause so that Miss Lewis could re-check her charts and then direct them accordingly. On top of this, their ears were endlessly pummelled by the rumble of colossal machines. It was exhausting, wearisome. The men's knees and elbows were soon raw and bleeding. In addition to that, the heat was unbelievable. Often the metal itself was scorching. But even when it wasn't, there was no ventilation or air conditioning, so the troops sweated copiously, gasped, grunted but stumbled relentlessly on, guided only by the light of their belt torches. And always, it seemed, there were more sections to pass along. Those that plunged suddenly downwards proved as difficult as those that ran vertically up, because in these cases gravity would frequently take over, and the men either slid or dropped—sometimes it was twelve feet or more before they hit the bottom.

"Captain," Lieutenant Briggs eventually said. "This is screwed-up. We can't be making any headway at all."

"This is the only sure route to the brain case," Howling replied.

"We know that for a fact, do we?"

"I can only follow the instructions I'm given."

"We're bloody-well losing time," the lieutenant argued, his tone impertinent.

Howling halted, turned and looked back at his second-in-command. In the stark torch-light, the junior officer was pale and sodden. His reddish hair hung in strands from under the rim of his helmet. His eyes, as before, had a crazed gleam.

"Are you going to keep it together, or what?" the captain quietly asked him.

Briggs's mouth twitched awkwardly. "It's just that—"

"I know what it is," the captain interrupted. "Now you deal with it, Marcus, or I will."

A tense moment passed, then they pressed on. Ten minutes later, they reached a T-junction, at which Miss Lewis halted them. "I understand you've got some plastic explosives, Captain?" she asked.

"Affirmative," he replied. "This is the place then?"

"Yes. It's sheet steel, but it's only half-an-inch thick. You should be able to blow a hole through it with relative ease."

Howling turned. "Jamie, pass the demolition."

"A word of warning, though," the woman added. "Beyond this point you mustn't even contemplate using explosives. On the other side of this wall, you'll be into what we call the inner works. The instruments in there are far too fragile and costly. You'll have to be extra careful."

"Don't worry, we're very careful," the captain said.

As instructed, they blew the bulkhead, then filed one by one through the smoking aperture into what looked like a maze of steel-mesh tunnels. The mesh protected ranks of computer panels, all chattering to themselves or displaying myriad patterns of variously coloured lights. The troops wove through it and, at the end, found a manhole cover, which they were able to lift. Below that, they were into a secondary water-ducting system. Again it consisted of single passageways, though these were wider and taller than those previous, tall enough in fact for the men to stand upright. There was a new problem here, however. These ducts were flooded.

One by one, the men jumped down, and found themselves waist-deep in cold, slopping seawater. Uncertain glances passed between them, but they pushed on. There were more twists, more turns. Inevitably, though, their route began to slope downwards, soon at a very steep gradient, until, perhaps twenty yards farther on, the water came right to the ceiling.

With the overall casualty counters racing up into the tens of thousands, divisional army commanders decided they'd had enough.

CALIBOS had reached the open countryside east of Launceston and was trampling farmland when it met its first serious resistance.

Six Challenger tanks, drawn from manoeuvres in Devon, were arrayed on a shallow, westwards-facing hillside. They commenced firing immediately the mechanism was sighted, using 120mm shells, which they concentrated on the gigantic creature's glittering metal legs. Despite their frustration, the tank-commanders knew that they couldn't risk striking its torso, though a very easy target that torso would have made. The closer the monster came, the more of the sky it seemed to fill, the greater the earth-tremors, the more and more people—not to mention horses, dogs, sheep and cows—came hobbling past, gibbering, gagging, frothing at the mouth.

The tanks continued to fire, leaping with the ferocious recoil of their L30 CHARM guns, flame and smoke ballooning from the ends of their barrels. Only one, however, scored a hit before the beast was upon them—for its final assault was delivered with greater speed and precision than even twenty-first century soldiers could imagine. Though the third leg on its left-hand side was severed at the lower knee joint, it still managed to spring forwards nine-hundred yards, and the next thing the cavalrymen knew it was descending on them like a global-killing asteroid. The shock of impact threw most of the tanks from their tracks. One was spun around sideways while in the process of firing. Its projectile impacted on the tank to its immediate right. The resulting explosion was catastrophic, a plume of flame soaring fifty feet into the air, fragments of burning steel hurtling in all directions.

In less than five seconds from the commencement of hostilities, only two of the six tanks were still operational. One attempted to rev forwards and pass directly under the monster, only for a gargantuan foot to smash down on top of it, pulverising it like play-dough; human guts squelched out from either side, shooting in ribbons through the mangled masses of wheels and caterpillar-tracks.

In a cloud of exhaust, the remaining tank turned tail and fled. It ploughed a hideous path through crowds of running, staggering people. Its gun turret swivelled around and the tank commander lifted the hatch...just in time to see CALIBOS sweep down with a mighty claw, pinch hold of the vehicle by its gun-barrel, lift it—though it weighed sixty tons—and then hurl it through the air. End over end it went, travelling hundreds of yards before crashing into a country cottage, the entire structure of which vanished in a cloud of choking dust and splintered wood.

"Oh God," said **Miss Lewis**, when Captain Howling reported the flooding in the passage. "Oh God. Don't you have any breathing apparatus?"

"Respirators," the skipper's voice replied, "but they're only air filters."

"Oh God."

"Think of something!" the general bellowed at her. "Jesus Christ, woman!"

Colonel Carson tried to reason with the CO, but he too looked weary and washed-out. Several moments before both men had been elated to hear that state-of-the-art energy-weapon technology might solve their problem; that a controlled explosion of the new pulse missile in close proximity to CALIBOS might neutralise the monster's computer systems without causing any structural damage. Very fleetingly, they'd thought they had a solution. But then word had come through from cabinet level that under no circumstances could an energy weapon be used. The pulse missile was untested, and the shockwaves it sent out might still cause damage to the mechanoid's ultra delicate brain-cortex.

"We can't just vent this?" Howling's voice queried.

"No," Miss Lewis said. "Not from where you are. And *we've* got no control at all."

"So?" the soldier pressed.

The scientist consulted her laptop. "According to my plans, that particular culvert is like an inverted horseshoe. It goes down, then up. The water must be at the same level on the other side."

"How far through?" Howling asked.

"Ninety-five metres!" said Private Matthias, wide-eyed.

"We can do it," Howling replied.

He'd already unfastened his chin-strap, and now took off his helmet, first detaching the mike and head-set, and shoving them into a sealable plastic pack. The rest of the men began to discard what equipment they didn't need. Their Kevlar body armour was designed to be light and flexible and was thus retained, as were weapons—but helmets could go, along with tool harnesses, bolt cutters, belt rigs, ration packs and respirators. Boots were then removed and fastened around necks by their laces.

Without waiting for further orders, Lieutenant Briggs hurried down the ramp towards the sloshing green water. The others followed, working their lungs slow and steady, to build up respiratory endurance. Then, one by one, they dived in.

This was more SBS territory than SAS, Howling thought as he frog-kicked his way down into the opaque gloom, but as part of their amphibious warfare training they'd all practised deep-range freestyle diving, and there wasn't a man in the team who couldn't hold his breath for five minutes or more. It was still a lengthy swim, however, and on occasion it proved unnerving. In the bobbing light of their torches, they regularly saw the remains of deep-sea life that had been trapped—once, no doubt, fantastical to look upon, but now, owing to the enormous pressure-change, little more than shrivelled knots of flesh and gelatin. More of a distraction to Howling was the state of Lieutenant Briggs. The younger officer was swimming ahead with frenzied force, swerving from side to side like a predatory seal, though, of course, lacking a seal's energy, resilience and lung capacity; in other words, wearing himself out even more. The guy was mentally all but gone. At this rate he'd be physically gone, too.

When they reached the other side, and replaced their boots and headsets, the skipper approached him. "You're on your last warning, Marcus," he said quietly.

Briggs looked around sharply.

Howling continued: "I'm not having you endangering the mission, not when thousands of other people's wives and children are being threatened too. The objective here is to locate and infiltrate the mechanoid's brain case, and then to deactivate the cortex. It won't be as simple as one-two-three, so the last thing I need now is my best man in a reckless race against the clock. Clear?"

Briggs stared at him. "Am I clear, lieutenant?"

"Clear, sir," the younger man said, evidently wanting to say something else.

The subaltern's new-found compliance was to be tested

to its utmost less than a minute later, however. They hoisted themselves through the next manhole, and found another open area crammed with machinery and complex instrumentation. The central feature of this space was a conveyance rack, along which passed a seemingly endless array of upright tubes. Each one was clear—made from some kind of translucent PVC—and brimming with fluid. Each one also contained a specimen.

A man, a woman, or a child.

They were all sealed in and fully submerged, and though many of them were visibly dissolving—one or two had already broken down into a partial chemical soup—not all of them appeared to be dead; here and there, a hand twitched, a pair of eyeballs rolled, a chest rose and fell as the heart inside it palpitated.

"Oh Jesus!" Briggs shouted. "Oh Jesus God!"

Even Howling went cold at the sight. He was a bachelor and had no children of his own. He couldn't begin to imagine what it must be like to see this and know that the perpetrator was now on its way toward the town where your family lived.

"The bloody heathen thing!" Sergeant Spears roared, his Geordie voice rising above the clangour of the machines.

"That's it!" Briggs screamed, slamming a fresh clip into his Kurtz. "This thing's dead! As of now, this thing's bleeding-well dead!"

They were so engrossed that none of them noticed the furtive movements in the labyrinthine cage-work directly overhead.

In the Ops Room, they sat and gazed in stunned disbelief at the twisted, tortured forms in the capsules—until suddenly, every screen was lit up by a glaring and prolonged flash of intense light, followed by an explosion of submachine gun fire.

For a crazy second, Miss Lewis thought that one of the men was shooting at the figures in the tubes, probably as an act of mercy. But then she realised that this wasn't the case at all, because a babel of hysterical shouts now blasted through her earpiece.

The team were under attack.

Instantly, the monitor connected to Sergeant Spears's shoulder-cam went blank.

The SAS team had been briefed beforehand about the antibody units, the warrior-machines that would attack them the moment they penetrated CALIBOS's inner works. They'd seen and studied diagrams of the creatures—mobile mechanisms that were much larger than either the maintenance-technicians or the lab-assistants, painted a gleaming jet-black so that when they came scuttling through their giant relative's innards they'd look more like black-widow spiders than crabs. They *were* crabs, however. More to the point, they were crabs of the most ferocious hunter-killer sort. Where CALIBOS's front pincers were essentially movable fingers, toothed but designed for gripping and holding, these things wielded vicious incisors whose sole purpose was for snipping and slicing. Where CALIBOS's exterior weapons consisted largely of snatch-and-grab devices, these creatures had disc-saws, needle-probes, pneumatic drills.

And now they were using them with maximum efficiency.

Four of them had come down on the intruders from above, surprise gifting them an awesome advantage. Sergeant Spears died first, when a pereopod—a spear-tipped foreleg—plunged clean through him from behind. Captain Howling responded quickly. He spun around, jammed the muzzle of his Kurtz into the middle of the monster's face—again delineated by two glowing red dots for eyes—and emptied his entire clip. But even from close-range, these antibodies were no pushover. As well as being larger, they were bulkier and far more heavily armoured than the previous automatons. Horribly, and somewhat gruesomely, they also carried clusters of smaller but no less fiendish versions of themselves on their backs, almost like mother crabs with broods of offspring. These demonic children scampered off the second crab the moment it touched down, and in less time than it takes to blink were all over Private Matthias.

Moments of utter chaos followed. Gunfire blazed in all directions. Tubes containing human specimens exploded. Flesh, bone and stinking humour sprayed over everyone. There were blinding, stroboscopic flashes, the ear-piercing screams of ricochets. One of the monsters reared up on its hind legs to grapple bodily with Briggs; the lieutenant smashed the butt of his spent Kurtz into its underside, kicked it backwards, then drew his Glock and blasted five rounds into its exposed circuitry. Howling was thrown against a wall of computer panelling. A pereopod stabbed down, intent on impaling him, only for the skipper to duck to one side and see it punch straight through the metal coating and into the electronics below; the antibody went rigid and began to pour out smoke as millions of volts were pumped through it.

Private Matthias, however, was having less success. Already slashed and bitten from head to foot, he opted to stumble away from his colleagues and draw a grenade. The smaller antibodies, six of which were still clamped firmly to him, were gleefully eviscerating him from the outside-in...when he flicked out the pin.

The detonation blew the small mechanoids to fragments, but tore the man in half as well, his upper torso slamming through yet another row of specimen tubes, sending their pitiful contents spewing out over the oily walkway.

General Buttering—lips flecked with froth—thrust Miss Lewis aside, snatched her headset and bawled into it himself. On the screens, only haphazard, cavorting images were visible through the murk: smoke, flames, flailing mechanised limbs, repeated strobe-like bursts of gunfire.

"Howling, what in God's name are you doing there!" the

general shrieked. "Get the hell out, man! Remember your training, cover-fire and fall back in twos ..."

The captain's response was broken by static: "Who'm I talking to now, over?"

"For God's sake get out of there! Jesus Christ Almighty, don't you see what kind of crisis we're dealing with here! We can't afford to lose your team as well."

Miss Lewis choked with horror as, very fleetingly, a gigantic crab-pincer flickered into view, clasping by one ankle the lower half of a truncated human being. There were more on-screen flashes, more roars of gunfire. Briefly, the sweat-sodden face of Lieutenant Briggs, shouting wildly, appeared on Captain Howling's screen.

"We need direction, over!" came the captain's voice.

"Just follow orders, soldier!" General Buttering hollered back at him.

The images on the screens capered wildly, but by the looks of them now, both Howling and Briggs—the only two left—were retreating side by side, pouring lead into a mass of piled and broken black armour.

"I haven't got a map," the captain said. "I need direction *now!*"

"Dear God in Heaven," the general howled, "can't you do anything—"

A karate-blow, delivered with a quick, crisp movement, struck the general on the side of the neck. He slumped down over the console, then slid sideways to the floor.

Colonel Carson handed the headset back to a very relieved Miss Lewis.

Following Miss Lewis's instructions, Howling and Briggs managed to make their escape to the next section by worming along a narrow aluminium conduit, which they were warned beforehand conducted occasional spurts of scalding-hot steam. After the fight with the antibodies, both men were prepared to take the risk. They slid on their bellies for perhaps fifty yards, before the captain, using his knife, was able to hack out a sufficiently large hole for them to crawl through.

Once again, they were in the midst of a multi-dimensioned framework of pipes and vessels, but another steel serviceway was visible ahead, and they clambered towards and onto it, eventually passing through a doorway. Beyond there lay a junction where banks of manual controls were located. To the immediate right, a narrow chute sloped down towards a glaring purple luminescence.

Miss Lewis's voice again sounded in Howling's ear: "Captain, you're right on the outside of the brain case. There's a reinforced door you'll have to dismantle, and on the other side of that a gridwork of laser beams, which you can only neutralise by keying in a series of binary codes I can give you once you get there."

"Received," Howling replied.

"Captain Howling," she said, once again struggling not to sound nervous, "you must work fast. New squads of antibodies will be homing in on you as we speak."

"Understood."

"First, go left," the woman instructed.

Howling moved, but Briggs stopped him, pointing down the shaft towards the purple light.

"Miss Lewis," Howling said, "there's an accessway to our right. We see a purple glow. Anything we should know about?"

"Ignore it," she replied. "Under no circumstances are you, or any members of your team, to go down there. That leads to the reactor vault."

"Understood." Howling set off, only for Briggs to stop him again.

"Sir," the lieutenant said quietly, still pointing towards the light. "That's where we want to be."

Howling was puzzled. "You heard the woman."

The lieutenant shook his head. "All this crap about dismantling doors, turning off laser-defence systems. It's going to take ages. And now we've got more antibodies coming."

Howling shrugged. "That's the job."

But Briggs stood stock-still. "I vote we blow the reactor."

Howling looked at him askance. "We'd be killed—along with thousands of others."

"Better than millions," came the taut reply. "Which is what'll happen if this bloody thing is allowed to carry on."

"Marcus," Howling said, using as placatory a tone as he could, having realised that the one thing he'd really feared over the last half-hour had finally occurred, "we don't even know that this thing's headed for Bristol any more."

"Whichever way it's going, it'll get there eventually."

The captain considered his words carefully. For the first time, his subordinate looked calm, composed, focussed. Not a good sign.

"Think where we've got to," the skipper said. "We're ten minutes from switching this monster off. Ten minutes, that's all."

"You hope."

"I guarantee," Howling replied. "Now we've worked together long enough for you to know when to trust me, yeah?"

A second passed—a slow, torturous second—then Briggs pursed his lips. And nodded.

Howling tried not to show his huge relief. "Okay, let's move."

He turned—and was promptly shot in the back.

CALIBOS was now advancing along the A30, the fast dual carriageway that ran around the northern edge of Dartmoor before veering southwards towards the teeming city of Exeter.

Once again, briefly, it was in an area of low population, and as a result, making swift progress. The best estimates of the chasing helicopter pilots were that it would reach the city limits in the next thirty minutes.

"Lieutenant Briggs!" Colonel Carson shouted into his mike. "Turn around right now and proceed with the mission as planned."

There was no response.

Miss Lewis was still staring with shock at Captain Howling's screen. It was operational but motionless; only a stretch of bloodied floorway was visible on it. Lieutenant Brigg's screen, on the other hand, showed that the junior officer was descending the ramp towards the reactor vault.

"Lieutenant Briggs," the colonel said again, "this is Colonel Carson. Turn around right now! That's an order!"

"He can't hear you," Miss Lewis said.

"He can hear me alright." The colonel ripped off his headset. "Is the reactor as well protected as the cortex?"

"Not really. There are two blast-doors. An inner one and an outer one, but he might be able to bypass them."

Carson grabbed up a telephone and tapped out a number. "Get me the minister urgently. No...do it now! I don't give a...Listen!" Carson rose to his feet, cheeks blazing. "I'll tell you how important it is! Let's talk about 'evacuating-the-whole-of-southern-England' important!"

The intense purple light that filled this most hazardous section of the entire CALIBOS infrastructure was extremely hard on the eye, but Lieutenant Briggs had become a man possessed.

He knew everyone thought he'd gone crazy, but as far as he was concerned there was a method to this madness that might yet save Jenny and little Carl. Nobody out there was running from this monster quickly enough, because they either didn't believe it or because they assumed it would somehow be stopped.

But an impending nuclear explosion would be very different. And an explosion down here, in Cornwall or Devon, especially a delayed explosion—because the reactor wouldn't overload immediately—would give places like Bristol, still a good distance away, ample time to evacuate. It was harsh, but it was the only possible chance for them, and so he pressed determinedly on.

He broke first through the antechamber door, by ripping apart its control-box and then rewiring it. Beyond that, he found a heavily shielded wall with an observation port, through which he could see the outer hull of the containment structure itself. Inside that was the pressuriser and the control rods. The entire assembly would have been shock-proofed to the nth degree. Even with his remaining seven grenades taped together and primed to go off at the same time, Briggs wasn't certain that he'd be able to rupture through to the core. But a row of condenser pipes was also visible, connecting with the structure and feeding water through to the steam generator. All he had to do was break those and the job was done.

He checked the control box on the second door, but finding it more complex than the first, cast his tools aside and unslung his MP5. The viewing port was fitted with tempered glass, but three shots from this most powerful of assault-rifles was all it took to shatter it.

*

Miss Lewis screamed: "Oh my God! Colonel, he's into the reactor vault."

Colonel Carson threw the telephone down and snatched up his headset again. "Lieutenant Briggs, I'm appealing to you...for pity's sake. Think what you're doing—causing a thermo-nuclear explosion on mainland Britain!"

Brigg's only reaction was to remove his own headset, and throw it on the floor.

At which point, the reactor vault's own antibody dropped from its ceiling perch.

Like the others, it was armoured with black plate and had a variety of lethal weapons at its disposal. Unlike the others, it had only one function, to protect the reactor...at all costs.

It landed directly on top of Briggs, and weighing as much as a Harley-Davidson, virtually smashed him flat. But broken and twisted beneath it, the soldier still had the strength to fight back. The MP5 had gone clattering to the far corner of the chamber, but he was able to draw his Glock again, wedge it into a gap between two segments of crab-armour, and fire repeatedly. It made no real difference. The malevolent robot-eyes gazed down into his from no distance, and a pincer clamped his gun arm by the elbow—with a wet CRUNCH, it snipped the limb in two.

Briggs shrieked loudly, but more from frustration than pain.

He was in pain, though—and the pain grew worse as the monster ground its weight on him, pressing his crushed pelvis into the steel floor. He beat at its shell with his one remaining hand, clawed at any loose piece of cabling he could see, trying even in his death throes to rip out its guts. He might have succeeded, had a probe-like lance not projected slowly from between the mechanoid's eyes, making contact with the centre of his forehead and, pushing on through, penetrating first his skull, then his brain.

In the Ops Room, they didn't know whether to be relieved or horrified as they stared at Briggs's now-blank monitor screen.

Miss Lewis finally broke the silence: "I must've missed ..." She glanced confusedly down at the plans, then up again. "At least, at least...we're spared...that."

Colonel Carson stripped off his sweat-sodden tie. "Yes, but unfortunately our friend can't be more than twenty miles from Exeter now, where he may kill at least as many people as an atomic bomb would."

Then, both at the same time, they spotted movement on one of the few remaining screens. They leaned forward to look—and saw that Captain Howling, who they'd assumed dead, was shifting about, in fact easing himself up into a sitting-posture.

Carson snatched his headset: "Captain Howling, this is Colonel Carson. How bad are you?"

"M...messed up," came a barely coherent response.

"Listen, John," Carson replied, "you're our only chance now. Briggs is dead, but he damn near blew us all to kingdom-come. You've got to continue with the mission—"

Carson fell silent. On screen, Howling was trying to stand.

It would have been difficult for Howling to follow the next set of instructions under normal circumstances—perhaps in a simulation-centre, with no pressure whatsoever. But right now he was grievously wounded and still had to negotiate passages that were lurching and tilting like a fairground ride.

Even so, he dragged off his gloves, dumped his Kurtz and his MP5, and, armed only with the bare essentials—his Glock, his knife, a spare grenade and a small took-kit hanging from his belt—he proceeded as per Miss Lewis's directions. He fell many times en route, but at last reached the 'brain case door', which was sealed like an airlock. He then had to manually remove its bolts and hinges, a task that took much longer than it should have done. At last, however, the door fell forward from its frame, and Howling saw a narrow service corridor, which ran for about thirty yards before ending abruptly in an access bay. He leaned weakly against the jamb as Miss Lewis reminded him that this passage was filled with crisscrossing beams of invisible light so intensely hot that they'd slice his flesh and bone like butter. Thus began the complex procedure required to turn them off.

There was a key-panel just inside the door, and Howling started tapping in reams of numbers, an exercise made all the more difficult because, being so close to the magnetic cortex, communications were repeatedly breaking down. To make matters even worse, a faint clattering echo was fast approaching: the sound of large, multi-legged creatures racing through the labyrinthine tunnels to get here. This noise grew progressively louder, so that when the final code was keyed in, Howling blundered off down the passage, not heeding the woman's advice that he throw some piece of kit ahead, just to check that the entire system had been deactivated. Thankfully, his gamble paid off. No beams remained, and he entered the access-bay at the end of the passage unharmed, only to find himself gazing up a steel, turret-like shaft that rose forty feet at least, before terminating in an eerie blue luminescence.

He started up, but despite the hand and foot grips that had been installed, it was a slow, agonising climb. Several times, his consciousness began to ebb, while the pain in his back, and now in his chest as well, became so unbearable that frequently he could do nothing but hang there, breathing slow and steady, and trying not to get too alarmed at how much blood shot from his nostrils with each exhalation. He'd perhaps only covered thirty feet when he heard noises below: a furious clamour of steel on steel.

The next set of antibodies had finally arrived.

They wouldn't be able to follow him up here, of course, though their 'offspring' might. Howling climbed all the harder. He was now desperately tired; his body felt as though it weighed a ton. Overhead, the pearly blue light was much closer. It shone down on him like a heavenly radiance. But below, with a quick skitter of claws, the first of the miniature crabs came scuttling up in pursuit. The captain was only two feet from the top of the shaft when the tiny monster reached his legs, and straight away, began cutting and slashing at them, ripping through his tough army-issue trousers, scoring the flesh.

The soldier aimed blows at it with the soles and heels of his boots, but it sprang from side to side, evading then with acrobatic ease. He drew his Glock, knowing it would be impossible to get a clean shot off; in his state, he'd likely hit himself. Further below, he saw a second crab appear, and then a third.

Anger overcoming his pain, Howling flung the revolver down. It missed the first, but struck the second one smartly, sending it into a tumbling descent, legs pin-wheeling. As it fell, it collided with the third, and the both of them vanished from sight. The first of the beasts, however, had now climbed past the soldier's legs and was onto his torso, again slashing and ripping. Instead of wasting time trying to repel it, Howling sought to finish the climb. As a special-forces man he'd long ago been trained to mentally shut out pain. That wasn't entirely possible in this situation, but he did his best and now he'd almost reached the top of the turret, from which point, finally, clearly, he saw it—the brain cortex, suspended just overhead.

It was a beautiful crystalline structure, about the size and shape of a football, but glowing a fiery, iridescent blue and attached to the panels encircling it by myriad fibres—brain stems, Howling realised, nerve strands, each one whisker-thin, delicate and fragile as a gossamer thread.

And more than he could possibly count, let alone systematically disconnect.

The antibody was now onto his chest, hacking at what remained of his armour-plate, trying to expose his throat and neck. The soldier braced his back against the turret-side and began to beat at the thing with his fists, so that his hands and wrists took the brunt of its sniping, incisor-like claws. He snatched out his knife and smashed down with the hilt. One blow caught the monster on its shell, knocking it downwards a foot or so, but it kept hold—and again tore into him.

All they could see on the monitor, now fuzzy with static, was the

captain's ragged, wounded hands. The flesh and muscle hung in
strips from them as they threshed down on the antibody, which
came clambering up his chest again, its pinpoint eyes gleaming.
Even bathed in blue luminescence, it was a vision of pure evil.

"John," Miss Lewis said, trying to keep her voice steady.
"John, can you hear me?"

There was no reply, only a frantic grunting and hissing.

"John," she said again, "listen to me, please! I know you're
hurting terribly, but it's vitally important that I take you through
the process. You have to..."

But the words strangled themselves in her throat.

What she'd been trying to say was: "You have to disconnect
it, you have to follow the correct procedure, unplug the fibre
contacts in a strict and specific order."

But that was nonsensical, ludicrous.

"Smash it, John!" she said. "The damn thing's like an eggshell.
Just reach up and smash it!"

Colonel Carson glanced around at her, startled, but in the
space of a second the woman had become a tigress. And she
was beautiful in her rage, her hair in dark billows around her
shoulders, the eyes wild in her flawless, mocha face.

"Kill it, John!" she cried. "Kill it now!"

They finally brought Captain Howling out of the great hulking
structure that lay inert over several cornfields just to the north
of Exeter, three hours after it had suddenly—inexplicably to most
people—frozen rigid, then buckled at the knees and slumped to
earth.

The soldier was flat on a stretcher. His neck had been
immobilised; he was hooked to a drip and breathing through
a ventilator. Miss Lewis—the only civilian allowed inside the
military cordon that had immediately been thrown around the
colossal carcass—was in the Mobile Command Centre with
Colonel Carson and various other top brass, when she heard that
one of the search-and-recovery teams had finally located the sole
survivor of the mission.

She rushed outside as they carried him towards the waiting
military ambulance. Running through the dry August stubble
was difficult for her, in her heels and tight skirt, but she was
determined. When she finally came alongside the casualty, he
gazed up at her through watery, blood-shot eyes. His lips and
nostrils were caked with gore, but he still managed to speak:
"Miss Lewis?"

"Call me Joanie," she said, trying her best to smile.

"Joanie...I knew you'd be handsome—"

"Perhaps you shouldn't talk," she advised.

"Don't worry about me...you'll lose your job..."

She glanced around at the mountainous pile of wreckage.
It no longer looked destructive or malevolent; was little more in
appearance than a scrapheap, a forgotten relic of some obsolete

gargantuan hardware. But that was deceptive. They wouldn't leave this fallen Goliath to rust.

"Some job," she said quietly. "Anyway, how are you feeling?"

He half-smiled. "Believe it or not, I've been worse."

"I'm sorry about your men."

If it was possible for him to shrug, he did: "Ours is not to reason why..."

They had now reached the ambulance. Two khaki-clad troopers wearing brown berets—also SAS, Joanie Lewis realised—stood guard over it, rifles across their chests.

"Where will they treat you?" she asked him.

Now Howling smiled properly. "I could tell you, but I'd have to kill you."

They opened the ambulance doors and he reached out a thickly bandaged hand. She took it. His grip was weak, but he held onto her for as long as he could before a paramedic gently disentangled them and ordered the stretcher to be placed inside the vehicle.

As it trundled away, Colonel Carson appeared. He handed the woman a folded print-out. "A communiqué from Professor Tracker," he explained. "For your eyes only, I guess."

She opened the paper and read quickly through it. When she'd finished, she closed it again and stared into space. Her brow was faintly furrowed.

"Don't tell me our problems aren't over?" the colonel asked.

She seemed uncertain. "Remember I was speculating earlier that someone else might have reprogrammed CALIBOS?"

He nodded.

"We dismissed it, of course," she added. "We couldn't think who would have either the capability or the motivation."

Then she turned and gazed up at the vast, silent hulk; droves of gulls were now clustering on it, digging with their beaks among the barnacles and weed.

"Well," she added, "just before it was deactivated, Tampa detected a signal." She paused briefly. "It seems that CALIBOS knew its end was near. It transmitted a distress call—of the sort it was programmed to send to us if it ever ran into serious difficulties on the sea bed."

"It didn't send it to you, though?"

She shook her head.

"So...where?"

"We haven't got a specific location," she replied. "But we've got a vague geographic region."

"And?"

She looked back at him. "I'm afraid that's classified."

"Oh?"

"Not that I think it makes any difference." She strolled toward the Command Centre. "I doubt even the SAS are qualified to carry out missions...in the depths of the ocean abyss."

NEWBORN

ERIC SHAPIRO

I wake up in the hospital corridor. Crust in my eyes. Drool flattened on my cheek. Dear God, I hope I didn't miss the delivery. A moment passes. My wife howls from behind the heavy door. Good, she's screaming. My baby has yet to arrive.

My relief is cut short when I view my watch. It's seven in the morning! Pam has been in labour for well over sixty hours. This cannot be good. I approach the door and knock aggressively. Before long, I am face to face with a sub-attractive nurse. Pale face, green shower cap. I'd rather be looking at my wife's swollen womanhood.

"What is it, Mr Perkins?"

"Is Pam okay?"

Another howl jangles my nerves.

"Of course not. She's in extreme pain."

"I mean, is this normal? This has been going on for *days*."

"With all due respect, Mr Perkins, you were asked to wait out here."

"I know, but that was on Tuesday. I'm beginning to develop the feeling that something is wrong."

The nurse slaps me across the face. She wipes my drool off on her pant leg.

"Mr Perkins, your cooperation is essential here."

"Please, Miss um..." I read her nametag. "...Barbara...I don't mean to cause any trouble. I'm just very concerned about my wife. I'm beginning to miss her."

Barbara inhales deeply. She looks me in the eyes and shakes her head. She says, "There are certain things we cannot tell you at this juncture, Mr Perkins."

"Like what, for example?"

Barbara opens her mouth, then stalls. "Nice try."

I snap my fingers.

"Perhaps you would like to go to the cafeteria for a soda?"

"Forgive me for saying so, Barbara, but I've had enough soda this week to last me a lifetime."

The door behind Barbara opens and out walks a fully decorated general. He gives me a quick salute and turns to Barbara. "Is this the husband?" he asks.

Barbara nods quickly.

The general removes his sunglasses and looks me over. He gives me a long, violent hug and says, "God be with you, my son."

Then the general sticks his fingers in his mouth and whistles. Six soldiers march out through the door, single-file, decked out in camouflaged military gear. I briefly fantasise about grabbing one of their rifles and charging inside, but I'm sure that doing so would result in my death or imprisonment.

Barbara gulps, as if I wasn't supposed to see the military personnel walking by. I lean in close to her, assaulting her with my morning breath: "My suspicion has peaked, Barbara. If you don't tell me what's going on around here, I'll be forced to alert the authorities."

"Most of the authorities have already been alerted, Mr Perkins."

An instant headache parts my skull. "Then why not tell me, for God's sake?"

At that moment, the local police commissioner exits my wife's delivery room. I recognise his face from the newspaper. He turns to Barbara, strokes his moustache. "Is this the husband?" he asks.

Barbara nods quickly.

The commissioner kisses me full on the lips and says, "Don't you worry, my friend. Things will work out just fine. It may take several years of adjusting, but you'll adapt. Keep hope alive!"

I shake up and down. "Hope for *what*?"

The commissioner opens his mouth to reply, but his mood changes and he begins to weep. He crawls away on all fours.

I grab Barbara by the collar, so close to her I can taste her. "If you don't tell me what is going on this instant, I am going to have a nervous breakdown!"

Barbara is visibly disturbed by my behaviour. She croaks, "That's why we haven't told you."

"Why?"

"Because we were afraid that you would have a nervous breakdown."

I let go of her collar and she snaps against the closed door. The pressure in my head is relentless. I yell, "Well, there's no preventing it now! You might as well just tell me!"

The door opens yet again. Out walks Dr Saperstein, the cretin who originally told me to wait in the hall. He's overseen Pam's entire pregnancy. I step backwards from him, fearing a hug or a kiss. Saperstein puts his hand on my shoulder. His palm is covered with slime. He says to me, "I understand what it is that you're concerned about, Sheldon."

"Well, that makes one of us."

"Two of us. Barbara understands also."

Barbara nods at me.

Saperstein goes on, "If you'll join me in my office, I'll be pleased to put an end to this suspense."

"Is my wife okay?"

"No, I'm afraid not."

He takes me by the elbow and says, "Let's go."

Saperstein's office has always horrified me. I don't much care for his photographs of fetuses, nor am I fond of his "Captain Vagina" trophy. I dare not ask him how or where he received it.

The doctor tells me to have a seat. He hands me a wet towel and I clean my face. I find some mints in my pocket and pop them in my mouth. Saperstein sits upon the front corner of his desk.

"Sheldon, has your wife ever had an affair?"

My heart crunches. "Why? Is the child of a different ethnicity?"

"That's putting it mildly."

"Doc, you're killing me here. Please."

"Okay, um...this is not easy to explain—"

"You don't say."

"—but your wife is giving birth to an enormous bird."

The room twirls around. The next thing I know, Saperstein and I are both on the ground. I am punching him in the face. A great deal of blood is at hand. In between punches, he tells me, "S ome...how...we...knew...you...would...re...act...this...way..."

Saperstein cracks me clean in the jaw. A sharp, strong blow. I tumble backwards.

The doctor stands over me. He plants his boot on my neck and shouts, "I understand you're upset, but it's no use taking it out on me!"

"Fair enough! Bring that bitch Barbara in here!"

Saperstein bends over and scoops me up by my shirt. We stand face to face. The lower half of his face is bright red. The top half is dominated by his bulging eyes. "I need you to be as calm as possible right now."

He drops me back in my chair and returns to his seat on the desk. My breath is uncontrollable.

"I'm sorry about your nose."

"That's all right. It's nothing I'm not accustomed to." His blood rains all over the floor. "During the past twenty hours, the beak has been steadily coming into view."

I cover my mouth with my hand. "Dear God."

"Now, we are doing our best to keep Pam comfortable. She is, however, in a great deal of pain."

"How big will this bird be, doctor?"

Saperstein gives my question some thought. He puts a finger to his blood-soaked lips. "Have you ever seen an SUV?"

My feet leave the floor and dangle in mid-air. "The bird will be *the size of an SUV?*"

The doctor cannot help but laugh. "No, Sheldon. Its *beak* is the size of an SUV. We predict the bird will be roughly eighty feet tall, with a wingspan of one hundred and sixty feet."

I can't help myself. I grab Saperstein's "Captain Vagina" trophy from his mantle and crack it over his head. It falls to the floor in two pieces. The doctor is not phased.

"Are you okay?" I ask him.

"I'm fine. I anticipated that reaction." A trickle of dark fluid runs down Saperstein's forehead. "I'll get some stitches after our chat."

I hold onto his desk to maintain my balance. "Will my wife survive this?"

"Unfortunately…yes."

My heart leaps, then drops. "Why is that unfortunate?"

"Because she'll be paralysed from the eyes down."

I vomit soda all over the doctor's hands. He wipes them off on his blotter, obscuring his schedule for the coming week. "The question remains, Sheldon: Has your wife ever had an affair?"

I fall into the chair. "None that I know of."

"Hmm…no large birds have ever phoned your apartment?"

I rack my brain. It's quite difficult to think. Nonetheless, I recall a bizarre late-night phone call from a year ago:

"Hello?" I said.

"Chirp."

"Hello? Who is this?"

"Chirp, chirp."

"I'm sorry, but I believe you have the wrong number."

"Chirp, this is Brutus, chirp, chirp."

I hung up and never questioned it.

When I relay my story to Saperstein, his eyes well up with tears. "Don't feel sorry for me, doc," I say, placing a hand on his shoulder.

He shakes his head. "I don't feel sorry for you. I just think I have a concussion."

"Oh. I apologise."

"No, it's not your fault. Blame it all on Pam. If you want my opinion, she brought this upon all of us."

Goddamn her. My sweet, beloved Pam. How could she betray me so? I wonder if anger on my part would be appropriate, given the punishment she's already enduring.

"If you want to go in and talk to her, you had better do so now. She'll be paralysed and unable to reply by noon. Shortly after that, we'll be taking her upstairs for a rooftop delivery."

Upon entering the delivery room, the first thing I notice is the infant's beak. The beak's orange colour brings theme parks to mind, for it is very bright and stimulating. Twenty or so doctors, nurses, and civilians cease hurrying about and look at me. Among them is a man I believe to be our mayor, but I don't bother to ask him. A young male nurse touches my arm and says, "I'm so happy that I'm not you."

I smile and thank him.

Slowly, carefully, I make my way over to Pam's upper body. Her skin is so green that it blends in with her sheets. I pet her moist forehead. "How could you do it, Pam? How could you betray my trust?"

She clears her throat and squeals, "I never betrayed you, Sheldon."

I turn and look at the emerging beak. Quite bold of her to lie, considering the evidence. "You can drop the façade, Pam. I'm not angry with you."

Coughs emerge from deep within her. "You're not?"

"No. Truly I'm not. I'm just happy you're alive."

The others are listening closely.

"Pretty soon I'll be as good as dead."

"Not to me, Pam. To my mind, you will always be worthy. I will be loyal to you till the end of time."

A blonde nurse towels the tears from her eyes. Pam, too, is crying. She reaches for my hand; so innocently and adorably, the way she did back when we were dating. She licks her chapped lips and says, "Does that mean I can't move in with Brutus?"

I ask the blonde for some tranquilisers and a baseball bat.

Park Rot

SKIP PEEL

David Braggle, Vice President of Theme Park Operations, might have felt beauty in the touch of morning air, were he that type of man. Millions had stood where he now stood and felt it. Every day they experienced it. But Vice President Braggle had been hired in from the outside and had never visited Thrill Acres before he found professional interest in it. Ordinarily he never parked in the main lot, only in his backstage executive space. He never entered through the main turnstiles, but brought family and friends through hidden side entrances. Standing there at 8 am, and spying the coasters and towers over the tops of trees, offered him no excitement. To many the atmosphere outside a theme park is quite intense, but Braggle paid no heed to it.

For twenty years the main parking lot of Thrill Acres had filled to capacity by mid-morning, but that day Braggle stood alone in the lot beside his car. He felt nervous, which suited his temperament, and grouchy, which suited him better. While waiting he turned over financial ledgers in his head, and wondered how much longer the Company could afford to keep Thrill Acres closed.

A large industrial van sped across the lot. Braggle adjusted his tie, tried to look professional, and succeeded. Looking professional was the only thing in his career he was really good at doing.

The van pulled into one of thousands of empty spaces, and its rear doors flew open. Out from a den of scientific equipment stepped a slender Japanese man, much younger than Braggle. Behind him stood several even younger Japanese men, who remained silent.

"Good morning," the man greeted with an accent, though he spoke English well. "I am Kazuo Tabuchi, Field Representative and Chief Case Handler for the Sekiyama Group's International Enterprises Division. I'm here to destroy a monster!"

Case Handler Tabuchi said the last part with business-like flippancy, yet there seemed a hint of pleasure in his tone.

"You're the man we need," Braggle replied, eagerly shaking Tabuchi's hand. "I'm David Braggle, Vice President of Theme Park Operations here at Thrill Acres. Will you come with me, please?"

Braggle proudly gestured toward his car, but Tabuchi seemed unimpressed. He said something in curt Japanese to his assistants, and stepped into the vehicle. As Braggle drove across the lot, the assistants followed in the van.

"We appreciate that Sekiyama responded so quickly," Braggle began. "Have you been to our park?"

"Not in America." Tabuchi replied.

"Well, welcome to Thrill Acres, where over 100 thrills await you," Braggle spoke in the manner heard in the park's recent commercials.

"You have 100 rides?" Tabuchi asked.

"We have 100 *thrills*, not rides. I'm proud to say that since I've been Vice President I've been able to significantly reduce our operating cost by decreasing what rides we could. But, yes, there are 100 thrills, including the thrill of eating a Misty-Twisty Pretzel, our newest food item, or the thrill of this year's newest attraction, the Wild Daisy Gardening Spectacular!"

Tabuchi seemed further unimpressed and examined the perimeter of the park idly as they drove around it. "I've been to Thrill Acres Japan. They say it's bigger than the American one."

"The Japanese park may have more rides," Braggle answered defensively, "but here in the US we have more square footage. There's more acres in the US Thrill Acres!"

"You like red roller coasters," Tabuchi commented, as they turned down a street of industrial buildings behind the park. "Everywhere I see a red roller coaster."

"That red coaster is all *one* coaster: Tyranny, King of the Roller Coasters, Thrill Acres' premiere ride, the ruler of our dozen other coasters. Tyranny is the longest roller coaster in the world, covering the whole park and going through every section. Our designers say the ride lasts twenty minutes—I wouldn't know as I've never been on it myself because I don't like roller coasters. But my office has a great Plan going. Since most coasters top out at three minutes, we want to separate Tyranny into two coasters, thus creating what would be both the first and second longest roller coasters in the world. Then Thrill Acres could hold both records and have two rides. Don't you think that's a great idea?"

Tabuchi said nothing.

"For twenty years Thrill Acres has had the reputation for being an extreme park," Braggle continued, "with the most intense attractions in the world. We became known in this industry as 'The Dark Park,' because everything was creepy and weird here. Thrill Acres did start as a seasonal Halloween attraction, but now we want to change our image. We want to continue two decades of success by becoming more kiddy friendly and lighthearted, fluffy and bright. Here's my office." Braggle pulled his car before an executive bungalow.

"So, Mr Tabuchi," Braggle added as they left the car, "can you do what you've offered regarding our problem?"

"Yes, the monster." Tabuchi seemed unconcerned. "You stated in the initial call that it's some kind of mechanical weapon?"

"It's a robot, not a weapon. Can your firm stop it?"

"Most of our contract work is with governments," Tabuchi

explained as Braggle led him into an office conference room, "but we'll take any client willing and able to pay, such as your financially lucrative company. Sekiyama Group contracts daikaiju elimination in and outside of Japan. We've many satisfied clients. I've just returned from South America where, for a nation that must remain contractually undisclosed, we eliminated a giant winged serpent that was terrorising the countryside—some kind of devil or god come back for revenge, they said. We destroyed it. What monster do *you* have, Mr Braggle?"

Braggle placed a promotional poster on an easel. Tabuchi gasped something in Japanese.

"This is what we're dealing with," Braggle said. The poster presented a gigantic green ogre. Rows of triangular scales hung over the body. Thick clawed hands extended from the muscular arms and shoulders. Green hair sprang all directions from the head as though trying to mimic some monstrous Einstein. Its eyes glowed red and the brutish mouth held perfect rows of silver metallic teeth. The rendering showed the monster lumbering through a swamp in the park where a castle and Tyranny, King of the Roller Coasters, decorated the landscape.

"This thing wasn't my idea at all," Braggle explained. "I only signed onto it to appease the designers and get their minds off making new rides. They called it an *Automated Interactive Character*. It would wander the park independent of any one place, though they designed it for the park's Medieval Village and called it Grendel—a silly name!"

"Ah, Grendel!" exclaimed Tabuchi.

"You've heard of it?"

"Surely you study World Literature in America," Tabuchi remarked. "Grendel was the monster in the Nordic epic *Beowulf*. It ate men until the hero Beowulf challenged it and tore off its arm."

"Yes, the designers did say something to that effect in the proposal," Braggle mumbled. "I must've slept through the meeting."

"I will be sad to destroy such a fabulous machine," Tabuchi sighed. "Do you have any photographs? And I need to see the original designs."

As he spoke, Braggle fished out photos of the partially completed monster, along with promotional sketches. "We were beginning park redesign during the slow season, when the monster, which hadn't opened to the public yet, appeared and started rampaging through the park. We evacuated staff and visitors and are settling lawsuits out of court. Security brought in guns, which were useless and did no damage. The executive board are terrified that Grendel will escape and start real trouble in the outside world—though it hasn't left the park. We still have no control over it ourselves, but at least it's stopped smashing things."

"Your military couldn't deal with it? That is usually attempted before anyone calls us."

"This is private property," Braggle explained softly. "We didn't report the situation to the local government or federal authorities. The political situation is delicate, what with our tax breaks and favoured zoning. We decided outsourcing to your company would be best if it allowed us to stop the monster without upsetting governmental partners or ruining our public image for Extreme Safety. The world at large believes Thrill Acres has closed for ride rehabs."

"I still need Grendel's designs," said Tabuchi.

"We haven't been able to uncover them." Braggle shrugged apologetically. "For professional and financial reasons, we downsized our engineering and design staff, who failed to understand that this is a business. The designers currently employed never worked on Grendel, and we have found nothing in the files at Creative Content. The designs were misplaced. They'll turn up eventually."

"Mr Braggle," Tabuchi sighed, clearly baffled by such inefficiency, "as the Company Vice President, can you tell me about the Grendel robot? How is it powered and charged? What is the reflex speed and rotary torque of its joints? Does it possess significant tensile strength? As to operation, is it preprogrammed from within a hard drive stored internally in its chassis, or is there a method of remote control by direct radio transmission or perhaps a GPS connection?"

"I wouldn't know." Braggle adopted an even-more professional air to cover his ignorance. "Those designers can never explain anything properly when they give a presentation."

"I'll have my crew research your monster Grendel on the internet," Tabuchi grumbled as he pulled out a two-way radio. "You can find almost anything there. Do you at least know where Grendel is now?"

"Sitting in the middle of Thrill Acres," Braggle offered, "like it owns the place."

"Seems he does," said Tabuchi. "Until my Exterminator arrives, at any rate."

Vice President Braggle and Case Handler Tabuchi waited near the main turnstiles of Thrill Acres. Tabuchi was adjusting knobs on what he called a "High Frequency Transmitter", which controlled the "Exterminating Instrument" about to arrive.

"Couldn't this monster come in a truck?" Braggle asked.

"At thirty-five metres high and weighing seventy-five tons, no truck could handle it." Tabuchi stared into the distance. "We ship him overseas in a cruiser outfitted for the purpose, but he must cross land himself. Don't be concerned, Mr Braggle. Itara travels fast."

"Does it get feisty?"

"Itara is docile, when I want him to be."

"I don't like your monster tramping across the state," said

Braggle. "News might leak out, and people will panic."

"Itara will be fine," Tabuchi assured him. "He could run across your country in two days at top speed and barely be noticed. Itara has never damaged any property or person while travelling. Destruction is only permitted during the extermination period. Excuse me."

Tabuchi answered his buzzing radio in hurried Japanese. When finished, he beamed a smile. "He is outside the park, Mr Braggle, reportedly a mile away, and has succeeded in keeping public and governmental attention to a minimum. He'll be here any second. A mile is nothing to him."

Tabuchi adjusted his High Frequency Transmitter. Braggle felt the ground rumble as shaking trees parted across the parking lot. A gigantic bipedal creature stepped through, lumbered across the lot, and thudded to a halt some hundred feet in front of them. With heavy hot breaths, it waited for a command, standing as tall as the coasters in the park.

The monster was a hulking amalgam of familiar yet bizarre flesh. Any child might have guessed its pieces, yet an adult would have been horrified by them. The thing was mad science at its most intense, as if the Sekiyama Corporation of Japan had made in this monster a statement of revenge against the mad science so long ago visited upon its own people.

The creature's foremost impression was incredible strength: massive in the shoulders and back, almost no neck, and a pack of muscle down through the biceps and triceps of its long arms. The head was feline, with ears drawn back fiercely, green cat-like pupils, and a whiskered muzzle. Long canines bulged from its black lips. The monster had opposable digits among its fingers, yet padded palms and long claws. Almost no hair grew from the beast's hide except for a few bristly patches on its back. Its skin was rough-hewn like armour plating—reptilian and scaly. The creature had no tail.

"This is Itara, Mr Braggle," Tabuchi explained. "Our daikaiju. Our Exterminator!"

"What is … It?" Braggle asked, hardly comfortable.

"He's my own invention," Tabuchi proclaimed proudly. "It took five years to design him. I can't explain the entire process— that's proprietary—but he is a clone. I combined selected positive characteristics from three animals for maximum efficiency. He has the sheer strength, foundational upright balance and hand dexterity of a gorilla; his speed, flexibility, eyesight, hearing, smell and general cunning and ferocity all come from the genetic makeup of a tiger; and he needed a blind aggressiveness, a complete tolerance of pain and a protective hide, qualities which were provided in the dragon-like charm of an alligator. Itara is beautiful, is he not?"

"It's something all right," Braggle wheezed, "but why'd you give 'It' such a boring name. That's it? It's just 'It?'"

"Not 'It'," Tabuchi laughed. "He is Itara, or *Ita*. In my language the word means 'pain'."

"Nice," Braggle mumbled. "So what do we do with it?"

"Mr Braggle," Tabuchi said with a smile as they entered the main turnstiles of Thrill Acres, "I need you to clear your theme park of all personnel—as a safety precaution."

"We got everybody out days ago," Braggle replied. "Doing so cut payroll, and eliminated the chance of lawsuits if our loose monster stepped on or tried to eat an employee."

"If Grendel is a robot," Tabuchi queried, "how could it eat anyone?"

"I didn't mean it would actually...." Braggle began in an aggravated manner. "Look, just do your job!"

"You're certain there's no control centre for Grendel's operation?" Tabuchi asked again. "It'd be easier if my Exterminator could storm that building and shut down the mecha, rather than engaging in direct conflict."

"All power to the main central computer is disabled." Braggle frowned. "For whatever reason, Grendel is still running. We don't want any more damage. The robot has done enough. Just stop it!"

Walking calmly through the Main Entrance Plaza of Thrill Acres, Tabuchi adjusted a knob on his silent High Frequency Transmitter. The monster Itara took a wide step over the entrance turnstiles and followed them, knocking an information booth into pieces as it shuffled past.

"Is your monster going to destroy much?" Braggle muttered.

"Have you ever seen a daikaiju battle?" Tabuchi responded.

"No."

"What will happen, will happen." Tabuchi completed this statement with an almost respectful bow. "Please take me to where Grendel lurks."

And so they entered the heart of the park, the cloned monstrosity lumbering behind them.

Thrill Acres was considered a preeminent American theme park for good reason. It had retained its carnival and midway roots, but had broken free of that cheesiness enough to be beautiful and inspiring in a quaint surreal way. In recreating Ancient Greece, the Amazonian Jungles or Feudal Asia, the talent behind the park was distinctive. It was no sprawling maze filled with a hodge-podge of rides. Everything made sense. As a theme park, Thrill Acres lived. With Tyranny, King of the Roller Coasters, rising above all, it was organic, an art in three dimensions.

Yet something seemed askew in the Medieval section of the park. Braggle and Tabuchi approached a gothic castle that stood forebodingly on a craggy hill, the former Haunted Fortress. It would have been awesome and alluring, except that most of the black stonework had been repainted an obnoxious yellow. Surrounding the altered castle were the remains of three construction cranes, all twisted into shapes reminiscent of the park's pretzels.

"We can walk through the Fortress," Braggle explained, "but your monster must go around it. I want to be careful—the repaint cost 2 million dollars. Imagine if we had to fix a turret."

Tabuchi said nothing, adjusted the dials on his Transmitter, and followed his client through the archway. The Fortress seemed barren now that all its gargoyles had been removed in accord with the park's new image. Meanwhile, the mighty Clone slunk around through the moat.

Passing over a drawbridge, the Medieval Village, Classic Carnival, and Space Port Thrill sprawled before them, all with more rides than could easily be counted. Nothing operated in the eerie quiet. No music played. No smells of candy and hot dogs graced the air. What looked to have been some rather garish buildings had been smashed, handiwork of the monster Grendel. Far across a lake, a giant wooden roller coaster remained half standing. The remnant that had survived was a black colour, while what lay splintered like scattered toothpicks was pink. More construction cranes were half sunk in the lake.

"What happened?" Tabuchi asked, pointing to the coaster. "More of Grendel's destruction?"

"Yes," Braggle sighed. "That's was our only wooden coaster. It was called the Black Death for years, but it needed a makeover. It won't be opening again anytime soon."

"Quiet please," Tabuchi shushed him suddenly. "I see Grendel, and since we don't know how he functions, he might detect us."

By the lake, amid a cluster of smashed trees, rising higher than the nearby tracks of the Tyranny coaster, the Robot sat hunched and still, as though it had been shut down. Grendel seemed unreal with all that green hair standing out from its head, and serrated rows of metallic teeth smiling like two parallel saws glimmering in the sunlight.

"What do we do?" Braggle asked under his breath.

"Itara is programmed with basic behaviours that give a trained, conditioned response," Tabuchi explained. "I'll prompt him to shove the robot into the lake. If Grendel has delicate mechanics, the water should short circuit him, doing little other damage, shouldn't it?"

"I don't know," Braggle whispered, trying to hide behind Tabuchi. "Everything here is designed for the rain. Just do what you have to, and get rid of that piece of junk!"

Tabuchi looked at his client with a cultural misunderstanding that in other places and times could lead to wars. Then, focusing back on his cloned monster, he pushed a Transmitter button.

A deep and unearthly noise rumbled from the chest of the Clone. Snarling like a zoo-full of predators, the energetic beast bounded from behind the Fortress and into the Medieval Village. The ground shook. Still Grendel did not move. Itara tore through some trees, claws forward, and crashed powerfully against the lifeless monster, sending it sprawling into the lake with a splash that sent water gushing tsunami-like to every shore. As the waves settled, the Clone lingered, waiting to discover if more aggression would be needed.

"On target!" Tabuchi cried, walking down into the Village while Braggle followed. "See, Mr Braggle! Itara knows his business. The Robot hasn't moved and should stay down now. It would pay to learn more about your own product, so you can fix problems like this and make upgrades. Inefficiency is as deadly in business as— "

Tabuchi fell silent as a shadow fell over them; Grendel had risen, blocking out the morning sun. Water dripped from the scaly hide that rippled like lumps of carpet over its frame. Moving awkwardly, its joints locked as a result of its mechanical skeleton, the Robot straightened to its full height and waited, ready for action. A strange cry sounded from an implanted electronic speaker in its forehead and its eyes glowed fiercely, visible even in the bright daylight.

Itara seemed naturally curious of its opponent but did not act, having received no orders—Tabuchi was frozen in place, in awe of the Robot.

Then, with the noise of servos and hydraulics activating, Grendel strode through the water, both fists punching upward in a tremendous motion from the hinge of its shoulders. Torque sent the Clone smashing backwards through the track of the red coaster Tyranny and another black steel coaster, roaring out its fury as it stumbled onto a tent-top building in the Classic Carnival section of the park.

"We've never faced an enemy with such power!" cried Tabuchi.

Braggle sighed in dismay. "Is your Clone beaten then?"

"Don't worry. If Itara is not mortally wounded, he will mount a fierce counterattack."

"Watch out for my park!" Braggle shouted suddenly. In springing to its feet the Clone had smashed a carousel and an arcade to splinters. Grendel approached, swinging punches wildly; Itara crouched like a cat and scratched at the Robot's chest. The park monster fell back several yards, though it seemed otherwise unaffected. Taking the initiative, the Clone charged, but Grendel stood unmoving and grabbed its living enemy in a mechanical vice lock. The creatures spun in circles, stepping on buildings that had housed coin tosses and squirt-gun races.

"What's happening?!" Braggle demanded. "Why isn't your monster doing anything?"

"Give him a chance!" Tabuchi snapped. "He's very smart."

Still in a headlock, Itara lifted Grendel by the legs and ran, slamming into a tower called the Frenzied Free Fall or Triple F—twice as tall as either monster. A groan sounded from its base, as though the foundations of the earth had cracked. The tower swayed, then fell, smashing through more of the omnipresent Tyranny coaster. Grendel straightened up, a huge dent where its head had smacked the tower. The Clone worked on catching its breath.

"The Triple F!" Braggle cried. "One of our top thrill rides! I wasn't planning on closing that. This is bad."

The Robot picked up the 200-foot tower in its arms and wielded it like some gigantic lance.

"Spectacular!" Tabuchi's admiration of his creature's robotic rival was obvious.

The Clone ducked under the Triple F tower as Grendel swung it with deadly force. Before the Robot could counter-swing, the living beast grabbed the other end, and growling, wrenched the weapon from its enemy. Itara swung it hard in return, and Grendel was unable to dodge. The blow sent the Robot skidding through a banquet hall, to land at the base of a Gondola Skycab station.

Itara dropped the heavy tower and with deep breaths smashed through more rides to where his enemy lay motionless.

"Careful, Itara!" Tabuchi warned aloud, as though his creation could hear and understand. "The Robot has deceived you once already. But you can finish him with your animal cunning!"

The expression on Itara's half-ape half-feline face was one of fierce concentration, as though puzzling how to kill the synthetic creature not even alive. In contrast, Grendel reacted mindlessly; he leapt, grabbed and threw the Clone into some trees. Then with still faster speed, the Robot pulled the metal cable that held the Skycabs out from its anchoring tower and power station. Electrical sparks flew—everywhere the Skycabs ran in the park they smashed to the concrete and shattered.

Grendel wrapped the cable around the scaly throat of the Clone, pulling it tight in a death choke. The living monster thrashed violently, strongly, yet Grendel held firm.

"This monster battles with great skill," Tabuchi said with solemnity. "There is genius behind it! Itara may not escape."

"If your monster dies," Braggle insisted firmly, "the Company's not paying a cent!"

Gurgles came from the Clone as it struggled, yet it could not reach its enemy nor break free from the steel cable. With what was almost a smile, Grendel pulled back harder. Itara's eyes bulged and its clawed feet kicked in death throes. By chance, one foot smashed into the transformer powering the Skycabs. There was a terrific *pop!* and, covered by plumes of sparks, both monsters quivered and shook, thousands of volts coursing through the foot of the Clone and into both of the combatants. Itara bled at the ears, and one of Grendel's red eyeballs shattered with a flash. Both monsters fell free of the transformer and landed lifeless on the ground.

Tabuchi ran onto the battlefield. Careless of danger, he examined his Clone anxiously, avoiding the sparks that still flew out of the transformer.

As Braggle caught up with him, Tabuchi turned with relief. "It's okay. Itara is breathing without labour, so I believe he'll survive. No wounds seem mortal. His body can absorb that shock. And look at your Robot! He's defeated this time!"

"I guess I was going to close this Gondola ride anyway," Braggle sighed. "It's not a premiere attraction and costs a fortune to operate. But all this damage! The CEO is going to kill me. I don't think—"

Braggle stopped as Tabuchi collapsed suddenly. "What—?" he began, before a terrible pain in the back of his head chopped off the words, and all went black.

Braggle's head hurt and his face was wet. Words rang in his ears as he struggled back into consciousness.

"You idiot! Wake up! I want to talk to you!"

He sat upright but could not move. His hands were free, yet something heavy gripped his shoulders and pulled tight across his chest.

"Wake up!" the voice continued. It sounded familiar. He heard a squirting sound and his face felt wetter. He squinted. Water ran down his cheeks. A Thrill Acres Misting Fan was spraying his face...

"Vice President Braggle, are you awake?" asked a second voice, this one Tabushi's. The Japanese Case Handler sat clamped alongside him under the shoulder restraints of a roller coaster.

"Yes," Braggle grumbled. The jet-black coaster car sat docked high in a scaffold launch station. Braggle failed to recognise the coaster, for he knew little more about his theme park than what he'd seen on the map in his office.

"Do you know this man?" Tabuchi asked.

Braggle gazed towards the ride's empty queue. A bright-eyed man stood there alone, the misting fan in his hand, leaning against the railing. Though Braggle typically noticed people about as well as he did his theme park, he did recognise this man.

What Tabuchi saw was a man whose forty-something graying hair flowed unkempt in the light breeze, yet whose youthful countenance smiled as though his face were accustomed to it. His eyes, so bright and alive, analysed everything with excitement. This man was always thinking. He could never stop thinking, stop dreaming, stop imagining. To stop was not in his nature, clearly.

"I know you," Braggle announced. "Don't I?"

"I'd hope so." The man's voice was powerful, full of character and experience, like some master storyteller, ready to weave a tale and mesmerise any audience.

"You're Skyler Blue, aren't you?" Braggle said, his head still aching.

"Yes," the man replied with a laugh. "I'm Skyler Blue, Senior Engineer and Creative Content Designer for Thrill Acres."

"Ex-Senior Engineer," Braggle corrected.

"By your records, perhaps," Skyler Blue replied, with the hint of a frown transforming his smile, "but that doesn't make me any less than I am, any more than it makes you any more than you are, Mr Braggle."

"What are you talking about?" Braggle asked. "What hit me? My head hurts. Get me out of this thing!"

"I'm pleased to meet you, sir," Skyler said, addressing Tabuchi and ignoring Braggle. "I've been to your country and you have some spectacular theme parks. And you *do* know how to run them. Tell me, is that fantastic monster yours?"

"The Itara?" Tabuchi answered, pleased by his captor's praise. "Yes, I envisioned it, planned it, designed, grew, and trained it."

"My compliments," the Senior Designer said with genuine emotion. "It's wonderful. It should be in a zoo. I'm sorry for attacking it, but you did strike first. That creature is a genetically synthesised creation, isn't it? I noticed both cat and crocodile in it."

"Tiger, Alligator, and Gorilla. You must be the creator of the Grendel mecha. A brilliant mixture of the new and the old. I'm impressed."

"Thank you," Skyler replied. "Grendel's my design. I've designed many things here."

"Enough crap!" Braggle demanded. "I don't care who made what. Mr Blue, let us loose!"

"Sorry, Mr Braggle. I'm not going to do that."

Braggle struggled against his restraints. "Release me now, Blue, or I'll fire..." Here Braggle paused awkwardly.

"You'll fire me?" Skyler said with a grin. "It's a little late for that."

"Blue," Braggle argued, trying to remain calm, "as an ex-employee, you shouldn't have access to the park. Besides, we've had to evacuate. There's no one here but us and these monsters."

"Don't you understand?" Tabuchi interrupted. "This man created Grendel, and so he also controls it."

"That's right." Skyler held up a device with knobs, two large levers, and a small screen. "This is my remote brain for Grendel. I designed it with complete override function, so even if the main control at computer central were functional, I'd still have prime direction. It hardly matters; nobody working in Creative Content Division these days would know enough to do anything about controlling Grendel anyway."

"Why are you doing this, Blue?" Braggle growled snidely. "Sour grapes about losing your job? Still angry over our creative differences?"

"Creative differences?" Skyler laughed. "You never had anything creative to be different about! Your ideas of creating are to save a buck at all costs or unleash another layer of bureaucracy. Tell me, just sitting there, what ride is this?"

"One of our roller coasters," Braggle grumbled.

"*Our* roller coasters, is it?" Skyler echoed. "Which one?"

"How would I know?" Braggle frowned. "There's so many in the park, and one's as good as another."

"Can't you figure it out?" Skyler cried with a hint of madness evident in his strained temples. "Look! Notice the safety stops in the shape of gallows! Here, replicas of medieval weaponry all painfully researched for accuracy. See the hooded dummy up in the monitoring station! What's that look like to you?" And here Skyler Blue leaned down in Braggle's face. "Can't you figure out, even if you never rode this thing? This is the Executioner!"

"The Executioner, yeah, that's right," Braggle mumbled.

"The Executioner!" Skyler yelled. "The first quadruple loop coaster in this part of the country! A coaster I designed to be 'the most sadistic coaster ever' in that it makes the rider believe his life is in constant jeopardy. A coaster consistently ranked in the top ten American coasters for six years running, last year at number three! A coaster which last year celebrated its 10th anniversary!"

"Okay!" Braggle shouted. "So it's the Executioner, and I've never ridden it! Can you blame me if I don't like roller coasters? What about it?"

"You didn't know *what* coaster it was, and you're Vice President of the park!" Skyler cried, grimacing. "You sit in your office sipping coffee and earning six figures, and you make life and death decisions for this grand park, but you're clueless. You don't care about any of it, yet you have the power to take the hearts of everyone who loves this place and trample them in the dirt. People want to bring their grandchildren here someday, and take them through the rides they enjoyed as kids, like the Goblin Gardens, the world's greatest funhouse maze. But you turned it into a greenhouse. You take our beautiful Haunted Fortress and paint it tacky yellow! You take the Black Death and paint it pink! What sense does that make, thematically or visually? Were you going to call it the Pink Death? Are you insane?"

"We were thinking Pink Thunder," Braggle shrugged. "It's more gender inclusive."

"It's still awful!" Skyler shouted. "Redoing crappy rides, like replacing a Scrambler with a themed log flume—that's improvement. But you destroy things. You say a classic ride is too expensive to operate, so you gut it and make it a character-greeting location. You turn masterpieces into garbage, like a tawdry tourist painting a moustache on the Mona Lisa. You may not respect the artistry of a theme park, but much of the world does. Talented people designed the 'breathtaking wonders' of Thrill Acres, but you've got those 'wonders' falling right and left. You took Ghouls of Hades—the greatest dark ride of all time…did you ever see the animalistic architectural design in there?—you took Ghouls of Hades, and changed it into the Family Fun Bears' Frolic! How could you? God save us all!"

Skyler Blue seemed at breaking point, his voice rising higher into a raspy squeak. His eyes bulged, while his face turned bright red. Tabuchi sat open-mouthed, dumbfounded by the man's enthusiastic ravings. But Braggle merely continued debating as though he were in a board meeting.

"All done to better the park's image and lighten things. Mr

Blue, you can't have a theme-park attraction these days called Ghouls of Hades."

Skyler Blue stomped over to the Executioner's lost-and-found bin and pulled out a ragged plush toy—an infamous Family Fun Bear—and looked it over with the disgust someone else might offer to a diseased cockroach.

"You say that," Skyler growled, "because you think that up in your executive offices. You don't know what real people want. Ghouls of Hades was fine for twenty years, and none complained except Thrill Acre's corporate idiots. In fact, none complained until you changed it. And boy, did they complain then, but you guys don't care.

"Look," he continued, holding up the Family Fun Bear, "you took a fabulous, fantastic ride that speaks to our subconscious, deals with our inner fears and shortcomings, a ride so spectacular in its timeless story and classical design elements ... it even had a killer soundtrack; well, you took it, and you exchange it for what? This, this ..." Skyler Blue stuttered as he shook the stuffed bear with passion, "... you traded it for this crap! This absolute garbage!"

Furiously, Skyler tore the head from the Family Fun Bear. Stuffing flew everywhere.

"Mr Blue," Braggle explained as the white fluff settled, "the Family Fun Bears represent an important merchandising sponsorship for the park, and are the hottest thing for the under-five set these days. They may fade away tomorrow, but then we can cheaply change out the ride for whatever's next. The new Bear ride might represent a slight decrease in our base attendance and perhaps temporarily tarnish our perceived popularity according to our main fan base—who will still come anyway—but it's great for profits. Those merchandising tie-ins are gold. Everybody wants a theme park tie-in these days. It's trendy."

"It's tasteless," Skyler barked.

"Your opinions," Braggle continued, "cost you and your colleagues your jobs. If you'd taken pay cuts and minimised budgets, and made plans for financially responsible attraction makeovers, then you'd still work here, and you'd still have a voice."

"I have a voice now!" Skyler said. "I've stopped paint jobs and removed lesser abominations. I've saved the Family Fun Bears' Frolic, because I haven't the heart to destroy the former Ghouls of Hades building, but I think I'll smash that awful ride today. It'll make so many fans happy when they learn that the Family Fun Bears are gone. And that's what Thrill Acres is about, making people happy."

"There's nothing you can do to change my mind, Blue," Braggle barked. "Let us go!"

"Oh no!" Skyler insisted. "There's much I can do. You may have tried to shut off the park's power, but I got this coaster running ... my coaster, my Executioner."

Skyler hit a switch and the launch platform rumbled. Both captives heard the clanking of an incline chain track in the distance.

"Are you going to ride us on this until we puke?" Braggle asked. "Is that your idea of torture?"

"Mr Braggle..." Skyler knelt patiently beside the Vice President. "Those fighting monsters smashed the end of the Executioner's track. I'm saddened because I love this roller coaster, but that circumstance gives the Executioner the opportunity to live up to its name. I've disabled the automatic safety systems. This thing is going to run today, no matter what happens."

Braggle fell strangely silent and licked his dry lips. He had suddenly found himself with enough imagination to anticipate what this meant.

"I designed the Executioner," Skyler recollected, "to look like it could kill you, but it has a perfect safety record. No one's been injured on it. Today two people will spoil that record, and be, let's say, 'executed'."

Skyler turned to Tabuchi. "To you, sir, I must say this: I'm sorry, but guilt by association, you know. Have a pleasant ride."

Skyler Blue hit the launch switch, and the coaster began to roll.

"Here!" he added, tossing a leg of the Family Fun Bear into Braggle's lap, "Take that with you as a mascot!"

The Executioner headed towards the first incline to make its final run, slinking through a dungeon replica filled with torture devices. With a grunt, Tabuchi pulled on his shoulder and slid half his body out of the restraint.

"You're supposed to remain seated on these things," Braggle said, as the coaster locked into position to begin its steep ascent, and spears shot in and out of the stonework over their heads.

"I have an idea!" Tabuchi twisted to reach into his hip pocket. "Mr Braggle, how long is this ride?

Braggle had closed his eyes, for at the apex of the incline stood a replica of a Guillotine. With each clank and lurch of the coaster, the blade shook and fell an inch, all timed to look dangerous, while being completely safe. A bloody sign read, 'Keep your head down'.

"I see the end!" Tabuchi cried. "I must hold tightly!" As the coaster peaked some hundred feet in the air, he saw a loop, a corkscrew, another loop, and then an extent of smashed track. Tabuchi's back hung outside the coaster, while he faced sideways towards Braggle.

"We're gonna die!" Braggle screamed, gripping the restraints, as the coaster plunged past an imitation wrecked coaster full of dummy skeleton riders, through a false door in the stonework, and into a cave.

"Banzai!" Tabuchi shouted as the coaster zoomed under swinging axes, swords and other threats of decapitation; he appeared to enjoy the ride in spite of the circumstances. "Listen, my friend! Itara may be conscious. We are not defeated. Blue took my controller, but like him, I keep an emergency overrider spare."

Braggle only shrieked as the coaster banked into its first loop. Tabuchi grasped his restraint with one arm, but the G-forces of the loop kept him planted in his seat. Once the coaster settled into a snaking run through a forest of hangman's nooses, Tabuchi spoke again.

"I can set my controller to give Itara a mixed signal, both Call and Retrieve. If he's awake, he might save us before we reach the end."

Tabuchi struggled with one hand in his pocket as the coaster spun into a corkscrew around a wicked-looking Medieval machine—a giant drill of wood and rusted iron, filled with rotating spikes. The coaster appeared to collide with the machine, but in reality missed it safely—yet Tabuchi flew out of his seat in shock. He held onto the shoulder restraint with all his wiry strength as they banked through the corkscrew. Tabuchi's leg barely missed the spikes; when the ride steadied, he scrambled to pull it back inside the coaster.

"Only one loop left!" he gasped. "I must call Itara now!"

He pulled a smaller version of his Transmitter from his pocket, and adjusted a few buttons with his nimble fingers. Needing to give this awkward action such focused attention, he failed to notice the track bank sharply to the right. As he smashed against his seat, he shouted something in Japanese and lost hold of his Transmitter. With the dumb luck that had so far led him successfully through life, Braggle reached out in blind terror and caught the device in a desperately clenched fist.

"Hold on to that!" Tabuchi cried. "It's activated, but I can't get it off you now."

Braggle said nothing, his unblinking eyes dry from the wind. The coaster slowed momentarily as it passed through a mill between two gigantic buzzsaws, while a third buzzsaw from the roof spun at their heads. An accelerator in the track sent the coaster flying, and as Braggle screamed, the buzzsaw rose out of their way and they charged into the last loop. Just beyond lay the destroyed track.

"Where's Itara!" Tabuchi cried, pressed upside down against his seat. "Only seconds left!"

There was a terrific bump as they cleared the twisted metal. Flying off the track was a thrill new to the ride, the last thrill they would ever have.

Both men screamed.

Tabuchi saw the Transmitter still in Braggle's hand, the trees as a green blur, and then the motion of something brown and massive.

The coaster lurched to an halt with the sound of crunching metal. Coaster cars from behind them flew over their heads. Braggle snapped forward, saved by the shoulder restraint. Tabuchi held on, spared by his own strength, his light weight, and some give in the coaster car.

Everything went still.

They had not fallen to the pavement, but hung suspended seventy feet in the air. Braggle whimpered, for on his side of the car the mutated face of Itara glared at them with gigantic cat eyes; the monster had received the transmission after all and had caught them in its claw. Braggle grasped the device, nearly crushing it, while the creature's hot breath stirred his hair. The coaster car rocked back and forth in Itara's grasp.

"Don't move!" Tabuchi said quietly.

"He's going to eat us!" Braggle cried.

"Don't touch any of the dials on the Transmitter!" Tabuchi warned. "He's been given a Call and Retrieve signal, but it could register an Attack Call. Itara is aggressive!"

Tabuchi crawled over to Braggle, as the Clone gave a gruff growl, watching. Caked blood clung about Itara's ears and head. Tabuchi wrenched the Transmitter from Braggle's frozen fingers.

When Tabuchi adjusted a dial, Itara lowered the scratched and dented coaster onto the concrete amid the other smashed cars, then backed away. Tabuchi slipped out.

"Help me!" Braggle panted.

Tabuchi found the safety restraint release lever near the twisted wheels. He pulled hard and with a clank the shoulder restraints rose. Braggle slumped over and Tabuchi pulled him free.

"I'm ready to leave," Braggle gasped, barely able to stand.

"Not yet!" Tabuchi scanned the wreckage. "We must find your employee. He tried to kill us, and I will not walk away without honour. The Grendel mecha may be operational—that man cannot escape with it. We have our weapon and must keep him from his. Come with me!"

Braggle could barely walk, but followed without argument. Itara's heavy footsteps thumped along behind them as Tabuchi marched back towards the smashed Skycab station looking for Grendel's body. While passing the Space Port Thrill section of the park, an object sailed through the air and landed at their feet.

"You might like to keep that," came Skyler Blue's voice from above them. He stood on a large neon sign that read 'Mars Bazaar'. Tabuchi's original Transmitter lay broken on the concrete.

"It's impressive," Skyler shouted, "that your creature could withstand the voltage thrown at him. He's strongly built, but I bet he's hurting. Grendel's similar injuries required work to get him going, but a Robot doesn't *feel* its busted fuses."

The former Senior Engineer raised his Grendel controller. Looming over the building stood the Robot, with one eye missing and wires hanging from its neck. It roared an electronic challenge with enough feeling to seem alive. Skyler jammed the two levers of his controller in opposite directions, and Grendel's arms flailed outward in a fierce gesture.

Tabuchi kicked the broken Transmitter away and held up his

spare controller. "We accept your challenge!" he proclaimed.

The hissing Clone charged, remembering its enemy. Claws and teeth tore into the polymer scales of the Robot as it stumbled backwards, making no defense but neither falling. Snarling and shredding, Itara pulled a patch of skin from the Robot, revealing a flat metallic surface underneath.

Above the Mars Bazaar, Skyler's fingers danced over his controller. As the Clone chewed at the false flesh, Grendel grabbed Itara by the head and neck, and snapped it into a building labeled "Star Bumps."

Tabuchi raced ahead, trying to keep line of sight with his monster. He turned a corner and just dodged a bumper car that skidded across the concrete and into the glass window of a restaurant. Itara was throwing Star Bumps vehicles at Grendel, pointlessly but impressively, as each hit the Robot in the face.

Broken cars piled at Grendel's feet, and before long Itara succeeded in exhausting itself.

"Don't leave me alone!" Braggle cried as he caught up with Tabuchi.

"Since there's nothing you can tell me about the Grendel mecha, Mr Braggle," Tabuchi said, "I'll aim for the head. There's always significance in a head."

A giant rocket rose twenty feet above the tallest structure in Space Port Thrill. Tabuchi spun a dial on his Transmitter; Itara leapt onto the building, wrenched the rocket from the construct that held it, and, as Grendel charged, drove the rocket in a downward stabbing motion. The durable steel split Grendel's head and lodged in it like a stuck arrow.

Grendel's eyes, hair, teeth, and speaker system shattered and fell away, until only some metallic shielding, with the rocket embedded in it, remained. Without pause, the Robot thrust its head forward and jammed the rear end of the rocket into its enemy's face. Itara's fangs cracked on one side and the Clone fell writhing to the ground, bleeding at the mouth.

The Robot threw punch after punch as Itara tried desperately to crawl out of reach. With the rocket still in its face and mouth speaker smashed, Grendel emitted no noise other than that of the motors moving in its body. The radio still strapped to Tabuchi's belt buzzed and he answered with a greeting in Japanese.

"My assistants," Tabuchi said moments later, "have uncovered a bootleg schematic for Grendel on the internet. The hard drive for his computer function is housed in the torso chassis. Itara must aim for his chest."

Grendel kicked the bloody Itara into another part of Tyranny, King of the Roller Coasters. A loop of red steel crashed down on the Clone, breaking into three pieces.

"If I can prompt him to use a tool," Tabuchi said while spinning dials on his Transmitter, "and remain on that command, there's a chance of destroying the Robot's operating system."

The Clone grabbed a piece of the coaster track, and drove the sharp edge of twisted steel through Grendel's chest. The metal pierced its hard plating and tore through the skin, emerging from its back and impaling the Robot.

Grendel, still active, swung a fist, but the Clone dodged the blow. The Robot found the extra weight of rocket and coaster track awkward to its balance and struggled to straighten itself. Itara drove another piece of the Tyranny coaster through the Robot's side.

Skyler Blue had designed Grendel with a CPU no bigger than a desktop computer. Even after a third piece of Tyranny was shoved into its mechanical guts, the Robot fought on, taking no time to remove the pieces. It struck the Clone with both arms, but Itara pulled off a fourth coaster piece and shoved it into Grendel with a frenzy. The Robot kept coming.

"There's no stopping it!" Braggle cried.

"I will!" Tabuchi insisted. "There's not much chest that we haven't penetrated."

The Robot, looking like a red porcupine with a space rocket head, grabbed the frisky Clone by its neck in a vice grip. As they crashed into the Alien Water Warp flume ride, the Robot shoved Itara's head into the main water reservoir behind the saucer vehicle loading station. As though exhaustion and its wounds had finally become too much for it, Itara went utterly inert.

"Your monster's losing!" Braggle cried.

Tabuchi scowled grimly. "Not yet."

The Clone no longer moved. With pieces of red steel protruding from its body, Grendel stood, turned and marched off through several buildings. Braggle and Tabuchi then heard the gleeful voice of Skyler Blue.

"Sorry to kill your monster, but a winner is a winner. That was excellent though! We should build an arena in the park, and have monsters fight in it. Hey, Mr Braggle, I feel so good, I'm going to have Grendel go smash your Family Fun Bears, right now! Just for fun!"

While Skyler raced from the roof to watch the destruction, Tabuchi slowly adjusted a dial on his Transmitter.

Itara stirred. The Clone, bloody and wet, blinked its angry eyes.

"A fake-out?" said Braggle.

"Itara is part alligator," Tabuchi explained, "and can hold his breath longer than was needed."

With Skyler's attention directed towards Grendel and the Family Fun Bears, Tabuchi programmed his Clone to tear up another shaft of red roller coaster. Then Itara charged after Grendel like the tiger it partly was, and speared the Robot through its torso yet again.

This time Grendel stood erect, spasming as his motors misfired. Then his neck, arms and legs began randomly contracting. With leg rotors out of control, the flailing monster tore through rides and shops. After a few minutes, however, it slowed, sparks flew from every joint, and with a lurch and a whine of failing engines, Grendel fell forward and collapsed before an exceptionally ugly building. A poorly painted, giant 2-D Family Fun Bear smiled down over the Robot's wreckage.

Tabuchi and Braggle ran to the scene of destruction and found Skyler hunched over, mumbling to himself, "Fun Bears! I hate those stinkin' Fun Bears."

At dusk Vice President Braggle stood chewing his thumbnail. Security, medics and a custodial crew were in the park. The once-Senior Engineer and Creative Content Designer Skyler Blue had been strapped to a gurney for his own safety; Thrill Acres First Aid did not have a straight jacket available.

"Please!" Skyler cried to the medic as they slid him into the ambulance, "Don't take me to those Family Fun Bears! Anything but them! I don't want to see the Family Fun Bears ever again!"

As Skyler's cries faded into the distance, Braggle was startled by Case Handler Tabuchi, who had been conferring with his associates and had now come up behind him.

"Mr Braggle," Tabuchi said, "I know you're busy with cleaning and repair, but on behalf of Sekiyama Group, it has been my pleasure to be of service."

"Thank you, I guess," Braggle answered, still stunned by the day's events.

"And here," Tabuchi added, "is your bill. You will find it itemised."

Braggle grew as pale as he had been on the roller coaster. After studying the bill, which was in US dollars and not Japanese yen as he had first hoped, he stumbled after Tabuchi in a daze.

"Excuse me, but is this really the bill?"

"Yes," Tabuchi replied firmly.

Braggle swallowed. "Mr Tabuchi, what forms of payment do you take?"

"The usual," Tabuchi said. "Whatever you prefer as long as the amount is deposited in our account."

Braggle nodded grimly, imagining his next board meeting. He looked at the smashed trees, the twisted pieces of coasters and the smoke rising from rubble that once represented a horde of thrills.

"Tell me," he finally managed, "would you accept a 900-million-dollar theme park?"

FOSSILS

DG VALDRON

A stopped outside my penthouse the other morning as I lay in bed. His weathered face, profiled through the picture window, startled me. He seemed close enough to touch.

I sat up slowly, many thoughts running through my mind, and reached for the camera I had fortuitously left by my nightstand.

Was the picture window one-way glass? I didn't know, but it didn't seem likely. Could *A* see through it? Could *A*'s eye make out a human shape through it? Perhaps *A*, like a dog or some other predator, focused best on movement?

With *A* and the others like him, there are only questions and an occasional lethal answer.

Still, I reached for the camera. *A* stood there immobile like a statue. With shaking hands I fitted the zoom lens, adjusted the focus and snapped off image after image, saving them to the chip. The click of the shutter and whine of the electrics were unbearably loud to me. At one point, I thought I saw *A*'s ear twitch—but it was merely his weight shifting.

I ran out of image slots and so just sat in bed, waiting for that baleful profile to turn towards me. But it didn't.

After five minutes, *A* took another step and passed from view.

I lay back, uttering a prayer to gods I no longer believed in.

I do not believe in gods, but if there are such entities, they do not require my belief to exist.

A exists; he does not require our belief.

When I was a little boy in school, they taught us about dinosaurs and fossils.

Fossils are made when, ever so slowly, little bits of mineral take the place of organic material like bone or wood. Eventually, the whole thing is nothing but mineral, stone taking the place of what had once been alive.

Sometimes there is no living matter to replace, just an impression left behind like a footprint and filled in by time. All dinosaurs, we were told, are known only by fossils.

I remember the little girl in the desk in front of mine putting up her hand and asking "What about *A* ?"

While waiting for the image slots to save into the art drive, I loaded the camera with a new chip and finished inspecting my lenses.

After a quick breakfast of canned shrimp, I headed down the stairs to the main floor. I contemplated taking the elevator, but A was in the neighbourhood, and the noise of machinery might attract his attention.

Probably not, but you never know.

The Kaiju are reported to be extremely sensitive, though to what, no one is quite sure. Magnetic fields, electrical current, sound waves, light and darkness: who could know for certain?

A was out of sight by the time I'd reached the main floor and exited into the street. I walked up to one of his footprints.

It was fourteen metres long by seven wide, and approximately two metres deep in the centre. The edges were barely crumbling, the detail superb.

Briefly I considered taking a picture of it. But I already had more than enough pictures of A's footprints and there was no additional context that would lend the image interest or perspective.

I looked down the street. A had been walking west. Three strides from the penthouse had taken A to the end of the street, where he turned left. I felt another seismic tremor as A, beyond my line of sight, took his next step.

But I'd had enough of A for the time being; I began walking east.

It was a fine new day in deserted Tokyo.

I spent the rest of that day breaking into apartments. In one, I watched a television documentary on a battery-powered set. It was about the refugee camps. I found myself wondering if any of the people I saw in the documentary were the ones who had lived in this apartment.

Afterwards I went shopping in the Kyoru family grocery. The produce was off, but the dry goods and canned fruit were abundant. From there, I took my selections to the Konishawa-Saru restaurant. It was a little dusty and the kitchen was disordered, but I managed well enough.

The Konishawa had been a four-star restaurant, but I wouldn't give it better than three stars tonight. The regular chef must be off, I decided.

Man is an arrogant beast, I sometimes think. We are like ants building our nests by the seashore, believing we have mastered eternity. Then the next wave comes and takes it all away.

We forget how small we are next to the world. Foolishly, we imagine that the fact of our existence is proof of our divinity.

We thought we were the masters of the Earth.

In 1952 we discovered that we were wrong.

In 1952 A came, the first of the Kaiju.

The next day, I stumbled across a group of people in the boulevard of Cherry Blossoms. I was startled; sometimes I would go for days without seeing anyone.

They were all gathered around an object near the centre of the boulevard.

Down the centre, of course, *A*'s tail had dragged, crushing groves of trees to matchsticks.

Diffidently, I walked up to them. I find I am unused to company, these days.

One of them looked up and called to me. I knew him: Ryushi, the physicist.

"Kenjiro," Ryushi called, "come and take a photograph of what we have found!"

The object was leaf-shaped, two metres long, one and a half across, smooth and glossy black. It was convex, with a sharply curving hook at one end. I took four pictures from different angles. One shot had Ryushi in it to show scale.

One of the others, Manabe, had found a length of pipe and began levering the object over. While he did this, I punched in a subtext to accompany the images I had taken.

"Is it hot?" Genma asked. Genma was one of our resident mad poets.

"Only mildly radioactive," Akira said. "Equivalent to a few months normal exposure. Also, slightly above ambient temperature."

I lifted an eyebrow, but did not look up. He must have touched it, to know the warmth. Reckless. But then, we are all reckless to be here at all.

That was enough for me. I joined Manabe at his labours, grunting as we flipped it over. The concave side was gray with layers of ridges, as if it had partially melted. I ran my hand over its surface.

"It's a scale," said the woman, unnecessarily. I looked up at her.

"It's a piece of—"

She almost said the name, but Manabe hushed her. We do not speak the name, ever. Call us superstitious. Would you call a God by a simple name? The Kaiju are too vast for names.

A is *A*. Nothing more need be said.

"It's a piece of *A*," Manabe finished for her.

Her name was Sumiko. I discovered this as we sat on a bench and watched the army helicopter cart away the scale.

She was new to deserted Tokyo, just arrived. She was a philosopher and she has been diagnosed with cancer.

A philosopher here to study *A*? I should be shocked, but I find nothing surprises me any more. Perhaps more than scientists, it is philosophers who are needed to grapple with the existence of *A* and his kind.

Politely, I told her the name of my mortality. I told her of yesterday's encounter with *A* and invited her to my penthouse to look at my stills.

Graciously, she accepted my invitations.

In the distance, we heard *A*'s lonely roar.

*

There are probably less than ten thousand people living in deserted Tokyo. Counting everyone. Counting mad poets, artists, photographers, journalists, eccentrics and scientists of every stripe, soldiers, police, thieves, looters, opportunists as well as simple fools and madmen. Although perhaps we are all fools and madmen to be here.

And of course, there is *A*.

A is in Tokyo. But does *A* live? Perhaps that depends on what you define as life. I read a biology text once which set out seven basic criteria to determine whether something is truly alive.

I am not sure that *A* fulfills all the requirements.

But in morose moments, I am not sure that I do, either.

The test of life is whether it can reproduce itself.

"This is a sumptuous home," Sumiko says, as I prepare supper in the penthouse. We'd taken the elevator up. *A* is far from us. "You must be a very wealthy man."

I cough, discretely wiping droplets of blood from my lips with a handkerchief. I let the stained cloth drop into a waste basket.

"The comforts of a city are at our fingertips," I tell her. "The least we can do is enjoy it."

She seems mildly shocked by my veiled admission of breaking and entering.

In the movies, looters are shot on sight. In deserted Tokyo, there is nothing petty thievery and vandalism can accomplish that approaches *A*'s awful potential.

Out in the refugee camps, Tokyo—the real Tokyo of people—continues as best it can. Men in cloth tents buy and sell fortunes and children play in the grass outside.

Perhaps I should suggest this to Genma. He could make a poem from it.

"Would you sleep in the Emperor's bed?" she asks.

It seems the authorities have allocated to her a modest apartment, and like a good Japanese, she has not thought to question it.

Why? In an empty city, I could sleep in a different penthouse every night.

"Only if you were to join me," I tell her.

She blushes and drops her eyes.

I am touched.

At dinner, of course, I am a perfect gentleman. Our conversation is animated and polite. Although he is always in our minds, we never mention *A*.

I chose this penthouse because of the magnificent view of the harbour. You can see all the way from the docks and shipyards in the south, to the houseboats, now largely absent, and waterfront palaces ringing the north.

On the east side of the penthouse we watch *A* in the harbour far away. He stands in the water, like some savagely thrown outcrop of rough volcanic rock. A storm caught in a moment of time, rendered in stone. Not a bad description of A.

He has not moved in two hours, save for the long ridged dorsal fin on his back. It rises and falls slowly, glowing. It always glows, although the effect is best observed at night. In stormy weather, St Elmo's fire dances along its tips.

Once he did not move for four days. I recorded it with time lapse photography and a battery of four cameras on tripods, tied into the household power source and downloading directly into a dedicated artdrive.

Later, I watched the accelerated record, clouds flicking past, day turning to night in minutes. A stood there like a god, impervious to time.

Perhaps A is a god. I will have to remind myself to ask Sumiko for her views on this.

The light is poor for photography tonight, and in any event, I have many, many, many images of A at the harbour. I do not use my camera. Normally, at this hour, I retire to the bedroom and tend to my lenses.

But tonight, I have a guest.

Sumiko does not tire of watching A. I am happy to pass the time in idle conversation.

"Each of the Kaiju are different," I say. "A is obviously derived from a dinosaur, but which one?"

Not all dinosaurs, it seems, are known from fossils. Or perhaps there are simply different sorts of fossils.

"A tyrannosaur?" Sumiko replies, startling me for a second.

"A common fallacy," I point out. "Actually, the Korean Kaiju is thought to be a tyrannosaurid, but most learned opinion places A's origins in the Jurassic rather the Cretaceous period."

"She's so huge," Sumiko whispers. "She seems to glow."

I notice that she refers to A as female. It is a matter of preference, I suppose. Irrelevant in the end. A transcends all things.

In fact, A does glow, not just the dorsal fin but all of it, but so softly you can only see it on moonless nights. All of the Kaiju, radioactive monsters that they are, glow.

A begins to move suddenly, lumbering among the docks. We hear a distant crashing as A pulls a wharf down.

"What is she doing?" Sumiko asks.

"A's building a nest."

A first surfaced in 1952, striding onto Japan and burning his way through Tokyo. The pleasant wide boulevards of modern Tokyo are the legacies of A's wholesale destruction. And of the Americans.

We battled fiercely, side by side with the Americans, until A returned to the cold waters.

We thought we'd won.

But A returned a few years later. Then, one by one, the rest of the Kaiju appeared up and down the Asian coast, with a few stragglers in North America and Europe.

A has been sighted fourteen times since then. We learned that the Kaiju could not be destroyed. So, when *A*, after fourteen years of relatively peaceful behaviour, surfaced and began to head for Tokyo, the city was evacuated. After all, *A* would leave eventually at his will; he has always done so, so we assume he will do so again.

He has only ever left at his will.

We wait for *A* to leave so we can have our city back.

A's image fills the wall I use for a projection screen. I enhance and magnify, zooming in on the teeth. After moments of blurriness, they come into focus, splitscreen close-ups of upper and lower dentition.

The teeth are a dirty white, built up in jagged layers like concrete inexpertly sculpted. Spikes radiate outwards from the edges. But upper and lower teeth curve in what we recognise as the classic carnivore's dentition. The upper teeth are smaller, with rounded tips and longer spikes radiating from the borders.

I check my readouts; the average size of the seven teeth in the frame is three metres.

"It's so strange," Sumiko says. "I guess I expected them to be smooth."

"Perhaps they were, originally," I say. "But awesome processes have been at work to create a being so vast. My guess is that they are smooth inside the mouth. Those spikes facing outward along the edges are probably melted from the creature's bolt."

"The plasma breath," she says.

"Not plasma," I correct. "Ionised steam, superheated to 10,000 degrees and ejected at something like five thousand pounds per square inch, coursing with energy, discharging in small arc flashes." Other Kaiju discharge fire or bolts or beams or glowing breath, but there is something about *A*'s bursts of destruction, the colour of dark storms concentrated, hurtling from his mouth, godly lightning dancing within. It's breathtaking to see. And sufficient to cut a battleship in half.

In 1968 the US fourth fleet, led by the battleship *New Jersey* and the aircraft carrier *Montana*, encountered *A* off the Kuril islands.

In a pitched battle lasting less than a day, *A* sliced apart the carrier, punched holes in the battleship, and sent three quarters of the fleet to the bottom of the sea, taking no significant damage himself.

A hydrogen bomb was dispatched, but by the time the bomber arrived, *A* was deep beneath the ocean.

I was ten years old when it happened, a little boy from Fukio province, and I remembered cheering to hear of the Americans humbled.

"Tell me about your book," I ask her over lunch. Days have passed and she is a frequent visitor now. For that reason, I seldom go out in the mornings, instead preparing for her midday visit.

I was surprised to learn that she had written a book. I thought

I'd read all the books on the Kaiju. I was surprised that I'd missed hers.

"It was only a thesis," she says modestly, "published with limited circulation."

I wait politely, sipping my tea.

"It dealt with how human societies construct the concept of the Kaiju."

"You think perhaps they are fictional?" I ask, just politely enough not to be mocking.

We both glance at the bowl on the table between us, at the seismic ripples of *A*'s latest footfall. Generally, he takes five-to-ten minutes between one step and the next, although he can move much faster. Much, much faster.

"The phenomena of the Kaiju," she says carefully, "are real enough, as is the phenomena of storm and waves. But we must ask what society makes of these phenomena. Once storms were thought to be living things, embodiments of the will of the gods."

There is an odd precision to these words. I wonder if she is quoting her thesis.

"Now we have the Kaiju. Are they the will of the gods? Science gone wrong? Simple animals? Are they even alive, or is that simply something we need to believe of them? What something is or does, and what we think it is—these may be different things."

"I find," I say softly, "that the fact of *A* overwhelms anything I might say or think of him."

Still, her words echo thoughts of my own.

The first Kaiju I ever saw was *C* on Okinawa Island. This was in 1975 when it had become known as the peaceful Kaiju.

A normally slow-moving quadruped, just a couple of hundred metres long, it had surfaced in 1964. After its now famous confrontations with *A* in 1965 and *M* in 1966 it had settled down to a sedentary peaceful existence, devouring groves in isolated areas.

There was, of course, no evidence that it needed the trees for sustenance. That seemed to have been archaic biological programming at work. The needs of the Kaiju are obscure. They do not seem to breathe or eat as we do. *A* seems as comfortable kilometres underwater as he is in downtown Tokyo on dry land.

In any case, *C* was remarkably placid for a Kaiju, taking no notice of the approach of humans.

As must be inevitable, a clandestine tourist trade arose. I, with a group of wild young friends, went to see the monster.

I remember that we had been drinking on the way and making many a joke. I was flirting, then, with a young woman I would, ultimately, never sleep with.

Everything changed when it came into view.

How to describe the mind-warping immensity of it? We all fell silent. It was as though we had come to some titanic European renaissance cathedral. A living cathedral.

Even then, I knew that while *C* was a respectable-sized Kaiju, it was far from the greatest. It was less than a quarter of the mass of *A*, for example.

For an hour, we watched it. Then, recovering some of my boldness from the journey, I walked right up to it, and leaned nonchalantly against a leg that could have crushed a small house. Being there, touching it, was a bizarre sensation that lasted a moment, until the creature decided to move. Then I ran like a rabbit.

In my files there is a picture of me leaning against it. I have a cocky insouciant grin. It is not a good picture of *C*, however. Since then, I have taken many better pictures of the Kaiju, and particularly of *A*.

The guide was beside himself at my actions, of course. It was radioactive, and forbidden to approach so close.

That moment changed my life; from then on, the Kaiju would be my obsession. The relationship foundered, especially after it was found that I was sterile. I have often wondered if that was the result of the encounter, or if I had always been this way.

Perhaps, this, ultimately, was where my leukemia came from.

I encounter Ryushi on my walk today.

I am not pleased.

I find that, except for Sumiko, I have little use for human company.

I ignore him, but he insists on following me around and chattering like a monkey.

"Have you heard from Geological Survey?" he asks. "They found a post-nuclear site in the Gobi desert?"

I shrugged.

"It dates to the Jurassic. This might have been the birthplace of *A*, possibly some of the others."

Finally, I stop.

"I do not care where they come from," I tell him.

Behind his thick glasses, his little boy face looks shocked.

"It does not matter whether *A* was born in a lake of fire, or found under a cabbage leaf, Ryushi. *A* is here now."

"But—"

"Haven't you ever experienced it, Ryushi?" I ask him. "Or have you merely measured. Such a creature mocks our pretensions. It does not care about your measurements. It does not care what we think. There is no past. There is no future. There is only the now, and in the now, there is only *A*."

These are more words than I have ever spoken to Ryushi. Embarrassed at my anger and at my passion, I walk away quickly. Ryushi stays behind.

Later, I find *A* exquisitely framed between two tall buildings. He is once again motionless and torpid. Breaking into the first building, I climb, taking several shots of *A* from the windows of each floor. I fill chip after chip.

However, as I am climbing down, intending to capture him from the angles of the opposite building, *A* rouses again and walks ponderously away. His tail brushes the building I am in. The structure rocks and the front part collapses away like a veil of sand. It is several hours before I can safely find my way out.

It is night when I finally arrive home. I collapse on the bed, exhausted, not even downloading my chips. They can wait until tomorrow.

"Where does A come from?" Sumiko asks as these latest pictures of *A* are displayed on the wall. This used to be a banquet room, but I find it serves well as a projection area. I line the walls and ceiling with projected images.

Sumiko lies on her belly, naked on the futon. I lie beside her, with my arm thrown possessively across her shoulders. In my hand, the control triggers and manipulates the sequence of images.

We have consummated our relationship. It was messy and wet and not at all safe. But then, in deserted Tokyo, what have we to fear?

Certainly not a virus.

As we made love, as I was inside her, I remember wondering if our cancers touched as well. Perhaps on some level beneath passionate flesh, rogue tissue, cells in riot, made contact, kissed, embraced, exchanged information.

But there will be no issue. Not from us, nor from our cancers.

I consider her question.

"It is hard to say in *A*'s case. Clearly, he is derived from dinosaurs. Some of the Kaiju are easy. *C* for example, is an ankylosaurid. *O* in Taiwan is obviously a tyrannosaurian. But *A*?"

"A stegosaur?" she offers. "Or perhaps a spinosaurus."

"The dorsal fins? The relatively small head on a long neck? The small forelimbs compared to the hind?" I offer. "That's one theory."

"But remember those teeth I showed you," I remind her. "Carnivore teeth. I tend to think he's something of the allosaur line, possibly something not yet discovered."

"And the dorsal plate, those fins, that runs down her back?" she asks.

I shrug. "Obviously part of *A*'s cooling system. Possibly it's a Kaiju growth, or maybe a mutation in the original creature. Perhaps a species of allosaurians developed dorsal plates independently, and we haven't found them yet. It has been known to happen."

There are strange things beneath the Earth. Sometimes they rise up.

The thirty-six known Kaiju constitute a taxonomist nightmare. Most are clearly reptiles, relatively identifiable offshoots of archosaur lines such as dinosaurs. Their origins are placed between eighty- and two-hundred million years ago. A few, however, are mammals of substantially more recent vintage. One is a bird of unknown provenance. One is a vastly mutated coelacanth. Another is a five-tentacled octopus. Four are arguably, impossibly, insects or arthropods. Three cannot be classified.

"When the Kaiju first came..." Sumiko is reading from her book. We are sitting on the east side of the penthouse, watching *A* slowly make its way to the waters. "...We identified them with the atom bomb. Because they were radioactive and wrought great destruction, we believed that they were the spawn of the American's atomic testing. Mutated animals, but more than that, we saw them as symbols of foreign recklessness and destruction.

"Many in the scientific community accepted this thesis, in spite of the obviously ancient traits of several.

"Only the Americans, with their lingering guilt over Hiroshima and Nagasaki, and their commitment to nuclear arsenals rejected this view.

"The Americans had tamed the atom. In doing so, they believed they had controlled the fundamental forces of nature. To the Americans, the Kaiju were simply a form of nature, of animal. Ultimately, they were merely an engineering problem to be assessed and solved."

That, I thought, rolling the words around in my head, was probably before the fourth fleet.

All of the Kaiju share certain traits. Their immense size: the smallest of them dwarf the largest blue whales. Colossal mass: often measured in thousands of tons.

Most are found somewhere along the Pacific ring of fire. The few exceptions appear to derive from other volcanic areas. In some undetermined way, plate tectonics seems to play a part in their cosmic biology.

The Kaiju are invariably highly radioactive and their defenses and offenses often incorporate this radioactivity. Their flesh does not appear to be composed of living matter as we understand it. They are best likened to walking nuclear reactors.

The Kaiju appear to be very territorial, often ranging widely to confront each other.

The Kaiju have frequently attacked human sites and inst-allations. It is uncertain why. Some feel that it is a simple matter of humanity being so widespread that no matter where the Kaiju go—and they go where they will—they encounter us. Others argue that the sheer size of man-made sites and constructions invoke their territorial urges. Still others point to a wide range of emanations—sonic, electrical, magnetic—that might attract their attention.

Some simply say that they are the will of the gods.

Who can be sure?

Once, when I was much less a hermit, only newly arrived in deserted Tokyo, the mad poet Genma confided his theory to me.

"Seismics," he said, drawing the word out over an exhalation of marijuana.

He passed the cigarette to me and I puffed politely, looking at him with curiosity.

"It was the nuclear tests that woke the monsters," he continued. "But not the radiation, not even the electromagnetic pulse, as everyone thinks. It was the seismics."

He grinned. "The seismic waves of the nuclear blasts mimicked those of a cometary bombardment."

He blew smoke rings.

"Tell me, Kenjiro, have you ever heard of cyclic extinction, of the slate wiped clean every seventeen million years. They blame cometary or meteor bombardment, but let's be reasonable; that wouldn't wipe out everything all over the world.

"It's the Kaiju. Every seventeen million years the comets come to wake the Kaiju, who sterilise the world for the next cycle of life.

"We've woken them early; that's why they are confused. Now we wait to see if they'll go back to sleep or wake fully."

"What if they wake fully?" I asked.

Manabe simply sucked a lungful of smoke from his cigarette and let it out, laughing crazily.

"Where does A come from?" Sumiko asks.

It seems to me that she has asked this question before.

We are in bed again. Our cancers have engaged in sweaty intercourse, carrying their human parts along.

I look at the ceiling.

"I will tell you the theory. Have you ever heard of post-nuclear sites?" I ask.

"Atom bomb craters?"

"No. The first one was discovered in Africa, almost thirty years ago. It was a kind of natural atomic pile. Several others have been identified, all dead for millions of years, of course."

She levers herself up on one arm to look at me. I admire the slight sway of her small breasts.

"How can that be?"

I am surprised at how little she knows of material things. The choice of the philosopher, I suppose.

"Radioactive materials are always decaying. In the future, there will be less. That means, in the past, there was more. A million years ago, there were twice as many radioactives in the Earth as there are now. Ten million years before that, twice as many as then, and so on.

"In some places, these radioactive materials were washed down streams. They accumulated and concentrated in ponds and lakes. Most times, this came to nothing.

"But sometimes these concentrations built, fission actually took place. Nuclear reactions began, accelerating the decay of some elements, creating new ones. Fed by streams, moderated by rainfalls and dehydration, the processes were remarkably like those in modern nuclear plants."

"This is very interesting," she tells me, "but what does it have to do with the Kaiju, with *A*?"

"Animals drink in those ponds and streams. They are poisoned by radiation. Many die. Some probably die in the water. Their bodies occasionally floating down to the bottom of the nuclear ponds.

"What a strange environment it must be. There are no bacteria to speed the normal processes of decomposition. Instead, the tissues are saturated in radioactive soup, base elements, free neutrons, heavy metals and incandescent vapours. The long-shattered strands of DNA are joined by ions of lead and graphite, uranium or silicon. Our bodies, our cells are merely chemical factories. Who is to say that an effective chemical factory might not be converted to a nuclear one?

"Slowly the dead beast wakes to a new kind of existence. Its body accreting new elements, new internal fires light. A self-perpetuating, feedback-based system refines and expands through pathways already made, it perfects itself, growing slowly but without limit."

"Kenjiro," she whispers, "do you think it is true?"

I laugh. I have seen *A*.

"It doesn't matter," I tell her.

The next time I see Sumiko, she is pale and shaking. I almost expect her hair to turn white. I take her home. Her teeth chatter, she is not aware of my touch. I bathe her and dry her and sit with her until she speaks.

Her story is not, at first, coherent.

She had been out on the Emperor's way, towards the Ministry of Finance. *A* passed by.

That was all.

A had been moving quickly, barely pausing between steps. Sumiko had stopped and looked up, and there, through the branches of leafless trees, she had seen *A* looming above her. She had looked up at one hundred and fifty metres of scaled not-flesh, a titanic construction of not-bone and not-sinew, as it gracefully passed her.

It took seven steps to the Ministry of Finance, vaporised several structures with an incandescent roar, and proceeded through the burning wreckage without once hesitating.

It takes her two hours to relate this.

I feel a kind of cruel and burning satisfaction.

This is *A*, not some footprint, not a discarded scale by the roadside, or a picture or a figure softened by miles of distance. Not some abstract metaphor explored in dry academia.

She has seen *A*, finally. Seen the truth of *A*. A vastness that drives out all thought, all knowledge, all comprehension.

Eventually she goes to sleep.

I step out onto the west deck of the penthouse. I feel *A*'s footfalls in the night, less than five minutes apart. *A* roars once.

He's restless tonight.

I had a dream once.

A and the other Kaiju walked the Earth under a vast red sun. It was a barren world, without gust of wind, without oceans, without life. Even the moon was but a ring of dust. The Kaiju walked, the last things on Earth, eternal and unchanging. Listening to things only they could hear. Following things only they could see.

"**The failure in Vietnam...**" Again, Sumiko reads from her manuscript. "And the destruction of the fourth fleet were just two of the factors contributing to the collapse of American optimism in the seventies. Perhaps equally significant was the first of a series of bracing recessions, their slow economic decline and eventual eclipse by other nations."

I must be honest and say that I find much of it abstruse and tedious. It is of interest only to other philosophers, and perhaps not many of them. But her early sections show traces of flash and insight. I make her read it to me, hoping it will help her regain herself.

She will never completely recover from the sight of *A*, of course. None of us will.

She belongs here now, in deserted Tokyo, with the lost and the mad.

"The seventies marked the end of the various constructions and devices to control or defend against the Kaiju. Barriers, electric walls, laser shields—some of these had experienced limited success. But all had proven ineffective against one or another of the Kaiju. Their appearance or use often seemed to goad the creatures.

"Nor could the great beasts be killed. It had become apparent that nothing short of a nuclear explosion might be sufficient to destroy one of them. More, it had become equally apparent that killing a Kaiju would merely liberate its atomic reactions from internal regulation. It posed more problems than the creature itself.

"Instead, unable to resolve the problem of the Kaiju as animals, the perception of them changed. From spawn of the atom, to wild beasts, they came to be perceived as simply a force of nature. The Kaiju were like hurricanes and earthquakes: powerful, unstoppable, irrational, but ultimately transient.

"As the eighties developed, the strategy became increasingly one of avoidance. When a Kaiju approached, the town or city was simply evacuated. When the Kaiju departed, as they invariably did, the population returned or reconstructed elsewhere.

"Interestingly, this strategy of dealing with Kaiju such as *A*..." I watch her involuntary shiver, "...appears to be strongly predicated on the perception of the Kaiju as, in their ultimate form, inanimate. This is a perception, oddly enough, not supported by initial evaluations, but rather, one forced upon us through our inability to properly intellectualise the phenomena..."

Sumiko begins to cry. Closing the book, her face contorts, tears streaming down her cheeks. Great racking sobs tear out of her. I hold her until it passes.

I wish I felt more.

That night, I wake to find her sitting cross-legged in bed, staring at me. Our eyes lock.

"I don't want to be like you," she says finally. Her voice is soft and full of regret.

"It is too late," I tell her.

I roll over and go to sleep.

In the morning, when I wake, she is gone.

I busy myself, caring for my lenses, organising my art drives. She does not appear for lunch. Finally, I go out to look for *A*.

A has wandered out into the suburbs. It is time for the assault on the nest. It has been in the planning, off and on, for months. We are all called in.

I go with Sumiko. She says little now. A coldness has entered our relationship. I suspect that we never will sleep in the Emperor's bed together.

"Do you know what Manabe calls you?" she said to me the other day.

"Man of stone," she said.

Ryushi is there, eyes too large behind bottle-thick glasses. He flashes his myopic grin as he hands out radiation suits.

I know what Ryushi is all about. He is like the blind men in the story of the elephant. He has persuaded himself that blindness, the restriction of his vision, will help him see more clearly. The truth is merely that he does not see at all.

Are we so different?

Radiation suits are a needless precaution for such as we. But I put mine on anyway, to please Ryushi. It is not every day that you venture into the dragon's lair.

Farther on, there are men I do not know. They are dispensing rock-climbing gear. They seem experienced.

We are broken into teams, climbing the mounds that *A* has thrown up around its nest. It is not a difficult climb, even though the slopes are steep and the debris is often unstable.

But it is disturbing. We grapple upon the crushed and melted remains of buildings and automobiles, past artifacts as small as a doll's hand, or as out of place as a computer keyboard. All of it mixed willy-nilly with total indifference to any human schematic.

There is nothing living here, not seagulls or rats or weeds. Nothing can live here.

I am almost afraid of what we will find on the other side.

As it turns out, the other side is just more of the same. It is as if someone has taken all the artifacts of human civilisation, stirred them in some great cauldron, and used them to build a Martian landscape. It is a strange and inhuman world we walk through. It dwarfs us with *A*'s unseen presence.

The geiger counter is going wild.

In several places, there are deep pools of unknown liquid glowing in many colours. Samples are taken. From the corners of our eyes, we see furtive movements: *A*'s parasites, creatures like fleas or ticks, but half the size of a man. These things live freely here.

This is not a place for human beings.

Finally, in the centre, we come to the ovoids. They are covered loosely with debris.

"Possibly droppings," Ryushi says.

"Eggs," Sumiko says.

"Impossible," I say. Life reproduces, that is what life is. That which reproduces. The Kaiju are not alive.

"Eggs," Sumiko says.

"No," I say, "they must be sterile, like hens' eggs. Products of an ancient biology gone wrong."

"Eggs," Sumiko says.

The others are shaken, I can see that.

They are trying to absorb this new development.

"I am leaving," Sumiko tells me as we have one of our now-infrequent lunches.

"Why?" I ask bluntly, fearing the reply.

"They've found a new Kaiju, buried on the Kamchatka peninsula. I've joined the expeditionary force."

I absorb this news quietly.

"Seismic surveys discovered it. We think it is dead. There is much to discover."

Impossible, I think, a Kaiju cannot die. It is forever.

Kaiju cannot reproduce, the thought lashes me. Reproduction is a mark of life, without life, there is no death.

I find I have little to say, as she leaves. It is not as if I need her, or anyone else. She is right. I am a man of stone.

How did I get this way?

What have the Kaiju done to me?

I have another dream.

I dream of *A* in her nest in the ruins of deserted Tokyo, brooding eternally, relentlessly, over glowing eggs which may never hatch. Perhaps this is truly *A*, a being torn from the belly of time, holding a moment preserved.

Perhaps this is what a god is.

I dream of the Americans, antlike and confused, stirred by the knowledge of the eggs. They are flying through the air. They bring their own god, another instant torn from the belly of time. A scream of birth/death/love/hate/marriage...

Its name is H.

KUNGMIN HORANGI: THE PEOPLE'S TIGER

CODY GOODFELLOW

The churning black surf of the Pacific Ocean spouted fifty feet into the air as something very large stirred in the depths at the mouth of the San Francisco Bay. A news helicopter that had ventured too close got swooped up and crashed into southbound traffic lanes on the Golden Gate Bridge. Army and Navy choppers buzzed like mayflies over the geyser, dropping marker flares and spraying red fans of incendiary shells. Nothing seemed to slow the invader, which torpedoed in on a collision course with the Old Ferry Building at the head of Market Street.

All along the waterfront, crews of artillery and mobile missile batteries eagerly peered into the roiling silver mist for their first glimpse of the adversary itself. Behind them, legions of protestors filled the streets from the woodland grounds of the old Presidio Army Base to the Embarcadero and the heart of the Financial District, tens of thousands of furious, banner-waving marchers pressing against the embattled lines of riot-control police. They had come to denounce the federal crackdown on the labour unions, the withdrawal of government assistance and the twenty-eight per cent unemployment rate—but the spectacle unfolding in the water could not be resisted.

A missile battery atop the ferry terminal sparked to life with a salvo of lightning spears that turned the black surface of the bay into a dome of white-hot steam. Waves of scalding seawater swamped the docks, but then the bubbles subsided. The cheers of the soldiers spread up and down the waterfront, drowning out their CO's irate barking and the chanting of the protestors.

It was a brief victory; something exploded out of the water, and for just a moment, the entire city held its breath as it struggled, with its childlike collective mind of a half million or so, to understand just what it was looking at.

Then, amidst the massed shrieking of the sudden inferno pouring down on the flaming invader and its own unearthly howls of tormented rage, hundreds among the crowd began to cheer for the monster.

The command centre of the Joint Forces Mobile Command fell silent as General Skilling entered with his retinue. "Get back to work!" he barked, and the airmen resumed running around as if the deck of the C-98 Supernaut cargo plane were covered in hot coals.

Skilling cast a jaundiced eye over the panorama of the big board, the global map jigsawed together from the composite vision of several hundred defense and private satellites and the exploded diagram of the world's media coverage. Most of two hundred screens played the images coming in from the flock of helicopters circling over San Francisco.

When he absolutely had to, Skilling turned to the man nearly everyone in the room had been mooning over when he entered: Commander Wesley Corben, the most visible officer in the Air Force's Special Counteroperations Detachment and the pilot of America's most closely guarded weapon. If he was on the scene, then the emergency was clearly under control.

Commander Corben ignored him, gazing out the window at the runway lights of Alameda Naval Air Station and a wing of F-18s scrambling off the flight line.

"This is everything we feared, Commander," said a voice from the speaker on the General's desk. Though he had never heard it so raw with exhaustion and nerves, he recognised it well enough.

"We're up to the task, Mr President," the pilot said, glancing at Skilling. "Both of us."

"Mr President, if I may," General Skilling broke in, "Commander Corben hasn't been fully briefed, but once he has been, I think he'll agree that the situation is under control, without the need for... extraordinary measures."

"Have it your way, General, but you boys swore up and down you could stop it at sea."

"Bring me up to speed, General," Corben said quietly, "and I'll decide whether turning the Army loose in the middle of San Francisco is a better idea than deploying Steve."

Skilling winced. He hated to hear the name spoken and glared down nearby technicians who had perked up at the word. "My opinion of your... weapons program is a matter of record—"

"General! They've got a visual!"

All eyes turned to the monitors, where a gargantuan tower of flames staggered across Market Street, kicking tanks and armoured personnel carriers out of its path like a burning drunk in a toy store. Suddenly, incredibly, the sixty-foot flaming behemoth sprang high into the air, clearing a row of warehouses, and vanished into the frothing Bay.

"This is most unprecedented!" shouted Dr Murai, the team's resident kaijuologist. "I've never seen anything so large move so fast. Only Dr Otaku could create such a weapon."

Commander Corben ran for the exit. Skilling did not try to stop him. "Well, Mr President," the general prompted, "I guess you know what this means."

"If that thing out there is the one they call Kungmin Horangi, then I guess it means we're now at war with North Korea as well. Don't these damn Commies know when they've been licked? What the hell does that crazy name mean, anyhow?"

Skilling bit his lip. Half the intelligence community was listening in. "Some shitwit at the Pentagon says it means 'People's Tiger'."

The President's snorting, signal-distorting laugh turned heads throughout the command centre. "A tiger? Is that what it's supposed to be? Goddamn, those commies never get anything right."

Commander Corben sprinted across the runway to the enormous hangar where his team lounged, lobbing a football and watching the news. Without a word, they took their positions to prepare for the launch. Corben zipped into his flight-suit and stepped into the shadowy, cathedral-sized space. In the centre, an enormous American flag hung from the domed rafters, screening off most of the hangar.

Lt Mullin walked alongside, briefing him on the pre-flight check. "The new armaments are loaded, the new Hellfires are quicker on lock-on, like you wanted, but the blowback is worse, so don't go punching anyone with them. The armour's been overhauled, again, but that fibreglass shit's gotta go. It's giving him a rash."

"What about the approach?"

"They don't want you to cross on foot. Reckon the Bay Bridge can't take it."

"Did you show them our numbers?"

"Sure, but the Richmond Bridge is already falling apart, and they don't want to risk an accident. He's gotta go over in the harness."

Corben cursed. "And the other...problem?"

"Electrolytes are bumped up to optimum, but he's still running like a faucet. The doc says he'll adjust to the new diet, but they don't want to run antibiotics on him so soon before—"

"Another upgrade? He's not a goddamned machine. He's—"

"I know, Wes, we feel the same way, but to them he's a weapon. They don't even call him a 'he,' anymore. And you know what they keep saying—"

"I know, I know. *He volunteered for this.* As if any of us knew what 'this' would be."

"Oh, and I tried to get *her* to leave before you deployed, but—"

Corben stopped, fussing with the readouts on his helmet. "I'll take care of it, Ben. She deserves better than to get thrown out by the guards."

Lt Mullin patted him on the shoulder, checked the optic jacks running from Corben's helmet to the CPU on the back of the suit, gave him a thumbs-up and went back to a safe distance.

Corben slipped behind the flag and stopped, as he always did, to offer a prayer for himself, and for Steve. Then he opened his eyes and ascended the stairs parked beside Steve's temple.

Steve lay on his back in the hangar. All the computers and gantries and medical equipment had been cleared out to give him room to get up.

At the top of the stairs, Laura waited, just like always, beside the open hatch bored out of Steve's right temple. The guards had orders to keep her out, but no one could look Steve's widow in the eye and deny her.

She lifted her black lace veil and poured those eyes all over him. "He's afraid, Wes."

"He's not afraid, Laura. He's—" A machine, a weapon, a meat puppet... "He was never afraid of anything in his life."

Laura got closer, her perfume burning in his nose. "He loved his country, you know that. He loved you, Wes. He loved me—a little bit less maybe. He wasn't afraid for himself, but now..."

"There's nothing to worry about. It's some mutt hunk of kaiju-shit from North Korea. It's probably already dead; this is just a photo op." He shook her off, but her real perfume—her sweat, her tears—made it hard to remember where he was.

"It's not the fighting," Laura tried to catch his eyes. "He's afraid of what he's becoming. He knew that this mission... doing this made him a symbol, like the astronauts. They're changing him again, aren't they?"

"They want him to win. That's his job, now. He has to adapt. We all do..."

He brushed past her, but her arms caught him, running over the countless sockets that would bind him to her husband. He pulled away. He couldn't make himself do it again, any more than he could forget that she wanted him for the same reason the Pentagon did.

"Try to get on with your life," he told her.

"I thought we were trying," she said, and he looked away. "The Army doesn't consider him dead, but they don't pay his salary. And—we're... Steve was Catholic... I can't even..."

Corben climbed in. "They'll understand when you do, Laura. Try not to be here when we get back."

"Give him my love, won't you?"

Corben slammed the hatch and initiated the pre-wake checks. Steve's EEG was a minimalist tundra of limbic activity with momentary temporal lobe storms, but nothing to worry about. Everything that was Steve had been scooped out of the front of his skull to make room for the cockpit. Cables snaked from the bulkhead and slotted into their respective ports on the suit. Corben tingled as those cables shoehorned his brain into the sleeping giant.

"Commander, this is your eleven o'clock wake-up call. The Green Meanies are waiting outside, and Steve's late for work."

Corben nodded at the marching columns of status lights on his smart visor. The phantom sensations of godlike power swept all the garbage out of his mind as he got into character.

"Roger that, Ben. Steve's online in three…two…"

He hit the switch.

Steve opened his eyes. Light burned until the visor calibrated his response and winched down his pupils. He rose to his feet, slowly, like a coma patient. His helmet brushed the hanging halogen lamps, forcing him to hunch over double to step out onto the runway.

The night sky was clear above, but an opaque canopy of fog enveloped San Francisco down to the double-decker Bay Bridge. From the heart of the fog came a constant flash and dull, rolling pops of ordnance being expended in an all-out war. Colt was developing a 90mm revolver for Steve to use, and a telephone pole-sized police baton that delivered a fifty-thousand-volt shock was on the drawing boards at the Pentagon, but for now, he was expected to beat whatever was raising hell over there with his hands and feet and some Hellfire missiles salvaged from a junked Apache helicopter.

Steve checked the harness on his heavily armoured torso, and hooked into the web of cables running back to two enormous cargo helicopters idling before him. At his thumb's up, they lifted and spread out until the cables stood taut, rotors growling in mutiny at the nine-ton payload.

He braced himself and rolled his shoulders, tried to scratch the rash on his back. At last, the cables twanged and the tarmac dropped away. Aloft, the helicopters double-timed, lurching into the wind over Treasure Island and along the Bay Bridge, where hundreds stuck in traffic honked and shouted his name. The wind pried at the seams of his Kevlar bodysuit, the battlements upon his shoulders and head, seeking any path to steal his strength.

Wes Corben dissolved like aspirin inside Steve, shivering at the wind and straining to see out of Steve's eyes into the shroud over the battle. Even as his thermal overlays gave up on the blizzard of fire and smoke, his radiation scans fed him an outline of something larger than Steve, and faster, and—beyond that, he had no fucking idea what he was looking at.

"Have a nice day at the office, dear," a chopper pilot chirped in his ear, and the cables cut loose high above the impossible, burning thing that even now looked up to watch him falling.

And then—and this always drove Corben batshit when it happened, but Mullin swore they couldn't find the bug—Steve's life flashed before his eyes.

When kaiju synthesis technology disseminated to all the extremist nations of the world, it sparked a renaissance of rogue state misbehavior. If plutonium and anthrax were effective means of asserting one's will upon the world stage, then the revival of some sleeping monstrosity—or the creation of a new one—was a golden dream of random havoc.

Not to be left behind by kaiju-mongers in China and Africa, the United States embarked on its own Megamorphic Weaponization project. No renegade sauropods or lumbering cybernetic chimerae could serve as a symbol of American military might, however—the people of the world's last great superpower would never rally behind a monster. At least subconsciously grasping the return of pagan idolatry that lay at the roots of the kaiju arms race, they strove to create a hero; to, in their own well-spun words, "put a human face, an all-American face, on the kaiju crisis". So they asked for volunteers.

Major Steve Arness had done so, as they never tired of reminding his wife, and had passed the rigorous screening process. They needed someone strong and fast, with excellent reflexes, with Golden Age astronaut looks that would translate into action figures, kid's pajamas and beach towels and shit. Steve was perfect.

Using gene therapy and nanomites, they reprogrammed Steve's mitochondrial DNA, and he grew. Within six months, he stood sixty-four feet tall.

His doctors pleaded with the Pentagon scientists to consider the potential for replication errors during this reckless growth, particularly in the brain, which stopped growing by age three in normal human development. To grow from three pounds to the volume of a V-8 engine block is traumatic enough for any organism, but how much more so for the most complex aggregation of matter in the known universe, the human brain? Very soon after his treatments stopped, Steve went totally insane. He devolved to a bestial shell of the confident Navy pilot who had volunteered for this project—and left them no choice.

After escaping from the Florida island where he was interred, he destroyed Cape Canaveral and twelve helicopters and a company of infantry before a TOW missile lobotomy felled him. Incredibly, he survived, though in a coma. Wheels began spinning, and the catastrophic setback became an unprecedented opportunity.

Neurosurgeons, structural engineers and computer designers flew to the island, and set about fixing him. The cavity in Steve's forebrain was filled with a mainframe that routed all his nervous impulses to a cockpit just above Steve's eyes. The man who controlled Steve would receive all the data of Steve's experience as raw reality; his reactions drove Steve's body as an amplified version of his own. That man would have to be an extraordinary pilot, as good as Steve himself had once been, for he would have to become Steve. Wes Corben had not wanted to volunteer for the project, but he did, because he could not bear the thought of a stranger inside his best friend's head.

Steve hit the ground and sank up to his ankles on a grassy palisade overlooking the Bay. The street was seeded with burning cars and military debris, and a fusillade of tracers sprayed out of the nearest cross-street. Protestors swarmed the sidewalks around his feet, waving banners and throwing rocks and bottles as they sought shelter from the meta-Biblical conflict raging above their heads.

A chorus of spotters buzzed in his ears that the enemy was closing in on his position, but he just stood there. The thing had been right under him when he dropped. How did something so big move so fast?

The building in front of him, an eight-storey office complex, sagged and spat glass as all its eastern-exposure windows shattered. Steve looked up at the titanic black shape perched on the roof just as it sprang at his face.

He tried to roll with the impact and throw the attacker over his head, but it slammed into his chest, crushing his lungs flat. Its talons got inside his arms and shredded his armour.

Pain whited out the scene. Corben almost succumbed before the dampers reduced Steve's pain-incentive triggers and told him what was wrong. Steve was laid out on his back in the street, armour and bodysuit torn wide open, the attacker straddling his chest like a dog about to bury a bone in his abdomen.

With a noisome trumpet blast that somehow cut through the din of war all around, Steve's irritable, bacteria-infested bowel cramped up and sounded a war charge. The monster flinched and shrank away, as if offended by the outburst. Galvanised, Steve brought one leg up as hard as he could between its hind legs, hoping the kaiju specialists had striven for authenticity, and levered its mammoth bulk up and as far away as he could.

The creature flailed at the air, sailing over three waterfront blocks, smashing to earth on an unfortunate retro diner and plowing across the street into the deserted stalls of the farmer's market in front of the Ferry Terminal. At last, Steve got a good look at it.

Even with its pelt burned off, Kungmin Horangi was clearly supposed to be a tiger, perhaps a new strain of the giant sabertooths the Chinese had revived from fossils and turned loose in Tibet. But its hide was a sickening mass of polyps and blisters, with arrays of envenomed quills sprouting in radiating patterns down its spine from its head, or where there was supposed to be a head. Nice try, North Korea.

Then it roared at him, and he understood that, blasphemy though it was, this was no mistake. It was the offspring of a fundamentally perverse union of land and sea fauna. But why? Why would anyone cross a tiger with a sea cucumber?

He soon found out. The head peeled open and splayed out like a banana, a thrashing mane of fanged tentacles around a gaping maw filled with busy mandibles. Its eyes, he saw, were everywhere, on the tentacles and all over its body, so that even as it recovered from the impact, it lashed out at a tank parked behind it and stomped its turret in, kicking it through the lobby window of a Japanese bank. Then it charged.

Steve snatched up the nearest solid object—a tour bus containing BC/DC, Canada's foremost AC/DC cover band—and hurled it at the oncoming monster. Kungmin Horangi changed course, talons digging into the solid masonry façade of the old US Mint, and vaulted off it. Steve barely dodged, reached out and gripped one of its tentacles as it passed, making ready to whip it around and smash it into the street.

But the plan fell apart before the pain even reached the dazed synapses of Steve's pilot. The thorny tentacle razored through Steve's gloves, into the muscle between the bones of his fingers and out the other side, as the monster tore past him and took his hand with it, ripping off the flesh like a glove.

Steve stared at his naked bones and let out a yelp of confusion. The spotters screamed in his ears, but he heard only the sound of his own building agony as it roared out of him and shattered the last intact windows on the avenue.

The Red Korean kaiju skidded to a halt a block away. The street buckled under it, brown sewage percolating up out of smashed pipes around its massive paws. The monstrous hybrid relaxed, as though Steve were already dead and it could destroy the city at its leisure. It shot one paw out at the walls of a glass skyscraper and smashed something inside—a cat stalking a mouse through a dollhouse. Steve recognised the building: the Transamerica Pyramid, always a favourite with disaster movies.

Blood loss and encroaching shock made red warning lights blink all around the periphery of his vision, but Steve focused only on the enemy. "Weapons hot," he growled, raising his intact arm to point at the thing now engaged in smashing open the Pyramid's neighbours like an anteater ravaging termite mounds. "Fox one, fox two," he said, and Hellfire missiles arced out of the gauntlet on his forearm.

Where they hit, the sun seemed to peek out of a hole in the night, and then the whole avenue was awash in fire that reduced the air itself to ash.

"Fox three, four…" Steve emptied the remainder of his arsenal into the flaming mound, but he knew that no matter how hot he burned it, no matter how many pieces he blew it into, it would come back, and keep coming, and coming—

And now, the news: *In the wake of the disastrous San Francisco attack, the true extent of the damage inflicted upon the city is only now coming to light. While the kaiju invader Kungmin Horangi broke down the physical security systems of an undisclosed number of bank headquarters in the city's financial district, an army of hackers descended on the unprotected servers and deleted whole banks of financial records, credit reports and loan documents. An emergency meeting of the FDIC and SEC this morning was closed to the public, but critics predict that at least four major banks will be forced to freeze all holdings and declare bankruptcy, until such* *time as the records can be retrieved. While his press secretary delivered the painful news that the federal budget is already too tight to allow for more emergency aid, the President made this brief statement, while enjoying a round of golf with friends and campaign boosters at Cocoa Beach:*

"We are at war, and the enemy is within our borders, as well as all around us. People will have to make sacrifices. Real Americans won't have to be told twice."

The President's golf game was cut short by the approaching Hurricane Manuel, but he still got to fire the inaugural round at Florida's first indoor duck hunting arena. The President and his party bagged fourteen mallards, and poked fun at his troubles by naming one of the two ducks he shot in a cage match 'Kungmin', and the other, 'Kim'—

It had not been Kim Jong Il's intention to initiate a sneak attack on the United States. The last thing he wanted was for posterity to associate North Korea with the conniving cowardice of the Nipponese devils at Pearl Harbor. If only the American President had taken his repeated warnings seriously...

At first his plan was only a frustrated whim—to turn a kaiju loose on his decadent cousins to the south, and force the Americans to show their impotence, or their insanity...it mattered not, so long as something finally happened. A modest plan, but the Supreme Leader's restless dreams of even a shabby reconstituted dinosaur were out of his poor nation's reach. All this changed when he stole the inestimable Dr Otaku and set him to work; the dream had become the creation of a symbol of North Korea's adamantine resolve, an avatar of the People to shake the palaces of the world to dust. The notorious Nipponese kaijuologist only smiled and bowed and disappeared into his lab, saying, "I will hold a mirror up to your state, and give your reflection life."

The world laughed when it heard what North Korea was doing. With half of the capitol in darkness, with disease and famine claiming nearly as many per annum as had the war that split their great nation in half, Kim was spending all their money on a desperate weapons project, using a kidnapped—and certifiably mad—scientist to make a monster.

But Kim had never listened to the world. If his rule, by the same rigorous Stalinist doctrine he inherited from his omnipotent father, was painted as incompetent tyranny by the chattering swine of the outside world, he would not deign to explain himself. Though Dr Otaku escaped to China only six months into the project—in a capsule within a giant earthworm of his own devising—the specimen in the brine tanks in his lab grew nevertheless, stunted and grotesque, yes, but it became more than he ever dared to imagine.

Kim awakened to a revelation, and dreamed a new dream of eliminating hunger and teaching the world about the true benefits of communism, but the world would not stop laughing long enough to listen. They cackled at the destruction of Kungmin Horangi in San Francisco, but soon they would hear, and see, and taste—and they would know.

In the heart of his palatial fortress at Pyongyang, Kim Jong Il swilled Hennessy, raged at his Playstation and waited for the world to apologise.

General Skilling hated using the laser pointer, but he'd found it was the only way to keep the President's attention. "As you know, sir, one year ago, North Korea was accused by the UN Security Council of running a biological weapons program. Nobody thought they'd ever pose a threat to anyone but themselves, but there was some speculation that China had financed them.

"Kim Jong Il refused to address the charges, but then Dr Otaku disappeared—"

"He wanted the head egghead for his monster factory."

"Correct, sir," Admiral Beecher cut in. "Kim is a freak for the old kaiju flicks, and when the Japs cracked the recombinant kaiju genome, he shit himself with envy, and went on a shopping spree. He did the same thing to get some movies made, a few years back."

Skilling waggled the pointer in the President's eyes. "Well, this morning, sir, we received this tape. It was postmarked two weeks ago, but it was sent parcel rate."

A screen lit up at the centre of the big board. A plump face filled the screen, eyes flashing like Siamese fighting fish behind the convex lenses of monumental goo-goo goggles. Pulling out in spastic jerks, the camera framed Kim Jong Il at a podium before a window overlooking the snowcapped mountains of the Amnok-Kang river valley, near the Chinese border. Behind him, an elderly Japanese man in a spotless white lab coat smiled and nodded, his nimble fingers dancing as if they worked the strings of a marionette.

"That's Dr Otaku. Kim's people took him from his fortified lab on Mt Fuji."

For once, the President was all ears. "Was he brainwashed?"

"You be the judge of who brainwashed whom."

The dictator appeared tired, but smiled benignly at the clockwork soldiers flanking him at the podium. Though heavily sweetened with digital studio effects, his voice was still the querulous falsetto of a cat trying to frighten a rival as he squawked through the hostile English-language script. "To those who believe that Communism is dead, Great Comrade Kim Jong Il offers this lesson. Communism is sharing, no more and no less, from each according to his means, to each according to his needs. And so, people of the so-called Free World, we share the gift of the People's Tiger with you."

The video cut out.

The President pounded the table. "What I want to know is, why was this such a goddamned surprise? We knew he was cooking up something, we knew he had the know-how, and he warned us—"

"He warned *you*, Mr President, but—"

"The man's some kind of goddamned nut, with all the crazy crap that comes out of his mouth. 'The People's Tiger is coming?' What were we supposed to make of that happy horseshit?"

Admiral Beecher, reluctantly, stepped in. "It would appear, sir, that we did have some advance contact..."

The President smelled the fumble and pounced on it. "What? Who dropped the ball?"

"Our nuclear submarine Akron, on patrol in the Sea of Japan, pinged an unidentified object larger than itself a week ago. It emitted no hull or engine noise, so the captain assumed it was a hostile kaiju, and torpedoed it. The target was presumed destroyed."

"Why the hell wasn't I told?"

Beecher looked around for support, but they'd all been thrown under that bus too many times. "Well, it, um... it was in the daily briefings to the Joint Chiefs, but it looked like a non-starter. No action alerts, no response from your people—"

"Well, now we know different, don't we?"

"Yes, sir. We've since collected waterborne tissue samples on the beaches near Aomori and Sapporo, but it's difficult to account for all of the mass because..."

"Because what? Out with it!"

Beecher spent, General Skilling took back the laser pointer. "People have been eating it, Mr President."

That cracked the President up. "Lord, those Japs'll eat anything, won't they?"

"Sir, your morning briefing of yesterday details the same problem in San Francisco—"

"What? What page is that on?"

"Fourteen–A, sir, in the bright red box? Army recovery efforts were hampered by the protestors, some of whom appear to have been pinko fifth columnists, and they led a salvage of the remains."

"What do you mean, 'salvage?'"

"The protests were about federal aid, sir, about food for the poor. The meat of the kaiju was roasted by Steve's, ah, overzealous attack, and distributed over dozens of city blocks by the explosion. It is resistant to decay and, by all accounts, the flesh of the monster is, ah..."

"Spit it out!"

"Well, it's said to be delicious."

In South Korea, the US Army maintained a high state of alert, awaiting an order to begin the mad minute they'd been trained for—showering North Korea with missiles. But due to the desperate peace brokered by South Korea's president, and China's promise that any attack on her poor neighbour would draw a nuclear response, a shaky truce held. But at home, a new radical movement formed and, almost overnight, escalated into an all-out insurgency.

When the unwashed hippie hordes of the UC Berkeley student body staged a sit-in at which the meat of Kungmin Horangi was offered as a sacrament, the police cracked down, but nobody took it seriously. When the same thing happened at Stanford's crypto-conservative Hoover Institute four days later, they started to worry. Police raids on Communist soup kitchens all over the Bay Area turned up a distribution network for the kaiju meat. Within a week, thirty-eight such establishments were shut down, and nearly three tons of the monster's flesh was confiscated and removed to labs across the country for study. What they learned in the next twenty-four hours made them freeze or burn all samples and order a news blackout.

When left in a medium of seawater and organic nutrients, the flesh replicated itself and grew. The proprietors of the soup kitchens—card-carrying Communists all—were interrogated and extolled the virtues of the meat as an inexhaustible food staple, a gift from the peace-loving people of North Korea.

Their customers, however, were a different matter. The poor and hipsters alike, drawn to the necessity or novelty of free kaiju cuisine, reported that it had properties far beyond its flavour and astounding nutritional content. Eating the meat opened gates in the brain, boosting endorphins and serotonin output, creating a euphoric yet alert state which one imprisoned kaiju chef described as "like Christmas morning, where you love everyone and want to share everything". This witness had particular clout, as he was a decorated artillery officer and survivor of the San Francisco attack, who snatched up and cooked a feast of kaiju meat for his Army buddies as a goof. "If this is what Communism was supposed to be about, then have we ever been barking up the wrong tree!" he declared, even as he was taken out and shot.

The government's aggressive publicity campaign to depict the meat as drugged, poisoned or radioactive seemed to fall on deaf ears. Spontaneous demonstrations of thousands blocked every law enforcement attempt to root out the trade in kaiju meat, and kitchens opened in Los Angeles, Portland, Seattle and Las Vegas—the latter of which suffered most grievously from the effect, as tourists discovered the futile stupidity of gambling and simply shared their money, and hotels opened their doors to the homeless.

The government tried, as well, to block the plague of websites devoted to kaiju cuisine and philosophy, most of which came not from North Korea, but from Japan, where the phenomenon had already saturated the community via the meat that washed ashore at Sapporo. In retaliation, domestic and foreign hackers alike descended on the federal servers in earnest, so that the NCIC criminal database was wiped clean of all records, and the New York Stock Exchange seized up and began rattling off kaiju recipes.

The next month saw the kaiju kitchens spread across the nation and out of the liberal underground, into the faltering middle-class mainstream. With more banks in default or freezing their accounts in the wake of the database collapse, unemployment climbed to nearly half the population, and social agencies were swamped and sank without issuing a single cheque. Employees at fast-food franchises were caught preparing kaiju meat for unsuspecting customers, and the suburban hinterlands began to simmer with political unrest and unconditional love. The news stopped showing the riots, as police clubs fell more and more on the heads of cornfed Republicans and even other cops who had succumbed to the forbidden flesh.

No matter what draconian measures the government imposed—martial law and curfews in the cities, roadblocks and roving gangs of National Guardsmen torching burger joints with flamethrowers everywhere else—the madness spread, and people pig-headedly, defiantly, continued to share.

Commander Wes Corben spent the next month running Steve through physical therapy in Florida, and so had little time to read the news. He received the Congressional Medal of Honor from his hospital bed, recovering from a concussion and the psychosomatic shock of losing Steve's hand.

He pushed for a robotic prosthetic, but was outmaneuvered by the project scientists, who wanted to try out a sauropod regeneration virus they'd harvested from the remains of one of Japan's lesser-known kaiju plagues.

The treatment bore immediate fruit; within hours, Steve's cauterised stump sprouted with new buds of bone sheathed in noisily dividing cells, and before the week was out, a hand, of sorts, had grown to replace the one sheared off by the monster. That his skin broke out in shingles like the scales of a dinosaur only intrigued them more, and when Steve began to grow a tail, they were ecstatic. They talked about pushing the envelope— Steve Mk2, armies of dino-Steves stomping through Pyongyang, eating everything and everyone in their path on the long road to Beijing—

The only battle Corben won was over Steve's incontinence; they resumed antibiotics and stopped feeding him by stomach tubes. But Corben had to run Steve's meal each day, herding the brain-dead behemoth through whole pods of steamed orca and hockey-rink-sized portions of cornbread.

He came back to his motel room off-base to find Laura waiting for him. She still wore her widow's weeds, but she shed them soon enough even as he worked the key in the door. Too tired from days on end inside a dead man's head, too beaten down to argue, he let her in, and kept his mouth shut when she called him *Steve*. He told himself he was defending his friend's memory by refusing to do it where she really wanted to, in the cramped confines of Steve's cockpit.

Afterwards, he lay in bed, wondering what day it was. The phone rang. Laura turned over, sighed in her sleep, whispered a sibilant name. He picked up the phone.

"Scramble, code red, Commander. Steve's late for work."

Corben slid off the bed and stepped into his crumpled pants. "Steve's still in therapy from the changes. He's not ready to walk around the block yet—"

"Too damned bad is what they say. We need him. Tiger-Cucumber's back."

"As near as we can tell, the bastards hoarded a ton of the meat, and incubated it near Norfolk, right under our goddamned noses." General Skilling caught his breath as he paced alongside Commander Corben in the hangar at Bolling Air Force Base. As before, helicopters circled over the water outside, dogging something moving fast upstream to the confluence of the Potomac and the Anacostia rivers, at the heart of Washington, DC.

Lilliputian scientists and technicians crawled all over Steve, disconnecting catheters and hoses and running the final pre-wake check. Corben eyed Steve nervously, seeing the changes in full bloom for the first time. Steve lay propped on his side to accommodate his new tail, as long as he was tall, spilling out onto the runway. His bone structure had begun to warp, muscles to sculpt themselves into a very different kind of body. An ugly brainwave soured Corben's alert frame of mind: a drawing-board sketch of King Kong versus Godzilla in a genetic blender, with Steve's apple-pie freckled, Tom-Sawyer face slapped onto the hideous final product.

"How do you know there's only one?" Corben asked.

"We'll cross *that* bridge if and when we come to it. Those asses in Congress have finally seen the light, and they've voted the funding to expand the program. We won't make the same mistakes again."

Looking over the chainmail mesh of serrated scales spilling down Steve's oddly hunched back, Corben could only mumble: "Who wouldn't volunteer for this?"

Skilling saluted him and nudged him up the stairs. At least Laura wasn't here. She was still asleep in the motel room—and he knew what she was dreaming.

Corben climbed into Steve's head and fired it up without running through the checks. Steve lumbered to his feet, trampling a lot of million-dollar equipment and more than a few fleeing technicians. Though heavier than ever, he felt even more powerful, his centre of gravity lower and wider thanks to the balancing tail, which slashed the runway clear with a will of its own, and drove Steve in a bounding, simian gait that was only half voluntary.

There had been much wrangling, at the start of the program, over where to locate the pilot. Some had demanded that Steve be run by remote, but security concerns and human practicality had won out. Steve had been a Golden Gloves boxer in his youth, and muscle memory and superb reflexes made his head the safest place to be when he ran amok.

Though much of the data Steve's nerves poured into his brain was utterly alien, Corben became Steve like never before as he loped across the paved expanse of the airbase, skirting the waiting helicopters and running down to the river. Here, he could already see the churning waters parting as his adversary burst from the gray Potomac and waded into the Capitol on the opposite bank.

Steve hit the water and kicked across in twenty strokes, his tail propelling him like a speedboat to the shore of East Potomac Park. In the silvery light of the overcast morning, the obscene profile of the enemy loomed over the Capitol Mall—Kungmin Horangi, reborn.

Steve took note of how it moved among the white sepulchral houses of government. In its wake, only selected targets were destroyed: the Mint, the Federal Trade Commission and the fortress of the Internal Revenue Service were flattened, while the monster leapt high over the Smithsonian castle and gamboled across the open greensward, cutting a wide berth around the bureaucratic temples and museums, in open contempt for the helicopters raining missiles with depleted uranium shells down on it.

Then Steve came out onto the Mall, and saw that the green was packed with protesters. Hundreds of thousands of men and women of every class and persuasion shouted and sang and cheered the kaiju invader. It traipsed over their heads like their collective dream of a champion made flesh, somehow never stepping on a single tiny body.

The damage to its fiery, jet-striped pelt was hardly negligible— gigantic gobbets of flesh sprayed and spattered the Mall, and teeming hordes of protesters overran the barricades to carry them off or devour them on the spot.

Locked on the monster, Steve led it so he aimed at a projected ghost of its probable path and launched a volley of missiles. Bigger than ever, easily eighty-feet long, the monster launched itself into the air and the missiles strafed the Smithsonian and made a blazing pyre of the US Forest Service.

"Power down your missiles, Wes! Repeat, power down, you're blowing up government property!"

"Do you want to win or not?" Corben barked, and Steve rushed the monster.

Protesters milled around his feet as he strode through their midst, spearing his ankles and feet and tail with the shafts of their picket signs. Screaming, "Whose side are you on?" Steve stomped them until the lawn was a swamp of liquefied sedition, and broomed the Mall with his tail until the fortress of the Department of Justice and the marble walls of the National Archive wept blood and human shrapnel.

Kungmin Horangi met his charge rearing up on its hind legs,

head splayed open and fang-studded tentacles questing for his
face. Steve slipped under the wriggling worms and drove his fists
into its blubbery chest. His tail darted behind and swiped the
monster's legs out from under it. Dragging it off-balance as he
once had his opponents in judo, Steve heaved the writhing bulk
over his hip, sent it hurtling across Constitution Avenue.

Even before it landed, Steve was racing after the airborne
abortion and pounced on it where it came to rest, snatched a
nosy news chopper out of the sky by its tail and smashed the
monster with it until the whirling rotors broke off and the fuselage
exploded like a cheap guitar on its sorry excuse for a head.

As Kungmin Horangi crumpled and lay prone against the
toppled tower of the Old Post Office, great slits yawned open all
down its neck and flanks and gave forth a faint but growing hiss.
Cautiously, Steve crouched behind the rubble of the IRS; in stark
disregard for every known principle of physics or biology, these
monsters almost always had some sort of energy weapon. He
waited to see what it would produce.

An eerie keening sound escaped from the gill-slits, and Steve
went dead-stick, oblivious to Corben's spastic gyrations in the
cockpit. Steve's nervous network broadcast only static, while
sensations like fluttering moths in his stomach—feelings!—
swamped the mainframe. Out of the unlovely orifices of this
monstrous abomination, in the thick of a titanic battle, came the
celestial sound of a chorus of children.

They sang in Korean, but the longing, loving voices sailed their
message straight through the benighted backwaters of Corben's
brain. These children, reared on Spartan rations and Stalinist
dogma, sang of their dream of a world where everyone shared,
and loved one another, as a family should. They offered this awful,
awesome thing, from which the recording of their song spewed
like the tune of an icecream truck, as a gift, and the harbinger of
a new golden age of humankind.

In their thousands, the surviving protesters poked up out of
the rubble like shoots of grass and took up the alien chorus.

Steve grabbed up tanks and cars and fistfuls of shrieking
protesters and threw them at the crumpled form, rushed up
behind it and planted a kick in its flanks. The monster was
lofted high over the Capitol, flipping end over end as the crowd
went wild in his ears, cheers and screams about evacuating the
President—

Steve fell on the monster again, plunged his taloned saurian
paw into its cratered, rubbery hide above its cartilaginous ribs.
Venomous spines pricked him all over, skin going numb and
swelling purple-black blisters the size of watermelons. Thrashing
tentacles flayed the scales off his back and pumped a potpourri
of toxins into his flesh, but he blanked it out as he squeezed
something deep inside that pumped like a heart until he popped
it, then slashed the muscles beneath its right foreleg.

The monster sagged under Steve, who wrenched the useless

limb out of its socket like a drumstick and rammed it into the frantically gnawing mandibles. The tentacles swallowed up his arm and stripped it to the bone again, but the echinoderm mouth ruthlessly chewed up its own severed forelimb, and rivers of sweet-and-sour ichor showered the White House lawn as the colossal combatants grappled, the syrupy song of the children skipping but still burbling out of its speaker-gills.

"What do you taste like, eh, you Commie motherfucker?" Steve roared.

Kungmin Horangi went limp in his arms, then swelled up like an emergency airbag. Steve struggled to get free, but his destroyed arm was still trapped in the barbed gullet of the monster. A blast of hot air and briny broth escaped, and Steve's nostrils caught it and told Wes that its aroma was not at all unpleasant.

Then Kungmin Horangi exploded.

Steve's arm ripped free amid a torrent of soft tissue, mountains of stomachs and intestines and glands the size of school buses lay out on the lawn and festooned the south portico of the White House, and still it kept coming, an endless, gory horn of plenty.

And Corben had to admit that he had never smelled anything so sweet in all his life.

With a Herculean effort of pure will, he pulled back on Steve to retreat from the situation. The Red Korean kaiju was limping away, deathly slow, towards the Potomac, and Steve had to get back to the hangar. He was bleeding, dying—

But the controls wouldn't respond. Corben felt himself go into a kind of paralysis, as Steve moved of his own volition towards the steaming pile of innards. Reaching it, he began to shovel them into his gaping mouth with his intact hand.

"Steve, for God's sake, it's Communism! Stop eating it!" Corben yelled. He yanked on the manual overrides and punched the emergency sleep sequence, but to no avail. Steve went on gobbling up the monster's digestive tract, which it had expelled after the fashion of its secondary parent species, the resourceful sea cucumber.

And even as Corben fought to pull Steve back, the cables running into his suit fed him the taste and the texture, the gelatinous, spicy, tangy succulence of it, not unlike kimchi or pickled octopus, but tempered by the pleasantly gamy murk of tiger meat, and the briny, womb-like glow of collective well-being, of universal rightness, of belonging to a harmonious whole, that began to spread out from his stomach.

Corben coded the self-destruct sequence, ripped the leads out of his suit and undogged the hatch, all the while telling himself he was not hungry, he was not going to eat it—

"You're an American hero, Steve," Corben begged one last time, "you're like a god to them. Why can't you stop?"

A familiar voice pounded on his eardrums, and shocked Corben so that he threw himself head-first out of the cockpit. Though Steve was hunkered down on his knees over the diminishing pile of guts, Corben still fell thirty feet to the immaculately manicured White House lawn, the echo of that voice still ringing in his ears.

"Why can't you stop fucking my wife, Wes?"

Corben's arm folded under him and he hit his head so hard he saw stars, but he rolled to sit up at the sound of a helicopter touching down in front of the west portico.

High above him, the explosive charges embedded beneath the cockpit detonated, blowing the domed roof off Steve's skull in a furious monsoon of bone shards and hunks of flaming brain. Steve's hand stalled at his mouth, a colossal rope of intestine slithering free and draping itself across his lap.

A party of dour Secret Service agents in black suits hustled out the West Wing exit and crossed the lawn, but halfway to the chopper, their ranks broke and a shorter man in shirtsleeves came running up to Corben.

"Do I smell barbecue?" shouted the President.

"No, Mr President, it'll brainwash you!" Corben went for his sidearm, oblivious to Secret Service agents painting laser dots on him and running to shield the President.

"Naw, I'm not touching that disgusting foreign Commie crap, but it does give me an idea." The President engaged that matinee-idol squint that denoted frontier grit and cowboy resolve, that somewhat alarming facial tic which, alone, had carried him in the southern states. "If that sea cucumber shit makes people turn pinko, then we just need an antidote, right? Fight fire with fire."

Picking his way across the debris-strewn lawn, the President stood in the shadow of Steve, still kneeling upright, though his convertible head belched smoke like an uneasy volcano. "Yes sir, a taste of true-blue courage, of independence and strength and faith, to remind them what it means to be Americans."

The leader of the free world knelt and scooped up a fillet of brain, still sizzling in its own juices.

"Smells like veal from my Daddy's ranch," he said, and took a bite.

Corben crawled up to the President, but a Secret Service agent stepped on his neck and pried his pistol from his hand. "Please, Mr President, don't! He wouldn't want—"

The President grinned. "Nonsense, boy, he knew what his duty was, when he signed up for it. Any red-blooded American with half the heart he had would jump at the chance. And, Jesus, take a look at him! Whatever it is, it sure ain't cannibalism..."

The President bethought himself a moment, then flagged down his chief of staff. "Now, get my Interfaith Council on the horn, and have them stand by for something big. And get me every cloning specialist you can, and some lab space, and some vats. And, you know, we're gonna need a helluva big grill..."

THE GREATER DEATH
OF SAITO SAKU

RICHARD HARLAND

Saito Saku awoke early on the day of his dying. It had rained overnight, and the air was warm and humid. Outside his window, the birds had begun their early morning song. He licked dry lips and remembered: the *gokami* had come to the Hot Pools.

His head was full of cobwebs. At fifty years old, he found it difficult to snap instantly alert. Too much easy living, not good for a bushido warrior. Today he would have to pay for it. He stretched and sat up in the dim light.

Not that anyone had said what was expected of him, not in so many words. The first news had come from his daughter, running up wide-eyed to repeat a muddled rumour. "Be calm, Aoi," he had told her; and when she'd asked what he was going to do, he had answered "Wait". He had waited until an hour after sunset, when the official deputation of mayor and villagers appeared.

The bowls of tea had been shaking in their hands as they told him the facts. It was a fully-grown *gokami*, a legend come to life. No one had seen it arrive—the traditional belief was that the fire-beasts flew down from the Burning Land. This one was reported as standing twice as high as the tallest cedar in Oirinji Forest. It was a monster such as he'd never expected to encounter in his own lifetime.

No, they hadn't said what was expected of him. But he understood. For twenty-five years, as protector of Kitake and its three smaller satellite villages, he had accepted their gifts: a splendid house, a fine wife, status and respect. He was expected to keep his end of the bargain.

He went out to the cistern in the courtyard. The leaves of the laurel trees glittered in the early light. He washed face and hands, then fastened his hair in a top-knot. At least he could look the part, even if he could no longer play it.

Ryosen had left a towel for him on top of the chest by the steps. Perfectly folded, fragrant with the smell of jasmine. Everything ready and in its place. Yes, he thought, he had been fortunate in his wife.

His morning meal was also in its place, laid on the mat on the outside verandah. The lotus-root tea, the bowl of eggflower broth, the salted rice cake and the honeyed rice cake. He sat and ate slowly, thoughtfully. The tree frogs were belling in the bamboo thickets, but his ears were focused on sounds within the house. He could hear the discreet movements of Ryosen and Aoi as they went about their household activities.

He felt more sorry for them than for himself. They had shared in his status as warrior and protector, always holding their heads high. But after today, every accumulated grudge would be visited upon them. Who would take their side when he was gone? He would be the failed protector, and his family would suffer a loss of face because of his defeat.

Occasionally, there were other sounds, too: a faint sniffling, followed by someone whispering *Shush, shush, shush.* It must be Aoi swallowing back her tears, Ryosen trying to quieten her down. Just ten years old, but already his daughter grasped the reality of the situation. She knew that her father had no hope against a fully-grown fire-beast.

Finishing his meal, he went to the room where he kept his weapons. Swords, staves, bows, breastplates and corselets of mail: all the equipment of a samurai warrior. But very little of it would serve against this opponent. Dismissing the heavy armour, he donned a costume of silk and soft leather. Better to remain mobile.

As for weapons, a bow and arrows would be ineffectual, a long-bladed sword too cumbersome. In the end, he chose a short sword and a barb that fitted onto the shaft of a spear. Of all his weapons, the inward-working barb was the only one that he thought might actually kill a *gokami.*

He took time and trouble over his preparations. He owed it to the villagers to put up the best possible fight. He went to the shrine in the family room to offer his prayers and prepare himself mentally. He stayed until he was perfectly balanced, perfectly composed.

His one regret was that Aoi and Ryosen didn't come to farewell him. Yet he understood their reasons. If Aoi couldn't control her tears, if Ryosen couldn't believe in his triumph, then they wouldn't weaken his spirit by letting him see their doubts. A warrior had to exclude the fear of death from his mind.

The day was warming as he walked out along the path. His mandarin trees were a mass of blossom, his azaleas hadn't yet come into flower. This part of the garden he had planted and tended himself. Perhaps he should have been a gardener...

The village was stirring, but not with its usual early morning bustle. No children playing, no groups of gossips. As he followed the single road, he could see people on their verandahs, watching in silence. It was as though the whole village was in mourning.

But not for him. They were in mourning for their own forthcoming exile. With the *gokami* at the Hot Pools, they would have to abandon their fields and decamp to a safer region. The decision would probably be taken as soon as their protector had been defeated.

No one called out to him, no one made eye contact. Two women were drawing water from the well, but they moved off as he approached. He was sure they hadn't finished filling their buckets.

They were ashamed of him, he realised. Ashamed that their samurai warrior was unable to fulfil his duty. They'd maintained him for so long, they'd almost forgotten his advancing age. But with the coming of the fire-beast, suddenly they saw him as he was. They were ashamed to have so little to show for all their gifts.

He understood their thinking too well to be angry with them. They didn't want to look him in the face, when he was the embodiment of their own mistake. For their sake, he wished he could have been a younger man, fitter and more vigorous.

He walked on in the silence. There was only the drone of flies, the dry scraping of crickets. He sniffed and caught a distinct tang of sulphur, blowing in the breeze from the direction of the Hot Pools.

He held himself very upright, with eyes fixed straight ahead. Only once did he cast a sideways glance, as he passed the mayor's house. Higo no Usemi and his family were all there, watching and waiting. Higo pointedly turned his head and looked away. Disowning him!

And yet, how often Higo had boasted about the deeds of the village's hired warrior! Small enough deeds, in truth: pursuing troublesome bandits, confronting a rabble of fleeing mercenaries, threatening the Fukori water thieves. But the prestige of its warrior raised the prestige of the village, the prestige of the village raised the prestige of its mayor. Higo's boasting had grown even as the actual deeds receded into the past.

Now, though, it would be the end of an era. Higo couldn't survive as mayor when the village was forced to re-locate. Everything would change, but Saito wouldn't be around to see it.

He lengthened his stride. It was no concern of his any more. The Hot Pools were half an hour's walk away.

The volcanic zone was in a state of exceptional activity. There was steam everywhere, and a stink of sulphur so strong that he almost gagged. Even the surrounding rock felt warm underfoot.

Weapons at the ready, he moved forward into the steam. Since volcanic heat was a fire-beast's natural environment, he guessed that the *gokami* would be in the very middle of the pools. For him, the heat and steam was just one more handicap in the unequal combat.

The pools were circular and shallow, some lukewarm, some hot, some almost boiling. Here and there stood massive boulders of pumice flung up by powerful geysers from below. Even as he advanced, a new geyser shot suddenly into the air. He heard it before he saw it: a mighty upwards rush that came back down with a smack of spray across the rock.

The *gokami* appeared as a darkness through the steam, like a hill shrouded by clouds. The reports hadn't exaggerated: it was truly twice as high as the tallest cedar in Oirinji Forest.

He calmed his breathing, slowed his heartbeat. Fear was as irrelevant as hope. He must study his opponent and work out the most favourable strategy. At present, he couldn't even tell where its head was.

He continued forward until he could see huge bronze scales like plates of overlapping metal. He was looking up at its hind legs and back. He ran through the lines of an old poem in his mind.

Nature unnatural, forged with heat,   Living in armour, the great fire-beast.

Waves surged across from pool to pool as another geyser shot up nearby. What was the *gokami* doing with its head? It seemed to be digging down into the ground.

Of course, seeking for volcanic heat! And the heat was rising to meet it! It was disturbing the crust of solid rock, encouraging the instability below.

He chose his ground for combat: the largest area of flat rock between the pools. He laid out his weapons, then went in search of a suitable boulder, as heavy as he could throw. The *gokami* still wasn't aware of him.

Returning with a spherical chunk of pumice, he measured his distance, then ran up, accelerating pace by pace. When he came level with his weapons, he hurled the chunk at the monster's hind leg.

There was a resounding clang! The scales weren't only bronze in colour, they were real metal!

The great body moved fast. Saito stooped to snatch up his sword and barb. He had just turned to face the head when the tail came at him out of nowhere. It knocked him flat and rolled him into the ground.

Crushed and battered, he hung onto his weapons while the weight passed over.

No time to count his bruises. He knew what would happen next. By the time he staggered to his feet, the tail was already sweeping back in reverse direction.

In a blur of bronze, it rushed at him. He bent at the knees and sprang upwards. Perfect timing! One step climbing, one step on top. As the surface sped under his feet, he kept his balance and dropped down on the other side.

The fire-beast shifted position, rotating further around. Saito looked up and saw a shadowy spade shape descending through clouds of steam. High above him was the monster's head.

His first impression was of glowing metal wreathed in smoke. Its snout was still hot from digging in volcanic rock. As he watched, the glow faded from orange to dull red, like a poker lifted from a fire.

Was it looking at him? The head was faceted in sharp planes like a cut stone. It was so heavily armoured, he couldn't see the eyes.

Look for vulnerable spots, he told himself. Shape your attack to your strengths and its weaknesses.

But it had had no weaknesses. It was magnificent. As a warrior, he couldn't help admiring its terrible beauty. His own imperfections were lost in the contemplation of its power. He forgot his stiffening muscles, his slowing reactions, his aging bones.

It was the embodiment of everything he had striven to become. He had trained in the use of weapons, but the *gokami* was a weapon in itself. He had learned to fight without conscious thought, but it had never known anything else. It was absolutely simple, noble in its simplicity.

He worshipped it—and attacked it. Raising his weapons, he ran forward with a ritual battlecry.

A great claw descended over him. Metal screeched, the air filled with rock-dust. The points of the talon struck deep into the ground all around. He was enclosed as if in a cage.

But the sheer size of the claw gave him a chance. The talons couldn't close to squeeze so small a body. He slipped out between the razor-sharp edges, pivoted, then plunged his sword into a chink between two overlapping scales.

Useless. He slid the sword in up to the hilt, and still touched only metal.

The talons moved, the chink between the scales closed up. The swordblade warped, splintered, then snapped clean off. He discarded the hilt and backed away.

He felt almost elevated by this proof of the fire-beast's power. In a strange way, he wanted it to be supreme, invincible.

The ground shook as the monster shifted again. He heard new geysers burst into life behind him, he was aware of hot steam and spattering drops of water. But he couldn't turn to look. Step by step, he continued to back away. Would the *gokami* strike with its head or its claws?

This time it was the other claw. It swung at him sideways, a casual flick. The force of the flick lifted him off the ground and sent him flying through the air. He fell backwards into a pool of scalding water.

He screamed in agony as the skin was stripped from his back. Then screamed again as a geyser erupted beneath him. He had a dim sense of being tossed high, high, high ...

It was the end—he couldn't survive such pain. His flesh was incandescent. When he landed on something hard and smooth, he hardly realised he hadn't come back down to the ground.

He looked out on a world of bronze. Shining plates like overlapping roofs, even larger than the scales lower down. He was in the valley between the fire-beast's shoulder-blades, just behind its neck.

It was so unlikely that his mind couldn't respond. He only wanted to get on with his dying. He had fought to the best of his ability, he had fought like a man half his age. He had earned the right to die.

The fire-beast was swinging its head to the left and right, searching for its tiny attacker. But it couldn't twist far enough to see him on the back of its neck. In any case, its search was directed mainly towards the ground.

No, no one could ask any more of him. But when he saw the gaps in the *gokami*'s armour, he knew he could ask more of himself. He had discovered its weakness after all.

The gaps appeared when it flexed its neck. The scales were less tight-fitting here, and lifted as they rode over one another. He could slip his barb into one of those gaps—if he could manage to crawl that far.

His body was a mass of pain, as if he'd been skinned alive. He picked out one particular gap and dragged himself forward on elbows and knees. The gap opened when the monster's neck swung to the left, closed when it swung to the right.

It was wide open when he reached it. He thrust his barb into the space between the metal plates. The barb met no living tissue. He pushed in with his arm, as far as he could. Still nothing,

He would have to crawl bodily inside. He rolled his head sideways and slid himself into the gap. Head and shoulders, deeper and deeper. The upper plate scraped against his back until he almost passed out.

Then the tip of his barb encountered something that wasn't hard and impenetrable, something yielding and gristly. He summoned his remaining strength and drove the barb home.

Saito had been dreaming. Long dreams of days and nights and days again. He had been thundering across landscapes, stamping over forests and fields, crushing everything in his path. He had dreamed of huge strides and tremendous speed—and a small inner wound that wouldn't stop stinging.

Awakening now, he couldn't remember the details, only the mood. Power and strength and a kind of grandeur...

He lay on his belly in the dark, rising and falling to the rhythm of a distant *thump-thump-thump*. So the fire-beast was in motion, and he was still half-buried between its scales. The thing in his hand must be the spear shaft. But what was the sticky wetness?

It was all over him. He could even taste its strange metallic tang in his mouth. Then he realised: he was lying in the fire-beast's blood. He must have swallowed it, must have nearly drowned in it.

He worked his way backwards and emerged into the open. Daylight burst over his head and made him squint. It was late afternoon, and the sun's beams came in low and level. Where they caught on the scales was a dazzle of gold and bronze.

He sat up. The blood was a dried-out river running back

over the scales. Dried-out, but with fresh red rivulets in it too. He looked more closely and saw specks of glitter in the red. Not ordinary animal blood, but bearing a sediment of bright metal.

Curious, he touched the ridges where the blood had coagulated. They were black on the surface, but hard and gleaming underneath. Encrustations of true bronze! Nature unnatural! He remembered the beginning of the old poem. The *gokami* grew metal armour out of its own bloodstream.

He looked to the source of the river. The wound wouldn't heal, he knew. The barb had detached from the end of the spear shaft and was now working its way deeper and deeper in. With its serrated flukes, it would creep through organs and soft tissue until it pierced the mighty heart.

A pang shot through him at the thought. Sharp and stabbing, close to his own heart. He dropped the spear shaft and turned the other way.

His gaze followed the trail of blood to where it vanished from view, beyond the shoulder-blades. He raised himself on all fours and began to crawl along the trail.

It was odd that he experienced no pain. He remembered how the scalding geyser had stripped the skin from his back, thighs and calves. He was covered in so much blood, he couldn't see his own wounds. But he hardly even felt his body any more. Perhaps the monster's blood had a protective, numbing effect?

The scales rocked under him, the shoulder-blades rose and fell. The fire-beast was running with enormous strides. He passed beyond the shoulder blades and looked out over its back.

The river of blood dropped down onto the great smooth curve of the wing-case, then fanned out over the side. Black and red, with metallic corrugations. It was hard to believe the *gokami* was still upright, let alone running, after all the blood it had lost.

He looked out further, over the landscape. Seen from this height, everything was very tiny. They were travelling across low hills forested with beech and pine trees. Irregular fields of millet occupied the pockets of flatter ground. Most of the slopes were now in shadow. It was an unfamiliar landscape, very different to the area around Kitake.

There were human figures, too. They fled from the *gokami* across fields, along paths, crying in shrill voices. Sometimes they fell flat on their faces, sometimes they made gestures of prayer or despair. Their panic seemed to increase even after the danger had passed. He felt no sympathy for them. Their behaviour was alien and vaguely ridiculous, like small pale monkeys.

He had felt the same way about them in his dreams, he recalled. Insignificant figures like small pale monkeys. He had seen so many of them scamper away from his thundering footsteps...

It occurred to him then that his dreams had been something more than dreams. They were too close to reality not to be real. But it wasn't his own reality. He had dreamed what the *gokami* had experienced.

Yes, days and nights and days again. Travelling across immense distances. Heading towards some goal. What goal? His dreams gave him only the mood, the inkling.

He turned and crawled back up the trail of blood. There was more bright red in it now, pumping out in spurt after spurt. Arterial blood. Inside the great body, the barb was approaching its goal. Which goal would come first?

He left the trail and climbed the base of the fire-beast's neck. The sun was sinking behind him, the sky darkening to a stormy plum colour ahead. But there was a light in the darkness, a fiery orange glow.

Volcanoes! He looked out around the curve of the neck and saw a great chain of cones across the horizon. Bare of all vegetation, ash-grey with streaks of smouldering red and sulphurous yellow. Already he seemed to smell the smoky fumes.

A second verse of the old poem rose to his mind:

Born in the depths of Mount Chiyo-san   Home of the monsters in the Burning Land.

Home, home, home. Truly, he felt that he was coming home. The mood of his dreams was his own mood now.

Another stab of pain exploded in his chest. His heartbeat shuddered, then recovered.

The pain couldn't stop him. He would die, but he wouldn't die of that. He would die in his own way, a greater death. The proper death of a fire-beast.

Whatever he had been, he was no more. Past and future narrowed to a single moment. The moment of standing on the rim of Chiyo-san, of unfurling his wings, of making the death leap. Heart bursting as he plummeted into the molten depths. He wanted to give himself back, to be un-made, un-forged.

The glow on the horizon lit up with a sudden gout of flame. From out of the middle of the Burning Land came tongues of red and yellow fire. A moment later, he heard the rumble, felt its vibration through the ground.

Mount Chiyo-san was bidding him welcome.

Very soon now.

He lengthened his stride.

LIKE A BUG UNDERFOOT

CHUCK MCKENZIE

So when I finally get down to Centrelink, I find it's been trodden on the previous day. Piles of shattered masonry surround a giant paw-shaped depression where the building used to be. There's a security guy standing out front (guarding what?) so I ask him which Big Beastie did it. He says he doesn't know, and his expression says he doesn't care. I tell him I've come to fill out a dole form. He says I can't do it here. I say, well obviously, but can he tell me where I'm s'posed to go now? He says he's buggered if he knows. I suggest he uses his walkie-talkie to ask someone who *does* know. He suggests I piss off. Prick. At least he's being *paid* to do bugger-all. I'm taking out insurance on the next regular DJ gig I land, instead of assuming my employer's covered for damage by Giant Monsters. Act of God, my arse.

I walk all the way back to the flat. Shitbox car needs a new engine. Could've taken the bus, but that $3.50 might be buying me lunch next week. Should only be an hour-long walk, but when I get to Annandale I find it's in the process of getting stomped, with the Army blocking access and redirecting traffic all the way out to Balmain. Up ahead I can see the 'Beastie—something like a T-Rex with tentacles—striding back and forth through the local shopping district. Back and forth, left to right, 'Beastie chased by helicopters, helicopters chased by 'Beastie. Don't recognise it. Might be a new one. I try chatting up the officer manning the roadblock: Any chance I could slip through? 'Beastie's not likely to notice a lone pedestrian. She says it's against orders. Translation: we don't want your next-of-kin to sue. So I take the two-hour detour, grinding my teeth as the noise of the 'Beastie's rampage slowly fades into the distance.

Can someone just tell me where the hell they're coming from? Bastards appear out of nowhere, rampage through an improbably localised area, then vanish. Last month the scientists were talking about wormholes to alternate universes. Before that, it was genetic engineering. Wish they'd just admit they don't have a bloody clue, and concentrate on swatting the bastards.

Dad blames the Japanese. For everything.

There's another bill shoved under the door when I get back (like they think I'll ignore it if they put it in the letterbox). Still can't bring myself to call the place 'home': a dark, mouldy, six-by-six-metre hole with fleas in the carpet. And now I can't even afford the lousy $150 a week it costs to rent this shithole.

Just one thing makes it worth being here: Tina. Only been going out for three weeks—still at the never-stop-shagging stage—and she's already moved in. I could use some stress-relief right now. Talk afterwards, get things off my chest. Great girl. But she's got a shift at the salon today, won't be back 'til after seven.

Still, gives me a chance to take stock of my finances, something I should've done as soon as I got retrenched. So: I know I've got about $200 left in my bank account. $5 in my wallet. Thought I had about $20 in change stashed in the kitchen drawer, but there's nothing there now. Must've frittered it away somehow. Practically broke. So—with no idea when I'm going to be able to put in a dole application—I figure it's time to hit the parents for a loan.

Not before looking at every other possible option first, of course. I've already hocked most of my valuables. I'd consider working as an escort (I hear the money's good), but I know what Tina would say. Old-fashioned girl, and I love her for it.

'Love'?

Well, if it feels right...

So it's the parents. And honest-to-god, I would rather stick needles in my eyes than make this call, but I'm desperate.

I haven't used the phone in a week, and I'm surprised to find it still working. Then I remember it's the *power* that's on Final Demand. The phone's on Reminder, and the gas isn't due for two weeks. Haven't lived in a place fitted with gas before, and I don't like it. It's bad enough the service gets shut down every time the pipeline gets stomped, but the next time some fire-breathing 'Beastie strolls past, the whole place could go up. The building superintendent—old guy living downstairs—reckons the agent's been promising to switch to electricity any day now. Sure. And then the rent'll skyrocket to cover the cost.

The call to Melbourne takes bloody ages to get through. A recorded voice waffles on about how they're experiencing delays due to circumstances beyond their control; code-speak for *some friggin' huge mutant reptile just burned our exchange to the ground.* But eventually the phone rings.

Dad answers. Mum I can get around without too much of a lecture, but dad's a tough nut. Lately he seems to *expect* me to stuff up, as if I ceased to be an adult the moment I left his field of supervision. So I just get straight to the point and ask for a loan, promising to pay him back ASAP.

"Well," he says, "it's not as if we have that sort of money just lying around. And you never paid back the removalist's fee to Sydney." Ouch. We both know he's never getting *that* money back.

"Listen," I say, "I *am* looking for work. There's just nothing available at the moment." All the local clubs have resident DJs booked already. But Sydney's a party town. Something'll come up.

"Local papers are full of ads for wait staff. I imagine it's the same in Sydney."

Boom. The room shakes slightly. Sirens begin to wail in the distance.

"Look, if I've gotta wait tables to pay the rent, that's fine," I lie. "But until I *find* a waiting job, I still need a loan."

Boom.

A sigh. "How much did you say you needed?" I tell him again. "Just about enough to pay off your debts and get back home, eh?" *Where we can keep an eye on you.*

BOOM! Car alarms are going off nearby.

It's like talking to a brick wall. He's always been like this: it doesn't matter what I say, nothing's going to change his view. So we argue 'round in circles, going over the same ground again and again, until I blow my top. But I *need* that loan, so I try to keep my cool. "Dad, I can't just move back to Melbourne. I live in Sydney now." Lame. "Something's bound to come along soon."

BOOM! Plaster dust trickles from the ceiling.

So what now? Maybe the famous *if only you'd worked harder at school* speech? Or *if only you'd put away some savings before moving out?* But instead, dad asks what all the noise is at my end. I tell him. He goes quiet for a moment, then tells me I'm always welcome back home, and he'll transfer the funds right away. Thanks, dad, gotta go, can't afford these STD calls right now. I hang up, angry and ashamed.

BOOM! The floor rolls under my feet. An ear-splitting screech rattles cracked panes. Against my better judgement I step to the window, and catch a glimpse of the 'Beastie as it strides past the flat. Not the Annandale-smasher, but about the same size, big as an office block. Massive legs pound holes in the road. Upper limbs wave spastically, like some nightmare *Thunderbirds* puppet. Rage-reddened eyeballs roll above a slavering, snaggle-toothed maw. Noxious secretions bubble between immense scales. Dog-sized parasitic insects skitter across heaving flanks. The smell is overpowering; sickly-sweet and cloying, like the reptile house at the zoo.

Fighter jets roar overhead. The 'Beastie screams again. A long spiked tail lashes out, and I jump back. *Crunch.* The building shakes, powdered masonry fogging the air.

And then it's gone.

Boom. Quieter now. The stench fades, but there's another smell—heady and choking, like methylated spirits. *Shit!* I throw open the window, then check the stove, but I can't tell whether it's leaking or not. The smell slowly dissipates, but I'm still rattled. Do I need to call someone? Tina would know what to do. Maybe one of the neighbours...?

I open the front door. Most of the other tenants are out on the stairwell already. The super's just coming back inside to tell everyone the 'Beastie's moving away towards Liverpool Road. Everybody nods, retreating back into their hovels without comment.

The old guy catches my eye. "Close one, eh? Tarrakis—he's a nasty one." He smiles self-consciously. "Grandkids collect the trading cards."

"I think I've got a gas leak."

"Want me to give the gas company a call?"

"Cheers." I nod and start to close the door.

"Shame about the building, isn't it?"

"Yeah. Still, could've brought the whole place down, eh?"

"No, I mean ... Oh." He squirms. "Didn't you get the letter from council?"

I shake my head. I probably did, but I always bin council correspondence. It's usually campaign crap. "Why, what's up?"

"They're going to knock the building down. Cracks in the foundations, from all the monsters stomping around. Not safe anymore."

The situation suddenly feels unreal, like I'm having a bad dream. "But—what happens to *us?*"

He shrugs. "*I've* lived here twenty-five years, you know ..."

"Yeah, well," I say, and begin to shut the door again.

"Oh, by the way," he says quickly, "there were some gentlemen here earlier, asked me to tell you—"

Debt-collectors. Great. I shut the door.

Shit. *Shit.*

The phone rings. Christ! Now what?

It's the cops.

"Do you know a girl named Tina Ashton?"

The back of my neck begins to prickle. "She's my girlfriend—is she okay?"

"Ah, listen mate, we've arrested her in connection with a series of thefts and frauds."

Boom.

My lip curls involuntarily. "Nah, listen, there must be some kind of mistake—"

"Yeah, you're about the fifth bloke I've heard that from. We've been after her for ages. Moves in with a bloke, gives him some tall story about her circumstances, then pisses off with his cash."

Boom.

"Had any money go missing? Cheques?"

"I ... don't know."

"Could you take a look for me?"

I put the phone down and pull my chequebook out of the (suspiciously) change-free kitchen drawer. The book looks intact. I smirk with relief. Then I notice a sliver-thin gap at the back of the tightly bound stack of cheques. My throat constricts. I flick to the back of the book. A single tell-tale fleck of paper peeks out from the spine, where several cheques have been torn out, stub and all.

Boom.

I pause, feeling nauseated. My head seems to spin. Then I pick up the phone again. "Ah ..."

"Thought so," says the cop. "Probably drawn against your

account with a forged signature. Better check with your bank. I bet she's cleared you out..."

His voice drones on, but my ears are full of white noise.

Boom.

"...need you to come in and make a statement."

Tears are streaming down my cheeks.

"You there, mate?"

I draw a shuddering breath. "I...I mean, are you *sure?* I was going to meet her folks next week—"

The cop laughs explosively. "Aw, sorry mate, I'm not laughing at *you.* It's just that we've been after this girl for a long time, and some of the bullshit stories she's been telling... Her folks are *dead,* mate. Died when Wollongong got stomped."

BOOM.

"So when d'you reckon you could come in and make a statement?"

With the car out of commission, I beg a lift.

"Sure, mate. We'll get someone over tomorrow." A pause. "By the way—I know this is a personal question, but...you *have* been sleeping with her, I s'pose?"

"Yes?"

"Okay. Look, ah, you should get an AIDS test."

I can't think of anything to say.

BOOM.

The room trembles as I hang up the phone. My heart pounds, breath coming in short, sharp gasps. Numbness grips me, adrenalin icing my veins. I feel light-headed and weak. The room seems to fade, patchy contrasts of light and shade pressing in, muffling the outside world.

BOOM!

A dull shriek pierces the fog. The window darkens. Helicopters buzz angrily overhead. The smell of alien flesh and petroleum combines to nauseating effect.

I *loved* her. Only three weeks, but...

And now—

It hits without warning, like a tsunami. Rage. White heat burns my face. I stagger, trying to scream, choking as my mouth fills with spittle. I want to tear the room apart. I want to crush, destroy, kill. Until everything lies in ruin. Until the pain goes away. But the rage is too great; I writhe impotently under its weight, unable to move, unable to breathe—

BOOM!

The impact releases me. Shrieking my hatred, I run to the door, slam it open, pound down the stairs to the street and out into the middle of the road. I stand there, shaking uncontrollably, mucus bubbling from my eyes, nose and mouth: the Hulk in trendy clubwear, roaring defiance at this shitheap of a world, fists clenched, ready to lay waste to all before me.

"*Come on, you bastards! Come on! Come on, I'll* kill *you, you bastards! Arrghhhhhh!*"

The 'Beastie looms over me, unconcerned, perhaps not even aware, as if I were a bug underfoot.

The thought enrages me beyond all reason. I scream again, ready to sink my nails into reptilian flesh—

This, I suddenly realise, is the 'Beasties' secret. Rage. Raw emotion, providing power enough to move monsters through time and space, to fuel rampages through brick and mortar and steel, to shield against the arsenals of humankind, the agonies of everyday life—

I grin savagely, glaring upwards, arms thrown wide in open challenge.

"Have a go, you bastard! Come on, have a go! I'll rip your bloody head off! Come on—do your fucking worst!"

A mighty foot descends, blotting out the world.

READ IT IN THE HEADLINES!

GARTH NIX

**ARCHAEOLOGISTS ENTER
FORBIDDEN TOMB!**

ARCHAEOLOGISTS FLEE FORBIDDEN TOMB!
TOMB FORBIDDEN FOR GOOD REASON

**GUARDIAN CREATURE
'DEFINITELY WILL NOT LEAVE' ANCIENT TOMB,
SAY ARCHEOLOGISTS**

GUARDIAN CREATURE LEAVES TOMB!
EXPERTS RE-CHECK TOMB TEXTS

PUBLIC SAFETY ANNOUNCEMENT
NORTH OF RIVER: LEAVE NOW

NAVY WILL STOP GUARDIAN CREATURE

"IT TUNNELLED RIGHT UNDER THE RIVER!"

**"GEECEE" KILLS 18
NAVY KILLS 2,117**

PUBLIC SAFETY ANNOUNCEMENT:
LIST OF SUBURBS TO BE EVACUATED

GENERAL NASHER:
"WE WILL DESTROY THAT THING!"

GEECEE ON RAMPAGE!

PROTESTORS DISRUPT GENERAL'S FUNERAL

PUBLIC SAFETY ANNOUNCEMENT:
NEW EVACUATIONS

PROFESSOR PENHOOD:
CREATURE NEEDS 'GOOD' HEART

THREE HEARTS **OR** *THREE TOES*?
TRANSLATION DISPUTED

GEECEE HEADING SOUTH-WEST

GEECEE *FIVE-TOED* **SAYS STOMPING SURVIVOR**

WHAT DOES IT WANT? THE PUBLIC ASKS

IT WANTS THE ARCHAEOLOGISTS!

MISSILE ATTACK KILLS 856
GEECEE UNHARMED

CREATURE RESPONSE TACTICS CRITICISED

PROFESSOR PENHOOD SAYS GEECEE HAS *HEART OF IRON*

IRON AND GOLD HEARTS MUST BE SWAPPED,
SAYS PENHOOD

GEECEE KILLS THIRD-LAST ARCHAEOLOGIST

ARCHAEOLOGISTS FERRISH AND DANCER
APOLOGISE TO CITY

DANCER GOES DOWN GEECEE GULLET
FERRISH HIDDEN FOR OWN SAFETY

GEECEE DIGS UP SECRET BASE BELOW CITY!

RESIDENTS PROTEST EXISTENCE OF SECRET NUCLEAR
ARSENAL:
GEECEE DIGGING CONTINUES

PROFESSOR PENHOOD RETURNS FROM TOMB

SIX TON HEART OF GOLD MOVED TO HELIBASE

DR FERRISH DEAD. *IS THIS THE END?*

PENHOOD SAYS RELATIVES OF ARCHAEOLOGISTS AT RISK

GEECEE MAKES GOULASH OF THIRD COUSIN

IT THINKS WE'RE ALL RELATED!

MASS PANIC.
MAYOR URGES CALM.

PROF TO DROP HEART BY HELICOPTER

HELICOPTER SPAT OUT OF THE SKY!
PENHOOD SURVIVES CRASH!

HEART RETRIEVED FROM
SMASHED HELI IN CRUSHED DELI

HEART ATTACK!
ARMOURED SEMI TO SMASH INTO GEECEE!

EJECTION SEAT SLIM CHANCE FOR HERO PROF.

PROF'S FIANCEE RETURNS RING

PUBLIC SAFETY ANNOUNCEMENT:
GET OUT OF THE CITY!

H-HOUR FOR HOT-ROD HEART TRANSPLANT

DID HEART HIT?

PLUME OF SMOKE AND DUST 5KM HIGH
PENHOOD'S PARACHUTE NOT SEEN

PENHOOD EMERGES FROM RUINS!

IT WORKED!

SUCCESS?
GEECEE DORMANT DOWNTOWN!

MAYOR, CITIZENS FURIOUS WITH PENHOOD
BILLIONS LOST IN REAL ESTATE VALUES

HI-TECH PERIMETER GOES UP AROUND CITY CENTRE

PENHOOD SUED BY PROPERTY OWNERS, CITY,
REAL ESTATE ORGANISATIONS

INVESTIGATIVE COMMISSION EMPANELLED:
PROFESSOR PENHOOD ARRESTED

PROSECUTORS DEMAND LIFE IMPRISONMENT FOR
PENHOOD

PENHOOD SENTENCED TOMORROW

**MYSTERIOUS GOUT OF
RADIOACTIVE STEAM IN CHANNEL**

**GIANT UNDERWATER SHADOW
MOVING TOWARDS CITY!**

GET GEECEE TO GUARD US! DEMANDS FRIGHTENED PUBLIC

PENHOOD RELEASED!

PUBLIC SAFETY ANNOUNCEMENTS
Ten page list...

THE QUIET AGRARIAN

PETRI SINDA

He caught Gorgeous George lying on the beach with all the indolence of a sunbaking iguana—admittedly one with glandular problems. Since his skin had the consistency of an unbaked potato, from a distance his huge form appeared unreal—an unconvincing crayon sketch—especially when silhouetted against the wrinkled sugarloaf karst peaks of the Cat Ba Archipelago. If anything, it was this optical protest that proved to Marvin he was back home in Vietnam.

Not that it was home *per se*, but he'd spent enough time away from Tuscaloosa to call *any* place he'd lived in for more than four years home. Collectively, this delocalised "home" stretched from Khmeristan to the island of Raivavae: a linear continuum, ideally, with strictly no repeats. (That was middle age increasingly pushing for fresh kicks…Marvin was overdue for his mid-life crisis and didn't dare skip it.)

Yet, somehow, these homes now seemed nothing more than memories strung like shrunken heads on a necklace for personal experiences.

So, here he was, taking a step backwards to 'Nam, once again consorting with unnatural giants. He'd always suspected it might become habit-forming.

Aspiring to wave to George, he cupped his hands and yelled, "See you soon enough!" The tourists from the nearby Doson Resort looked up but he drew nothing from Gorgeous George himself. The big guy's chest merely expanded and subsided like a circus tent taking up the play from a steady breeze. Would it have killed them to have given him a jolly green skin tone?

One look was enough for now. George was still here, and he was still gorgeous. Marvin hopped back in the cyclo and told the driver to head for the ferry back to Haiphong.

There was a surprise waiting for him at a patio table of the Mystery Karaoke Hotel, the first joint he'd picked after stepping out of the Giant Bat Bus Terminal. The surprise weighed about 104 kilos and came sunburnt in that hue only Australians knew how to (or wanted to) perfect. The surprise offered him another surprise: a pint of something called Little Creatures Sparkling Pale Ale.

"Russell?"

"Whassamatter, forgot how ta say g'day?" Russell made his point by leaning over and flipping a pint glass towards Marvin so that the latter had to catch it, swing it, swig it in one motion. This Marvin did, and he was a better man for it. "That's the way. Call me Russ, okay? Too hot to stand by formalities."

Indeed it was. They were surrounded by the torrid essences of perspiring bodies, their own novice skins wincing under a humid noonday sun. Russ detected a droning overhead. Drilling around at random, a swollen cloud of mosquitoes drifted overhead, ready to drop on them like falling netting. You had to learn to wear mosquitoes like a second skin.

The circumstances prompted time-travelling; already his head buzzed with memories of yard-sculling contests back in their Bond University days. Russell Betheridge had placed quite high in the Beerocracy. Prime Ministerial material, some had opined.

"Did you know I was due here?" Marvin asked, peeved.

Russ shrugged. "Whenever I blow in to Gookville I ask after *any* honky white folk. Found you on Guestsearch, but ya weren't here so I thought, y'know, I'd treat the liver to the old duelling contest."

Marvin grinned. "Is that right? And who's winning?"

Russ gestured off-handedly. "My doctor."

Marvin ventured to ask, "So what sees you around these parts? I thought the Daintree'd make you sick of the tropics."

Russ somehow unrumpled himself in his seat and set his ale down straight. "Look, I've kicked the failure-habit, okay? It ain't fancy but I've been stringing for a tropical rainfall-measuring project as an atmospheric chemist. Boss HQ wantsta sew up the model on how cloud micro-organisms and carbonyls manipulate cloud formation, rainfall...you name it."

"What's the game? Weather control?"

Russ slapped his thighs, glued his palms there as if ready to *sproing* himself out of an ejector-seat. "Marvey, I'm just a big F-aholic, remember. They've never even shown me a *brochure* of the Big Picture. This—" He took a wild look around "—is the shit-hottest gig I've had for *years*! Believe that? Years!" Russ turned his palms face up as if in supplication. Overdoing the hard-luck angle a bit, Marvin would have thought. Pride must suffer most from changes in fortune.

He recalled their undergraduate yahooness, and Russ' wild streak, how he'd been a fun-seeking missile with a mind to prove it, happy to direct his excess energy anywhere, anytime. Recently, however...well, life could be a tough market to crack. Marvin looked closer. Those wisps of grey hair. The coarse-textured lips. The dented white box of his skull showing through. His condition angered him. *Pity* angered him. Marvin looked aside, discomfited to have made the identification. He took an angry swipe at the pint glass and swallowed half of it in one go. "That's the way! That's the way!" he heard Russ cry, like a jockey flogging on his steed. What a sorry-ass creature.

A waiter ambled about, trying to attract guests to "Grilled Eel At Reasonable Prices!" Russ wagged a crooked finger to call him over. Marvin reached across and spritely slapped his hand. "Don't be like that. You're not summoning an animal, you know."

"Oh, I supposeda get the finger-lingo right, aye?" He brought his hand next to his ear and aped the screwing-in-lightbulb gesture, then snorted and roared for more beer. The waiter responded with his own doubtful screwing-in-lightbulb opinion of the situation. He knew Russ's current liver-content better than Russ did.

Russ began spewing profanities so Marvin stood up and grabbed a collar lapel. Time to get him out of there before he stunk out his own good name at the hotel. Now he remembered why they'd never really stayed in touch.

Nevertheless, turning him away would be cheap. Instead, he thought hard for a way to help him out. "Promise to take some Antibooze and I'll give you the grand tour around my work. Guaranteed to restore your ambitions squeaky clean."

"Beats having to stare at these monkeys."

Marvin gave him a shove to show him the general way.

As they walked, Marvin shunted away thoughts of the guy by his side. He reminisced about the Vietnamese first accepting George. In particular, the time George went waddling out to tend to a Mnong village—the kids quit fishing from the bomb craters and chased after him. They dragged out bazooka megaphones and, seemingly with puppetmaster access to his ganglia, compelled this seven-storey posable dummy to model for their art class. This battery of little Svengalis ordered him to lift his knee *so*, make a teapot handle with his elbow like *that*. Finally, they settled on George holding a ballet pose while they painted his size-210 feet with paintbombs.

Objecting did not occur to George. His was to do or die, not to reason why.

And do he did. Each season, his ecological remediations improved. The nation rallied around him. With his role as caretaker of the nation consolidated, in an absolute sense Gorgeous George *was* Vietnam.

The hems of the passersby never touched the spongy mud that stood in for Haiphong streets; the ghostly white conelike *ao dais* just floated serenely past in glaring contrast to Russ and Marvin: the implacable squelch of mud-boots.

Some electric fishermen overtook them on Nguyen Tri Phuong. They utilised pitchforks electrified by car batteries strapped around their waists. Head spinning, Russ drank in the sight of all the white silk trousers, cheongsam and blue silk mandarin coats passing by. Everywhere the twitter of gossip as they made their way towards Marvin's office at AgriGnosis, or AgriKnow, as the workers preferred to call it, contemptuous of their marketing division's idea of an appealing trademark.

"Hey sport, you ain't said what you do there."

Russ drank from a bottle as they walked.

Marvin scratched behind an ear. "Well, I was on the first brainscan team, and had an affinity bond with Gorgeous George in particular—"

" 'Gorgeous George'…wasn't that some boxer?"

"Like I'd know. At any rate, these days I'm strictly freelance. Mostly I light out from the Centre for Microcontamination Control in Tuc—"

"Oi! You know Cameron Byrne?"

Marvin made a face. "Can't say I do."

"Oh. Don't sweat it. Go on." He drained his bottle and flicked the last drops out across the road. For a moment, Marvin thought he was going to underhand it beneath one of the roadside stalls.

"Yeah, well, Congress wants three old-timers to do a progress report on AgriKnow: there's 14 billion globos *each* invested in these guys."

"That's what I don't get. Isn't it cheaper to go with Jap robots?"

Congress was thrashing out the same debate. The Japanese solution to looking after their aging populace wasn't ever going to feature the mass importation of foreign carers. Instead, they kicked their robot industry into hyperdrive and within a decade saw their industrial base go supercritical. The resulting economies of scale allowed them to saturate the global market in cheap robots. Some felt the "Robot Economy" threatened the established order. From hell to breakfast, societies were no longer conforming to Pareto's Law.

"Well, let's see. Just as China's about to become a Superpower, Japan powers ahead with its Robot Economy. So robots get banned in all Chinese Protectorates. Including Vietnam."

"But *these* giant monsters are all a-ok by the Mandarins?" he asked doubtfully, complete with shit-eating grin. "What can your cutie do that robots can't?"

Marvin wolf-whistled. "If only you knew. He's the ultimate can-do man. Simian Redesign squeezed a thousand utilities into him. He's a biomass eater for a start—by all rights he should be the poster boy for The Global Appetite Consortium. See, George has a hundred specialised guts for sorting nutrients from the standing crop biomass he munches. He batches up GM-enriched neo-protein SupaHumus. Customises fungi and blue-green algae to help nitrogen fixation. Extrudes root capillary systems right throughout a crop, making a three-dee map of the subsurface—a fractal soil examination at high rez. This lets him calculate the *exact* duty of water it can take; helps him redesign its ideal chemical and water transport system. *He saves provinces at a time, Russell.* Single-handedly helps the nation recover from typhoon or drought. Supports tens of thousands of people throughout Bac Bo. *Singlehandedly.* Ah, the other Georges mosey around from Laos to Khmeristan, but the Vietnamese are damn lucky to have him all to themselves: he's in tune with their land, their needs. I swear Gorgeous George *cares*, and that makes all the difference to yield."

"But I'd heard they're dumb as a box of hammers!"

"True, George's so big he puts dinosaurs to shame. Brain's a lot bigger, but he still runs into the same motor impulse time-lag problem. Shares the same solution, too: fifteen ganglia distributed throughout his body to coordinate everything. Not enough, usually; every now and then he requires guidance. So, grafted to each ganglion is a telefactor circuit, mated to some microtubules. We access him by remote, man a ganglion each and give a little correction whenever the overseer computer detects he's going a bit wobbly—and bingo, he's fresh as a daisy."

Marvin fretted those occasions when his neural traffic phased out of equilibrium. Gorgeous George sometimes went *this* way when he thought he'd told his legs to go *that* way—suddenly he'd find himself playing Twister with himself in a dirty paddock, with tourists somehow always present to capture this kinky act and spam it onto the Net. Whatever people had originally presumed Gorgeous George was for, he was now considered a skilled comic mime in the super-heavyweight division.

"Sounds perfect!" Russell chimed in incredulously.

Marvin sighed, massaged his eyelids as if to release unwelcome images trapped there. "The Georges are imperfect organisms. We know that. Augmenting Splices is an imperfect art, and emergent, quirky little things always crop up. But, you know, these glitches kinda make George human."

"If you say so. Can I see him then?"

Marvin laughed. "He's taking a nap by the beach, but I'll show you around his brain once we make office."

"Time for a beer before then?" Russ whined plaintively, only half-joking.

Marvin clapped him on the shoulder. "It's the strength of your convictions *I* admire. C'mon, move it!"

The Brain Lab was a tad empty at the moment. Only four people manned consoles on the far side of the room, screened off behind a chest-high partition. He took a step inside but stopped Russ from joining him.

All four walls were lined with flatscreens displaying neural telemetry coming in realtime from Gorgeous George. There were at least two adjacent ones for each ganglion, so that stereoscopic displays could be produced even if the VRML coding crashed. Grafted to the microtubules alongside George's telefactor implants were forty or so tiny phase-contrast imagers. They exploited x-ray refraction to peek into George's ganglionic activity at a hundred times the resolution of the best hospital fMRI scanners. Twenty petaflop computers took the telemetry and reinterpreted it for human senses. At his shoulder, Russ whistled.

Marvin followed his gaze and noticed the eighteen telefactor rigs tasked for direct neural hotwiring. Oh, it was going to be good back in the hotseat, riding pillion in George's brain, feeling his sensorium vasten to match George's scale. Riding pillion, the powerful feeling of vastness came from the sheer bodily distance that George's sensory-motor traffic had to travel. Body-expanding, rather than mind-expanding.

Yet, with all this one-to-one isomorphism with George's mentality, there was really no sense of human intelligence. He just wasn't... *there.*

He heard imperious footsteps clipping along towards them. Dr Josephine Campbell intercepted them just inside the doorway, her eyes automatically flying to the guest badges they'd had to pin on back at reception. She wore florid glasses: an old-fashioned affectation? They shook hands. She said nothing.

"I'm Doctor Marvin Brandau—I know I'm a few days early but I just wanted to show the joint to my best mate here. This is Russell Betheridge."

Dr Campbell reached out and curtly shook Russ's hand. Russ didn't let go. Bending over, forcing her ear close, he whispered, "Don't pay him any attention. *You* can be my best mate!" He let go and stood back, a cocky smile playing about his lips.

Marvin clapped him roughly on the shoulder. "My best-behaving buddy here has been seeing the glass half-empty of late. One session with Gorgeous George should set him right. I'm certain George's successes are single-handedly influencing the regional air-sea cycles Marv's atmospheric science team'll be studying. I'd like to give him guest-access to our data. Prove George is the living avatar of Gaia."

Russ shrugged free of him. "That why you're busy showing off? You weren't even *plannin'* on introducing me to the ladies?"

"Dr Campbell? Care to set him straight?" Marvin leaned back against a workbench and crossed his arms, smiling mildly.

"I can spare a few minutes... for your *mate.*" She kept a straight face. "The government wanted to free up the seventy per cent of people who used to work in Agribiz. Enter Big George, stage left. In-skin, he's got the tools for everything. His exoskin lays down a semipermeable membrane which can selectively remove nutrients from the watertable; it retracts into his body when he's done. He houses microbial fuel cells in his guts, fuelled by the proteins and lipids in the sewerage he scoffs down; what's more, he breaks down the organic waste while he's at it—he's a walking sewerage-treatment plant!" She flashed them a triumphant smile.

"Waste not, want not." Russ issued with meek conviction.

"Our George has got over a hundred specialised guts—"

Marvin cut in. "Yes. Told him."

"Is that right? You mention his specialised teats?" Turning to Russ, she announced: "Livestock depend on his teats. They like his AgriCola best."

Russ jumped to ask, "Do you have a sampler?"

"Uh...it's not exactly recommended for humans," she said, nevertheless signalling a willingness to make an exception in Russ' case. "Anyway. George. The American War against Vietnam. Ecocide. TCDD dioxins. George filters the dioxins *out* of the contamination hotspots."

"Whoa, again please? He digs them outta the—?"

"No, no...George visits a village and unspools as many filter-umbilici as they need—say a hundred villagers at a time. He keeps changing their oil until he cleans out their environment. He's a regular one-man Gaia." She began counting off on her fingers. "Also does land reclamation, pollution amelioration, coordinates the conservation of raw materials, handles pomology, oleiriculture...but there's only four Georges for the whole of SEAsia. Pity Team Gaia cost more than five aircraft carriers." She turned to face Marvin squarely. "That's why it's crucial our good work here be supported. *Congressionally.*"

Marvin spread his hands out in the air. "Hey, ditto—same side, remember?"

"But you've *been* back home. Infected by the politics."

He challenged her. "You're what, caught up in rumours about a UNA...?"

Russ tapped him on the shoulder. "Speak English. Or failing that, Confederate."

Marvin shrugged the hand aside. "Never mind. That's enough of that. Doctor, mind if I give him a quick joyride in the hotseat?" Dr Campbell's look indicated just how thrilled she was but she simply nodded, flipped her fringe away from her eyes and strode out. Russ nudged him in the ribs and whispered, "I think she likes you ... "

"Tell me everything."

Russ eased into the hotseat. Several see-through screens swooped in to shroud his head. Signal transients from George's biometric ID tags ghosted across the screens in green-gold flickers—phase-contrast radiology scans of his vital organs. One by one his somatic signatures clocked in, a checklist undergoing autoverification. Reaching in front of Russ, Marvin play-tapped on a virtual keyboard and disabled extraneous features until all that remained were Brain Atlases of each of George's fifteen neural ganglia. By observing the changing fireflies of neural activity sparking at each loci, and cross-referencing all that coalescent flux with the interpretational software, you could tell what George was doing twenty-one kilometres away.

He was no longer sunning himself on Doson beach. He had gone out for his afternoon constitutional. Good for him.

"Judging by the climb of those chemical gradients, I think he's readying himself to transfer apomictic traits to some crop plants."

Keen as a puppy, Russ fished after explanation. "He regulates them, too? Stops accidental gene transfer? Your Boy Wonder takes it all upon himself, doesn't he? What's he ask in return?"

"A good scratch behind the ears."

Russ mused, "Aren't the best crop strains hybrids from seeds produced by apomictic plants?"

"These days, sure. George maps the crops, catalogues them, resets the *elongate* gene that controls apomixis, tracks their performance...farmers here are set for life if their hybrid crops can keep cloning themselves. George is the ultimate green-thumb—that's why he's so gorgeous. And he's great with kids. Some days he lets them ride on his shoulder, or hold onto his ears."

"So you gonna let *me* ride him or not?"

Marvin stopped, gave him a lopsided smile. "Certainly." He reached up and drew down an elastic cord. Taped to the taut cord was a ring bristling with fibreoptics: if he let go it coiled a few centimetres back towards the ceiling. "Go on, close your eyes." Marvin initiated a few safety-test sweeps of Russ's temporal lobes and neocortex. A maze of retinal overlays gridded in over the active screens. Russ conserved his breathing, the room suddenly hushed as a cathedral. Marvin enabled the telefactor rig to mingle Russ's presence with George's, but set it on passive so Russ couldn't influence George without warning. He waited until he heard the satisfied sigh of awe. No one had yet managed to control their emotions the first time they affinity-bonded to George. *To spy on someone else's mind from the inside...*

Marvin checked over the interpretational display, following the amorous plethora of neural fireflies as they weaved their nests of purpose and causality inside Russell/George. The sinuous exploration of a will temporarily combined, submerged within the presence of its limits. Marvin was a voyeur once-removed, eavesdropping on someone eavesdropping on another consciousness, hoping something of the displaced mystery would rub off on him, like sympathetic magic. It was like art.

He led himself away, unwilling to present the slightest distraction. Besides, he was slightly jealous of first-timers. He was one of those people who could only see a film once, the first time. Without surprises, consciousness promptly relapsed into a glorified screensaver. (What loop played while *he* slept?)

He pottered around the office and reacquainted himself with the consoles, excited about the upgrades.

A flash clipped him from behind, simultaneous with a minute boom of sound that ripped through him like a tide through soggy paper. He stood paralysed for a moment, then he was running through the doorway, peering left and right. A black mushroom cloud about a metre high rose from a slightly buckled wall panel. Were the circuit bundles inside connected to the telefactor gear? He called out behind him, "Russ! Better get out!" No one else had yet arrived—he had to grab the fire extinguisher himself. Swearing, he did the job. Other workers joined him once he was done.

"What was that!"

"You tell me. Hey, get that guy out of the bull harness! Get him out of it!" Marvin waved away smoke.

Russ didn't appear. Annoyed, he strode over to take care of the recalcitrant prick himself, only to collide with him in the doorway. "Let's blow this scene, mate. Something's squeezed out all the juice."

Marvin sighed. "Okay. Done." He turned to the workers prying open the affected panel. "We're going. If you gentlemen could convey my regrets to Josephine...and tell her I didn't touch anything."

They waved him away, unlikely to have heard a thing. Marvin turned to Russ and said, "Let's grab that beer."

"I feel a bit ripped-off. You owe me big time."

Marvin replied with a silent sip.

They were drinking Budweisers—his choice—at the Emotion Cybercafé, listening to the *tring-ring* of passing cyclos while idly sampling a platter of Laughing Cow Cheese. French doors had been opened out to give the joint more air. Sunlight already glazed the lip of their table. Inside, the blades of the air-conditioning fans in the ceiling sluggishly recycled the humidity. They were modelled after Huey chopper blades. In the corner sat three men passing around a bong. It was in a crashdive and trailing bongsmoke...a scale-model of a B-52 fuselage. Painted flames trailed from the nosecone...the prestige of The American War lofty as ever.

Russ had been goading him into inquiring what the hell had torn his life apart, but Marvin had no interest in taking that bait. Desperation angered him, too. The afternoon had become stillborn, invested with a silence of deep apartness.

"I need a drink!" Russ exclaimed, slapping the table too hard. A drink in the sun is worth two in the shade. He reached out to a passing kid, one of the owner's young sons. "Hi! Listen, more beer, aye? Two! Two!" He held up the necessary number of fingers. The boy waited, impassive. Russ tousled the boy's hair. The boy squirmed free and ran away, excitedly crying out.

Marvin leaned over and hissed at him: "Fer Christ's sake, man—don't touch kids on the head! This is mostly Buddhist country!"

"Marvey...? How izzit Yanks always say Bhoo-dah? Can't you hear vowels well? It's short, sharp; rhymes with 'good'. Say after me: *Bood*...TAAHH...!"

"I mean it. The head is sacred. And don't point your feet anyone's way—it's goddamned rude."

"Let me guess: it's the 'lowest' part of the body."

"Thought so! You're only stupid when you want to be." Russ shrugged proudly. Marvin said, "Man, you're an idiot-savant who missed out on the savant."

Russ accepted this flattery with a bow. He said, "As flowers, we disgrace ourselves; as shit, ah, we excel incomparable!" He gave the last word a French lilt. He signed off with the sentiment: "How we live depends on the glitches."

Marvin thought for a moment, remembering. "Ex Australis semper aliquid novi," he said.

"And you call *me* pretentious!" He reached for his bottle, once again saw it was empty; swore.

" 'There's always something new out of Australia.' "

"*That* I'd like to drink to." He put his hands on his knees and rocked forward in his rattan chair as if about to spring up. Suddenly, nothing happened.

Examining Russ, the strange hard nemesis of his face, Marvin noticed Russ' eyes alight from his and fix on something behind. Creeped out, Marvin whirled around. He saw a young girl in school uniform. She was reading steadily, holding a book in front of her face as she crossed the road. The traffic careened past her, around her, without effort, without fuss or abuse, while she remained coolly oblivious. Aloof. Serenely death-defying. Her eyes wonderfully wide, but only in regard for whatever she was reading.

Marvin hadn't felt his heart beat so fast in ages. A chill flashed through him. *What could she* possibly *be reading...*

He turned to see Russ trying to catch her eye. He had his fingers crossed, raised in the air: trying to summon a prostitute. He recalled the Aussie penchant for treating SEAsia as their personal whorehouse.

"Russell... it's obvious you're walking flypaper for demons. Do me a favour and don't disgust me for five minutes. What do you say?"

Russ caught himself, lowered his hand. Sheepish, but a bit put out, he complained, "Once, whores cost a ciggie a night."

Marvin got up to buy more beer. He tried to enter the bar but a plug of cigarette smoke forced him back. He coughed, wet his fingertips to rinse his eyes, and tried again. He brought back two beers of some Chinese brand. Incongruous volumes of cigarette smoke followed him outside, like ailing wraiths begging for favours.

They drank in silence. The heat was sour. Everyone succumbed. Under the shop awning across the street was an old man of about eighty. Sitting down cross-legged, he resembled a tangle of sticks. Marvin wondered whether his dream-slow movements were impaired by too many whiffs of opium—or was that cups of green tea? One of the *doi bui*, he diagnosed; the "dust of life".

Gossip gargled back and forth across both sides of the street, audible even above the road traffic. Neon slogans in a dozen languages crowded the shopfront windows, intermingling in a neo-hybrid gestalt that went far beyond "Spanglish". Many of the signs were emblematic of fancified million-dollar-bills. The United States may never have conquered Vietnam but Tourism certainly had. Vietnam was a many-headed perpetual-motion machine testing the limits of change. Marvin was glad: it gave him the same kick as Hong Kong.

At last Russ broke the spell by asking, "So how long you gonna camp out here? I'm probably pulling up stumps in ten, fifteen days."

Marvin wiped his hand through his hair. "Christ, I don't know. A fortnight with each George should do it, I guess."

"We'll have time to catch up again?" Marvin pretended he hadn't heard. Russ continued, "Say, how *fast* can you pull up stumps if everything goes pear-shaped?"

"What are you yabbering about?"

"Like…the States' imminent second war with China…the return blow for the injustice of flaking out in the first one."

Marvin scoffed. "Not that China won either!"

Russ agreed. "No, no; Taiwan should never have nuked Three Gorges Dam."

"Mmm. No one expected that. A twentieth of China killed with one missile? That still leaves, what, a billion pissed-off hornets for their armed forces to choose from?"

"Yeah, real smart tactical move, that, giving Taiwan red button on their nukes. *'The concise exercise of democracy'*," Russ intoned with presidential pomp. An old euphemism for any surgical military strike. Russ was right. Because of that one ecological supercatastrophe, a future war was guaranteed. Russ noticed something in his face.

"You don't think you'll win the next one either?" he demanded with some concern.

"Nope."

Clink. A depressing toast. They knocked back half a bottle each. Russ met his eye. "We can blow this little world apart with firecrackers," he claimed, as if inviting Marvin to sign a pact. Marvin nodded back. "I *know*. History's *forgotten* quicker than it's made."

"Oh, that's right, analyse the Christ out of it," he replied, disgusted. Marvin caught the squirt of fury in his eye. He found himself emanating shame for some reason. What? He'd missed something. God, he was sick of being subjected to these endless needles in his ears.

"Too much improvement is worse than none at all," Russ continued with rock steady conviction.

"Russell…what on Christ's earth are you on about?" He let all the tiredness in his body come out at once. His body was starting to reject Russell. He was an emotional toxin.

"Me? What about you and your Repetitive Belief Injury? Christ this, Christ that…God above must be real proud of ya, most loyal of his dogs…"

That was enough for Marvin. He jolted into life and stood up, fists balled. Russell, insanely enough, looked up with zeal, his pupils fat with bloodlust.

Marvin was about to grab him when he noticed his beer bottle shaking with jewelled bands of interference. They criss-crossed to and fro, shuddering to a slow and steady beat. Possibilities immediately raced through his head. Had one of the minefields crept into town? When one went off, others tended to get jealous and leapt to join in.

"Russ, maybe we—"

"Maybe you shut your trap and please tell me that's Fat George."

Russ pointed behind him. And up. Marvin looked.

"Ah, the Gorgeousaurus himself...and Russ? George ain't fat." As they whispered, neither took their eyes off the huge dark shape now lumbering through the streets several blocks away, parallel to the Cam River. In fact, for all they knew, George could be wading *in* the Cam.

"Someone who weighs, what, a hundred-fourteen tonnes ain't fat in your book?"

Marvin noted that Russ unconsciously considered George a *someone* rather than a *something*. A rarity, where Spliced avatars were concerned: 75% human tended to be viewed the same as 0% human.

Russ rubbed his bristly chin. "That's Tiny George, aye?" he said, somewhat in the way Aussies dubbed redheads Bluey. "He's a li'l beauty. A barefoot original. Uhm, wasn't he educated at a Montessori School for Overdevelopers?"

Marvin remembered the first footage he'd ever seen of the young Gorgeous George. The paparazzi had found him lying doggo among a classroom of late-teen basketball giants until his learning problem was finally noticed. He'd been a couple of months old at that stage. Neither Simian Redesign or Somaplastic Industries had given out clues to what he would one day become.

They heard whistles, cheers, sirens floating out over the rooftops. Gorgeous George had attracted one of his crowds of wild admirers. That usually meant one thing: his ganglia were temporarily out of synch.

Smooth governance of so many brains simply was not a 100%-of-the-time proposition. George was awash in an ocean of stormy nerves. Flux overvolts tugged to and fro at his ganglia, driving spurious voltages through the fuses. Surges raced through his neural labyrinth. George could get lost in the funhouse before he knew it, subjected to a snarl of warped mirrors. Motor navigation became a game of Snakes and Ladders. Delusions of omnipotence swept the ganglia as each limb rashly set its own agenda. East turned into west; south defected to the north; and, however much George bent over low to peer through his legs, he always found down a long way to the top.

He, in some strange power's employ, did not move in a rigorous line. Curvilinear motion had mounted a coup and overthrown every sensible causal regime. In short, George was having Elvis problems.

Slowly, his legs began to wobble—nay, gyrate! He traded forward motion for Brownian motion and still ended up short-changed. His feet wobbled independently of his legs, like someone on skates whose wheelnuts had been loosened. Before long, the Elvis action in his pelvis would send the whole left leg flying off into the crowd.

No, George certainly was not waddling in the Cam like a duck (not yet, anyway), but he was wading through a river of bodies, and the bodies were mostly children. The whole mass turned onto Tran Phu as one, heading right towards them. The sound level jumped.

Russ smirked and said, "So I'll call him 'Le Hombre Invisible' then?" Marvin ignored him. Tryhard.

The inevitable happened. George's legs tripped over each other. He came down like a Russian orbital booster. Marvin protected his ears. Hooting in triumph, as if they'd accomplished this through massed force of will, the children rushed in to throng George: tragedy abhors a vacuum at least as much as comedy. Common knowledge reigned that, once Big George was horizontal and surrounded by little fast-moving things, he was programmed not to get up, or move, based on the sure likelihood of accidentally squishing someone. The police procedure was to whisk the area clear and set up a safe perimeter. All the while George would have to sit there with forbearance, submitting to a barrage of laughter or paintbombs. Eggs, if he was lucky.

Marvin could pick out a near-subsonic moan that only he recognised as George in distress. The distress of humiliation. George didn't feel much, Simian Redesign always claimed, but Marvin was convinced you didn't need emotions to possess a sense of dignity. He was a cognitive theorist, and he wanted to get his cognitive theorising brain out of there before it did any more thinking. What he did want was to get back into the rig, feel what George was going through. He decided. He slapped Russ on the back and handed him his unfinished bottle. "I'm done. See you around."

Russ turned to him, his brow knitted in concern. "To appease the gods, shouldn't we arrange a shotgun wedding with Godzilla?"

"I'll have my boys sneak a look into his datebook."

His dream guest-starred dozens of Georges of all ages and sizes finding themselves trapped inside the limestone karst rocks of Halong Bay, as if the karsts were blocks within which sculptures of George awaited discovery. Indeed, when the dream tides came in they washed the limestone excess away, revealing these Georges within, at last freeing them to breathe and move. And yet, as the tides renewed themselves, Marvin noticed they were in fact washing the Georges away too, leaving behind gaping nothings...

...and he found himself awake, an alarm-bell tearing his skull to shreds from the inside. He had trouble pulling himself together. A tinny voice kept chiming, "Dr Josephine Campbell calling ..."

That fixed him: his HeadMenu waking him with a priority interrupt, a massive injection of neurotransmitters into his hypothalamus, where alertness was regulated. However, since he was caught between different circadian rhythms, the high was artificial. His vision lurched dramatically. So did the rest of him for that matter. It was afternoon, and alcohol-assisted siesta time at that. Russell had managed to lure him out to yet another liquid lunch at a Beer-cuddle Bar, after he'd promised himself not to.

Josephine was yelling:

"George's gone crazy. He's tearing the docklands apart! Just get to the Lab." And gone.

Groggy with parasomnia, Marvin tried to understand. He winked in and out. Microsleeps beckoned.

The Lab? To hell with *that*. He got dressed. Lit out for the Harbour. He wanted to see this for himself.

Reconditioned junks and boats chugged across the harbour by Southend Pier, only now they had something new to avoid besides flat-bottomed *thuyen thung*.

George was wading in the middle of the Harbour, arms suspended out in front of him, a gesture uncompleted. Waterfalls dripped from his elbows. He appeared calm, and seemed to have recovered. Marvin had arrived too late. He was glad. Mostly. Even as an old Russian saying came back to him—"When giants dance it's best mice get out of the way"—a sickening excitement clutching his stomach testified he would've liked to have seen him in full flight.

He had his HeadMenu call Dr Campbell. "I'm at the riverfront. Show's over. George looks like he's in shock, though. What's the telemetry saying?"

"Don't kid yourself. His traces are a regular Himalaya. Watch him! He's due and peaking."

Marvin whirled round. George was beating his head.

"Oh shit...Josephine, *what happened?*"

"Epileptic seizure, near as we can tell. Look, I have to man the rig." Her voice turned to steel. "You get right here. We're short." She broke off.

George raised a foot onto the pierside. Climbing up, he saw the shorefront Maritime Museum, a knock-off of the prototype of its kind in Fremantle, Western Australia. Struck by its menacing resemblance to the bugs he was programmed to eradicate as enemies of the soil, he bellowed in outrage and charged it.

Marvin grabbed a quick look at the museum. From this angle he, too, saw a resemblance to a five-storey bug trying to crawl off the port and escape into the sea, warehouses entangled in its appendages. An honest mistake anyone could make. But Gorgeous George could be ruthless; he wasn't about to let it escape.

He piledrived into the museum and peeled half of it open, then the metal piled up into an artistic new conformation and began to resist. George stopped, seized one of the derricks just behind the museum—kookily positioned to mimic antennae, Marvin felt sure—and snapped it off. He rammed it into the back of the Maritime Museum's carapace, triumphantly pinning it to the dockyard. He put one foot on its back and flicked his head back and forth, bellowing incoherent victory. Then he began to flay it at leisure. George peeled open a sweeping roof assembly to get to the delicate marrow within...and found other li'l two-legged bugs inside, scurrying to and fro in a panic that would have shamed termites. Eeuuuww...how distasteful! His ganglia were not programmed to hurt two-legged weevils like these. Frustrated, he tossed the bug-shell aside. Puzzled, flexing his fingers, he looked far out to sea, still roused to action. Absentmindedly, George broke off the bug's other feeler and toyed with it at the corners of his mouth, in the manner of his two-legged friends just after they had eaten. The bug had probably been indigestible anyway.

Nevertheless, his head still hurt.

At extreme magnification, he spotted something out to sea.

Marvin pulse-burst Josephine in a hurry. "Hit the cut-outs! I don't care, pull the core pins! Just isolate the ganglia." He broke off.

What George saw out to sea was the resting body of an outrageously oversized mosquito. Its legs were folded in under itself, sticking straight down into the sea. What did it think it was, daring to grow as big as he? Comprehension dawned on him. Where had it stolen so much blood to grow so big? From the little people, his two-legged friends, that's where! His brain boiled! He had to teach it a lesson!

Furious, he picked up the rest of the Maritime Museum, slamdunked it into the sea as if putting away rubbish, and strode off into the harbour towards the oil rig.

A few paces out, he simply stopped. He swayed. Tottered. Arms outflung, he fell backwards, parting the Cam River like the Red Sea. A warehouse found itself rakishly wearing a Chinese junk like an exotic hat at a fashion contest.

Becalmed, George floated sunny-side up. Dr Campbell had succeeded.

Above him perched robot derricks, still swivelling about like giant preying mantises trying to choose between him and the container ships that were their customary fare. Marvin felt the urge to charge at them like Quixote, warning them off: "Leave George alone!"

The back lot behind AgriGnosis's Brain Lab had once been the Divine Calmness Bamboo Garden. Gorgeous George sat there nursing a four-tonne headache. Surrounding him was a Stonehenge's worth of neural transducers and imagers mounted on huge articulated servo-arms. Marvin found it hard to ignore George's unearthly subsonic moaning; it unsettled his bones. He sought out the Staff Supply Sergeant and found him in the rumpus room.

"Say, you got Gecko-strips?"

He certainly did.

Marvin took a few strips and double-ended them back on themselves, then slung some loops around his fingers. He hoisted his pack onto his back and walked up to George. He stretched upwards as far as he could reach, slapped his palms against George's hide and stuck there, clinging tenaciously. He reached down, lassoed two strips around the tip of his boots, and began scampering up George's flank, relying mostly on fingertips. While climbing, he mulled over his recent conversation with Josephine.

"Sorry, equilibrating his ganglia took longer than expected. Worse, he seems resistant to new programming. Something's screwy. I need you to go image his brain directly."

So here he was, climbing towards the black-box recorder in George's skull. The Gecko-strips carried synthetic kapton setae the size of Gecko hairs, exploiting the same intermolecular van der Waals force they relied upon. Marvin had rarely used them, but, without fail, he found hanging from glass by a few fingertips or climbing a slippery vertical surface exhilarating. The danger was in braking suddenly, straining ligaments, tearing muscles.

Tricky, but so god-damned-much *fun!*

George, feeling his presence, craned his neck to look down at him. Marvin waved sadly.

He clambered onto George's potato-soft head and steadied himself by hanging off an ear. He unpeeled the Gecko-strips and stuffed them in his pockets. He unslung his bag and pretended to set up a sub-millimetre wavelength imager. He didn't know who might be looking. He arranged the equipment in a ring to obscure the device he'd packed first, right in the centre of the pack.

Few outside Simian Redesign knew Gorgeous George had a trapdoor in his skull: a port that gave highband-access to the key telemetry on his consciousness. He was looking for a specific period. The neural activity tracing the onset of George's epileptic fugue. He found that period, downloaded it into his personal slate, then backed it up in his HeadMenu. That was Josephine satisfied. But his real purpose here was to install Forecast v8.83.

From the moment Josephine mentioned epilepsy, Marvin had wondered how he could protect Gorgeous George. Forecast seemed the best bet. It would record his brain activity and work up a profile, alert for activity that approximated any onset of epilepsy. Forecast averaged eight minutes advance notice. The recommended procedure was to immediately lie down. Yet lying down on the spot might prove problematic for George, if he happened to be strolling past a childcare centre or a pottery business. (If only he could guide George to a polling booth in time.) With George, *any* advance notice that he was brewing up a Mt Saint Helens would be worth it. Before he finished up, he retasked the black box's telefactor utility to transmit the warning telemetry to his slate only, burst-pulsed and encrypted.

As he descended (too fast! too fast!), he wondered if George would ever let him ride on his shoulders while he ran across farmlands, his arms out by his side like a toy 747.

Even before he took himself aside and reviewed the data, he posed the question: Was someone scapegoating George by telefactored manipulation of his ganglia?

He uploaded the black-box data to Madhusree Siddiqu, his longtimer in the Department of Homeland Security. It didn't take her many days to get back to him.

There had been an anomalous download to George's ganglia. Propagating slowly, surreptitiously, it had delayed for many days before linking together to execute its program. The initial download most closely matched the day of Russell's first visit to the Lab. His disarming tendency to ask Marvin a whole bunch of dumb questions. That circuit fry-up...how it had removed everyone from the room but Russell, stuck alone in the telefactor rig. But who had provided the ganglionic phage?

Marvin contacted the Centre for Microcontamination Control and searched for a "Cameron Byrne". The traces were scant, but recent. He was a lobbyist for Chinese agronomics. Come campaign-donation time, his wallet waged a fierce war on behalf of tariff reductions.

Russell had longstanding Sinophile interests, come to think of it. In his honours years he'd gone to Shanghai on student exchange. Why there, of all China, Marvin had never known. Considering how cosmopolitan Shanghai was, he might as well have chosen Tokyo or Hong Kong. That was when they'd drifted apart. Who knew whom Russell had turned into behind his back?

He shook with anger, furious with himself for being such a soft target. However, he could now say: "I know what's going on."

If Russell could demonstrate that George was as vulnerable to hacking as Japanese robots had on occasion proven to be, discrediting US agritech, China could sweep in and "save" Vietnam, legitimising its claim over the "Protectorate" in the process, as it had tried with Taiwan...

...And Australia could rush in and pick up the four Georges for a song, retask them to sniff out uranium in Kakadu National Park. Russell worked for ASIO. Had to. He was chairing some espionage against his US allies. For his Sino allies instead. The "Great Game" well afoot.

Marvin reviewed current Australian public opinion. Over the last decade, a dangerous level of grass-roots sentiment had swelled up in favour of Australia's emplacement in SEAsia, rather than holding out as another bastion of honky whiteness. LiberalFamilyFirst could well be smelling the wind, preparing to tack. Marvin was a touch surprised, considering the historically essential conservatism of the Aussie character. But, well, one thing he knew was that government existed for government's sake alone. In any line-up where principles that justified screwing over the public were considered, staying elected always came first. Therefore, Russell the proxy agent engineering an agrimarket crash. A precision sniper amidst panic raiders.

For a moment, Marvin faltered, wondering if the police would agree to put out an APB on him. Then he rediscovered his purpose. To get even.

He made some enquiries with Revenge Unlimited and ended up signing a Contract.

All of which proved too late.

It was late morning when the alarm from Forecast vibrated inside his skull. A nightmare on speed-dial. Marvin dropped what he was doing and got his HeadMenu to paste the pre-epileptic telemetry over his visual field. A rollicking rollercoaster of zigzagging spikes, building to a frantic Rocky Mountains. The seismograph of a disintegrating soul. Eight minutes, he hoped. He put in the warning call to Dr Campbell.

All too late. Earthquake.

Marvin flung himself under a doorframe before he realised *no, not earthquake*. He opened a window and flinched as a massive concussion blast drove through the streets like an air hammer. Then he raced up the stairs to the roof.

Gorgeous George was destroying buildings close to the Du Hang Pagoda. Down went the Century Riverside. Vertical Quay housed thirty-odd Skyhoppers in its bays. Big George smashed it, too, toppling it over before a single hopper could swoop free. Electrical arcs whipped the air in flailing Catherine wheels. He tore through the residential suburb, leaving buildings tipping to and fro like houseboats in a stormy bay, his eyes wide with a greed to destroy. Then George stumbled, battered at his head, at his arms and legs, as if trying to put out invisible spotfires. He rolled round and around, collapsing apartments beneath him like boxes of playing cards. Splinters jetted out in explosive clouds. Did he have fleas? Was he itchy? Parasites? What was wrong? *Was he feeling sexy?* His frolicking about did seem rather sensual…

The residents disagreed. They fled the area screaming, but death lashed down on them.

Marvin had never before seen a seven-storey *grand mal* seizure; now guaranteed never to forget. A look of agonised comprehension spoiled over his face. This was the end for George. Pets with rabies had to be destroyed.

Could Dr Campbell muster a pull-out in time? He called.

"Forget that, you idiot! Get here with first aid and *help out!*"

Of course.

Doing triage with a hundred-tonne homicidal maniac contaminating the makeshift OR proved an anxious proposition.

While among the garbled corpses, he took care to sidestep the individual rubble of their skeletons, but, distracted, Marvin couldn't avoid stepping on slippery bones. He thought he could help one victim, until he reached behind the man's skull and found it all disarranged like a rotten squash. He found Dr Campbell tapping him on the shoulder, asking him to help replace slippery tubes of intestines back inside a girl, but she died the moment he touched her.

Not a few of the Vietnamese recognised him and excoriated him while he treated them.

The work was hard going. But as he treated wounds, spraying antiseptic blue gel directly onto affected organs, a difficult idea worried at him. He dredged up what he knew of anti-angiogenesis and managed to recall how this programmable gel could be tweaked to suffocate fibroids and tumours by blocking their blood supplies. He bumped into Dr Campbell again and quickly explained his idea. George's ganglia had to be physically taken out of the picture. Not by killing them—that was murdering George—but killing the organic telefactor devices mated to the ganglia. The seizures would stop propagating back and forth. He'd probably lapse into coma, but at least he'd stop reducing the amount of available real estate.

He had to try it. Anything to save George.

Dr Campbell tried to stop him quitting the makeshift OR, but he broke free. Time to find that Staff Supply Sergeant again.

Russell and his shit-eating grin found him first. He leaned out from a wall by one straight arm.

"I've no time for you," Marvin spat out in disgust. He shoved at the arm but it didn't budge. The man was stronger than he appeared. "What's the matter, Marvey?" Again Marvin yanked at the arm. Russell relented, raising the arm like a boom gate, but as he did a change overcame him, arresting Marvin mid-step. He was not the same man. He was Christopher Reeve changing from Clarke Kent to Superman before your eyes. His posture was that of a professional, a uniform-without-a-uniform.

"You won't find anything, mate. In a few minutes an EMP-bomb will wipe all data for klicks around. I go trackless in this world and you aren't about to mess that up." Russell stood like a commando spoiling for a fight.

Defiant, but increasingly helpless, Marvin sighed, "I just want to halt the seizures, okay?"

Russell smirked sceptically. "You can't accomplish anything. Face facts. You're just not a player here."

Sick of this childishness, Marvin tried brushing past him. Before he knew it, his head was ringing. Concrete stung his cheeks where his face was mashed against a wall. The pressure eased and Marvin slid straight downwards. Gingerly he felt his jawbone.

"...Shit. Here," he heard from somewhere above. He felt arms yank him to his feet. Russell glanced embarrassedly up and down the corridor, brushed Marvin's shirt creases straight.

Gulping, Marvin wheezed out: "When did you grow balls and become an ASIO adventurist?"

Russell hesitated, looked down, smiled to the ground and, when he looked up, nodded. Marvin recognised him for the first time since university. "Okay, you pinged me as ASIO, fine. I'm only gonna tell you this because no one can verify a fuckin' word you'll say. ASIO, yes, that's my junior sponsor, but my real patron is Japanese robotics. Freelance industrial espionage is far more lucrative than the public sector, as you should well appreciate."

Marvin's head was pounding. "I don't get it."

"You don't…? Let's say the Japs want *someone* to demonstrate that even the organic consciousnesses of Splices are hackable. Guess what then? They'll product-launch their new generation of quantum-encrypted cyber brains in their autumn mass-robot release—that's what then. Great publicity. High reassurance factor." Marvin had never seen anyone look so smug, not even politicians hours away from dumping their running mates.

It all fell into place. *Russell had played him for a patsy beyond his wildest dreams.* He'd *relied* on Marvin to catch him out, finger him as a traitor and point the bad finger towards China.

With him the ready-made fall guy.

Slowly, he eeked out: "So this is all a money thing?"

Russell let rip a roar. "Isn't everything? It's why anyone joins LiberalFamilyFirst! ASIO is the fast track to the best business contacts going. But I'm all sweet now, so I'm getting out of the Patriotism Game."

"Governments take traitors seriously. They'll—"

"Mate…they're *all* like me back home!"

But Marvin was thinking more of Revenge Unlimited, and their exceptional success statistics when it came to long-distance payback.

"Marvey, you fail to appreciate the bigger picture here. For years our dear mates the Libs have been lobbying for an end to the UN. *Your* country—" Here Russell jabbed a finger into his chest. "—wouldn't dream of undoing all that progress. It helps that we're working to the same blueprint. Chinese engagement *has* to be discredited before all these Leftist bastards pollute our great country. The milksops of your sad 'Reality-based Community' have done enough damage, thank you. I mean, who wants to have peace in a universe of everlasting blah? No, the States are the only model for us—a great model. We want in. Deeper in. Since our FTA, we—I mean LiberalFamilyFirst—have been collecting a pretty big lobby group in Washington, pushing to let Australia join in as your 52nd State."

"Oh yeah, sure," Marvin murmured distractedly, rather amused. "Just like Israel: Li'l Spanner wants to work the Big Spanner. How cute!" What a Foolocracy.

Russell clipped out his next words with military precision. "It will buy some leverage for *the real launch*. Favourable PR, hands linked across the world, etcetera. Aww, don't look *stupid*. Quit fucking around already; make a push for it! Go! Inaugurate the United Nations of America: the world is waiting!...Well, maybe not the whole world, but the part that counts. Us." He thumped his patriotic Australian chest. "Know our new logo? '*Men Able to Turn the Soil of a New Way*'."

"Yeah, you sure are dedicated to finding new ways to turn soil into grave-plots, I'll give you that much."

Pitying this recalcitrant defeatism, Russell hollowly clapped him on the back goodbye. Then he sauntered past him as if he'd never seen him at all.

Marvin could still hear George brawling with the buildings outside. There was still time.

Marvin took something for the pain, collected a pair of Quickwalker boots and more Gecko-strips and scrambled off after George, the polymer gel already reprogrammed. He cursed Russell for delaying him. At least he had lied about the EMP. Just trying to wrong-foot him.

He found George on his back, turning weakly from side to side, the seizures fading. He paused to consider how to smuggle George out of—

Another source of rumbling came to his ears. Helicopter rotors. And, not too far behind, an armoured military convoy. He began to sprint as fast as his little powered legs would take him.

As always, far far too late. A plasma-cannon squirted a hairline ray hot as the sun at George, peeling his shoulder open to the collarbone. He whirled in pain, saw the tank, and in one motion plucked the roof from a building nearby and lobbed it at his assailant. It disappeared. Four simultaneous detonations mauled George then, boxing him in flame and debris. Lucky misses all. But he had mere seconds to live.

George turned and ran.

Attaboy! That's the ticket! Who said he was dumb? Bravo! Then Marvin was running after him.

The titanium heels of the Quickwalkers housed engines driving hydraulic pistons that could propel people along at forty kilometres per hour. Marvin made fifty. He kept George in sight as he tore through the cardboard of Lach Tray Stadium and escaped past the Lake of the Restored Sword, leaving the artillery well behind. The helicopters were another matter. They pestered him with small arms fire and the occasional RPG.

George improvised. He yanked an old tree from the ground, twirled it into matchwood between his hands, stuffed the lot in his cheeks and expelled, *hard*. The shrapnel tore the sky apart and one helicopter along with it. Gone, simply reduced to aerial confetti that fell with a heavy clatter. Lightly peppered, the other helicopters reconsidered their positions and decided forty kilometres away was a respectful distance to maintain.

George was going to make it. Would he swim beyond Vietnamese territorial waters? Or hide out in the highlands of Quang Ninh Province? Martin saw him reach the city limits. *He was going to get away scot-free.*

A cloud of dark smoke kicked up around George's feet, startling him. For some reason he shielded his face and staggered. Then the sound wave hit Marvin. A mine. He'd stepped on a mine.

Heart racing in beat stampede, Marvin stopped and topped out the magnification in his optics. It...didn't look *too* bad. The foot was intact, mostly. It would slow him down though; and in the sea attract sharks. Better he lead George to the—

Then he had it! His dream! He remembered his dream! *Hide George in a cave in the Cat Ba Archipelago.* The limestone karst formations were home to plenty of caves. There was still a chance, a big chance—

When the next mine went off, Marvin conceded. He waited ten seconds. Sure enough, the ground ahead writhed as if agitated by gigantic grasshoppers.

Gorgeous George had blundered into an intelligent minefield.

He'd survived to walk away from the first one.

So the minefield had followed him.

The last was a comic, unintentional consequence. Marvin knew the US had commissioned these "self-healing minefields" to foil specialists who cleared minefields. Each smart-mine had ultrasonic sensors and radios to communicate its position with its neighbours. When someone stepped close and cruelly forced a mine to sacrifice itself, the others reorganised their positions to accommodate the empty spot. Piston-driven feet flipped them three metres through the air. They hopped about in this fashion until they once again achieved a roughly equidistant formation. This took ten seconds at most, and was as beautiful a sight as it was thrilling. The Chinese had sent them hopping across Bac Bo for years now, but never before so close to the coast.

This minefield, continually sensing dropouts in its numbers, worked hard to plug the gaps. Every time George moved he ran into more mines, which created more gaps to fill...George was soon caught in a homicidal vicious circle. The intelligent minefield pursued him in this dumb way, hounding him, tenacious as a dog, despite the rapid depletion of its numbers.

Finally, George outpaced the minefield. But the cost had been far too great.

Opaque waterfalls of blood cascaded from a dozen gristly wounds. Devastated, Marvin stared at unrecognisable blobs of flesh that jiggled up and down as they swung from ligaments now stretched too thin. Whenever George paused, they twisted in the wind like demented weathervanes. Marvin noticed craters with bone floating around inside.

George knew what was happening. He stood waiting for the last mine to finish him off. After a minute, he comprehended he had outwitted the minefield. "No..." Marvin gulped out, as George stepped back towards the minefield. He hesitated, turned around, then resumed his slow painful haul to the coast. He had to drag himself over the earth, sad as a mutilated elephant.

George's progress was now pretty slow, but who could stop him? Marvin followed to track his death. No one deserved to die alone.

At top speed, the Quickwalkers gave Marvin a four-metre stride. The buoyant suspension gave him an amazing sensation of flight, as if the Earth had lost most of its gravity. He loped along in slow motion, the wind serene upon his face. He felt a rare bodily peace. Such horrible contrast to George: he didn't dream of downloading George's vitals. However, he deliberated how long he himself could go on; the boot tanks only held enough fuel for 30 kilometres.

Villagers jeered them as they passed. Some threw projectiles. The most inspired threw Molotov cocktails or sticky burning oil rags. Marvin guessed that, with his faithfully accompanying presence, he was sentimentalising a monster that had just half-destroyed their local city. They pelted him for his ongoing insult to humanity.

We are all alone, he became convinced. He looked to George; he wanted to matter to him.

But doubted he did.

The beach was still hazed behind faintly jewelled mist when George arrived. From here, the unearthly karst peaks resembled nothing more than the Pillars of Creation in the Eagle Nebula, only earthbound in dark limestone. Marvin blinked, cleared this brief fling of cosmic vertigo.

George slumped over as soon as he reached the beach. Spray tossed up in the air and engulfed him in a momentary white shroud. Stretched out, half in, half out of the water, he cranked his head about to face Marvin, a face that understood the dignity it bore. Marvin's heart lurched to a stop, and he had to close his eyes. Reopening them took considerable effort.

Marvin took up station five metres away. He removed his Quickwalkers and planted his feet on the tideline. He enjoyed the surf enveloping his naked skin. He did not withdraw his feet when the surf turned red and coagulated to his soles. But he began to avoid those wonderfully wide, unblinking, turquoise-flecked eyes. Serenely death-defying. Strange how he'd never really paid attention to their subtle little colourations. Minute by minute the eyelids drooped and folded their colours away.

He thought about how, primitive as George's brain was, in some respects it nevertheless contained a model of him, drawn from their seasonal relationship over the years. How *much* of George's brain was hardwired with a "Marvin Brandauness"? Did a little Marvin sleep among the folds of George's brain? He thought: *How much of me will perish along with you?*

Perhaps no one really died alone after all.

Was his soul yet touched by the black? He felt like climbing up on George and going to sleep on his back, sealing an ear to his skin to dowse for his heartbeat.

Living with death on a beautiful beach. A state perhaps incomparable for futility, but he could never abandon George. He didn't move throughout deathwatch—simply listened to the parallel murmurs of the waves; slow, like the sluggish beat of an unwell heart.

Deathwatch: Marvin pictured giving out pairs of glasses with the lenses blacked out.

George's ganglia began to short out one by one; everywhere his body was rocked by brain lightning, severing the ganglia from each other. Disconnected tremors jumped about so that he twitched like an unoccupied reflex machine. He was crumbling apart. Marvin had never seen its like. Before his eyes, George was shaking apart into a mass of seizures. Worse, as death spread exponentially through him, it subdivided his brains into fifteen separate cells of solitude. Gorgeous George would die alone, at least fifteen, sixteen times over.

Marvin shivered. No one had ever died like this.

He could not tell whether hours passed, or many minutes. Clouds moved in to break up the uniform radiance of the mist. His awareness fell on the creased lines of monochrome foam as they surfed up the beach, fizzling on the sand like spittle from a drowning victim. Marvin felt himself slowing down until he was a thousand years old, matching the geological calm of the rocks as they stood sentinel with him.

Then George died with a mighty rush. Marvin found himself unable to eavesdrop on this most awful apotheosis. He sought out the sea, the super-eminent karst peaks. Yet he caught movement springing from George's corpse. He followed a yellow glow sweeping out over the sands, watching as it penetrated rock after rock until it soaked inside the karst towers, absorbed. Impregnated with light, a silent aurora crowned their peaks: the flickering wings of a spirit so powerful its wake had scraped out a path through the rough fabric of the world itself. Then the glow elapsed, winked out, and he understood he'd been looking at a train of bright afterimages from a gap in the cloud cover, nothing more. Optical trickery. Vietnam magic again. There was no spirit. No soul. Gorgeous George was dead.

He remained there some time more until the sky darkened. After each wave receded, he had to re-identify the thing on the beach. The slimy death gas issuing from the flesh was becoming hard to ignore, particularly by scavengers. He hated thinking about the maggots swimming about inside him.

He ventured some elegiac words: *"He strove beyond his—"* But gave up, words suddenly so fake, flimsy. He felt reduced to a boy again. Helpless, raw, devastated by the loss of a lifelong pet. He couldn't stand it.

He thought of the Buddhist Festival dedicated to all those who died without descendents.

He recalled how he had told Russell the head was sacred to them. Finally, he knew it was time to stand up. It was done. Over. He heard a sound by George's thighs. Walking over, he discovered a pig lapping and slurping at the remains. He did nothing. Exhausted, he shambled over to Gorgeous George's head and stretched out trembling fingertips; a loitering attempt to be near the unique constellations of his thoughts. However, there was nothing but dead sky inside. He gave a bitter squeeze and left.

•

Years later rumours winged their way around the world; weird rainbow seaweed had begun to drape the beach and the karst outcrops. The tides arrived as successive deposits of rainbows, cumulative heaps that forever changed the colouration of the beach. The general opinion was that some portion of George's protein nanomachines had seeped down into the shore and cannibalised enough energy to survive on some crude level, desperate to conserve their programming. As ever, even to the least of him, Gorgeous George remained the quiet agrarian, unwilling to abandon his obligations.

Marvin knew that one day he would have to go back home and check out what those rumours were made of.

In Final Battle

IAIN TRIFFITT

Everything else had been tried: proselytising, land warfare, biological warfare and finally diplomacy. Yet still the three major religions—Judaism, Christianity and Islam—could not reach a compromise. There was only room for one of them on the planet, and so it was decided to resolve the question once and for all by the only means left: giant robot prophets would battle each other to the death.

A massive stadium was built in the radioactive waste that lay across the Tigris and Euphrates Rivers. All one million seats were filled by true believers of the respective faiths. The final battle between the cyberprophets was to be televised throughout the world, however—except in the Islamic territories where it would only be broadcast over radio, so that the faithful would not have to gaze on the image of MechaMohammed.

First blood, or in this case oil, went to the sixty-foot CyberChrist and its stigmata beams, which turned the full polyethelene beard of the RoboRabbi into a raging fire. But the Judaic robot was not daunted. Enraged, it spun its Blazing Dreidal of Doom, five-foot-thick spinning chains ripping the Papally blessed titanium from the CyberChrist's legs. The CyberChrist toppled over into the dirt of the stadium, and lay prostrate at the feet of the MechaMohammed.

The MechaMohammed unsheathed its Mighty Sword of Jihad and brought it down on the head of the CyberChrist. The CyberChrist activated its Rotating Crown of Thorns, shredding the Mighty Sword of Jihad into a million razor-sharp shards, the bulk of which embedded themselves in the RoboRabbi. The latter uttered a tiny metallic *oy vey* before exploding into a million pieces.

The CyberChrist struggled to its feet, a panel opening in its chest. From within itself it pulled a fifty-foot glowing crucifix. Startled, the MechaMohammed took a giant step backwards as the CyberChrist swung the cross at its head. But the blow connected and sparks flew from the Islamic terror's turbanned cranium. The MechaMohammed grabbed the CyberChrist by the ears and headbutted it.

At that moment a shadow fell across the two combatants, a huge shape blocking out the sun. Cheers erupted from a gaggle

of eco-terrorists who had smuggled themselves into the audience.
At last their own prophet had arrived! Its massive saurian head
turned heavenward as it let out an incredible roar that destroyed
the hearing of the worldwide audience and overloaded the
broadcasting equipment.

The prophet of Gaia stomped MechaMohammed and
CyberChrist into a thousand fragments. Then it turned its pitiless
gaze on the audience. The Gaians' cries of joy turned to screams
of terror as their prophet scooped them into its maw. After sating
itself on the remainder of the audience, it lumbered back towards
the Gulf, shitting human refuse along the refertilised Crescent.

THE UNLAWFUL PRIEST OF TODESFALL

PENELOPE LOVE

The two travellers, exhausted from days without rest, stumbled out of the unclean wood onto the brow of a desolate hill. Their clothes, reduced to filthy rags, were sodden with sweat in the afternoon's heat. The rains were close but it was not their time yet. The whole landscape sweltered in the oppressive humidity, and pleaded mutely for release. Olan Season haze softened distances and rose in long lazy wreaths of clouds that hid sight of the sky. Before them swept a wide vale of tawny cropland descending to the city state of Uerth on the shores of the Lake Everlasting, created long ago by the damming of the Uerth river. The travellers' cracked lips pursed with thirst at the sight of the water. But on that blue and placid surface no sails showed.

The city-states of Uerth were once a collection of isolated, fortified towns, but now they were all grown together. The huge city bristled with towers of the nobility, and was generously slabbed with the fat full squares of warehouses and crammed granaries. But there was no movement, no clamour of people and animals, no reassuring, living stink. No smoke rose to soil the soft haze. The city-suburb of Zaijian, the last and least of the city-states of Uerth, lay before them, abandoned mute and defenceless to its last agony.

"Where is everybody? Has Todesfall arrived and gone already?" cried Asneath, sick with dismay. She was a small, bony, plain, fair-haired woman, her large green eyes grey-ringed with weariness, her white face taut with strain. She wore torn and stained rags, once Frir's robes of gold-trimmed green. Around her neck hung Frir's amulet, a small greenstone with the circle and the sickle carved on it.

"No. There! Look!" Baoqian exulted. He was tall brawny bronzed man, twice his companion's size, with a slab face and shaved head. His muscled body was naked to the waist, covered in Olan's blue tattoos, and an immense axe was strapped on his back. He pointed with a thick finger at a dark shape that filled half the horizon, the merciful haze a veil between the living and full sight of Todesfall's face. It was so large, Asneath had simply missed it, assumed it was a mountain or thunder cloud. She felt despair seize her as she realised for the first time how colossal Todesfall was. She strained her eyes to pierce the haze, even though she dreaded what she might see. She had so hoped, so hoped, for she knew not what, some gift or freak of the gods that would save them—but what could save them from this? Todesfall was immense, beyond mortal hope of moving.

Then Asneath screamed, for the shape lurched nearer, all at once, tearing aside the haze like a veil and for a moment giving them clear sight of all except its face. Baoqian seized hold of Asneath, reflexively, as a vast tremor shook the ground. In the city below, paving stones gaped like lover's lips. Stone walls rippled like water, water reared into walls and some fair towers fell to ruin, with distant, pitiful roars.

An immense statue of black obsidian strode through the lake towards Zaijian. Yet, for all the terror of its unimaginable height and inconceivable weight, the statue had chubby arms with the useless plump little fingers of infancy. It had dimpled knees, and above a babe's adorable penis rose a curved soft swell around the bulging belly button—all clearly visible, even from this distance, because of vast size in which they were etched in unyielding obsidian. The face hidden by haze was undoubtedly chubby, too. The watchers could imagine the rounded cheeks and soft features, the dimpled nose and double chin. Imagination pictured the face more vividly than the real thing.

The statue moved slowly, so each footfall took hours, so slow that it threw mere human watchers into an agony of impatience to watch it. Yet each step took it countless miles. When a footfall landed, the land ran like water and the water reared like land. The statue stepped, the towers fell, the aftershocks tumbled one after the other like echoes. The travellers neither moved nor spoke until all was still again.

"Let go of me," Asneath said then, in a voice that cut ice blocks from the summer heat.

Baoqian let go at once. "Todesfall is much bigger than I thought," he said, weakly.

"Of course, idiot," Asneath snapped. Baoqian had saved her life, but his insistence that they echo the ritual relationship between Olan and Frir grated away her gratitude. Now he voiced her fears exactly and in that moment she hated him. "That's what they all said, all of them that are dead. He *grows*," she said.

"If all is as they said, there is still hope." Baoqian dealt with dread of death better than Asneath. He was trained to deal with it, and meditating on Olan kept him calm and inspired within the world wreck. Besides, once the statue stopped the haze blurred its dreadful outline once again. He remembered his god could deal with everything, even this. "One day Olan went hunting—" he began.

"Can't you do anything besides tell stupid Olan stories! Can't you actually say something comforting for once!" Asneath shrieked.

Baoqian subsided, hurt.

Asneath closed her eyes, each freckle standing out like a

scream on her white face. She remembered Baoqian had saved her life. She remembered she needed his help. She remembered that he had tried to sleep with her only once, and given up when she resisted. She murmured a prayer to Frir, and Frir gave her strength. She opened her eyes. "I didn't mean to be rude. I'm sorry. When do you think Todesfall will arrive?" she resumed, on a calmer note.

"Soon. Tomorrow or the next day," Baoqian guessed.

"He must not. He must not!" Asneath choked.

All the world was wrong, and some said the Great Ending was at hand. The gods had deserted them. Olan and Frir had answered prayers for help only by saying the right aid would come to the right souls at the right time and place. Rimbaud the bat, Rimbaud the crone, bringer of rebirth, was gone from her moon-roost. At night the moon's face shone broad and white, with no shadow upon it. That was bad, for Rimbaud left the living only in times of great death, when many souls needed her help on their way through the dying lands to new life. And all because Todesfall walked where he should not.

Todesfall was the son of Olan and Frir. He had killed his mother when he was born, and cost his father much trouble to fetch her back again. Todesfall, the Dark Child, kills all he touches and knows not why for he has no more understanding than a day-old child. His father had to banish him to his own realm of Dying for the sake of the world.

In the Dying lands, you must wait until Todesfall comes for you, until you see his face. The sight wipes all memory away, and then you are on to your next life and the lonely land of Dying is behind you till next time. Although it is said that sometimes he will relent if you appeal to him in his mother's name, even though she left him alone in a strange land. Only Todesfall dwells in the realm of Dying, alone and forever, forever and alone. And that is where he is supposed to remain.

"We must find the well in the north square, as we were told," Asneath said, trying to be brisk. "Then this will be over, one way or another."

Baoqian nodded. But he did not step forward. The city below would hold many dead. The dead were born of the Dance of Death, and they wanted you to join in. There lay the problem.

The Dance of Death was simple, a half dozen steps. A child could learn it. You danced and whispered your enemy's name, and in the night your enemy died. The Dance started in Zaijian some months ago, and spread from there to the rest of the world. It brought on a terrible time, a dying time, when many were found to have enemies that deserved none. But then this statue of Todesfall started to walk and the Dance of Death ceased to work, so all saw the dance was a spell created for the statue's benefit.

The statue was far away then, in the north, in the vale of the White Shang. It had been smaller then, much smaller—no bigger, it was said, than a baby. It was hidden in a temple of the lawful priests of Todesfall, those who ease the path of the dying into Todesfall's dark land, who lay out the dead, and guard their graves. No one outside the temple knew of the statue, for it is forbidden to make an image of Todesfall for fear the god will like it and will walk. Instead, by law, the priests are compelled to worship a block of obsidian.

The statue grew as it walked. At first it was slow, a step a day. At first the growth was not large, one inch, two, three. The lawful priests of Todesfall tried to keep it hidden. But one day its head broke through the dome of the temple and they could keep it secret no more. Then those that were killed by the Dance of Death came back. They found their slayers and carried them away.

The living tried to break the statue and could not. They tried to wall it in. That failed. Every night the dead returned and danced around the statue with their murderers still living in their arms, murderers who called for help until they died themselves, then fetched their families and friends to join their merry jig. The more that died, the bigger the statue grew. The only way to slay the risen dead was to chop off their heads, and they came in such waves that even the stoutest warrior could only slay so many before being seized by eager hordes and whirled away.

By then the statue had passed from the White Shang, where it caused much distress, through the Moon marshes to the city-states of Uerth, which rose in horror and dismay. The living fled. The Lady of Frir of the White Shang, and Lord Utan of the Five Duchies summoned a great assembly of the most powerful lords and warriors to decide how to deal with it. The Lady of Frir had seen the statue depart. Her gentle soul craved to heal all, even Todesfall. Lord Utan was the most powerful lord of the Five Duchies to the east of Uerth. His lands lay next in the path of the statue's advance. The assembly had the lawful priests of Todesfall brought before them, in chains for their treason in making such a statue when its dangers were so well known.

The lawful priests of Todesfall pleaded for their lives. They had not made the statue, they said. It had been made by their most hated foe, the unlawful priest of Todesfall. Centuries ago they had taken the statue from the unlawful priest to destroy it, but could not and so decided to keep it hidden. None in the assembly had heard of this unlawful priest and the lawful priests were put to sore trial. But they held fast, and at last the assembly saw that only raw fear had induced the priests to tell of their ancient and bitter and secret enemy.

The lawful priests said the unlawful priest dwelt in Zaijian, the last and least of the city-states of Uerth as he had since centuries past when once that city-state was rich and great. He did not live in the way of common men, but lived in death. For that reason he was constantly in sight of Todesfall's face. They said this with great malice and deep grievance, and the assembly saw that the lawful priests hated their unlawful fellow for his constant state of bliss. *That which is dead should stay dead*, the lawful priests said.

It was he who made that statue, long ago, they vowed, and he who had sent the Dance of Death, *to fetch the statue back.*

Everyone knew the statue was heading straight to Zaijian. And also the Dance of Death had spread from there, as all could well remember.

The lawful priests told all they had learned of the unlawful priest. He was carefully hidden by his zealous followers, the best assassins and poisoners and embalmers in the world. They had learned the way to make contact with his followers, and the answers to the three questions his followers asked before they welcomed any guests. The lawful priests said the only way to stop the statue was to kill the unlawful priest. They would not reveal the three answers, for they hoped to use them to bargain for their lives. Instead they appealed to the White Lady, the beautiful, the good, the merciful.

When Lord Utan saw they would speak no more, he had all but one of the lawful priests executed. The White Lady pleaded for their lives, but Lord Utan told her to obey him in this, as a wife does a husband, and she bowed her head. Lord Utan took the last lawful priest with them on their journey, to show them the way to the unlawful priest and give the three answers. He assembled a host of his finest warriors, and the Lady of Frir took dozens of her priestesses to tend to the wounded. The world's greatest assassins and poisoners, they reasoned, would not give up their priest without a fight. They marched quickly for Zaijian.

Asneath and Baoqian were with the company, but neither had an important part to play until Lord Utan went mad. Green pus came from his mouth and he killed the Lady of Frir and her priestesses. His own men killed him. They set him on a bier in due mourning, with his battle-axe in his hand, but that night he rose up again. All that were killed by him rose with him and attacked the living. The living wasted time in their confusion before remembering the only way to kill them was to lop off their heads. It is not easy for an Olan warrior to slay a Frir-maid, even when green pus drips from her lips and her hair flies bristling and her hands are claws. Asneath lived only because Baoqian and some of his companions found her early and set her between them.

At first the men fought in fierce disorder, shouting to Olan for aid, until Olan aided them. Their tattoos writhed. Blue aurochs of attack raged through them. Blue dragons of defence reared over them. They fell into the battle trance, their blades singing sweetly, their eyes vacant of all but Olan's blessing. They felt neither pain nor despair nor fear of dying. The battle raged fiercely, the balance see-sawing between the living and the dead. Horses and people screamed in darkness.

Asneath knew the smaller spells of healing, although not the great spells that return life. They are Rimbaud's alone. As her first stark terror ebbed, she held Frir's amulet in her hand and meditated upon the circle and the sickle. She felt strength and certainty return to her. Murmuring Frir's chants she touched the men's wounds. Their wounds mended. She saw when they were flagging and gave them fresh strength, until it seemed to them, in their battle trance, that Asneath *was* Frir, and to fail her meant the death of Life itself. But Death and Dark were strong and terrible, while Asneath's powers were weak and mortal. She could not save them. As the night lengthened, the men staggered and wearied and foamed at the mouth. The blue aurochs and dragons turned to pale ghosts, then ebbed entirely, and the men fought on with only their devotion to Olan to sustain them. And that was not enough. Gaps were torn in the ranks around Asneath. Finally only Baoqian remained. Then, at last, dawn saved them. The dead screeched when first light touched them. Their flesh hissed and smoked. They fled into the woods.

Baoqian leaned on his battle-axe amid the carnage. He and Asneath looked around at the camp, with tents fallen and fires smashed and scattered with corpses. They saw they were the only ones still living. All that great quest had fallen on them.

"But we do not know how to find the followers of the unlawful priest, or the three answers to give them," Asneath wailed.

The sound of her voice woke movement beneath a fallen tent. They pulled the fabric aside and saw the lawful priest of Todesfall beneath. His feet were still bound, but he had one hand free, clenched tight around a small crystal vial. Nothing living or dead had touched him, but he was hurt to the death. In the desperate fight the tent pole had snapped and pierced his chest. Yet he smiled sweetly, not at them but beyond them, as if behind them he saw an old friend, long cherished in absence, coming towards him again. Asneath shivered and turned around, but there was no one there. No one living. She gathered courage and knelt beside him. She murmured a prayer and touched her amulet. She felt Frir's holy strength pour through her, banishing her mortal weariness. She touched the wound in his chest. She felt Frir deny her. She rocked back on her heels in amazement. "Frir refuses to heal you," she exclaimed. "You must have done a great wrong."

His smile broadened. He released his grasp on the crystal vial. It spilled green pus that sizzled and killed the grass it soiled.

"That is the poison that killed Lord Utan," Asneath cried, amazed.

"He should have let my brothers live," he mumbled.

"You dog! You die!" Baoqian howled. He whirled his axe around his head.

"Hold!" Asneath cried. She threw herself between the lawful priest and the blade. "He is dying now," she cried. "He will see Todesfall's face soon enough, with or without your help. He can tell us how to find the unlawful priest, and the three answers," she explained.

Baoqian considered, then let her have her way, although he spat upon the dying man's upturned face before he strode away. Asneath knelt by the priest again. She saw by the look in his eyes that his friend behind her was very close and very welcome.

She did not have much time. She asked him where the unlawful priest of Todesfall could be found. He told her that a follower of the unlawful priest always waited by the well in the north square of Zaijain.

"Will killing the unlawful priest stop the statue?" she pleaded.

"If you do not kill him before the statue reaches him, then the lands of living and dying will become one," he gasped. "Then we face the Great Ending whose coming has many times been foretold but has always been held off somehow." He never took his eyes from that invisible one so uncomfortably close behind her. "In the Great Ending all who die will be reborn only in death. There will be no living soul left to worship so even the gods will die. The dead will dwell in darkness that has no end."

She saw he dreaded that Great Ending, and she believed him. Yet also she saw laughter lurking in his eyes as if at some private jest. She wondered what this meant and concluded he was not telling the entire truth about the unlawful priest. But she had no time left. She asked him for the three answers.

He spoke thin but clear. She had to bend close to hear. He told her the first question and the first answer, the second question and the second answer. He told her the third question and she waited a long time for the third answer before realising it would never come. For his smile became fixed and his gaze cleared. She screamed and snatched her hands over her face so she did not catch any glimpse of that Other face in the mirror of his eyes. At her cry, Baoqian came running. He had searched the camp and found some unspoiled supplies. So they journeyed on, pursued always by the dead who had once been their friends. So they came at last to Zaijian.

They entered the city by the north gate in the late afternoon. The north square was immediately inside the gates; Zaijian was not a large city. A four-sided well stood in the centre, slab-roofed, with steps to the water. No doubt in normal times a man could linger here long, unnoticed, in the bustle of the crowd, but now the man sitting by the well was the only living soul there. They hurried to meet him.

Asneath had told Baoqian she did not have the answer to the third question. They had decided on a plan.

The stranger rose as they approached and removed his hat, showing himself a long lanky individual with sandy hair, a beaked nose and mild eyes. He was wearing rags that had once been fine clothes and still had a certain air of shabby finery about him. Anything less like an embalmer, assassin or poisoner they could not expect to find. A well-to-do pickpocket perhaps. They drew to an astonished halt before him.

"You are alive," Asneath blurted out, before she could think of anything sensible to say.

He bowed, doffing his hat. "As you see. You must be thirsty." He offered them each a bowl of water to drink. The travellers licked parched lips, but hesitated. "It is not poisoned," he smiled.

Asneath murmured a Frir-prayer over the water, that would discolour it if it were tainted. But the water stayed clear. The thirsty travellers drank deep. "I am sorry for doubting your word," she said, setting the bowl down at last.

The man waved a dismissive hand. "You have reason. You are sent, I suppose, by the lawful priests to kill the proper priest of Todesfall."

Asneath stared in astonishment. Baoqian put his hand to his axe.

"I have expected you a long while. You are almost too late," the acolyte said. He turned to the statue that loomed over the city and blotted out the sky. Its foreshortened raised leg and foot approached, agonisingly slowly. It made the travellers fidget to look at it. Beyond, its torso reared into the clouded sky that hid sight of its head.

"Do I kill him?" Baoqian mouthed at Asneath, puzzled.

She shook her head, as the acolyte turned back to them. "Sir," she addressed him. "It is true that the lawful priests of Todesfall sent us here, but they betrayed us and killed our lord and lady. We seek to stop this statue before it brings about the Great Ending and we believe the unlawful priest was the one who started it walking. Will you not let us speak with him to find out the truth?"

The acolyte smiled at them, benevolently. "Of course, but first you have to answer three questions," he said.

"I am ready," Asneath said.

"What is the great poison, that is colourless, odourless and tasteless?" he asked.

Asneath felt a gush of relief. This was exactly as the lawful priest had told her. "Aqueta or little-water," she said, confidently.

The acolyte clapped his hands. "What are the seven noble poisons?" he asked.

Again relief filled her, for she knew the answer. "The seven noble poisons are aquafortis, arsenic and mercury, powder of diamonds." She paused, for she had heard the list but once, and memory groped for the next answer. As soon as she stopped, the acolyte started forward. She met his eyes and saw he was full of joy, of fondness for all life, that he bore not the slightest ill will to any living creature in the world, yet he would kill her if she forgot. It mattered not to him if he ended this life for her, when she had another, and another, an endless, inexhaustible supply to go on. Sweat sprang upon her skin, sweat that had nothing to do with the heat, and raw fear jogged her memory. "Lunar-caustic, great spiders and canthirides!" she gasped to the end.

"Two out of three. Well done. Here is the last. What is the name of the nameless god?" he asked.

Asneath's heart hammered even as she smiled and tried to

look confident, for she knew not the answer to the third question. Her plan seemed a feeble one now it was embarked on. "I am afraid I am feeling the heat," she said, apologetically. "It is on the tip of my tongue. I just cannot remember."

Out of the corner of her eye she saw Baoqian start to manoeuvre. But there was no need, not then. The acolyte threw up his long arms. "I am sorry to be so rude. I wouldn't be surprised if you had sunstroke," he said, and shot her a pleased look, as if wondering if she would die of it. "Come to our hall. You can sit in the shade and recover your wits. Then you can give your third answer."

She felt hopeful that her ready answers had dulled his suspicions.

He stepped back and whistled, high and shrill. A dozen shabby figures appeared from the surrounding streets. Baoqian stepped back against the well, axe raised. "Peace, friend," the acolyte said. "You have no need of that. We can kill you any time we like."

The men were a shabby bunch of outcasts whose belts were hung with swords and daggers and garrottes, with poisons and darts, with brain hooks and canopic jars. They swept Baoqian and Asneath through a broken grate into a low sewer on the south side of the square. The outcasts shot regretful looks over their shoulder as the statue disappeared from view but Asneath and Baoqian were glad to leave it behind. They were glad too for the shade and coolness of the thick stoned sewer, even though it stank. They splashed through fetid stormwater with a crust of filth, but the outcasts were beyond noticing and the travellers past caring. Asneath soon gave up the idea of trying to retrace their steps. She saw a dozen places where traps were set, some to stop entrance, some to stop exit, and she had no doubt as many more existed that she did not spot. Fear seized her as she realised she was going to die, that she was being hurried to no good ending. She prayed to Frir for strength. "I am not afraid of death," she told herself. She did not realise she spoke aloud, until the acolyte of Todesfall smiled.

"I do not fear death either," he encouraged her. "It bores me rather. On and on, life after life. No true end. Pointless, isn't it." She realised that in his own way he was trying to cheer her. "Even the gods are trapped in it. Frir gives life, Olan guards it, Rimbaud will keep pushing souls on to rebirth, whether they want it or not. Only Todesfall had the right idea and look what happened to him. We followers of the proper priest seek the End to rebirth."

"Then this statue is doing what you want, by bringing on the Great Ending," she said, remembering the words of the lawful priest.

"No, the statue does not bring the End. We will die but there will be no peace for us in Todesfall's dim land. Rimbaud, that blind old bat, will hunt us out and hurry us on, whether we would or not, but there will be no life to be born into. We will be reborn into death, and there is no second death from that. Then the gods will fail us. Even this present mindless dance is a better fate."

"Then why does your priest do this? Why did he start the statue on its course?"

"He did not start it," the acolyte said. "The lawful priests started it when they stole it. They feared his power. But they have made him a thousand times stronger." He jerked his chin in the direction of the invisible statue, as they entered a large open space beneath the city. Tall pillars dwarfed the ragged band that splashed beneath the fluted ceiling. It was no sewer, Asneath realised, but a long disused cistern from the days before the Uerth river was dammed into a lake, when Zaijian was far from the shore and still needed a water store. A smaller area, like a stage, was raised at one end. It was lit with candelabra holding dripping candles of what she hoped was pig fat. Beyond the lit stage a tunnel disappeared into darkness. The acolyte saw her looking.

"That is where our priest dwells," he explained.

Asneath winced at the thought of living in that dank hole. "Don't the dead come here?" she asked.

"They know we are as they are, and leave us be," the acolyte said, which didn't comfort her terribly.

She wondered if the unlawful priest watched from the darkness—a man who did not live as normal men, but lived in death. Her imagination fired, picturing a green zombie with putrid flesh, or a skull with jewelled eyes. She shuddered.

What was the name of the nameless god? The question hammered in her head as it had all through this short, doomed journey. It was ridiculous. How could a nameless god have a name? And besides, what did a nameless god have to do with Todesfall? Unless, the thought occurred to her, the nameless god had something to do with the End that the followers of Todesfall sought? Also, she was puzzled by the casual nature of the unlawful priest's acolytes. They had led them straight here, on the flimsiest of pretexts. They had let Baoqian keep his weapons. They did not fear for their priest. This was wrong. She glanced at Baoqian.

He nodded, once, thinking she was signalling to him to start his advance. He slipped to the side. The ragged men let him go. Yet something held him back from vaulting onto the stage at once, and charging into the dark tunnel with raised axe. Something terrible but helpless, like the ghost of a child, tugged at him with futile, fearful persistence. Something nagged at him about the nameless god, as it had since he had first heard of it. Something he almost but not quite remembered. It hovered in the shadows on the edge of his mind, watching him with bright eyes. He tried to banish the muddled image by concentrating on present danger. He hefted his axe, framing a prayer to Olan.

The acolyte sat casually on the edge of the raised stage. "Are you feeling better?" he asked Asneath. The others grouped around her.

"Yes, much better now I am out of the sun," Asneath said. She resisted the impulse to glance one last time at Baoqian. All of a sudden, now she was going to die, she was very fond of him. She did not wish she had slept with him, but she did wish she had been kinder, more patient, that she had not snapped at him, and that she had thanked him. She fixed her eyes on the acolyte, willing him to look at her, not at Baoqian. She clasped her amulet in her hand. Beneath her breath she murmured a very foolish, little spell of Frir, beloved of young women, that makes them more attractive to men.

Baoqian hesitated, not because he thought they would die. He might kill the unlawful priest, but he was sure his followers would not let him escape. He faced his fate squarely. He prayed to die unflinching, with Olan's name on his lips. But what secret kept the unlawful priest of Todesfall so safe that his followers did not fear for him? He glanced back, and was caught by Asneath's spell. She looked like Frir, white and slim. He did not know what to do. "Olan help me," he prayed.

And Olan gave him aid. The nameless god stepped from the shadows of his mind, bright and vivid, and bowed its antlered head. "I know! I know the answer!" He started back, then spun around and stared into the dark tunnel as a cry rang out of it.

"Dada, are you there?" The voice was high and shrill, not a man's, and held a careless edge of command. "You can't hide. I heard you. Come here now. I'm bored!" the voice called.

"In a moment, dear heart," the acolyte called back, casually. "I have guests." He stared at Baoqian, appraisingly. "What is the name of the nameless god?" he asked him.

"It is dead and its name can be said only in the dying lands. We who still live cannot name it," Baoqian said, confidently.

Dada clapped his hands. "Only Olan himself could have given you that answer. Congratulations," he said, dryly. "Here is our priest," he added.

"One two three, coming ready or not," a voice said from the dark tunnel. And then a white, white child stepped out. His hair was black as night, his eyes burned and his lips were red as blood. He was five years old and dead as stones. He stared in surprise at Baoqian with his big axe. "I don't like you. Go away!"

Baoqian did not budge.

"Make him go away," the child said to Dada, crossly.

"Remember we can make him go, but even you cannot bring him back," Dada said, gently.

"Oh he can stay then. I don't care," the child said. He turned his burning eyes to Asneath. A pleased smile flitted over his lips. "Ah, she wears a necklace like mama's," he said. He ran towards her, chubby arms outstretched. As he passed Baoqian the man gave a great gasp and called on Olan for strength. He raised his axe.

"Stop!" Asneath screeched. All her Frir-soul revolted at killing a child.

Baoqian froze, mid-swing. The child stopped and turned on Baoqian, hands on hips, without the smallest flicker of fear on his small, dead, imperious face.

"I really don't like him," he said to Dada. "He's mean. Like the men who made mama and I drink that nasty drink."

"He means the lawful priests of Todesfall," Dada explained.

"Will I dance at him?" the child asked, and none needed to ask what dance he meant.

"He made that dance up out of his own head. Just imagine," Dada said to Asneath, proud as any parent.

"He's not mean," Asneath stumbled desperately into the breach. "He was just playing. He wanted to give you a scare."

"You can't scare me. What's your name? My name is Qushi," the child said, pleased, without waiting for answer. "Do you want to meet mama? She's just in here."

"Just a moment," Asneath said. She turned to Baoqian in appeal, hoping he understood how she felt, her horror and her pity and her regret. "There must be another way that does not involve killing," she said. "And—and—how did you know the third answer," she asked him, softly.

He stared at her in pure horror then bowed his head and whispered. "One day Olan went hunting. His hounds started a stag with a human face and they hunted it through the world. It turned at bay at last in the poison wood, but as Olan raised his spear to slay it, it spoke to him with human tongue. 'Kill me,' it said, 'And the Great Ending is at hand."

"'Liar and coward,' Olan called it. 'What is your name."

"'Except in the dying land I have no name,' it answered. Then Olan saw it was a dead god living and stayed his hand."

She waited a long moment, but there was no more. He shuffled his feet, apologetically. "You can tell me more Olan stories anytime," she whispered.

This was so different to the rebuke that he expected that he jerked his eyes up to meet hers, blushed and gave her a pleased smile.

"Are you coming, hurry! Mama is waiting," the child interrupted before Baoqian could say anything more. Asneath climbed onto the stage. The child took her hand. His hand burned like cold flame.

The tunnel led to a small tomb lit by more smoking candles of pig grease. Gaily coloured toys lay in heaps of profusion, balls and drums, dancing marionettes and painted wooden animals. A woman lay on the tomb, a corpse preserved by the highest of embalming arts. She had coarse yellow hair, dressed with rich jewels, and her sharp pointed chin and nose showed her a shrew. But there were also lines of love and laughter about her eyes and mouth. One hand lay at her breast, beside an amulet of Frir, a cheap trinket. The fingers were heavy with rings, although the hand was red and chapped with toil. The corpse wore rich robes that Asneath was prepared to swear she had never worn in life. This was a poor woman who lay before her. Her other arm was outflung and a blanket and pillow lay askew beside it.

Asneath's flesh crept.

The child scrambled into his bed. "Mama has gone away and can't come back," he said. And Asneath saw the anger in his eyes, that his mother would leave him alone in a strange land.

"Believe me it was none of our doing," Dada said from behind her. "Our priest is reborn to his task, over and over. He knows who he is by his dreams. When he is grown a man he comes to us and undergoes the purification and ritual. He is with us in death until his body wears away, for all our arts. Then we store his relics with great care and wait for him to be reborn to us again. The lawful priests have always feared him but they waited their chance when he was weak. They found him when he was yet a boy and killed him and his mother, thinking that way to end his power. Did they think to fool Todesfall?"

"We all strive to be like our gods for that is the path to them. But he is too like and has opened a path for the god to come to him," Asneath said, in great fear. She saw Qushi's bafflement, his pain, his rage and his shame. She saw why he danced the Dance of Death and why the statue woke when he called it, and walked to meet him. He did not understand or care, no more than Todesfall, that he would have to kill the whole world to bring his mother back to him.

"Todesfall neither knows nor cares what he does, no more than a day-old child," Dada agreed. "But he shares our priest's pain, that he can never be with his mother again. That has made them one in spirit. When they meet in the flesh our world will join with Todesfall's. Life and death, hand in hand. Life in death, I mean. Then none will be safe, not even the gods themselves. Truly, the Great Ending is at hand."

"There must be a way," Asneath said. Her first thought, her first refuge, was prayer. Prayer to Frir. But wiser and greater folk than she had already tried that, and already failed. Prayer to Rimbaud, then? No, Rimbaud was goddess of rebirth, not death— besides, the goddess was absent from her moon-roost. Memory of the moon's blank face made her shiver. That only left Olan, the banisher, the betrayer.

"We must take him to his father's temple," she said. "The White Lady received this answer to her prayers, that the right aid would come at the right time and place to the right souls. If this is not the right time and place then what is?" she said. "We can only pray the right souls are near." She turned to the child. "Do you want to go and visit—?" She bit her lip rather than mention the father who tore Todesfall from his mother's grasp. "Someone you know," she finished.

"I will if you carry me," Qushi said. He held up plump arms.

Asneath picked him up. No heart beat beneath his breast, no breath rose and fell upon her cheek. He was cold, cold all over. She felt her skin prickle and numb. She felt her heart freeze. Yet he laughed and wriggled as if he were a living child, pleased to be carried in a woman's arms. "Faster," he called.

Then the ground trembled around them as another footfall shook their world. Overhead, towers fell. Within, the roof of the cistern groaned. Stones ground against one another. Stone dust trembled to the floor like rain.

Realising they had little time, Dada seized one of the candelabra to light their way. Baoqian came with them on the return journey, but the other acolytes ran ahead, eager to see the statue again. As they neared the surface they had to brace themselves against a second tremble in the earth, much nearer than before.

"But that is too soon," Dada said, amazed.

One of the acolytes came running down towards them, face aflame. "He is striding towards us much quicker than before," he cried, exultant, then dashed back out again.

They stepped out into the square. It was night, warm as milk, and the blank, fearful moon shone orange and swollen through the mists. The statue loomed over the city, blotted out the sky behind it. It was walking faster now, fast enough for mortals to see. One step while they stared, then two.

"We must be on the right path, for it seeks to stop us!" Asneath cried, relieved and terrified.

"Quick!" Dada led them forward. The statue needed only one or two more steps to overtake them.

They ran out onto a broad embankment overlooking the harbour. Earth shook and buildings tumbled. They saw the dead at last, thronging the lake shore, rejoicing in the arrival of their lord. The dead turned their faces towards them as they came into view, faces as blank and horrible as the empty moon. The statue loomed over the city, as a child looms over a toy. Another step and its bulk hid the moon.

"I see Olan's temple," Baoqian shouted. A big building, that must once have been handsome, stood on a prominent spot overlooking the harbour. He recognised the two pillars that stood before all temples to Olan, the legs of Olan they are called. Even as he shouted, the statue took its last step towards them, a step in real time, a hasty lurch that splashed into the shallow shore water. They all fell over at the impact. Buildings shuddered and collapsed. A wall of water reared from its footfall.

"Run!" Baoqian shouted. He thrust Asneath before him. Dada ran at his heels. The wave swilled behind them, overwhelming the embankment, dashing the dead away. Baoqian reached the twin pillars. He seized one, and caught Asneath and Qushi together with his free hand. Dada threw himself past them and inside the temple. The wave smashed past them, as if following him in. The wave shouldered the pillars, but it would take more than Todesfall's strength to unseat them.

Asneath was overwhelmed, baffled, deafened, blinded, choked. She was helpless against this wave, and if she had been alone it would have ripped her, flung her and dashed her senseless against the rocks. But Baoqian stood firm as the legs of

Olan. Then the wave broke over their heads and the ebb began. Baoqian roared and tightened his hold. At last the wave ebbed around their ankles, spent. Gasping, Baoqian released Asneath, who set Qushi down.

Qushi was outraged. "Now I am all wet," he said, as water poured from his mouth. The flood would have killed a living child. He would not let Asneath pick him up again, but ran ahead. "Where is Dada?" he said.

Behind them, the statue, with an awesome grinding, started to bend.

Within the temple was dim and austere and empty, wet to tall windows that let the orange moonlight in. On the north wall stood the altar, with two pillars before it, the arms of Olan. "Here I am," said a voice. They looked up to see Dada perched above the windows, just above the water line, clinging to the statue of a bat.

Rimbaud has no temples for she is always wandering about and has no time to settle down. Mostly she has shrines attached to Olan's temples, for the two met on Olan's travels to find his wife and became firm friends. It was the wily crone who thought of the way to fetch Frir back again. Where there is a shrine to Rimbaud there is sure to be a statue of a bat, and a few of her beloved bats. Even now, a dozen fruit bats circled around the ceiling, shrieking, disturbed by the giant wave and Dada's mad scramble to their refuge.

Qushi screamed with laughter. "What are you doing up there?"

"Trying to get down," Dada said, promptly.

"You are silly," Qushi said, affectionately.

"We must pray to Olan," Asneath said, turning to Baoqian, for she did not know how.

"A true warrior prays with his axe," Baoqian said, gruffly.

"Here's your chance, friend." From his perch, Dada gestured behind them. "I thought they had held off too long."

Asneath and Baoqian turned to see the dead pour through the door, as the wave had done. They came in silence, arms spread wide, ready to dance.

"Get to the altar!" Baoqian directed Asneath, readying his axe.

"They will do as I say," Qushi said, cocky, and raised his arms in command. Then he screamed. "My hands! They've gone!"

Asneath screamed with him. For his hands and arms had vanished, or so she thought, until she knelt and felt them. They were still there. They had gone black, not the colour, but in absence of light. As the statue neared, the form of the child was changing to that of his god. She picked him up. He felt lighter than before, his living weight draining from him. They ran to the altar and Baoqian stood before them, between the all-guarding arms of Olan.

The outraged bats screeched in the dome. Baoqian wielded

his axe, soul singing. A blue dragon spread wings above him; a blue auroch charged through him. The dead fell before him.

Dada jumped down to the ground and ran over to them. The dead ignored him. He turned cheerfully on them. "Can I lend you a hand?" he said, tearing off an arm. "Mind your head," caving in a skull. He tore a path through to the living.

Then the roof was swept away as a child sweeps his toys aside. The living crouched, hands over their heads in useless protection as boulders the size of horses rained around them. But the arms of Olan are a strong shield and no stones struck them. Then the statue looked in. The face was too far above to make out, in shadow, remote and dim, yet awe and dread froze them.

"Watch your step!" Dada said, catlike recovering his footing first, and bringing his boot down hard, on a femur. It cracked with a dry crunch.

Then the dead drew back, with a dry murmur, bowing in reverence to their lord. The dance was over.

A vast hand reached in through the roof, of black obsidian. It groped with the plump uncoordinated fingers of infancy. The child in Asneath's hold screamed as flesh swept from him. He shone darkly with utter absence of light, and he lifted in Asneath's arms. Or rather the living world seemed to bend around him, bend in to him, to oblivion.

"Mama! Mama!" he screamed.

A voice sighed with him, filled with the same feeling, a voice bigger than the world. "Mama, mama," the statue sighed, through the aeons.

"No!" Asneath cried, as Qushi rose towards the reaching obsidian hand. Or it rose to him or... Perspective altered in ways she could not comprehend. She clung to the dead child. She lifted with him, or the world left them behind. Dada seized her waist as she rose, and tried to hold them down.

The giant head lowered enough for them to see the face, a face larger than the city. But there was no face. There was only a frightful whirl, a vortex of power sucking life into that other place, that lonely land of Dying that lies so close to ours, marching hill to hill, dale to dale, heart to heart, skull to skull, and yet is so distant and so terrible.

"Todesfall! Lord!" Dada exclaimed in reverence, tears pouring down his cheeks. He sank to his knees, forgetting to hold Asneath.

Only Baoqian stood between them and it—Baoqian, the arms of Olan. Baoqian roared in rage and hopeless defiance. He screamed Olan's name and gave an impossible leap. A blue dragon reared over him, a blue auroch leaped through him, but he was a flea to the colossus that bestrode them. He swung his axe in a great arc. It was not a human movement, it was divine. It was a prayer. The blade shattered when it hit the obsidian. Then the hand swept him aside. He was crushed against the left arm of Olan, and slid dead and broken to the ground.

The hand seized Asneath and Qushi. Then the statue stood. They swung high, impossibly high above the world, and all the time Qushi squirmed in Asneath's arms and *changed*. Asneath clung to him, her face buried against his shoulder, hoping to shield him with flesh still human. But he was oozing from her arms and floating, and shining now, shining with blackness, drawing the world into him. "I must pray," she thought, but all she could think of was Baoqian. He was dead and she had never thanked him. The hand came to a halt. She knew they must stand high, high above the world, before the face. She dared not look. The cold breath from Dying flooded over her. "Frir! Frir!" she cried, as her last desperate grip failed. "Save us! Save him!"

And the gods answered her prayer. A voice too large to hear thundered in her ears, like the sea and sky a thousand times magnified. She was sure it spoke one slow, sure, remorseless word. "Hold."

The child in her arms grew heavy again, and ceased moving. She raised her head. She saw Qushi had taken on flesh once more, with normal pink skin. But his eyes were closed, he was limp in her hold and he was not breathing. Below the world was hidden beneath silver mist that curved to the horizon. Around them was cold darkness with the empty moon like a dead lamp lighting a cold black room.

She saw at once they had made a mistake. The statue of Todesfall had not become larger. It had stayed the same size it ever was. It was the world that had become small. Perspective had slipped, but now she saw the true state of things. For Olan restored everything. Olan towered over them, over the rim of the world. He was so large that half of him was hidden beneath the horizon. She could see only the upper part of his chest, heavily tattooed, and far above the shaved dome of his head gleamed above a face, stern and blurred. He was as large again to the statue as even the fondest father towers over his new born babe. And Olan was not fond. Olan's arms were folded. "Hold," one word, still rang in her ears, the echoes reverberating to a close.

For the right prayer had come to the right souls, at the right time and place, when Baoqian died fighting without hope, his battle axe shattered in his hand, when Asneath called on Frir instead of despair.

One glimpse. One word. Todesfall had to obey. That was all.

Perspective slipped with a sickening swoop and the world swam to its right size again. The statue was the size of a baby so there was no fall at all. Asneath knelt on the cold stones of Olan's temple with Qushi still in her arms. Dada stared at her, astonished. "Can it be? Have you won?" he asked.

"Child!" a woman called.

Asneath saw it was dawn for there was a golden light shining through the temple doors. There was a woman standing in the light, blinding, radiant. Asneath raised her hand to shield her eyes. She saw a poor woman, in rags. Her reaching hands were red and chapped with toil. She had a sharp, pointed chin and nose, that told a shrew. But her eyes were filled with all the love and laughter in the world.

"Mama!" Qushi squealed. He ran towards her, arms wide.

Then mother and child were gone. The light was gone. The body in Asneath's arms lay still, so still. Yet Asneath could not let him go, even though she knew his soul had gone on to where he so longed to go, back to his mother and better luck in his next life. But that did not help her in this one. She knelt over him and wept, wept for the living and the dead. After a long while, she became aware that Dada was kneeling next to her, that his blameless, murderous eyes were fixed on her.

She hiccuped out incoherent words, that she hoped he would not kill her.

"We are deeply in your debt," he hastened to assure her. "Look. You have returned our statue." He picked up the baby-sized statue and brought it to her to show her, cradling its heavy weight in his arms with care. But he shielded its face from her sight, so she never saw it.

"Hide it better this time, so the lawful priests will not find it," she managed.

"I don't think they will try that trick again," he said, cheerfully.

"I thought it was dawn," she sobbed, remembering. She wiped her tears and looked up through the shattered roof. She saw that the Frir-light had deceived her. It was deep night still. The moon was high, but she saw with joy that reassuring shadow was splashed across its face. "Look," she said, swallowing her sobs. "Rimbaud has returned to her roost."

So they knew the world had come perilously close to the Great Ending whose coming has many times been foretold yet has always held off somehow, but now the danger was past, and reassurance shone in the moon's shadowed face. Asneath climbed to her feet, decided to lay the dead boy down beside Baoqian. She turned to see an astonishing sight.

A dozen confused fruit bats had flown around the dome while the battle raged and great events shook their tiny, uncomprehending animal world. Now as silence fell they grew bold. They flew down into the hall of the temple and they circled above the crushed figure of a man. The sight filled them with strong, strange elation, feeling foreign to them. A feeling neither beast nor human but divine.

One by one, they flew to the pillar and crawled down, until the bravest of them brushed the dead man's face with his soft whiskers. The touch was too much for him and he drew back with a squeak of fear. They formed a strange illusion as they huddled there, a strange shadow on the pillar, like an old woman in a cloak. And stranger still, as the echo of the squeak died, the old woman shook her cloak and stepped from the stone.

The crone looked at Asneath, and Asneath fell to her knees

before the power of her bright eyes. She turned to Dada. "Blind old bat, am I?" she laughed, mockingly. He dared not meet her gaze.

She bent and touched the dead man beside her, and his crushed flesh healed. Asneath felt hope so great seize her that she thought she would choke. "Baoqian," the crone called, in a hoarse rasp. But he did not wake.

Asneath's wild hopes sank.

"No time to lie about, lazy bones," the crone scolded, and kicked Baoqian smartly in the ribs.

This time he woke, with a surprised grunt. He sat up and rubbed his face.

The shape of the crone collapsed back into bats, who flew in all directions with startled shrieks. But her voice rang out, strong and mocking as life itself. "You've traipsing enough to do yet before you earn your rest. Get up, get up, and live," Rimbaud said.

So he did.

Man in Suit!

J M SHILOH

Dr Kodai Nomura received the unmistakable omen of a very bad day when his morning drive to work took him straight through the shadow of Robo Banzaizer, the silent sentinel of Radian City that now stood defeated on the blood-red horizon, a small plume of black smoke still rising from its smashed-in head. Nomura could feel the heaviness of that shadow, darkening his hope as well as a long, humanoid-shaped swatch of downtown.

Things got even worse when the silver-haired old man unlocked the door to his laboratory to find his android assistant, Miki, crying. She was missing the entire lower half of her body, and what remained was sitting in a little red wagon that belonged to Mitsuru, Nomura's nine-year-old nephew. The ever-precocious lad stood nearby, gently patting Miki's shoulder.

"Uncle! Miki's lost her legs!" said Mitsuru. "Someone broke in and stole them last night when she was recharging."

"Blast!" said Dr Nomura. "They must have been after the gluteal fusion generator."

"Oh, Doctor!" Miki said. "I've been made useless. How can I do anything stuck in this wagon?" Miki bawled with such ferocity that synthetic tears shot out the sides of her eyes like tiny missiles.

"How could this happen?" Dr Nomura said. "I designed the security system myself. No one can get into this laboratory without—"

"No one, Dr Nomura?" a new voice said. "Not all your designs are foolproof."

Nomura knew who was behind him before he turned around. Major Matsumoto was back.

"The Major has come to help us, Uncle," said Mitsuru. "I let him in. He gave me a candy bar."

Matsumoto was not alone, of course. His two bumbling cronies, Ringo and Tomo, stood nearby. They poked nosily around various devices on the lab tables while their boss, ever the cipher, puffed on a cigarette and betrayed no interest in such wonders as the optican brain enlarger or the combination school bookbag/personal rocketpack (the new horror of Radian City parents).

"Get away from those devices!" Nomura yelled. "Last time you people messed around with my inventions, one of your soldiers ended up with the head of a seahorse."

"And we were grateful for your help in saving our city from the madman he became," Matsumoto said. "But we have other business to discuss. The break-in last night...this is a serious matter worth government attention. Perhaps I can be of some assistance."

Nomura knew Matsumoto's tone, and it betrayed him. As Miki looked up at the doctor with wide, hopeful eyes, Nomura turned back to the Major with a grimace.

"I think I may have some idea who was responsible, Major," he said with disgust. "Furthermore, I am guessing that in exchange for this so-called 'investigation', you will want something from me?"

Matsumoto laughed heartily, insincerely. "You know me too well, Doctor."

"I know your methods. And what you're capable of."

Matsumoto became suddenly serious, his spine straightening. "And you also know how dire our situation is. Now that he has defeated Robo Banzaizer, the monster Ragnaroka will surely return. His battle wounds will heal, and he will know that Radian City is no longer protected from his wrath. Does that not frighten you, doctor? It frightens me."

Ringo (left-hand crony) leaned around the Major's shoulder and said, "Believe me, it's serious if the Major is scared." Tomo (right-hand crony) did the same. "'Cause he's not scared of anything!"

Dr Nomura turned and rubbed his chin in thought. He walked over to the front window that overlooked the city, saw in the distance the gleaming, still form of Banzaizer, and remembered that final battle. The monster Ragnaroka had employed every weapon in his arsenal, from the swinging wrecking ball that hung from his right arm to the black, fleshy salaryman briefcase that grew from his left like a rectangular tumour; now and then the case's gaping maw would snap open, releasing pterodactyl-sized paper bats to flutter about the head of Banzaizer in an attempt to blind him from the monster's next blow. An additional distraction came from the TV monitor encased within Ragnaroka's torso, a hellish device that bombarded his enemies with enticing television commercials offering New and Improved products for the giant robot who has everything (*Fist Finder A-Go-Go! New GPS locates a lost rocket-punch anywhere on the globe!*). Yes, the beast was wily, but Robo Banzaizer had fought on. Brilliant red laser beams were fired, sleek blue missiles were launched, spinning Blades of Doom were spun.

And then the unthinkable happened. As thousands watched on TV from emergency bunkers, Ragnaroka froze mid-strike, his wrecking ball dropping carelessly to his side. The beast stared into the face of his enemy, suddenly noticing, for the first time in all their battles, the small glass-enclosed cockpit in the head of Robo Banzaizer, where sat the robot's young pilot, Go Musashi. Ragnaroka hesitated for a moment, then casually smashed in Banzaizer's head with one swift (and not even particularly forceful) blow from his left arm.

And like that, a city's hope died.

Dr Nomura wiped a tear from the corner of his eye and turned back to Major Matsumoto. "You know, Major, that I always help in any way I can. The damage to our city will be repaired by my nanobots. They will reconstruct our metropolis in exact detail, as they have countless times before."

Miki said, "In fact, Dr Nomura is working on an idea to replace the Pneumatic Escape Tubes with teleporters, if only we can get—"

"That's all very good, but something more is needed," Matsumoto said. "A way to defeat Ragnaroka, to—"

"No!" Nomura said. "I will never again use my scientific skills for military purposes. I created Banzaizer for you, and now it has cost the life of our city's hero. I will not let that happen again."

Matsumoto just smiled and gave a sly wink to Miki, who blushed like a schoolgirl (not the first or last time Dr Nomura would regret installing the emotion drive). "You didn't let me finish, doctor. I am not asking for weaponry," he said. "It is clear Ragnaroka cannot be defeated by military means. The best we can hope for is to *remove* the monster. And in that we suspect you can help us."

Dr Nomura's face paled with a sudden realisation. "What are you implying, Major?"

Matsumoto said, "Despite your attempts at secrecy, we are aware of your recent experimentation with what you call *ghost realities*... unreal worlds existing as phantoms on the boundaries of spacetime. Like you, we see great possibilities in this work. Possibilities for rendering such worlds temporarily real. If you *could* open a fissure to one of these parallel worlds, we might be able to lead Ragnaroka into its path—"

"Madness!" Dr Nomura yanked his thick glasses from his face. "What you propose is madness!"

"But Uncle," said young Mitsuru, "if it worked we could be rid of the monster forever."

"It's not that simple," Nomura said, wringing his hands. "It's not like opening a door to another room. It's playing with the very fabric of reality. Far too dangerous a thing to try on such a large scale."

Matsumoto walked over to a still-sniffling Miki and handed her a handkerchief. "Would you rather waste your time and scientific brilliance reconstructing poor Miki?" He patted Mitsuru on the head as the youngster munched the last bites of his chocolate bar. "Would you deny your nephew another opportunity to pull this glorious red wagon through the streets of Radian City? If Ragnaroka strikes again, there will be no more joy for the children."

Dr Nomura looked at Miki, her huge eyes shimmering with tears, and although he knew they were only a saline solution of his own creation, somehow contained within those crystal droplets were the hopes and fears of every man, woman and child in Radian City. They were all helpless in the face of the monster. But he, Dr Nomura, was not.

"All right. You win again, Major," said Dr Nomura. "I will help you. And may the Great Protector in the Stars forgive me if something goes wrong!"

Miki's trusting smile beamed, almost making up for the self-satisfied grins crossing the faces of Matsumoto and his men.

*

The next month was a busy one for Dr Nomura and his team; a month of Tesla coils and solar panels, soldiers in radiation suits and accidentally mutated dust bunnies, bubbling beakers and horrific controlled explosions of blue fire that could be seen from the moon. At the end of the fourth week, Dr Nomura handed his pocket tachyon generator back to Miki (who kept it safely protected in her sternum) and said, "It's done. Now we must wait, and pray."

The very next day, the call came through: soldiers guarding the beach had spotted a great boiling spot in the sea—the tell-tale sign that Ragnaroka's hibernation/healing period had ended. A rampage was due, and this time he would rise unopposed.

Or so he thought.

As the alert sounded throughout the city, thousands took to their Pneumatic Escape Tubes, shooting themselves through Dr Nomura's nanobot-constructed underground labyrinth of escape tunnels. As usual, a few stayed behind, for reasons ranging from the brave (journalists) to the insane (Ragnaroka cultists eager for self-sacrifice). And amidst the fleeing, a military escort rushed into the city square. Troops created a perimeter around the bronze statue of Go Musashi—the fifty-foot token of appreciation that had now become a memorial. At the base of the statue sat a boxy silver control panel, its console blinking, tentacle-like tubes emerging from all sides and trailing off to humming generators. Dr Nomura leaped from the Jeep as it pulled up to his invention and said, "Quickly! Quickly! He will soon emerge from the sea!" As Nomura made final calibrations to the machine, Matsumoto, still in the Jeep, lit a cigarette and barked a command to his bumbling cronies. Ringo and Tomo unloaded the little red wagon from the back and, one on each side, clumsily lifted Miki from the Jeep and placed her in the wagon.

"When can I have my wagon back?" asked little Mitsuru, his face smeared as usual with chocolate.

"As soon as your uncle saves the city, little friend," said the Major, "we'll get Miki put back together and you'll have your wagon."

"You'd better hope the Major never sees a military application for it, I'll tell you that," grumbled Nomura bitterly. He moved the great lever in the centre of the console, and a deep throb like the city's heartbeat emanated from their surroundings. All power in

Radian City was now being diverted to tear open a portal to a world once unreal.

"The power source is stabilised," Nomura said. "Now we need only get the monster within the target area."

They didn't have to wait long. Eight minutes later, Ragnaroka emerged from the dark womb of the sea, reborn and ready. His head, a fusion of flesh and metal, gleamed in the merciless sun like a five-pronged iron crown with blazing red eyes at the tips. His craggy purple body shot steam from its gills as he lumbered towards the shore, wrecking-ball arm swinging with his steps, salaryman briefcase at his side. Military trucks reported landfall and sped into the city ahead of the beast.

The nauseating thud of the monster's footsteps shook the ground for what seemed like ages to those waiting in the city square. When the behemoth finally came into view on the horizon, Dr Nomura felt Miki clutching his leg in fear, the wagon axle squeaking from her trembling. Mitsuru stopped munching his candy bar. Behind them, Ringo and Tomo stood petrified, hands on their sidearms for comfort. Major Matsumoto remained silent and unreadable—yet even his stoic countenance was betrayed by a single drop of sweat running down his temple.

The first great crash hit their ears—Ragnaroka was getting down to business. He took out the TV station with one swing of his wrecking ball, and from his front eye loosed a winding plasma beam straight into the Ragnaroka Temple, cleansing fifty-six more loyal worshippers from the Earth with his Blessed Atomic Fire. He kicked his way through a few smaller structures on the way to the city square, where Dr Nomura slowly placed his palm upon the red ignition button.

Ragnaroka, for all his faults, did possess one positive quality: he was witlessly predictable. He never missed a chance to obliterate his three favourite targets—the Art and History Museum, the Science and Technology Center, and Kikyu-Nomo Toys, Inc. The bright colours and brilliant geometry of downtown's most famous structures were irresistible to his destructive lust, and each had been rebuilt a dozen times by Nomura's nanobots.

This time, however, things would be different.

Nomura hit the button. The facades of the museum, the tech center, and the toy company broke apart at the seams and began to crumble, falling away in unison all around the monster. Dr Nomura had altered his nanobots' programming; this time the buildings were only clever shells concealing three identical, chrome-ringed warp generators. Ragnaroka paused and stared as golden, spinning globes atop each generator sent noodles of electricity into the air.

"He looks confused," said little Mitsuru.

"Put your safety goggles on, everyone!" said Dr Nomura, lifting the thick blue lenses to his own eyes.

On cue, crackling ribbons of red lightning snaked from one generator to the next, trapping Ragnaroka within an electric maelstrom. The world around the monster flashed negative, light becoming dark, dark becoming light, with an ear-bursting kettledrum crash. Finally, a perfect half-globe of popsicle-red light grew up around the area, obscuring from view everything within the radius of the three warp generators. Within that dome of mystery-energy, the boundary between the myriad worlds had been breached. A quick yellow flash and a tooth-shaking boom capped it all off.

As a quiet rumble faded into silence, plumes of smoke arose inside the target area. Dozens of eyes—belonging to soldiers, police, government agents—watched the scene. Dr Nomura slowly removed his safety goggles. Miki held her breath. The Major's cigarette had burned down to his fingertips.

When the smoke cleared, they would all know their city's future. Would the target area be empty? A huge, triangular swath of the city snatched away into another world? Or would something else be there in its place—a chunk of alien planet swapped with ours? Dr Nomura's old eyes were the last to decipher the murky shapes coming through the smoke. When he heard Miki gasp, he turned to see in her eyes a horror he had never before witnessed.

Looking back, Dr Nomura saw: the buildings inside the target area were still there. A swath of destroyed real estate leading to the beach was still there. And the great beast Ragnaroka was still there, feet planted firmly in the cracked asphalt, apparently unaffected.

Ragnaroka remained.

"I have ... failed," said Dr Nomura, quietly.

Ragnaroka broke the silence with a swing of his wrecking-ball arm, shattering generator number 1 into tinker-toy-like pieces that rained across the city.

"Back-up plan, activate!" yelled Matsumoto into his walkie-talkie. "Attack tanks, move in and lay down heavy fire! All other units retreat immediately!"

As the soldiers cleared out, dragging a dazed and tearful Dr Kodai Nomura with them, the Radian Attack Tank Brigade moved in. They opened fire on Ragnaroka with an arsenal that could easily obliterate a lesser foe.

Dr Nomura watched from the fleeing military transport as the tank missiles drew blue streaks of twisting smoke through the air, exploding into the great beast's hide in orange blossoms of fire. Then he heard the monster cry out in pain.

"Owwww, crap!" Ragnaroka said.

Dr Nomura looked at Matsumoto. Miki looked at Mitsuru. Ringo and Tomo looked at each other. "Hey," Tomo said, "did he just say 'crap'?"

"I never heard him *talk* before," said Ringo.

They turned back and kept watching. Ragnaroka was spinning around crazily, slapping himself with the briefcase to put out the tiny fires caused by the missiles. His other arm, the wrecking ball, swung wildly and hit the nearest building, a twenty-story structure that flew apart like balsa wood to reveal empty insides.

"Look at that building!" Mitsuru said. "There's nothing inside!"

Tomo said, "Dr Nomura, I thought your nanobots rebuilt the insides, too?"

"Yes, Doctor," added Matsumoto, "have you been cutting corners with the nanos this time?"

But he hadn't been. The nanobots had rebuilt the city as usual, with the exception of the three generator facades. Yet now, as Ragnaroka knocked down one building after another, all eyes could see that they were hollow. All fakes.

And pretty shabby ones at that.

"They look like models!" said Tomo.

"Owwwww! Dammit! Cut it out! Stop shooting!" said Ragnaroka, his voice muffled but understandable.

"Ignore him, men! Keep firing!" Matsumoto said into his walkie-talkie.

"Holy crap, that burns! Cut! Cut!" Ragnaroka said. Then he reached up and grabbed his head and pulled it clean off. The collective gasp from the onlookers was such that it seemed the city itself did a double-take.

"I... can't believe it," said Dr Kodai Nomura, for once utterly incapable of scientific reasoning.

"Can someone please tell me what's going on here?" Ragnaroka said, holding his monster head under one arm and running his other hand through the mass of sweat-matted hair that topped his real head, his human head.

Miki stammered, "He's... he's..."

"He's a man in a suit!" said little Mitsuru.

"I told you something would go wrong! But did you listen to me? Does anyone ever listen to me?" Dr Nomura was sprawled out in a chair with his hand on his forehead, Miki next to him in the wagon, softly holding his other hand. They were in Matsumoto's swank offices, where a spotting of grim faces seemed to dampen the deco colours of the room. It had been a mere three days since the incident, but it already seemed like years ago.

"You didn't tell us *this* would happen," said Major Matsumoto, taking a drink from his robot waitress, which consisted suspiciously of a pair of legs and a pelvis topped by a serving tray. "The people are blaming us now. They think Ragnaroka was a government hoax all along, that we used him to instill fear and keep the population under control." The Major held up that morning's newspaper, the headline screaming: *MAN IN SUIT!* Underneath was a fuzzy black-and-white picture of the man formerly regarded as the creature Ragnaroka, sitting cross-legged in his rubber suit, looking down at a smattering of military trucks and troops. If you looked really close you could make out a crane lifting a platform up to the giant's head, a platform containing the tiny figure of Dr Kodai Nomura. "You're in this, too, doctor," Matsumoto continued. "They think you built some sort of enlarging ray to grow a normal man into the fake monster."

"I can't help what people think," Nomura said. "They're going to come up with some theory or other if you won't tell them the truth."

"And how can we do that? How, without shattering the foundation of their individual little worlds?"

Nomura stood up and slowly walked over to the west window. "Perhaps you are right, Major," he said. "This man came from a world that was unreal to us until we opened that portal. A ghost universe. And yet in his world, there is no Radian City, and none of *us* are real. That in itself does not surprise me so much. It is easier to imagine a world in which I do not exist than a world in which I half-exist. But that is the case…in his world, I am present only as a fictional character. We are all characters in a film, an entertainment. There are no real monsters in his world, no robot champions like Robo Banzaizer. They are only stories, and we are the people in the stories."

"He said my name, in his world, is Yoshi Nakamura," Matsumoto said. "I am an actor. Or rather, there is an actor in his world who looks like me, who plays Major Matsumoto." The Major's face dropped. He stared at the floor, took a quick drink. "You are right, doctor. It is worse than not existing at all."

"And I suppose you are right, Major, that we cannot let the realisation of this reach the wider world," Nomura said. "No one should be confronted with such truths." Dr Nomura looked out the window and saw the man who was Ragnaroka, a simple man who called himself Yasuo Tanaka, sitting in the field behind the government complex. His expression was unreadable, his eyes murky as he stared into the setting sun, still unable to make sense of this new world. Below, a military truck was pulling up, its payload filled with fresh vegetables. Giant men must eat, after all.

Someone else was riding in that truck, Nomura now saw. It was little Mitsuru. In the short time since the questioning of the giant man began, Nomura's fearless nephew had started to become friends with this towering visitor from another earth. A connection had been made—perhaps the two worlds were not so alien after all.

Through Mitsuru, Dr Nomura had found that he, too, had empathy for the man in the suit, and the cogs in his mind began to turn. That news story, the hypothetical enlarging ray…nothing more than a reversed shrinking ray, really. Now might be the time to dust off that old prototype in the lab. Perhaps he could give the man called Yasuo Tanaka something akin to a normal life in this strange new universe.

And yet, he wondered, is this very act of benevolence a scripted scene in that other world? A pre-written destiny, conceived by human minds in a universe that is a ghost to him, enacted for real in a universe that is a ghost to them? Or is he the primary mover, does he unknowingly write the script for *them*, simply by living?

As he stared out the window at the tiny figure of Mitsuru being lifted by crane, as he saw the giant man give a small smile of recognition, Dr Nomura took comfort in one fact: as unsettling as their current situation was, they were now rid of the monster Ragnaroka. The plan had, in an unexpected way, worked.

The other world, Dr Nomura thought, wasn't so lucky.

"I'm Officer Nagai. What the hell's going on here?"

"We don't know," said the studio security guard. "When I got here people were running everywhere, screaming about a—"

The guard was interrupted by the sound of an explosion blowing out the north wall of Studio 23B. He and Officer Nagai covered their faces as splinters of wood and shards of glass rained down on them. All around people were fleeing the scene, the police cruisers and ambulances almost hitting several as they sped into the parking lot. A silver-haired old man wearing a white lab coat ran by, and Officer Nagai grabbed his arm. "Hey! Were you in there?" he said. "What's going on?"

"I don't know, it's crazy!" the old man said. "We were filming and the guy went nuts!"

"What guy?"

"The guy playing the monster. Something went wrong with the FX rig, an explosion. It was just supposed to spark but it turned into a huge red fireball. I can't believe anyone near it survived. Then the stuntman in the suit started tearing everything apart!" Behind them, a beam of red, snake-like energy shot from the smoking hole in the studio wall, blasting one of the police cars to scrap metal. Officer Nagai, the security guard, and the old man ducked down behind Nagai's car as shrapnel clinked and clanked everywhere.

"What the hell is he armed with anyway?" Nagai yelled.

"I don't know!" the old man said. "I thought the monster's powers were all special effects added later."

An unearthly roar silenced everyone, and all eyes and guns in the parking lot turned toward the smoke billowing from the hole in the wall. Slowly, the hulking shape of Ragnaroka, man-sized but still fear-inspiring, emerged through the gloom, steam shooting from his scaly body, his red eyes glowing with hideous energy. The TV monitor in his chest was playing a beer ad full of scantily clad women.

"He has a TV in his chest?" said Officer Nagai.

"It wasn't real!" said the old man. "I swear it wasn't real before! They superimposed the images in post-production."

Ragnaroka's left arm jerked, and his salaryman briefcase flew open, paper bats flying out and up into a circle above his head, then dive-bombing the cops and EMS teams.

"We're going to need back up!" Nagai yelled. "Let's get out of here!"

As they fled, the old man stopped, looking around in a

bewildered manner. Nagai asked him what was wrong.

"Jiro! Where is Jiro?"

"Who?"

"The kid who plays Mitsuru. I never saw him leave the building. Someone has to get in there and find him!"

As the old man pleaded with Officer Nagai, Ragnaroka flipped over another police car in the parking lot, fired another dazzling beam of energy from his red eye, and reveled in the glory of it all, in this new world put before him for destruction.

And inside Studio 23B, among the shattered glass and melted cameras, the flaming backdrops and overturned floodlights, a little boy in short pants emerged from hiding under the catering table, his mouth still smudged with chocolate. He could hear the chaos outside, the explosions and screams, the sirens and gunshots. He looked over to the abandoned set, where small flames licked the balsa wood model of Radian City, now half-destroyed. One of the warp generators had been knocked over, and the gold spray-painted garden globe that topped it had shattered into pieces like a Christmas ball.

But something was different. The boy walked over to the set, some buildings not reaching his shoulders, others towering a foot or two over his head. He leaned down and stared at a model office building. The front façade had been sheared off, exposing its insides. The boy couldn't remember things being this way before. Had the buildings always been so meticulously constructed? Weren't they just hollow balsa wood boxes? He reached in and touched tiny oak desks on which sat tinier nameplates. He saw tiny telephones and filing cabinets, tiny restroom facilities with streaming rolls of tiny toilet paper. The boy stared, astonished, at a diorama far more detailed and elaborate than any of the ones he'd built in his bedroom at home.

His gaze was distracted by a muffled cry, a small groaning sound coming from one of the offices. The boy lifted one of the tiny desks, and his eyes widened. A man was hiding under it—a man no more than two inches tall. He was wearing a shirt and tie, and a miniscule camera hung from his neck. Slowly and gently, the little boy reached down and picked up the tiny, tiny figure. The man's screams of horror were barely audible over the commotion outside.

He could crush the man in his palm, the boy knew. Would he do so? Would he pull the arms off the man like wings off a fly? He had no reason to, but he had the power.

The boy turned and walked away from the set, stepping over a hastily discarded script, the final pages of which were slowly burning away. And in his grasp, the tiny man looked up in dread and awe, fearfully awaiting the next move of this new, short-pants-clad terror—this young and curious *daikaiju*.

FOOTPRINT

DAVID CARROLL

There was a dull crumping sound and the scream of tearing metal, the squealing of brakes. Then a more human cacophony of pain and anger, perhaps despair. The shiver that ran through Odawara's hotel room and made his cutlery jitter seemed almost an afterthought.

He rose to see what was going on, although of course he knew. None of the human cries that drifted in with the dust were of surprise. His legs ached and a strip of skin under his right shoulder itched intolerably, as it had since he'd disembarked the plane. The cancer that was nestling comfortably above his balls felt like wet heat today, so different from Jerusalem's parched desert air. It was why he kept the balcony door open.

They said it would snow here, come winter, but he wasn't sure he believed it.

He was too old to be in this room, too old for this oldest of cities. The pain he heard rising from the street was only a brief distraction from the discomforts of his own body, and there was no fight or flight left in him—or so it seemed. Still, before looking down Ben Yehuda Street for the scene of devastation, he checked the sky. It was clear, and perhaps his heart did steady a little under that unbroken expanse of blue.

You shall not know the day nor the hour, said the banner. Michele checked her watch. It used to be a joke, then habit. Now she suspected it was ritual.

5:51 pm, her watch said. Also that it was the third of May, and that the beast was eleven kilometres away. She didn't have one of the new ones with its own GPS, only a receiver. She had never changed the default location on which the watch was centred, and now she was in Jerusalem, she didn't need to.

Eleven kilometres, which might be traversed in minutes or days, or never. For all anyone knew, the beast might turn around and head back the way it had come. *Oh no, there goes Tokyo,* as the song said.

After fifty years, she suspected not.

The banner was her landmark—this particular one, slung across the camera shop that was now closed and dark, possibly forever. The next stop was hers, and then a change of buses to get to North Talpiot. She pressed the indicator button, hearing the sharp *ding* and seeing the light at the front of the bus show up red: *atzor*.

9.8 kilometres, her watch said, and it gave her a chill—both that the beast had travelled that distance, and that the display had starting showing the decimal point.

She stood, and made her way to the front of the bus, sliding carefully, as you learned to do in certain cities, to minimise the chance of curious fingers sliding along curves. (Those curves weren't as high as once they'd been, but neither did she look her almost-forty years. The advantages of a misspent youth, perhaps.)

9.5 kilometres, as the bus slowed to a halt. Soon the direction would become important, too. Jerusalem or Bethlehem? Even now she felt the chill of premonition provoked by Yeat's now most-famous poem, the significant lines omnipresent in the Western world, and much of the Middle East as well. Not so much in Jerusalem though, since if you were going to scrawl graffiti about *what rough beast* you might as well travel the last seven kilometres south and do it in the birthplace itself.

But Michele had little faith in the premonition of poets, and thought she knew as much about the beast as anyone, let alone some guy who had died fifteen years before it had risen from Tokyo Bay. It was a city creature, and would have no time for the tacky and war-torn streets of Bethlehem (normal population: 25,000) when it could choose those built for 600,000 instead.

Though the bus had stopped, the indicator *ping*ed again, and the red light flashed its Hebrew: *stop*.

Then the bomb went off.

The corridors outside Odawara's room were darkened, and silent. Some doors had been left open (through one he saw the lights of a helicopter, descending fast), but not many. Jerusalem was by no means free of tourists, but not many of them were here, halfway between the Old City and the Givat Ram district, where most of the fortifications and bunkers were. Mount Shmuel, overlooking the city from the north west, was also likely to be crowded if the civic plans he had read about were as described.

The lift descended quietly and efficiently. It was a Japanese lift, he had already noticed. A younger man entered on the second floor (a more sensible location, of course, given the likelihood that the electricity would go), and the two studiously ignored each other.

The lobby was also shadowy, though the sole concierge had the radio on, listening to a terse and continuous commentary in Hebrew. He had a motor scooter, casually leaning against the stylish welcome desk, and the lobby doors were wide open, promising a quick exit.

Along with the world times behind the counter, various displays showed the beast's location, including an actual plasma-screen map, and as distance in metres from the Mount of Olives, the hotel itself, and the Church of the Nativity in Bethlehem. Odawara ignored all that, and went outside.

Michele wandered a little way down the street. There were helicopters. A man talked to her, but she couldn't understand what he said. "*Je suis infirmière,*" she told him, though soon afterwards realised he might not have understood her either. By that time he was gone. She hadn't seen him leave.

A seat lay in the road in front of her, twisted and blackened. Another was beyond it, in better condition and even upright, although far too low, having been torn from its metal supports. She looked at it longingly, but there was a foreleg and foot and sensible shoe lying on the ground between her and the chair, and she wandered off in another direction.

She thought she was going deaf, until she realised that the wailing woman she saw in front of her was simply being drowned out by the helicopters. That would explain the wind, too. Michele bent down, but the woman twisted out of her clumsy embrace and ran away.

She tried to take stock, work out where she was, and how she was doing, but it seemed a moving target.

"Any cuts?" a man said to her, in English. "Flying blood, bone fragments. AIDS. Hepatitis B C D...E F G...H I J K—" Then he was gone, too, and she thought he had been for a while. Her arm stung a little.

She staggered again, past the still-smouldering body of a teenager. An oxygen mask had been placed on the lacerated mess of his face, but she couldn't imagine that he needed it any more. There was another pair beyond the teenager: an older man (maybe Chinese) bent over a portly woman, who was trying to light a cigarette. The man looked in good health, as did the woman, apart from a strange stiffness in the movement of her hands. Michele approached them, and the man looked up, concern upon his face.

"I am a nurse," she said to him, careful to use English this time. And then she burst into tears.

The men and women about them, dressed in a uniform he could only describe as medical fatigues, moved efficiently and with purpose. Odawara approved. It made him feel young again, almost—back in his navy days. All those present were examined. The dead were ignored, the most grievously wounded put onto stretchers and then into the helicopters, the others given quick bandages and shots, as necessary, and then left where they lay. That was also familiar from the war. There was no time for burial rites or coddling tonight, not for the paramedics.

He watched as the choppers lifted and flew east, arcing north; his body tensed, almost in preparation to salute. It had been too long since he had flown, far too long, and helicopters were after his time regardless.

(He remembered seeing a helicopter in the War, a German Fa 61, it must have been, but by now he could not tell if it was a real memory or not.)

It was only then, turning his attention back to the shredded bus, that he realised the beast had not been here at all. It should have been obvious. He had stood in the footprints before—had stood in them and made a vow to defend his country.

Odawara picked his way to the shell of the bus and, finding the metal quite cool, hoisted himself gingerly into it, thankful his sense of smell had long faded. Blood was seared onto most surfaces, only a little tacky.

His training in explosives was decades old, but he still thought he picked the culprit. There was more of him than might be expected, given he was at the centre of such a powerful blast, for the human body can ride the wave better than the rigid structure of the vehicle. Still, his legs were completely absent and there was little of the rest of him that could not be described as rags. Like the other dead on this night, he had been ignored by the paramedics. Odawara looked carefully into the bomber's skewed and charcoaled face, and then alighted again, before the creaking structure gave way beneath him.

"I was part of the 3D Commune, *le Dos de Dieu,* you know?"

The elderly Asian gentleman across from Michele nodded, looking unsure. She tapped his business card against the table absently. He was Japanese, and worked at some company she had never heard of. According to the English side of the card, he was an Engineering Consultant.

The two of them were in a café, but apart from a dog resting beneath one of the tables, looking half-spooked, they were alone. A large *cholent* had been left simmering behind the counter for whomever wanted it, and instant coffee was close at hand. Somewhere she could hear some sort of generic Europop, as faint as the crackly public announcements broadcast from the east.

"It was deeply stupid, really. I know that. But—I missed Burma, got on in Bangladesh and we made the crossing to India. It was incredible, *magnifique.* We lost two-thirds of the group at the border, because everyone thought that the Indians were just going to bomb the crap out of it for sure, but they didn't. I guess they were still jumpy after China's *petite erreur.* We even let the others on again. Have you read Calver's *The Monkey on Your Back?"*

He nodded again.

"That captured it. All the drama, all the bitchiness, all the oxygen deprivation..." She grinned, but he didn't share the joke. "That was a review I read. Though it didn't really tell you how fit you had to be. We had this network of ropes up and down the beast's back, and getting anywhere was hell. Not to mention the humidity. But yeah, I didn't get far into India, and missed the really bad stuff later on. Nobody crossed with it into Pakistan, no matter what they tell you. Though that was a couple of years later, of course. '87 or something."

She looked at her watch, and saw it click from eleven to twelve kilometres. The beast was backing off, no doubt under the heavy firepower and diversionary tactics being thrown at it—or just because it felt like it. Its westward progress was hardly a straight line. Regardless, nobody would be riding its back this night.

She sighed, and got up to serve herself some more of the *cholent*, and started opening drawers, looking for biscuits or mints or something.

"Did I tell you I was from Bordeaux, originally anyway. I was studying in Paris before, you know, jumping on. I was doing nursing, like I said before."

He nodded, staying silent as he had been since the almost formalised greeting (and presentation of the card). She looked at him, suspiciously. "You are following this, *oui*? *Parles-tu anglais?*"

He just kept looking at her, patiently.

"*Vas donc te faire voir, vieux connard.* Did you understand that? Fuck you."

She threw her bowl over the counter, into the public area, and then strode out and into the street. Odawara sipped his coffee, and the dog snuck forward to lap at the spicy stew oozing from the shattered china.

The woman was hanging back, watching him. She was not trying to hide, simply waiting to see if she would be acknowledged. He raised his head and smiled some sort of welcome, but that was mostly reflex. If he wanted people, he would be with the crowds, not here, for in the last two days Ben Yehuda Street had been emptied still further.

The dog from the café had gone, too, and the *cholent* reduced to a dry and fly-ridden paste.

"Good evening," Odawara said carefully (some of the syllables slipping nonetheless).

"*Konnichi wa*," she said. "I thought you might be here. Sorry about all the drama. I was angry, and my English tends to run wild."

"You are from Paris?" he said.

"Yes."

He fell silent, but she seemed comfortable with that, which he liked.

"And you do not think the beast will reach your own capital?" he said eventually.

She laughed. "Not in my lifetime. It's not as far, but there's more to stomp on the way. Still, they've already worked out how to put the Eiffel Tower on a boat. I think we're going to follow the example of New Delhi, and just get everyone out of the way. None of this defending the promised land."

He nodded, and she laughed again, sounding brittle.

In the direction of the old city, the sweep of searchlights and the flitting of helicopters and the sounds of artillery fire was becoming frantic. There were great clouds of dust and smoke as well, and every now and again the lights and swirling darkness was occluded by a larger darkness, like a shadow.

They watched it together.

The household in the Jerusalem suburb of North Talpiot, south of the Old City and so far not in danger of being trampled upon, had four male and six female adults, six nationalities, no shared language, a complex web of sexual relations, a big map of the city with a variety of coloured pins attached, a floating population of pets, eleven radios, four laptops, two TVs (not including those attached to the network of XBoxes), two telescopes, two state-of-the-art video cameras and a comprehensive library of 'beast lore'.

Not that the inhabitants treated the appearance of the creature with flippancy. Reactions in the house ranged from religious awe to a sort of pedantic obsession with so-called facts that called for close observation and late-night theorising. All claimed to have ridden the beast, though it was sometimes hard to ascertain if that were true (those who made the claim falsely were universally derided as 'hangers on'). There were similar groups in the city as well, some with prestige and grant money, some with little more than a pair of binoculars.

Michele sat in one of the upstairs bedrooms, leafing idly through the book collection, the business card of the Japanese man in hand. When she had finally given the name on the card more than a glance, it had tugged something inside her. Tamotsu Odawara was famous for something, she was almost sure, but nothing was coming up, not on Google, not in *Daikaiju Complete* (and *she* was mentioned in that one, albeit only as a passing reference from the 3D days), and not in the indexes of all the more focused books surrounding her.

She was very tired and hot, and sometimes she was not sure if the city was shaking beneath her, or perhaps it was just the words blurring under her gaze, and sometimes she thought of her sons back in Paris—one in prison for driving under the influence of narcotics, one happily married and equally happy to ignore her entirely—and more often she thought of the bus and the warm hand at her back that had slapped her down and then screamed in her ear, and Japanese names floated through her mind, and she thought she was missing something obvious.

Reina came in muttering imprecations of violence in three languages.

Reina was almost ten years younger than Michele, but had also done medical training in her time, and together they had applied for a position in the emergency hospitals of the soon-to-be-besieged city. They had been politely told that *goyim* physicians were welcome to help at Mount Shmuel and similar camps, but not in Jerusalem itself.

It was Reina who had found the North Talpiot household, though perhaps it was Michele (and her inclusion in *Daikaiju Complete*) that cemented their residence. It was Reina who pointed out that staying in the city after what they'd been told pretty much gave the lie to any excuses they might have made on the way.

Reina wandered out again. Dennis came in soon after, asking after her.

"You should look under T," he said, glancing at Michele's notes, and then left.

With fluttering stomach, she looked up "Tamotsu, Odawara" in the big book, and realised why the name was familiar.

The city had an acrid feel to it this morning, and the electricity had finally given up in the hotel. People would wander down the streets occasionally, while helicopters and jets flew close overhead at all hours. Mostly it was silent, a tired wind blowing through deserted streets, with the hint of decay on its breath.

Cracks had appeared on many surfaces, often very fine, but sometimes dramatically wide.

The beast had passed to the north of the hotel yesterday evening, and Odawara had watched it from another room, its proud head silhouetted against a fading sky. Perhaps that meant it had finished with the Old City and parts East. Perhaps not.

This morning, Odawara would not have been able to describe what it was like to look upon it, in Japanese let alone English. In truth, he was not sure he knew. After it had become little more than a darkened bulge on the cityscape (deigning to dodge all the new-fangled weaponry designed specifically for it), he'd gone back to his room and passed darkened urine, painfully.

Breakfast was bottled water and a 'power' muesli bar, and then he climbed down the dimly lit stairs (even the emergency lights seemed ready to fade away to nothingness), out onto the street. The woman Michele was there, and he smiled at her.

"I found an article about you," she said, "in one of our scrapbooks. The *LA Times*, January 2002. *Kamikaze Pilot Derides 9-11 Hi-jackers*. Cowards and madmen, you called them."

Odawara blinked at this unexpected confrontation. But it was not too unexpected, for was that not how he had been defined for fifty years? A kamikaze pilot—a *failed* kamikaze pilot. "Quite right," he said.

If she meant to follow up with anything—an accusation or question was the usual next step—she faltered, looking lost. Together they walked up Ben Yehuda Street.

The remains of the bus were still there. Jerusalem's famous ability to sweep away the debris of suicide bombers was turned to other purposes, but at least the bodies were gone.

"Cocksucker," Michele eventually said. "I just don't know

what to think. It was like he *saved* me. He was behind me on the bus, and waited till I got off. I just want to rip his guts out for what he did, but..." She laughed, and now the bitterness was touched with mania. "But he even did that for me, already. Cock*sucker.*" She looked up at Odawara. "I can't stand it. I just can't."

They waited on the corner, whilst a building slowly crumbled a few blocks west.

It was Odawara's opinion that the suicide bomber had detonated himself by accident, for both the street and the bus had been mostly empty at the time. The further east he had travelled, the more damage he would have caused. Odawara suspected he was hoping for the Old City itself, slipping into the chaos as it prepared for siege against a far larger foe.

Would the Zionists be undermined by such damage at a critical time? He did not know (did not know what state the Old City was now in). It seemed unlikely to him.

So yes, the man had been a cocksucker, as the Americans said, and an incompetent one at that.

"My brother Nakajima died," he said softly. "He attacked a British ship called the *Formidable* off Sakishima, what you would call the Saki Islands. No one is sure if his plane was one that hit or not, but he did not come home, and was declared a hero of the Empire.

"Nine years later it was my turn. There were four of us. We swore upon the Empire, took the sacred libation, and sang a song of the samurai."

Umi yukaba, mizutsuku kabane. If I go away to sea, I shall return a corpse awash.

"Then we flew our planes, old *Zero-sen* fighters they had found somewhere, laden with explosives, and resolved to fly into the maw of the beast."

She was rapt in the story, he saw, though it was told clumsily by an old man, in a language he would never master, and was not even her own. Perhaps it was a good story, though it was the only one he had.

"I failed. It evaded my first pass, and clipped my wing with its claws. Any further attack I could make would have been clumsy and misguided, and I barely had enough stability to land."

She did not ask what the beast was like. He remembered she had lived upon it for a period (why?), and she would not need reminding that the Chinese had managed to get a nuclear weapon down the beast's throat, for all the good that did. But his story always ended the same way.

"I looked into its eye, as I dove towards it, and you know what I saw?"

"Nothing," she breathed.

He smiled, remembering what else she had read. "Yes, like I told the journalist. No intelligence, no anger, no peace. Just a void. That was what I said was in the heart of the hijackers, and in the heart of the man upon the bus."

She nodded, and put a hand upon his arm, as if it was she comforting him.

But he could not finish yet, much as he would want to. This was a new part of the story, and there seemed no escaping it, here in this oldest of cities.

"Japan did not treat me well, after I landed. I had not disgraced my vows, for the first rule of the kamikaze is not to be in a hurry to die. But it seemed I was a disgrace to my countrymen, for being willing to die for them. It was the way of the Empire, and the Empire had too recently fallen under the American heel. Since that time, I have done... nothing."

She looking into his own eyes, searchingly. There was a great roar from the south west, and a barrage of strange sounds that had not quite the cadence of modern artillery. They both turned briefly to look, and she checked her watch, as was her custom.

He sighed. Perhaps he would not have to say it after all.

"And here we are," she said. "Come here for no reason, except that we have seen the beast, and we are empty, and have not even anything to die for."

He nodded reluctantly, and she patted his arm again. After a while they went back up to his hotel room, for the view. To see the movement of the beast, if it had finished with Jerusalem, and, if so, where they would follow it next.

Thanks to Erwan de Diepenhede and Ian Mond for help with translation.

haikaiju

SEAN WILLIAMS

(4)

I am Daikaijo:
nature's larger-than-life friend.
The hills know my name.

I am Daikaijo:
friend of children; foe of Man.
I come when I'm called.

I am Daikaijo:
Red in eye, tooth, claw and tail.
I am Daikaijo:

Hear me roar.

THE TRAGICAL HISTORY OF GUIDOLON, THE GIANT SPACE CHICKEN

FRANK WU

MAIN CHARACTERS:

GUIDOLON, giant space chicken and film director
TRISURON, giant space Triceratops and production
    assistant/actress
JERORA, giant space jellyfish and production manager
OCTURON, giant space octopus and screenwriter
FRIBUGUS, giant flying monster and movie studio lackey

NOTE: The film is in black and white, like FEDERICO
          FELLINI's 8½ or the first Godzilla movie.

FADE IN:

EXT. MOUNTAINOUS SEASIDE, JAPAN — DAY

Ominous music. A MONSTER lumbers out of the water. He
    has a beak like an eagle, points that stick out
    horizontally from his cheeks, and bug eyes that glow
    angrily. The camera angle is low — the monster is
    massive, like the Colossus of Rhodes.

The monster opens his mouth, releasing a terrifying *basso
profundo* rarr.

As he rises from the waves, water sheds from his legs,
    swamping fishing boats the size of his toes.

An Art Deco train rumbles out of a tunnel. It is a
    double-decker, but it only comes up to the creature's
    ankle. He reaches down for the train when —

VOICE (o.s.): Cut! Cut! That's all wrong.

The monster straightens, arms akimbo, and lights a
    cigarette. The train falls off the track, landing on
    its side. It is obviously a toy. The monster looks
    up.

WHAT HE SEES:

Pan up to a model fishing village, then to sculpted hills.
Behind them is a painted backdrop of mountains
and sky. Above that are movie lights, among which
appears a second monster, GUIDOLON, to whom the voice
belongs. Both monsters have beaks, pointy cheeks and
big bug eyes, but their proportions differ. The first
monster is noble, Guidolon cartoony. Only Guidolon
has deelie boppers.

GUIDOLON (to first monster): **Takashi, if you're
going to play me, do it right. Your method
acting has become unsound.**

TAKASHI: **Pish! Need I remind my esteemed director
that I have performed both No plays and
Shakespeare before our Emperor?**

GUIDOLON: **Then tell me this: What's the difference
between a tragic hero and a comedic hero?**

TAKASHI: **That's easy. In a tragedy, the hero dies
at the end. In a comedy, he gets married.
How does this inform the making of your silly
monster movie?**

Zoom out to reveal the rest of:

THE MONSTER MOVIE SET

Populated by camera operators, grips, makeup artists,
etc., all of which are monsters. These include:

JERORA, Giant Space Jellyfish. He has a pulsating
translucent body and tentacles transparent as rice
noodles. Holding clipboards and pens, he is the film's
production manager.

OCTURON, Giant Space Octopus, and the screenwriter. He
holds script fragments in suckered tentacles.

TRISURON, female, Giant Space Triceratops. She has
three horns, one over each eye and one on the nose,
with a bony frill at the back of her head. She is a
production assistant and sometime actress.

As Guidolon and Takashi argue, Jerora, Octuron and
Trisuron glance back and forth at each other,
nervously.

Finally, Trisuron walks across the soundstage to

INT. A SOUND-PROOF PRODUCTION AND RECORDING BOOTH

With a glass window so she can see the movie set. Inside,
she picks up a rotary phone and dials with a horn.

TRISURON: **Get me Fribugus! It's an emergency!
They're at it again. Get Fribugus down here
fast! I'll try to hold things together!**

On the movie set:

GUIDOLON (beak quivering): **A monster movie, like
a Shakespearean tragedy, is all about hubris,
over-arching pride. Every tragic hero has a
flaw that both makes him great and ultimately
ruins him! Macbeth had ambition, which led
him to great achievement. But then he decided
to kill the king, which was bad. If you,
as a monster, had stayed in Monsterland,
you would've been king! But, by leaving
Monsterland and attacking Peopleland, you
overreach yourself and will eventually be
destroyed by men.**

TAKASHI (bug eyes glowing in exasperation): **How does
this relate to the annihilation of a train?**

GUIDOLON: **In destroying the train, you destroy
yourself.**

TAKASHI: **This is ridiculous! You're trying to make
this into a Shakespearean tragedy when it's
really just a silly little movie about ... a
giant space chicken!**

At those words, every monster stops whatever it is doing
and stares at Takashi and Guidolon.

OCTURON (to Jerora, nervously popping and
unpopping suction cups on his tentacles): **Uh-
uh. Now he's hit a nerve.**

TAKASHI (walking off set, pulling off his head to
reveal that he is a giant human being in a
monster suit): **I cannot abide this inanity.
Shrink me back down to human size. I'll be in
my trailer.**

GUIDOLON: **Did you hear what he called me? I am NOT
a giant space chicken! I am the Cosmic Avian
Avenger! I am not a giant space chicken!**

FADE OUT

Harp music to indicate dream sequence.

Sound effect — clanking sound of a mechanism lurching
forward, then jolting to a stop.

FADE IN:

EXT. BIRTHPLACE OF MONSTERS

Silver planks in a long row stretching into infinity, with
swirling mist. On each plank is a glowing BLOB of
protoplasm, each with two eyes but no other features.

A man sits on a marble throne facing the blobs. He wears
a robe from a Bible movie. Although he is Japanese,
glued to his face is a thick Moses beard of the type
Japanese people cannot grow. He is EIJI TSUBURAYA,
Godzilla's effects man. For Monsterkind, Mr Tsuburaya
is like unto God the Creator.

In one hand, Mr Tsuburaya holds a gnarled staff. In his lap, an Encyclopedia of Animals.

Sound Effect of the clanking again, and the planks lurch forward to bring a new BLOB before Mr Tsuburaya.

Mr TSUBURAYA (without looking up from book): **You will be like unto the Tyrannosaurus rex, mighty among dinosaurs. On your back, you will have decorative — but functional — plates, like a Stegosaurus, which will glow red hot before you unleash your radioactive fire breath.**

Foosh! The blob's eyes widen in delight and excitement. As Mr Tsuburaya lowers his staff, the blob turns into the monster. He rarrs, Mr Tsuburaya smiles, and the planks advance again.

A second BLOB appears before Mr Tsuburaya.

Mr TSUBURAYA (taking more time to look through his Encyclopedia): **You, my son, will be like unto a mighty alligator. You can shoot laser beams from your eyes and swallow artillery shells as if they were peanuts. Wind and wave obey your command!**

Foosh! It is done as Mr Tsuburaya orders. Blob #2 is transformed; the conveyor belt again lurches.

A third BLOB comes before Mr Tsuburaya.

BLOB #3 (pulsing with light to indicate speech): **What do I get to be? Maybe a giant snake? A giant pterodactyl?**

Mr Tsuburaya nervously looks through his book.

WHAT HE SEES:

The Encyclopedia is filled with photos of animals. Across each is scribbled the name of a monster.

Mr TSUBURAYA: Already done all those.

BLOB #3: How about a giant spider? I could spit radioactive silk. Or a giant flying robot? Giant space mummy?

Mr TSUBURAYA: Sorry. All the good monster ideas are taken.

BLOB #3: You've got to have something left!

Mr TSUBURAYA: OK — here we go. You will be —

Blob #3's eyes widen in terror. Mr Tsuburaya's magical staff descends, like a mighty oak falling on him in a dark forest.

Mr TSUBURAYA: A giant space chicken!

BLOB #3: Nooooooooooooooooooooooooo!

FADE OUT

Harp music to indicate end of dream sequence.

FADE IN:

INT. GUIDOLON'S TRAILER

With a writing table, chairs, a bed. The walls are
    covered with movie posters. One features a young
    Guidolon and is for the film THE OMEGA MONSTER —
    HORROR BEYOND IMAGINATION. Buried in the credits on
    other posters are the names Octuron, Jerora, Trisuron
    and Guidolon — though their faces do not appear.
    The names are circled and marked with stars and
    exclamation points.

Also scattered around the trailer are photos — in various
    combinations — of Trisuron, Guidolon, Octuron and
    Jerora.

Guidolon bursts into the trailer and rushes to his
    writing desk. He has been struggling to keep it
    together, and as he sits down in front of his manual
    Smith-Corona typewriter, he loses it.

GUIDOLON (sobbing, hiding big bug eyes with his
    claws): **I am not a giant space chicken! I am
    not a giant space chicken!**

TRISURON (o.s.): **I have an inordinate fondness for
    giant space chickens.**

GUIDOLON: Oh, babe ...

Camera pans to show Trisuron, sitting on a chair by the
    bed.

TRISURON (powdering sheen off her three horns):
    You've got to relax, honey.

GUIDOLON (deelie boppers wiggling): **This movie is
    my last chance... Maybe my dad was right. I
    should have stayed in medical school.**

TRISURON: Honey, it'll all work out in the end.

GUIDOLON: Babe, this movie's killing me.

**TRISURON: OK — I can help you take your mind
    off your problems. Let's re-enact the first
    Godzilla movie. You be Godzilla —** (falling on
    bed with arms out) **And I'll be Tokyo.**

Guidolon smiles at her for a moment. Then the blood
    drains from his pointy cheeks.

GUIDOLON: I'm sorry, babe. I can't... concentrate.

TRISURON: Then finish your stupid movie then!

Guidolon turns from her to his typewriter. Not because he
    wants to write, but because he does not want her to
    see him ashamed and impotent.

INT. MOVIE SET — VARIOUS SHOTS

Hustle and bustle. The crane operator swooshes the
camera like a fighter plane. Track is laid for a
dolly tracking between miniature buildings. Octuron,
with various script drafts, is talking to Takashi. A
technician, pliers in fangs, works on the wiring of a
tank model.

JERORA (o.s.): **Pyro! Are we ready for a big bang?
D.P., cameras 2 and 3 in place yet? Smoke
machines! All right. OK, the Maple Street set
is ready for destruction. Where's the talent?
Well, wake Takashi up and bring him back up
to giant size! Tell him the monster's due on
Maple Street!**

EXT. TOKYO IN FLAMES (VARIOUS SHOTS) — NIGHT

Takashi in Guidolon suit fighting jet planes — models
zipping along piano wire strung across the set.

One perfect shot of Takashi howling, then catching a
plane in his claws. He crushes it, and it explodes
satisfactorily.

Next shot: Another jet comes at Takashi, but Takashi
moves at the last moment, and the plane cartwheels
off the top of his head.

Then another plane explodes, but before Takashi has caught
it.

Then another jet zips by Takashi until it gets tangled in
its wires and hangs in mid-air, sideways, like a fly
caught in a web.

More planes swoop in, with explosions and smoke, and
Takashi's rubber suit catches fire and he falls
over, with Octuron running onto the set with an
extinguisher.

INT. SCREENING ROOM

We realise that these scenes were on a dailies reel
reviewed by Guidolon, Jerora, Octuron, Trisuron and
other monsters.

GUIDOLON (points on his cheeks drooping): **This
is the good stuff? You're not showing me a
blooper reel?**

OCTURON (octopus body deflating a bit): **If the
studio sees this, we're done.**

GUIDOLON: **OK, Jerora. Get everybody back to the
set and prep for today's shoot. We'll just
keep working until we get it right. Trisuron,
Octuron, Jerora, I really need you guys to
back me up.**

JERORA: **All right, everybody! Back to the set!
We've got a lot of hard work today!**

CLOSE UP:

Guidolon, despondent.

As Guidolon rises, Trisuron stops him. She waits until
the others have left. Then they talk, walking across
the SOUND STAGE toward the movie set.

TRISURON: Honey, I have the solution to our
production problems. I've asked Fribugus to
help us out here.

GUIDOLON (big bug eyes annoyed): Fribugus? He
kills every project he touches.

TRISURON: But he helps finish up movies in trouble.

GUIDOLON (deelie boppers frantic): We are not
in trouble! Not like... Like... Fribugus
was called in to work on THE DARKNESS, after
production had dragged on too long. It was
the worst bomb I've ever seen. Everything he
touches turns to crap.

TRISURON: But that movie wouldn't have been
finished at all without him.

GUIDOLON: How could you do this to me? To us?

TRISURON: I did this for us.

Their argument is interrupted by their arrival at:

INT. MOVIE SET

The monsters in the crew are not working on the film.
Jerora is playing a polka song on the accordion,
visible through his body. The monsters are all doing
"The Chicken Dance".

Guidolon stands at the edge of the set, stunned.
Trisuron's horns droop. Guidolon emits a rarr — not
frightening, but like a squealing piglet. The music
and dancing stop.

GUIDOLON: What is going on here?

Most of the monsters except Jerora slink away.

JERORA (translucent tentacles waving in air,
glowing brightly): Everyone has been so tense
lately. I thought if we could cut loose a
little, and pay tribute to you in song —

GUIDOLON (spittle flying from beak): I sent you
here to get things revved up! Not to put us
even more behind schedule!

JERORA: I'm really sorry, Guido. Takashi and the
boys thought it might be funny —

GUIDOLON: Yes, yes, "The Beer Barrel Polka".

Some of the monsters snicker.

GUIDOLON: What's so funny?

Monsters giggle that Guidolon doesn't know what song it is.

GUIDOLON: What is going on? Jerora!

JERORA (softly): We were doing "The Chicken Dance".

GUIDOLON (furious): "The Chicken Dance"? Jerora, how could you do this to me? You know how I feel! Fine, stab me in the back!

TRISURON: Honey, honey... Please stop over-reacting!

GUIDOLON (to Trisuron): And you...! (redirecting his fury at Jerora) You're fired! You'll never work in this town again! We are no longer friends.

JERORA: Guido, no, wait...

GUIDOLON: Get off of my set, you transparent Brutus.

The crew stand shocked, silent. All eyes watch Jerora as he dejectedly walks off the movie set. He pauses to shake tentacles with Octuron. Then he pauses again when he reaches Trisuron and Guidolon.

JERORA: Trisuron, you're the only one who can stop him. Before he destroys himself.

TRISURON: I'm not sure I can.

GUIDOLON: Jerora, you may slime away, you stringy ball of snot.

Jerora gives Trisuron a quick goodbye hug, further infuriating Guidolon. After he leaves:

TRISURON (poking him gently with a horn): Guido, can we talk in private?

GUIDOLON: Everybody take five! And when I get back, everyone better be ready to film!

INT. GUIDOLON'S TRAILER

GUIDOLON: How could that jellyfish do that to me?

Trisuron opens a black bag and pulls out a blender, which she plugs in. Then she pulls out an iceberg, and dumps it in the blender. Along with an entire lemon tree. And several large barrels labeled WHISKEY.

GUIDOLON: You think I'm going mad, don't you?

TRISURON (ignoring him): Nice relaxing drink. Ah, the secret ingredient.

Out of her bag she pulls Tokyo City Hall. She rips the top off and empties it like a packet of sugar,

pouring screaming people into the blender. Then she
hits PUREE.

Trisuron strains the drink into a glass and hands it to
Guidolon, who gulps it down.

GUIDOLON: You know why I had to fire him, don't
you?

TRISURON: He's been your friend for fifteen years.

GUIDOLON: Twenty. Which makes his treason that
much more —

TRISURON: And you're going to throw it all away
for a little joke?

GUIDOLON: The only thing that really matters is
finishing the movie.

TRISURON: The only thing?

GUIDOLON: Well, not the only thing.

TRISURON: You need help. Your lead actor hates
you. You've fired your production manager.
You're way behind schedule. What are you going
to do?

Their argument is interrupted by a CHEER coming from o.s.

GUIDOLON: Oh gosh. What now?

INT. MOVIE SET

The film crew monsters cheer ecstatically.

WHAT THEY SEE

Standing by the seashore is a winged MONSTER we have not
seen before. His profile is elegant, with a magnificent
crown of spikes. Iridescent sparkles shimmer across
his scaly skin.

With a blast of fire breath, he ignites the floor beneath
him. Flames shoot up, illuminating him from below.

WINGED MONSTER: I am Fribugus.

All the monsters — except Guidolon, Trisuron and Octuron
— cheer. Octuron rushes to Fribugus with a fire
extinguisher.

FRIBUGUS: I am here with the full authority of
Dengaku Studios. And their financial support.
You have a good movie, with only minor
troubles. I am here to help. I believe in
GUIDOLON, THE COSMIC AVIAN AVENGER! I believe
in Guidolon, your director! I believe in this
script! I believe in this crew! This movie
will be a blockbuster! It will be the first film
to win the Nobel Prize!

The cheer from the monsters is thunderous. Some monsters
come up to Fribugus — who is twice as tall as many

of the others — to kiss his hand. One monster crawls up on hands and knees, worshipful, like the bleeding woman who wanted to touch the hem of Jesus' cloak.

GUIDOLON: We're doomed.

INT. CONFERENCE ROOM — EARLY MORNING

Fribugus and Guidolon sit alone together. Spread before them are scripts and storyboards.

Fribugus' back is to the window, the dawn light behind him. To look at him is to behold the sun. Guidolon changes seats.

FRIBUGUS (folding his wings back to show he means business): OK, let's get this meeting over with. We've got a movie to finish.

GUIDOLON: Hold on. I always run these production meetings.

FRIBUGUS: You don't understand, you wattle-chinned chicken. If the studio calls me in, I'm in charge.

GUIDOLON: Just one second —

FRIBUGUS (fluttering wings threateningly): You fight me, you beaky freak, and I'll pull the purse strings faster than you can say GUIDOLON, THE COSMIC AVIAN AVENGER. You have a problem with that?

GUIDOLON (having a problem): No, I don't. I don't have any problems.

FRIBUGUS: That's not what I hear. Never get off the schedule. Darn right. You got off the schedule. (Concentric rings of tractor beams shoot from Fribugus' eyes, pulling a script from across the table) The story lurches herky-jerky from one improbability to the next. And it's not sexy enough.

GUIDOLON: Not sexy enough? The monster's naked!

FRIBUGUS: I'm not talking about the monster. Tell me about the scientist.

INT. SPACESHIP XK-OMEGA-9 BRIDGE — IN SPACE

As Guidolon narrates, we see four human (Japanese) crew members. They all wear orange jumpsuits, and helmets like motorcycle cops, circa 1970. They are indistinguishable, except for the scientist, Dr Okabe, who is wrinkled and gray.

GUIDOLON (o.s.): Dr Okabe is a master of all sciences, from anatomy to zoocryptoxeno-phrenology —

FRIBUGUS (o.s.): What does he look like?

GUIDOLON (o.s.): He's tough and sinewy, like
    Buster Crabbe with Albert Einstein hair.

INT. CONFERENCE ROOM — EARLY MORNING

FRIBUGUS: No no no.

GUIDOLON: We've already shot three scenes with him.

FRIBUGUS: Dr Okabe will be replaced by a girl.

INT. SPACESHIP BRIDGE — IN SPACE

As before, with beautiful blonde girl replacing Dr Okabe.
    In her presence, the other crewmen are even more
    indistinguishable.

FRIBUGUS (o.s.): Skinny like humans like them.

INT. CONFERENCE ROOM — EARLY MORNING

GUIDOLON: Why are you doing this?

FRIBUGUS: Not only monsters but humans watch these
    movies. She will appeal to the male 18 to 35
    demographic. You should study marketing. We'll
    call her... Lyta.

GUIDOLON: And who are we going to get to play...
    this Lyta... so late in production?

FRIBUGUS: Didn't Trisuron used to act?

GUIDOLON (grumbles)

FRIBUGUS: Purse strings!

GUIDOLON: Sorry.

FRIBUGUS: Yes, Trisuron will make a fine Lt.
    Commander Lyta White. (looking through script)
    OK. Good. Now. Tell me about these chicken
    attack scenes.

GUIDOLON: These are some of the best. For the
    audience to comprehend the tragedy of
    Guidolon's death, they have to realise the
    great potential that was lost...

INTERCUTTING:

VARIOUS SHOTS

GUIDOLON (o.s.): On this planet are billions of
    poultry, enslaved by the food industry... Led
    inextricably to ignoble deaths.

Stock footage of factories with chickens in rows of
    crates, stretching into infinity. Then, during a
    Thanksgiving feast, we see turkey legs snapped off at
    the knee.

GUIDOLON (o.s.): Guidolon will be their
    liberator...

We see grainy footage of chickens lined up in armies, like TRIUMPH OF THE WILL, but with chickens instead of Nazis.

GUIDOLON (o.s.): **Under Guidolon's leadership, they will rise up against their oppressors.**

We see the US President sitting in the oval office.

PRESIDENT JIMMY CARTER: **We suffer today from a crisis in confidence.**

A team of white chickens, and one killer rabbit, fly up from under the President's desk, attacking him, while he screams and flails with an oar.

GUIDOLON (o.s.): **Guidolon founds a chicken world order.**

We see Takashi in his Guidolon suit standing proudly before a huge flag decorated with stars and chicken heads.

INT. CONFERENCE ROOM — EARLY MORNING

GUIDOLON: **This is what drives him until it undoes him. Because, like any tragedy, the main character has to die at the end.**

FRIBUGUS: **Guidolon dies, yes, but chickens conquering the world? No no no. Why do I always have to be the voice of reason?**

GUIDOLON: **Without these scenes, how can Guidolon be the Cosmic Avian Avenger? Without these scenes, he's just... just...**

FRIBUGUS: **What?**

GUIDOLON: **A giant space chicken.**

FRIBUGUS: **You said it. Not me, you freak with a beak.** (tidies papers and stands) **I think that wraps it up. And Guidolon, don't forget. This is Dengaku Studios' movie. Always has been, always will be.**

INT. SPACESHIP BRIDGE — DAY

The bridge has windows in front, where Captain Takao and Lyta sit. On the sides are stations for the other two crewmen. The electronics are voltmeters, tachometers and knobs from an AM radio. Lyta is the only one not wearing a helmet, blonde hair falling into her face.

Takashi in Guidolon suit appears on the windows. Lyta screams a Fay Wray scream.

CAPTAIN TAKAO: **Target seven point eighteen point nine! Fire remote-controlled rocket missiles!**

Sound effect of missiles firing, with ship "lurching", as camera shakes and crew rock in their chairs.

CAPTAIN TAKAO: Die, monster, die!

The rockets explode against Takashi's scaly skin.

CREWMAN #1: The missiles have no effect!

LYTA (nods knowingly)

CAPTAIN TAKAO (piloting ship, as crewmen tilt):
Lyta, how did you know they wouldn't work?

LYTA: The monster is made of Guidolonium!

CAPTAIN TAKAO (pressing buttons for lasers):
What's that?

The monster howls, more annoyed by the lasers than
injured.

LYTA (looking into voltmeter): **These spectral
lines reveal that Guidolonium is an element
not on our periodical table! Therefore
Guidolon came into our solar system 15
trillion years ago!**

Takao continues firing lasers, despite their obvious
uselessness.

LYTA: **Guidolonium interacts with molecular oxygen
in our atmosphere, making Guidolonium oxide,
which is a dense, impenetrable shield!
Guidolon sheds explosions off his body, like
Turtle Wax sheds water off a car!**

CAPTAIN TAKAO: **How are we going to defeat this
creature? You're the scientist!**

LYTA: **Maybe if we can figure out how it got to
earth in the first place...**

CAPTAIN TAKAO: **You've got to think of something
or... it will conquer the world!** (pressing
laser button one last time)

FRIBUGUS (o.s.): Cut!

Pan from spaceship interior to reveal that it is part of
a

INT. SPACESHIP BRIDGE MOVIE SET

FRIBUGUS (wings fluttering contentedly): **Good job,
everybody! That catches us up some. Now get
some rest and we'll be back at it tomorrow!**

Lyta slinks like a sex kitten toward Guidolon.

ZOOM IN TO CLOSE UP:

On Lyta's hand as it moves toward the top of the zipper
running down the middle of her orange jumpsuit.

CLOSE UP:

On Guidolon, bug eyes open in delight.

EXTREME CLOSE UP

On Lyta's hand, pulling the zipper down, between her
    breasts. The jumpsuit falls to the stage floor,
    revealing a monster body underneath. Lyta reaches for
    her blonde hair and pulls. Her face mask comes off,
    revealing Trisuron. She takes off a hairnet, rubs her
    scalp and her three triceratops horns pop out. She
    loosens her girdle.

GUIDOLON: Hello, beautiful.

TRISURON (smiles at him): **How did I do?**

GUIDOLON (happiness draining from his face)

TRISURON (wiping her horns with a rag): **That bad?
    I thought it went pretty well.**

GUIDOLON: No, it's not that. You were great. Very
    believable as a human female. Only...

TRISURON: Honey, what?

GUIDOLON: This is going to sound stupid, but...

TRISURON: What?

GUIDOLON: You were so good that it reminded me
    what a talentless, irrelevant hack I've
    become. You make me look bad.

TRISURON: It's all about you, isn't it?

CUT TO:

CLOSE UP:

A clawed, scaly, irridescent hand draws an X through a
    page of the script.

FRIBUGUS (wings conveying his annoyance):
    Guidolon, tell me what this long speech is?

ZOOM OUT to show

INT. CONFERENCE ROOM — EARLY MORNING AGAIN

With Guidolon and Fribugus.

GUIDOLON: It's called a soliloquy.

FRIBUGUS: No no no. Monsters can't talk in
    movies. Not like in real life.

Fribugus rips up the pages of the script and throws
    them onto the floor. They scatter, like the pages
    of Willard's notes on Kurtz thrown in the river in
    APOCALYPSE NOW.

INT. SMALL CRAMPED OFFICE

Several monsters are typing mimeographs to copy the next
    day's shooting script.

Octuron stands over the shoulder of a monster typist
    named KENJI, who uses a NASA rocket as a pipe.

OCTURON (handing him handwritten pages): **These are changes for tomorrow's shoot.**

KENJI: You want this back in? Fribugus told me it was out.

OCTURON: When did you talk to him?

KENJI: Maybe an hour ago.

OCTURON: Well, that was the six o'clock version. This is the six-thirty. Let me see what you've got already.

KENJI (hands him some sheets)

OCTURON: Yeah, just type up these new changes and we'll be good to go.

Octuron turns to go, taking Kenji's sheets. As he leaves the office, Guidolon is waiting for him.

OCTURON: OK, I did what you wanted me to do. Your version's back in.

GUIDOLON: Good. Thanks a lot. I'm lucky you're my friend.

OCTURON (grumbles, octopus body quivering unhappily)

EXT. BURNING TOKYO — NIGHT

Tanks wind through narrow streets, blasting Takashi in Guidolon suit, but the explosions do nothing. Then he sees a small crowd of JAPANESE PEOPLE FLEEING.

Takashi unleashes a blast of fire breath. The people scream, bursting into flames. As the fires clear, we see that the blast has left shadows of the people on an alley wall — like the atomic blast at Hiroshima.

FRIBUGUS (o.s.): Cut! Cut!

Zoom out to reveal

EXT. BURNING TOKYO MOVIE SET

FRIBUGUS (wings fluttering, peeved): **That's not in my script! Script girl!**

Tractor beams shoot from Fribugus' eyes, pulling a SCRIPT GIRL MONSTER on roller skates, who hands him the day's shooting script.

FRIBUGUS: Guidolon, you switched scripts!

GUIDOLON (looking innocent)

FRIBUGUS: You're lucky I don't want to be re-writing when we could be shooting. (flipping through script) Every second we waste arguing is money down the drain. This crew doesn't work for free, you know? OK, well, I can

skip over some of this and salvage something
filmable. (wings quietly threatening) **Guidolon,
you win this one. But don't ever, I mean ever,
try this again.**

GUIDOLON (smiles to himself)

INT. SOUND STAGE

OCTURON (octopus body completely deflated): **I'm
sorry, boss. I can't take this anymore.**

GUIDOLON: **Do you need more money?**

OCTURON: **That would be good, but that's not it.**
(like James Dean in REBEL WITHOUT A CAUSE) **I'm
supposed to be the script writer, but then you
write one thing, he writes something else, and
then it all changes back again. You're tearing
me apart! We're re-writing and re-shooting the
beginning of the film. We're going backwards! I
have to take some time off. I'm sorry, Guido.**

GUIDOLON: **There's no way I can change your mind?**

OCTURON (shakes his head)

GUIDOLON: **Octuron — Thanks for everything, pal. I
really appreciate it.**

Octuron smiles and holds out a tentacle for Guidolon to
shake. Guidolon knocks the tentacle aside, giving
his friend a big squishy hug. Then Octuron walks
away, off the set.

Sad music.

**INTERCUTTING: INT. SPACESHIP BRIDGE and EXT. SPACESHIP
and FLYING SAUCER IN SPACE**

Rocketship XK-Omega-9 is sleek, though studded with more
fins, canards, winglets, and vertical stabilisers than
is strictly necessary. Its four engines constantly
spew flame as the ship returns from Mars. Captain
Takao, Lyta and the two crewmen sit on the bridge.

CREWMAN #1: **Captain! We have a blip!**

CREWMAN #2: **It's not like anything I've seen
before!**

A glowing flying saucer — shaped like an orange that's
been run over by a car — moves ominously toward the
rocketship.

LYTA: **Oh no! It's the Altairiarians! They've been
raiding our galaxy for centuries!**

CAPTAIN TAKAO: **Die, you Altairiarian scum, die!**

XK-Omega-9 fires missiles at the flying saucer. Massive
explosions, but the saucer is unharmed.

CAPTAIN TAKAO: Lyta, what can we do?

LYTA: Nothing! Let's get out of here!

CAPTAIN TAKAO: OK, then. Fire all laser cannons!

Lasers shoot out from the rocketship. They too are
ineffectual.

CAPTAIN TAKAO: Evasive maneuvers!

CREWMAN #1: Too late!

The flying saucer launches little white balls. As the
rocketship swerves, most of the balls miss or bounce
off to hull. Unexpectedly, they do not explode.

CAPTAIN TAKAO: What were those?

LYTA: I don't know, sir!

CAPTAIN TAKAO: They didn't explode!

CREWMAN #1: The flying saucer's getting away!

CREWMAN #2: Maybe it's retreating because all its
missiles were duds.

CREWMAN #1: Shouldn't we go after it?

CAPTAIN TAKAO: No, we barely have enough fuel to
get back to Earth. Let's go home.

CLOSE UP:

On the EXT. SPACESHIP XK-OMEGA-9. One white ball has
stuck to the hull. It pulses, quivering, as if alive.

ORSON WELLES, NARRATOR (v.o.): Unbeknownst to our
heroic crew, the flying saucer has planted
an alien egg on the earthmen's ship. But who
knows what terrors lie hidden inside this
space seed? Horrors beyond imagination.

The space egg contains two tiny ovals, which glow like
Guidolon's bug eyes.

INT. SOUND STAGE

FRIBUGUS: Cut! That's perfect. Now we're really
getting somewhere.

Trisuron and Guidolon stand in the shadows.

GUIDOLON: You've got to get him off the movie set
for me.

TRISURON: How?

GUIDOLON: I don't care. Tell him No. 1 wants to
see him.

TRISURON: You want me to lie to him? He's my friend.

GUIDOLON: Then what I am to you?

TRISURON: OK. I'll do it. You keep up this
    insanity, though, and...

GUIDOLON: And what?

Trisuron sighs and leaves. She whispers into Fribugus'
    ear and he hoots in delight.

FRIBUGUS: I gotta go! I'm going to see the
    boss! Everybody be good while I'm gone! (to
    Guidolon) Especially you.

Fribugus shoots reverse tractor beams at the floor,
    lifting off and flying away.

Guidolon finds the MONSTER D.P. (director of photography).

GUIDOLON: This is what I want you to. Empty all
    the cameras. Mark the film canisters we've shot
    today with a red X.

D.P.: But I just reloaded two cameras a few shots
    ago.

GUIDOLON: I want all that footage kept separate
    from what we shoot next.

D.P.: That's absurd, but you're the boss...

TRISURON: Guido, what are you doing?

GUIDOLON: All Fribugus' footage from today will
    be destroyed before it's developed at the film
    lab. And now that he's gone, I can re-shoot
    this scene the way I want to!

INTERCUTTING:

INT. SPACESHIP BRIDGE and EXT. SPACESHIP and

EXT. FLYING SAUCER IN SPACE and INT. FLYING SAUCER BRIDGE

The flying saucer appears in front of the rocketship.

CAPTAIN TAKAO: Fire all missiles!

Missiles explode against the saucer, which is
    undamaged and continues to zoom toward the
    rocketship.

We see the cockpit of the flying saucer, which is
    just like that of the XK-Omega-9, but with more
    Christmas lights. Takashi in his Guidolon suit
    pilots.

CREWMAN #2: He's gonna ram us!

CAPTAIN TAKAO: Fire all lasers!

The lasers bounce off the saucer's hull. As the ships
    are about to collide, with one claw Takashi presses a
    strange button.

They're all about to die, so Captain Takao stands and
    hugs Lyta. She doesn't mind. They watch through the

window, helplessly, as the saucer approaches closer and closer.

Then the saucer explodes.

The four crewmembers jump up and down, happy to be alive.

EXT. — SPACESHIP HULL — IN SPACE

Through the bridge windows, we see the crew celebrating, then we pan across the ship's hull and see a clawed foot on the hull. Takashi is standing on the rocketship, riding it like a surfboard. [Note for modelmakers: Takashi's height is two-thirds the rocketship's length.]

ORSON WELLES (v.o.): Unbeknownst to our heroic crew, the cosmic avian avenger has sacrificed his own ship. Now he can hitch a ride aboard their rocketship and on toward new lands to conquer...the late great planet Earth.

INT. SPACESHIP BRIDGE — IN SPACE, APPROACHING EARTH

SPACE COMMAND (o.s., filtered): This is United Earth Alliance Federal Space Command, please identify yourself.

CAPTAIN TAKAO: This is Spaceship XK-Omega-9. Do we have permission to land?

SPACE COMMAND (o.s., filtered): Permission to land granted. Coordinates seven point eighteen point nine. But your approach vector is off. Are you carrying extra weight?

CAPTAIN TAKAO: Negative. We collected only twenty pounds of Mars rocks.

SPACE COMMAND (o.s., filtered): I recommend visual inspection of the ship. You may have accumulated space debris.

Captain Takao points to crewman #1, who dons a spacesuit and crawls through a passageway.

EXT. HULL OF SPACESHIP

Crewman #1 opens a hatch on the top of the ship. Seeing Takashi towering above him, he screams.

CAPTAIN TAKAO (o.s., filtered): What's going on?

CREWMAN #1: It's a giant monster!

INT. SPACESHIP BRIDGE — IN SPACE

Crewman #1 stumbles onto the bridge, breathless, terrified.

CAPTAIN TAKAO: Lyta, you're the scientist! What do we do?

LYTA: Can we electrify the exterior hull of the ship?

CAPTAIN TAKAO: I don't know. I've been flying this baby for five years. We haven't needed to before.

CREWMAN #2 (looking at Rocketship Instruction Manual): Here it is! Page 7189!

CAPTAIN TAKAO: I don't see what that will do!

LYTA: No time to argue! Hurry! Do it now!

EXT. SPACESHIP — IN SPACE, NOW NEAR EARTH

The ship is now just entering the most tenuous part of the earth's atmosphere. Suddenly, sparks start crackling at Takashi's toes. He dances from one foot to the other and then falls from the ship.

LYTA (o.s.): Hurrah! The monster's gone!

INT. SPACESHIP BRIDGE — ENTERING EARTH'S ATMOSPHERE

CAPTAIN TAKAO: Lyta, I think that's it.

LYTA: What's it?

CAPTAIN TAKAO: That's my career. After this, I'm done fighting giant space monsters.

LYTA: What will you do?

CAPTAIN TAKAO: My family has some greenhouses near Kokonoe. They grow roses.

LYTA: It can take years to train a good rose bush.

CAPTAIN TAKAO: Yeah, years. Farming makes you feel really planted, settled. You like roses?

LYTA: Sir, I love roses!

They kiss.

EXT. MONSTER TAKASHI IN SPACE

The monster Takashi is now falling through the air. He is tumbling, seemingly burning up on re-entry.

ORSON WELLES (v.o.): Unbeknownst to the celebrating crew, the monster's skin interacts with oxygen to produce the densest molecule in the universe. A hard crust forms around him — a heat shield as he plummets to Earth.

The monster falls like a meteor through the sky, landing on the slope of a mountain. As he hits, he tucks in his shoulder and remembers to roll. His momentum is dissipated by hurtling down the mountain, leaving a swath of crushed burnt trees, until he tumbles into Tokyo bay, releasing a ball of steam.

GUIDOLON (o.s.): Cut!

INT. MOVIE SET

GUIDOLON: Oh, that was perfect! Isn't that a
    better way to explain Guidolon's origin? Now
    Guidolon isn't just a lackey of space aliens,
    but he decided himself to invade the earth.

PRODUCTION ASSISTANT #1 (coming up to Guidolon):
    Fribugus is on his way back.

GUIDOLON: OK, everybody! That's great! Get some
    sleep and we'll be back tomorrow. (to Prod.
    Asst. #1) Tell the D.P. to get the film to the
    lab. Except the stuff marked with red X's. He
    can just throw that away.

Production Assistant #1 walks over to the D.P.

PROD. ASST. #1: Guidolon said to develop the film
    right away. Except to throw away the stuff
    marked X.

D.P.: Every order Guidolon gives gets stranger and
    stranger.

The D.P. finishes unloading the film from a camera and
    hands the canister to the Prod. Assistant.

D.P.: You know where the film lab is, right?

PROD. ASST. #1 (not knowing): Yeah, of course I
    know.

Now carrying four canisters of film, the Production
    Assistant runs into Fribugus, who is just arriving.

FRIBUGUS: What do you have there?

PROD. ASST. #1: I'm on my way to the lab.

FRIBUGUS: This is all that we shot today? I
    guess Guidolon didn't get much done while I
    was gone.

PROD. ASST. #1: No, actually, this isn't all of
    it.

FRIBUGUS: Well, get your act together. Collect all
    the film we shot today and get it to the lab!
    All of it!

The young Prod. Asst. runs off. Fribugus finds Trisuron on
    the set.

FRIBUGUS: I thought you said No. 1 wanted to see
    me.

TRISURON: That was the message I was told to give
    you.

FRIBUGUS: Who told you that? It was Guidolon,
    wasn't it? Wasn't it?

TRISURON (nodding her head yes): No.

FRIBUGUS (pounds his clawed fist): Oh, that little

bird brain's gonna die! (calming down) **How did
the filming go while I was gone?**

TRISURON: It went pretty well, actually.

FRIBUGUS: Well, maybe while I was gone Guidolon
returned to reason.

CLOSE UP:

Guidolon behind the wheel of a dark-coloured golf cart.
The mouth under his beak is twisted into a maniacal,
obsessed grimace.

EXT. **BACK LOT OF MOVIE STUDIO — EVENING WITH OMINOUS
CLOUDS**

Prod. Asst. #1 carefully negotiates a white golf cart
between the buildings on the lot. He stops so a TECH
with a wheeled rack of costumes can pass. In the seat
beside him are film cans. Just as he is about to start
up, he is rammed from behind — by Guidolon's golf
cart. Startled, the Assistant floors his golf cart.
He whips around a corner, Guidolon in hot pursuit.
The Assistant is gunning the golf cart at top speed
(the equivalent of 15 mph). A PROP MISTRESS with a
bowl of fruit dives out of the way, tossing fruit
into the air. The Assistant and Guidolon rumble their
golf carts over the fruit, but a SOUNDMAN slips on a
banana peel. The Assistant looks back to laugh, but
as he turns around, he smashes straight into a wall.
Styrofoam bricks and rocks tumble down, burying him,
the cart and the film cans. Guidolon pulls up behind
him.

PROD. ASST. #1 (extricating himself from Styrofoam
bits): **Are you crazy?**

GUIDOLON (getting out of his cart): **No, I'm a
filmmaker.**

PROD. ASST. #1: **Oh, my gosh! It's you! What are
you doing?**

GUIDOLON: **Give me the film!**

PROD. ASST. #1: **Is that what this is all about?**
(shoves Styrofoam aside to find a can. He flings
it at Guidolon, but it is so heavy, it lands
at Guidolon's feet) **You can have it!** (flings
another at him, throwing harder and further.
Continues throwing canisters) **And this one!
And this!**

Guidolon is struck by a film canister, between top of bug
eye and base of deelie bopper. He gathers up the cans
off the ground. One marked with an X he rips open
with a screwdriver. He unravels the film, exposing it
to the sunlight.

PROD. ASST. #1: **You're out of your mind!**

GUIDOLON: No, I am taking control of my destiny.

PROD. ASST. #1: You people are crazy! And you're not even paying me for this job!

GUIDOLON (throwing some coins on the ground): There! That's your severance pay!

PROD. ASST. #1: Fine! I hope nobody ever sees your stupid movie! I hope you never make another movie in this town again, you pollo loco!

INT. GUIDOLON'S TRAILER — LATE

It is dark and sad. Guidolon looks at himself in the mirror; maybe he has become a monster. The movie posters with circled names of Guidolon, Trisuron, Jerora and Octuron are still on the walls. As are the photos. But Jerora and Octuron are gone now. The chair where Trisuron mixed a Tokyo City Hall is empty. Guidolon is all alone.

Guidolon realises he is sitting on something. He pulls from under him a copy of the script. Scrawled at the top is:

HONEY, I MISS YOU.

PLEASE COME BACK TO ME.

TRISURON

A knock at the door to the trailer.

FRIBUGUS (o.s., outside): You want to be in on the next shoot or not?

GUIDOLON: Start without me!

FRIBUGUS (o.s., outside): Suit yourself, you lazy buzzard!

We hear Fribugus fly away.

SLOWLY FADE TO BLACK

SLOWLY FADE UP

INT. GUIDOLON'S TRAILER — LATER

Guidolon has been there quite a while. Drinking. It's very dark now. He picks up a rotary telephone and dials it.

TRISURON (o.s., filtered): Hello? (Guidolon is silent, holding the phone against his ear in the dark, listening to Trisuron's voice) Hello? Who is this? OK, I'm hanging up now.

GUIDOLON: Babe, it's me.

TRISURON (pretending not to recognise the voice): Who is this?

GUIDOLON: I sat behind you in seventh grade

English. Uh, all year long I wanted to
talk to you. But I was distracted by too
much schoolwork. You probably thought I was
just some pencil-neck geek. I wasn't on the
football team or anything, but I was wondering
if you might... If you'd like to go out on a
date with me Friday night.

TRISURON (after an excruciatingly long pause): All
right, whatever.

INT. WILLIS O'BRIEN'S RESTAURANT — DINNER TIME

Willis O'Brien's is a swanky restaurant, with lots of
shiny crystal. A painting of King Kong hangs in the
foyer.

Trisuron and Guidolon sit at a table across from each
other. Trisuron wears diamond and gold rings, one
around each horn.

We hear other DINERS talk, as Trisuron and Guidolon are
silent. A WAITER arrives with a platter.

WAITER: Sizzling seafood?

Guidolon raises a claw, tentatively. The waiter places
the plate on the table, then coughs up a jet of
radioactive breath to set it afire. He walks away.

Guidolon and Trisuron share the tiniest of smiles.

GUIDOLON: Did I ever tell you that when I was
little, I used to barf up fireballs in my
sleep? Set my bed on fire once.

No reaction from Trisuron.

GUIDOLON: Thanks for agreeing to see me tonight.
Sorry I've been so out of sorts lately.

TRISURON: I heard about your... car accident. How
dramatic.

GUIDOLON: I've driven away everyone I care about.
Everyone I love.

TRISURON: That's about right.

GUIDOLON: Sorry.

TRISURON: You're not really sorry. We've made
movies before. Why is this one so important?
More important to you than Jerora or Octuron?
Or me?

GUIDOLON: It's not. It just seems that way.

TRISURON: Yeah.

GUIDOLON: Do you really want to know?

TRISURON: Yeah, I suppose.

GUIDOLON: OK. OK. As you know, I starred in

a little movie many years ago called THE
OMEGA MONSTER.

TRISURON: HORROR BEYOND IMAGINATION? Yessirree,
Bob, this I know.

GUIDOLON: It stunk, didn't it? But what I never
told you was that Dengaku studios wanted this
to be a new franchise.

WIPE TO:

EXT. TOKYO IN FLAMES — NIGHT

Guidolon — younger, slimmer, bouncier — ravages Tokyo,
pushing over building, stomping on tanks, smashing
jet fighters.

GUIDOLON (o.s.): And so they picked me, Guidolon,
the giant space chicken. I was going to
compete with Godzilla's movies.

INT. WILLIS O'BRIEN'S RESTAURANT

TRISURON: It wasn't a bad movie.

GUIDOLON: Nah, it was retarded. You know I was
married then?

TRISURON: To Gorgo.

GUIDOLON: Yes, and she had an affair and left me.

TRISURON: For Barugon.

GUIDOLON: Right. I didn't tell you that we got
a huge payout from the first movie, with
the promise of more when it did box office
boffo. She bought this big house. I didn't
mind, it made her happy. But then the movie
bombed. Maybe if I had made enough money,
she would have been happy. We'd have been
happy. But that didn't happen. We had to
sell her dream house. It was my fault. And
then she left. You know, I really loved
her. A long time ago.

TRISURON: You're better off without her.

GUIDOLON: But maybe she was right. Maybe I was too
wrapped up in my own projects. And maybe I'm
doing the same thing now. To you. To us.

Trisuron smiles to encourage him to make the right choice
now.

GUIDOLON: You have no idea.

WIPE TO:

INTERCUTTING:

EXT/INT SHOTS OF YOUNGER GUIDOLON, JERORA AND OCTURON

GUIDOLON (o.s.): One day me and Jerora and Octuron

are tearing up Sunset Strip. All three of us
have our own movies. The phone never stops
ringing. Then it all changes. None of our
movies gets tapped for a sequel. In a blink,
we're all divorced. Has-beens. I gained six
hundred pounds. We do nothing but drink.

We see Guidolon lying in a gutter in a stupor.

A LITTLE BOY and his MOM approach Guidolon.

LITTLE BOY: Look, mommy! The giant space chicken's
loaded!

INT. WILLIS O'BRIEN'S RESTAURANT

GUIDOLON: Maybe my career's over. Everything I've
struggled to achieve my whole life... is lying
in ruins. Irreparable, unfixable. But I'm OK
with that.

TRISURON: Oh, honey, I didn't know. I guess I
never really understood... You hadn't told me,
you hadn't let me into your world before...

GUIDOLON: I'm not good at sharing the most
pathetic parts of my personal history. But
now, now... Now everybody is nostalgic for the
past, even the past they never experienced in
the first place. Everybody wants to make new
versions of old TV shows and movies! This is
it! I get to finally make the movie about me
I always wanted! This is my movie, this is my
time, this is my chance.

TRISURON: Oh, honey...

GUIDOLON: And maybe this was my last chance. Now
I'll never work in this town again. It's all
over. I've lost the movie. I've lost you, I've
lost Jerora and Octuron. And...

TRISURON: And?

GUIDOLON: I wanted to make you proud of me. The
world's full of giant gorillas and giant fire-
breathing dinosaurs and cool monsters like
that. Why would you want to hang around with
some stupid space chicken?

TRISURON: Because I happen to love giant space
chicken movies. And I love giant space chickens.

GUIDOLON (tears streaming from his bug eyes)

The waiter reappears.

WAITER: Would anyone like dessert?

Guidolon shakes his teary-eyed head and the waiter walks
away.

TRISURON: Do you miss me?

GUIDOLON (nods silently, wipes beak)

TRISURON: Do you want to come back?

GUIDOLON (nods)

TRISURON: Come here.

GUIDOLON (gets out of his chair, collapses on
        the floor, head in Trisuron's lap. His pointy
        cheeks stab her in her scaly thigh, but she
        doesn't mind.): I love you.

TRISURON: I love you, too.

GUIDOLON: I even wrote a killer ending that stars
        you.

TRISURON: Oh, I don't care about that.

Both of them are crying. They hold each other for another
        long beat and then Trisuron can't wait any longer:

TRISURON: OK, now, tell me about this killer
        ending that I'm in.

DISSOLVE TO:

INT. SPACESHIP BRIDGE

CAPTAIN TAKAO: Evasive maneuvers!

Lyta, the Captain and the two crewmen lean in their
        seats. Then the ship turns completely upside-down,
        and they land awkwardly around the bridge. As the
        ship rights itself, the Captain grabs the controls.
        Lyta is in a corner, in pain.

LYTA: My leg! My leg!

The captain hits the AUTO PILOT button and comes over to
        her. Her leg is all red.

CAPTAIN TAKAO: Hey — this doesn't look like blood!
        It's ketchup!

LYTA: Hey — you're right!

She strikes him over the head with a pistol, knocking him
        out.

CREWMEN #1 and #2: What are you doing?

LYTA: Taking command.

With the gun, she motions the two crewmen backward. A
        glass hatch opens behind each. Lyta waves the gun
        and they enter, the hatches closing. They are marked
        ESCAPE POD #1 and #2. Lyta hits some buttons and the
        pods are jettisoned.

We hear a groan as the Captain rises from the floor. She
        points the gun at him.

CAPTAIN TAKAO: Lyta, I thought you —

LYTA: That's why I have to do this.

Lyta ushers the captain into a third escape pod. The glass hatch closes over him.

CAPTAIN TAKAO'S POV:

Lyta leaves a lipstick kiss on the glass hatch, and her mouth silently says "I LOVE YOU". Then the captain's pod shoots from the ship to safety.

CAPTAIN TAKAO (o. s.): Lyyyyytaaaaaaaa!

Lyta sits in the captain's chair and slaps the auto pilot off.

INTERCUT:

EXT. TOKYO BAY — NIGHT and INT. SPACESHIP BRIDGE — NIGHT

Lyta brings the ship under control and flies it right toward Takashi in his Guidolon suit.

The monster is rarring and shooting fireballs into the air. He stands waist-deep in Tokyo bay, and is preparing to devastate the city once again.

CAPTAIN TAKAO (o.s., filtered, from speaker on the control panel): Lyta! Lyta!

LYTA (into microphone): Hello, Captain.

CAPTAIN TAKAO (o.s., filtered): What are you doing?

LYTA: Only the outer crust of the monster is Guidolonium oxide. His insides are all still pure Guidolonium.

CAPTAIN TAKAO (o.s., filtered): I don't see how that helps us!

LYTA: The earth's atmosphere is only twenty-percent oxygen. If I can crash the ship into Tokyo bay, and then electrify the hull, that will electrolyse the water into oxygen and hydrogen. If I can raise the local oxygen level to forty per cent, he should turn into solid Guidolonium oxide.

CAPTAIN TAKAO (o.s., filtered): Won't that make the monster indestructible?

LYTA: Maybe against explosives. But it will also turn him so dense and so heavy that he will fall through the crust of the earth. He'll be crushed by the weight of the earth's mantle!

CAPTAIN TAKAO (o.s., filtered): That's so crazy, it just might work!

LYTA: But is it too crazy — or not crazy enough?

CAPTAIN TAKAO (o.s., filtered): **But you'll be killed!**

LYTA: Believe me, Captain, that's not my intention! I know of some rose gardens that could use a woman's touch!

Lyta crashes the ship into the bay, creating a wave that knocks Takashi down. He stumbles to his feet, water splashing around him. As the ship pitches wildly, Lyta hits some Christmas lights on the control panel.

Electrical arcs fly out of the ship and into the water. The water sizzles and boils, as Takashi howls.

Lyta makes her way across the lurching bridge and into the last escape pod.

CAPTAIN TAKAO (o.s., filtered): **Lyta, get out of there!**

Lyta fumbles for the panel inside the pod. Buttons say EJECT 1 and 2. She hits the first button, and a protective panel is blown off the top of the ship, uncovering the escape pod. She can now see through a second glass hatch at the top of the pod.

WHAT SHE SEES:

Takashi rarring above her, smashing his claws into the ship, as electrical arcs continue to shoot from the ship, frying the water.

She hits the second EJECT button. And nothing happens. She hits it again and again. Still, nothing happens.

LYTA: Aw, poo.

EXT. TOKYO BAY — NIGHT

A humongous explosion. Water and fire fly in every direction. Takashi has started to solidify into Guidolonium oxide, his arms stiff in front of him. He falls forward, crushing the remains of the exploded spaceship.

EXT. MANTLE OF THE EARTH — SIDE VIEW

Takashi is in agony as he falls through the crust of the earth. Water vaporises as it hits the red-hot magma. Ship wreckage tumbles down after him, exploding. Takashi claws at the lava and magma, but he can't get a hand-hold. Gravity is pulling him down. Tons of hot rocks pour down on his head. The lights in his glowing big bug eyes go out. The monster is dead.

EXT. TOKYO BAY — NEXT MORNING

The destruction of the monster has thrown up all sorts of rock, which have blocked Tokyo bay from the rest of the Pacific. In the middle of the empty bay is a huge hole, like a drain, where the monster fell through.

Captain Takao and the two crewmen walk along the bottom

of the bay. Beached oil tankers and sailboats are
scattered around. A fish flops, gasping in the mud.
Crewman #1 picks it up and tosses it, happily, into a
large puddle.

The men reach the edge of the hole and look down.

CREWMAN #1: 'Twas beauty killed the beast.

CREWMAN #2: And beast killed beauty.

CREWMAN #1: You know she loved you.

CAPTAIN TAKAO: But she loved life more.

The Captain has a bouquet of roses in his hand. He rears
back and throws it toward the pit. We FREEZE FRAME on
the bouquet suspended against the bright morning sky.

FADE TO BLACK

TITLE CARD:

"THE END"

CREDITS ROLL

INT. SCREENING ROOM

Lights come up. We have been watching a cut of the film,
along with Trisuron, Guidolon, Fribugus and other
monsters.

TRISURON: Oh, honey, that was wonderful!

GUIDOLON: I think it all worked out OK.

Trisuron snuggles up to Guidolon and kisses his pointy
cheek. Guidolon smiles, proudly.

FRIBUGUS: You can't have the girl die at the end.
Monster yes, girl no.

TRISURON: You want the girl rescued?

GUIDOLON (joking): Maybe she can be rescued by
midget wrestlers.

FRIBUGUS: I don't care. As long as she doesn't
die. And the movie needs more action. And more
funny bits.

GUIDOLON: The movie's fine the way it is!

FRIBUGUS: Nope. Those are the changes I want.

GUIDOLON: You're not going to oversee these
changes yourself?

FRIBUGUS: I've been called off this project, since
it's basically done, to go work on some other
films in trouble.

TRISURON: You're leaving?

FRIBUGUS: This was just a job to me. Catch ya
later.

Fribugus leaves.

GUIDOLON: I can't do this.

TRISURON: But I know some people who can help.

GUIDOLON: Who?

TRISURON: Maybe Jerora and Octuron.

GUIDOLON: Do they still want to be my friends?

TRISURON: Can you muster an apology?

INT. CONFERENCE ROOM — AFTERNOON

Octuron, Jerora, Trisuron and Guidolon sit at a small
    table, awkwardly eyeing each other. It's worse than
    marriage counseling.

TRISURON: OK, maybe, Guidolon, you can apologise
    to Jerora and Octuron. And maybe you guys can
    find something to apologise to Guidolon for.

Guidolon doesn't say anything. Trisuron elbows him. He
    still doesn't say anything.

JERORA (pointing translucent tentacle): Guido,
    you've been treating us like errand boys since
    this movie started.

OCTURON (pointing suckered tentacle): Yeah, you've
    walked all over us. Used us like grocery
    clerks.

GUIDOLON: Without me, you guys would be lying in a
    gutter. But some friends you guys turned out
    to be! When I need you the most, you take off!

TRISURON: Wait, you guys are supposed to talk
    through your misunderstandings...

JERORA: Guido, you are a self-important giant
    flightless bird with delusions of grandeur!

Guidolon rarrs heroically, more powerfully than before.
    Octuron's tentacles flail in the air, then he rushes
    Guidolon. Guidolon is knocked over, as Octuron wraps
    his tentacles around him. Jerora jumps on him, too.
    The three male monsters roll in a ball around the
    conference room, crushing the table. Script drafts,
    production notes and sketches fly around.

TRISURON: Guys! Guys!

Guidolon pecks at a tentacle — hard! — until Octuron lets
    go. Guidolon spits a fire ball at Jerora, and Jerora
    shoots electrical beams at Guidolon.

Finally, Guidolon, Octuron and Jerora are exhausted and
    lay in a pile, panting.

OCTURON (pulling himself upright): That was fun.

Jerora pulses and giggles.

GUIDOLON: You guys wanna be friends again?

JERORA: Sure.

OCTURON: Sounds great.

JERORA: What do we need to do to finish this movie?

GUIDOLON: More humor and more fight scenes and...

TRISURON: Hold on! Hold on! Honey, don't you need to apologise to them? And Jerora and Octuron, don't you need an apology from Guidolon?

Silence.

GUIDOLON: Hey guys, are we cool?

JERORA: Sure.

OCTURON: Yeah, why not?

GUIDOLON (explaining to Trisuron): We're guys.

The three male monsters nod at each other. Octuron goes around the room with a fire extinguisher.

TRISURON: I don't even know why I bother.

JERORA: More laughs? More battle scenes? I snuck in and saw a print of the movie. It seemed fine.

OCTURON: I don't know why we don't go over Fribugus' head to the top execs. Show 'em our version of the movie.

GUIDOLON: Oh, I have a better idea. Fribugus is a menace. We have to take care of him. It would be irresponsible to let him go — he'll just wreck someone else's movie.

JERORA: What do we do?

GUIDOLON: We make two versions of this film. One we just leave it the way it is, the way we like. The other version we incorporate all of Fribugus' suggestions.

JERORA: And they'll love our version and hate Fribugus' and kick him out of town.

GUIDOLON: Sounds great.

TRISURON: So I get rescued at the end?

GUIDOLON (joking): Yeah, by midget wrestlers.

All the monsters laugh.

OCTURON: That's funny.

JERORA: I like that.

GUIDOLON: So do I.

TRISURON: Midget wrestlers? In a monster movie?

Are you sure this a good idea?

OCTURON: No, no, the point is that it's a bad idea.

TRISURON: Hmm.

GUIDOLON: Maybe we have to destroy the movie in order to save it.

JERORA: How about midget Mexican wrestlers?

GUIDOLON: Octuron, can you write that?

OCTURON: Oh, Guido, once you add midget Mexican wrestlers to a film, the screenplay practically writes itself.

GUIDOLON (o.s.): And we could play the wrestlers ourselves to save money!

INTERCUTTING:

INT. SPACESHIP — VARIOUS SHOTS

OCTURON (o.s.): They'll work in the spaceship's engine room.

We see stereotypes of Mexicans. They are swarthy, unshaven; they wear bandoliers and soiled clothing. The three wrestlers are the monsters, dressed up, in an oversized set.

They are shoveling radium into atomic furnaces, like in FLASH GORDON.

JERORA (o.s.): And Fribugus said he wanted more humour. They could be comic relief, too!

The wrestlers hit each other with the shovels, then throw cream pies and bonk each other like the Three Stooges. They wrestle.

TRISURON (o.s.): And they rescue me?

We see Lyta trapped in the escape pod.

OCTURON: What if they came up to the bridge and saved her ...

The wrestlers cut open the malfunctioning escape pod with blow torches.

JERORA (o.s.): But they're still on the ship!

OCTURON (o.s.): Oh, I got it! They strap themselves to engines to escape!

The wrestlers carry Lyta into the engine room. They rope her to an engine. They press a button and the entire engine blows away, rocketing Lyta off to safety. Far away, she falls off the engine and tumbles through the air, landing in the arms of Captain Takao. They kiss.

Meanwhile, the water is electrolysed and the monster falls through the crust of the earth, to be crushed by molten rocks.

The wrestlers each strap themselves onto an engine and blast away from the monster and the explosions. They ride the engines like Slim Pickens at the end of Dr STRANGELOVE, only up and away from the explosion instead of down and into it.

The three midget Mexican wrestlers, who now have oversized sombreros and guitars, sit on the rocket engines as they shoot off into the sunset. They are playing a Mariachi version of "The Chicken Dance."

FADE TO BLACK

TITLE CARD:

"THE END"

CREDITS ROLL

INT. SCREENING ROOM

Lights come up. We realise we have been watching the movie along with Octuron, Jerora, Trisuron, Guidolon, Fribugus and a collection of stiff monsters in suits: the Dengaku Studios EXECUTIVES. One executive is a giant eyeball, with a tiny body in a suit attached. A second is a giant hagfish.

EXECUTIVE #1: That was the worst piece of drek that I have ever seen in my life.

EXECUTIVE #2: Drek!

GUIDOLON: Wait! Wait! We have another version of this film we want to show you!

EXECUTIVE #1: I don't think I could sit through —

GUIDOLON: This version was all based on suggestions made by Fribugus. He's responsible for this!

EXECUTIVE #1 (to Fribugus): **You, back to the mail room!**

EXECUTIVE #2: Mail room!

FRIBUGUS (wings shrink back very small)

EXECUTIVE #1: And, you, Guidolon, since you're the director... No. 1 will want to see you.

GUIDOLON: Is that good?

EXECUTIVE #1: No.

EXECUTIVE #2: He said no.

GUIDOLON: You haven't seen the better version of this movie!

Ignoring him, the executives all file out, leaving
     Fribugus, Octuron, Jerora, Trisuron and Guidolon.

FRIBUGUS: It took me three months to work my way out
     of the mail room last time. I hate you all.

Fribugus stomps out.

OCTURON: That didn't go as planned.

GUIDOLON: Well, if I get to talk to No. 1, I think
     I can convince him that that our version is
     the keeper.

INT. RECEPTION AREA OF DENGAKU STUDIOS — MORNING

The reception area is light and airy, with a spectacular
     waterfall where blue whales frolic.

Guidolon approaches the RECEPTIONIST, who is a slimy,
     dripping mass of ooze and toxic waste.

GUIDOLON: Hi, I'm here to see —

RECEPTIONIST: No. 1.

GUIDOLON: How did you know?

RECEPTIONIST: I'm paid to know these things.

GUIDOLON: I hear that No. 1 looks different to
     different viewers. What does he look like to
     you?

RECEPTIONIST: Oh, the Boss is a giant puppy. Likes
     to be scratched behind the ears. That's what
     he looks like to me.

A light blinks on her desk.

RECEPTIONIST: The Boss will see you now. (points
     an oily arm down a long dark hallway) Do you
     want last rites?

GUIDOLON: Should I?

RECEPTIONIST: I'm supposed to ask.

INT. ENTRANCE TO No. 1'S CHAMBER

Guidolon steps through the doorway, which resembles a
     guillotine.

INT. NO. 1'S CHAMBER

A frightful mix of fire and smoke. Art Deco pillars rise
     up so high that the ceiling itself — if there is one
     — disappears into the smoke and darkness.

Floodlights shine up at No. 1. He is three times as big
     as Guidolon. He is a pink cylinder with two bends in
     it. He looks like a giant middle finger.

GUIDOLON: Sir, thank you for inviting me into...

NO. 1: Silence!

The entire chamber shudders.

NO. 1: All I wanted from you was a simple monster
movie. And you insult me with this moronic
encyclopedia of ineptitude.

GUIDOLON: Did you see the other version, sir?

NO. 1: I didn't have to. Your movie is
irredeemable, boarish, malformed drivel. You
should be ashamed of yourself.

GUIDOLON: Maybe it's so bad it's good. It could be
a cult hit, a midnight movie.

NO. 1: That is not this studio's reputation. It
would be more economical to write this off
than to market this parade of idiocy.

GUIDOLON: My movie will never be released?

NO. 1: The negatives have already been melted down
for their silver. Guidolon, you don't deserve
to live.

GUIDOLON: Sir, was there nothing about my movie
that pleased you?

NO. 1: Yes, there was. I have a modicum of
fondness for the miniature wrestlers. But you
will never work in movies again. Now...be gone
from my sight!

GUIDOLON: Can I say one last thing, sir?

NO. 1: Yes.

GUIDOLON (screaming): OK — Get him, boys!

Octuron, Jerora and Trisuron crash through the walls.
Together, they tackle No. 1 and the five monsters roll
as a ball across the polished floor.

No. 1, being three times bigger than the others, breaks
free. He hops up and down like an enormous pogo
stick, trying to squish them. Jerora, being made of
carbon, spits uncut diamonds the size of icebergs at
No. 1, who tries to squash Jerora into a smear with
his fingernail. Then the friends charge the finger, and
together they crash through the wall into:

EXT — BACK LOT OF MOVIE STUDIO

Trisuron punches No. 1 over and over.

**TRISURON: And that's for insulting my sweetie's
movie!**

No. 1 is a steamroller, crushing the others. But the
monsters are merely pressed into the concrete, only
to extricate themselves and fight again. The monsters
burst through another wall into:

INT — MAIL ROOM

Tractor beams shoot from Fribugus' eyes, moving letters
and packages into mail slots. As the other monsters
crash in, mail flies everywhere.

FRIBUGUS (losing the letter in his clawed hand):
Dang! My check was in there!

Trisuron's two biggest horns swivel and point at Fribugus
like cannons. Fireballs shoot out and Fribugus falls
backward, boxes tumbling on him.

TRISURON: And that's for making my baby cry!

GUIDOLON: I'll take it from here!

Guidolon throws boxes aside, finding Fribugus with the
spikes on his head all a-sunder. Guidolon jumps up
and down on him, until he's satisfied. He claps his
hands, job done.

Then Guidolon rips apart packages in search of something
to throw at No. 1, only to find pillows, bunny
slippers and teddy bears. Then he finds one that holds
a huge solid globe of the world. He raises it above
his head.

NO. 1: You'll never work in this town again!

GUIDOLON: What do I care? I'm king of the world!

He brings the globe crashing down on No. 1, knocking him
out and destroying the world.

Fribugus rises from the debris. Jerora jumps up,
enveloping Fribugus' head. But the tractor beams
from his eyes pass right through Jerora's translucent
body, throwing Guidolon through the wall. Trisuron
rams Fribugus and they tumble outside, dislodging
Jerora.

EXT — BACK LOT OF MOVIE STUDIO

No. 1 stumbles through the wall. Octuron grabs the spikes
on Fribugus' head, redirecting the tractor beam.
No. 1 is lifted high into the air and then dropped,
painfully. Guidolon sweeps Fribugus' head across the
back lot, and buildings lurch toward him. Then he
sweeps across the sky and aims Fribugus' tractor beam
at the moon.

The moon is pulled closer and closer to the earth.

**TRISURON: How can you move the moon with a little
tractor beam?**

GUIDOLON: Everything in space is weightless.

The ground trembles. Tidal waves rise at the horizon. The
wind blows terrifically. Lightning fills the air, as
the moon looms larger and larger. Even small craters
are visible now, as are the Apollo landers. No. 1

stumbles toward Guidolon, the concrete breaking under
him.

GUIDOLON: **Everybody, get ready!**

Guidolon lets go of Fribugus and rears back, ready to
   lay a devastating blow on No. 1. The others gather
   around and together, in one coordinated effort, land
   four simultaneous upper-cuts on No. 1. The blow is so
   tremendous that No. 1 flies through the air, sailing
   past clouds and crashing onto the surface of the
   moon.

With a wink, Fribugus uses his reverse tractor beam to
   push the moon back. On the lunar surface No. 1 jumps
   up and down in protest, until the moon recedes to its
   normal position, a quarter million miles away.

At the back lot, lightning, wind and earthquakes subside.

FRIBUGUS: **He was my boss, but he was always a jerk
   to me, too. Can I join you guys?**

INT — SLEAZY BAR — NIGHT

Guidolon, Trisuron, Jerora, Octuron, and Fribugus sit at
   a booth. Empty beer mugs, shot glasses and pitchers
   are piled in front of them.

FRIBUGUS (motioning with fists): **Hah! Hah! Take
   that, No. 1!**

OCTURON: **We showed him who's boss!**

They all laugh.

TRISURON: **But what about your movie?**

GUIDOLON (sighing): **Gone, baby, gone. Melted, gone
   forever.**

FRIBUGUS: **Sorry, Guido. I was just doing my job.
   Your version really wasn't that bad. I was
   just trying to make a name for myself. Sorry.**

TRISURON: **It really could have been great.**

They all sigh, suddenly sad.

GUIDOLON: **Well, guys, I have everything I really
   wanted in this little room. Maybe that's the
   lesson that God wanted me to learn.**

Trisuron smiles.

JERORA: **But what are we going to do now?**

OCTURON: **Guido, you're the brains of our little
   group.**

JERORA: **Maybe we could start our own studio.**

TRISURON: **With what money? We poured a lot of our
   own money into making this movie. I doubt if**

the studio will reimburse us.

GUIDOLON: Jerora, do you have any cash?

JERORA: I used to have this drinking problem...

GUIDOLON: Yeah, I was there. How 'bout you, Fribugus? You have any money?

FRIBUGUS: The guy who signs my paychecks is on the moon.

OCTURON: I have some money.

GUIDOLON: How much?

Octuron spits out some ink, and writes a number on a napkin. The others are somewhat impressed.

GUIDOLON: Where did you get that kind of dough?

OCTURON: I sold the studio the rights to the midget Mexican wrestlers. They loved those little guys.

GUIDOLON: It's still not enough to make a movie...

OCTURON: I was thinking I could buy a new house. Maybe we could all live there together.

FRIBUGUS: I've got it! Instead of buying a house, maybe we can bring one down!

GUIDOLON: What are you talking about?

FRIBUGUS (wings wiggling excitedly): Maybe we can take this money and do what you always wanted to do in the first place! A Shakespearean monster tragedy!

INT. THEATRICAL STAGE

Jerora lies on the stage, translucent body quivering. He holds a golden chalice limply. His body pulses once, twice, and then the light goes out. Trisuron lies on the stage, a clawed hand on her chest. She too is still. Fribugus lies face down, rapier in hand.

Octuron is in a spot of light, looking at the dead bodies and the burning cityscape stretching into infinity.

At his feet falls Guidolon, dropping a rapier.

GUIDOLON (to Octuron): I am dead, Horatio.

Octuron stands behind him, holding a gold jacket. Guidolon crawls to Trisuron.

GUIDOLON: (to Trisuron): Wretched queen, adieu!

He stands, Octuron placing the jacket on his shoulders. Guidolon falls again, and the jacket slips off.

GUIDOLON: Oh, I die, Horatio. (coughing, stumbling): The...rest...is...silence...

The lights slowly dim in Guidolon's big bug eyes. Now he is still and his eyes are dark.

Octuron walks backward, draping the gold jacket over Guidolon. It is now a funeral shroud.

OCTURON: Good night, sweet prince. And flights of angels sing thee to thy rest!

The curtain falls. The audience gives thunderous applause.

As the curtain rises, Jerora, Octuron, Trisuron, Guidolon and Fribugus stand, arms linked. They bow. The applause grows louder, and Guidolon steps to the centre. The other four step to the side and applaud him. Guidolon and Trisuron are both now wearing wedding rings.

Flowers tumble through the air in slow motion, landing on the stage. An AUDIENCE MEMBER stands, rears back and throws a bouquet of roses to Guidolon. We FREEZE FRAME on the bouquet, mid-air, brilliantly lit by the theatrical lights. Fangs flash amid the petals.

FADE TO BLACK

TITLE CARD:

"THE END"

CREDITS ROLL while

a MINSTREL MONSTER plays "The Chicken Dance" on tabour and fife.

— THE END —

WONDERS 8 THROUGH 88

A BRIEF HISTORY OF THE LARGER-THAN-LIFE

BRIAN THOMAS

The psychologists of the world are always ready to explain our monsters to us. Frankenstein, vampires, werewolves, ghosts—there are stacks of books explaining the Jungian and Freudian underpinnings behind these supernatural creatures. Homer warned us about Monsters from the Id eons ago. But what about a much larger form of monster, the very daikaiju that we're all so interested in? Where does that nightmare come from? Is there a SuperId to match the SuperEgo, one that unleashed gigantic beasts to rampage across the landscape?

Psychologist Kyle D. Smith has described society's creation and fascination with daikaiju as "an exercise in Awe". Human beings crave stimulation, and a pretend encounter with such mighty beasts fulfills our need to get in touch with something beyond ourselves and our world. It can be simple escapism, the thrill of imagining beings greater than life, death and morality, or a humbling reminder of the vastness of the universe.

IN THE BEGINNING...

Of course, one reason that there hasn't been much psychobabble about giant monsters could be because, unlike other monsters, they are certifiably *real*. Our museums are full of the evidence. A hundred million years before certain hairy bipeds began to notice that they could keep a better eye out for predators if they stood up straight, our planet was teeming with giant monsters. If not for a cataclysmic event that wiped out most of them, who knows what they might have evolved into by now? With so many people fascinated by unearthed fossils of these beasts, it's no wonder most daikaiju stories are about some form of dinosaur.

MYTHS AND MONSTERS

Scientist try to tell us that every dinosaur died long before Man evolved, but something seems wrong with that theory. Whatever wiped out the dinosaurs surely couldn't have done the job so completely. Dinosaurs survived for so long that the Earth's surface was completely rearranged while they ruled the planet. It seems reasonable to assume that several species escaped extinction, at least for a few more million years.

Every society, from the Incas to the ancient Chinese to our modern web of international e-society, has its own legends of monsters. But the remarkable thing is that so many of them are so similar. Why do so many ancient legends describe dragons that are so alike in detail? Why do the sailors of so many nations encounter such similar sea monsters?

It's not unreasonable to assume that ancient people saw some animal in the wild, and their stories became exaggerated in legend. Reports of the rhinoceros were responsible for the unicorn myth. A "fire-breathing dragon" may come from a handed-down story about any large reptile with hot breath (if it hissed a lot, all the better). Sighting remnants of any species of winged reptile would give the dragon wings. But one way or another, the dragon became a fixture in the public consciousness in most societies.

Giants usually went along with dragons. People imagined their gods (and monsters) most often as more extreme versions of themselves, so the gods were made to tower over men. And the gods, requiring suitable opponents with which to battle, were opposed by even larger titans, demons and ogres, some of which represented various forces of the natural world.

EIGHTH WONDER OF THE LOST WORLD

Myth was set down on paper and became literature, and the monsters followed. Early science fiction and fantasy authors like Jules Verne and William Hope Hodgson pitted men against fantastic beasts in their stories, but the blueprint for the giant monster story came from Sir Arthur Conan Doyle, the creator of Sherlock Holmes. His novel *The Lost World* sent his number two series character Professor Challenger to a remote mesa in South America. On top of this mesa, Challenger's party found prehistoric creatures still living, untouched by time. After various adventures, the explorers return to London, bearing with them proof of their story in the form of a captive pterodactyl—which promptly escapes back into the wild.

Here we have the bare bones of the daikaiju tale, though various authors would split it into two archetypes. In one, a party of explorers visits a world of savage monsters, either in some hidden corner of the world or by journeying through time or space. In the other, a monster somehow arrives in our own civilisation, causing a great deal of trouble. Sometimes the second archetype is combined with the Frankenstein legend: the monster is created by Man, only to turn on its creator. But the most successful daikaiju stories have combined both archetypes.

While the printed word is not dead (you're reading this, aren't you?), it is in the cinema that the giant monster story flourished. And it's no wonder—actors up on a big theatre screen are already larger than life. As long as audiences were already looking up at something awesome, it was only natural to give them something they'd naturally look up at in the movies. At first, dinosaurs appeared only in trick films and comedies. In 1914, Winsor McCay attempted to succeed where Prof. Challenger failed by not only presenting his animated prehistoric beast *Gertie the Dinosaur* for exhibition, but teaching her to perform a few tricks as well. But though McCay interacted with his dinosaur, Gertie still remained onscreen in her own prehistoric world. It'd take another decade for the monsters to enter the modern age.

One of those making trick shorts with a prehistoric theme was an animator named Willis O'Brien. When First National Pictures made their adaptation of Conan Doyle's *The Lost World*, director Harry O. Hoyt—previously probably best known for re-editing adventure serials for re-release as feature films—was credited as being in charge, but it was O'Brien's special effects that drove the project and were responsible for its success. In the movie version, Challenger returns to London with a larger specimen than in the book, and a full grown apatosaurus rampages through the city streets, scaring folks before diving into the Thames.

As successful as the film version of *The Lost World* was, it was just a dry run for the most famous and most beloved giant monster movie of all time. Filmmakers Merian C. Cooper and Ernest B. Schoedsack were famous for their documentary features made in the wilder corners of the Earth, but distributors and critics complained about a lack of traditional character and story elements in their movies. The partners responded with an adaptation of A.E.W. Mason's adventure story *The Four Feathers*, but again were frustrated by the fact that most productions were going to sound. What they really wanted to do was make a movie about a big gorilla, the way they'd made elephants the stars of their previous film *Chang*. *Kong*, the story they came up with, started out as a reflection of their own experiences, with the team fictionalised as a character named Carl Denham who brings the big ape back alive to New York. However, with O'Brien added to the team, the similarities to *The Lost World* grew—the monkey got a lot bigger, and his native habitat became an island of prehistoric beasts.

But it's the things that make *King Kong* different that people remember most. For one thing, their captured monster had a lot more personality than any dinosaur. But what really caught the public imagination was the film's love story. Cooper and Schoedsack cast Fay Wray, the sexy young starlet from *The Four Feathers*, in the lead, and focused on a "beauty and the beast" angle that worked like nothing else ever had in movies. Kong, the fearsome SuperId, is defeated and chained when his attraction to beauty gets the best of him. Kong might have gotten away at several points in the story, but that impossible fascination with a strange blonde drove him to his doom.

The same filmmaking team would go ape again in the hastily prepared sequel *Son of Kong* and in the post-war effort *Mighty Joe Young*, but nothing they ever did could possibly match *King Kong*.

1950s: BEASTS EMERGE

Strangely, despite the incredible success of *Kong*, no one really attempted to replicate it until years later. There was a Superman cartoon made in the early 1940s in which the Man of Steel faces a dinosaur thawed from an iceberg that seems to have been very influential on daikaiju scenarios to come. But the biggest inspiration for giant monster movies was the atomic bomb. Like Superman's nemesis, 1953's *The Beast From 20,000 Fathoms* is a dinosaur preserved in ice. However, the Beast is thawed by an atomic bomb blast, and remains radioactive as it makes its way into New York City.

Beast, brought to life by O'Brien's former assistant Ray Harryhausen, set the pattern for a parade of atomic terrors that lurched onto theatre screens throughout the 1950s. First the menace strikes. Then scientists and military personnel investigate and, after a dangerous encounter, find that radiation is responsible for the monster or monsters. Efforts are made to destroy the monster in the wild—depth charges, bombs, poison gas, etc.—but nothing stops the menace from reaching a major city, where it proceeds directly to the nearest monument or landmark. After some destruction and mayhem, the heroes stay up all night thinking of a way to get rid of the critter.

This pattern, with some variation, served to entertain audiences buying tickets for *Them!*, *The Black Scorpion*, *The Monster That Challenged the World*, *The Deadly Mantis*, *Beginning of the End*, *Tarantula*, *The Amazing Colossal Man*, *It Came From Beneath the Sea* and many more. Sometimes the monsters came from the '50s' other big issue—outer space—as in *20 Million Miles to Earth* and *The Blob*, but for the most part 1950s movie monsters were spawned by a fear of atomic radiation.

If the citizens of the United States were quaking in fear of the atomic bomb, imagine how folks felt in Japan, where such bombs had actually been dropped. Or better yet, see for yourself by watching *Godzilla*. Producer Tomoyuki Tanaka had a contract with Toho Studios to make a big war epic in Korea, but when the deal fell through he needed a replacement project. With *Beast From 20,000 Fathoms* and a re-release of *King Kong* doing great business worldwide, a similar monster movie seemed to be a surefire money maker. In the hands of writer/director Ishiro Honda, that basic Man vs Monster tale took on a distinctly Japanese flavour. While *Godzilla* is a thrilling monster adventure, the overall impression is of regret and sadness over the part the nation played in World War II, with a general atmosphere of terror due to the awful firebombing and nuclear devastation every Japanese witnessed firsthand.

Of course, not much of this was translated into the American edition of the film, with any political commentary replaced with documentary-style guidance by actor Raymond Burr as a wire-service reporter. The fact that the dubbed, remodeled and retitled *Godzilla, King of the Monsters* was a big hit, even playing across Asia all over again, apparently sent a message to American distributors: Asian cinema means big bucks if altered extensively to disguise its foreign origin as much as possible. Only in recent years, as audiences have become savvy about how their entertainment has been mangled in the past, have Asian films begun to receive distribution in the USA uncut. Even diluted, *Godzilla* had an impact on the public, taking on the title given by the US distributor. When people think about a monster movie, a general image of Godzilla is what comes immediately to mind.

MONSTERLAND

Over the course of the 1950s and '60s, the Japanese came to almost totally dominate the field of giant monster movies. Occasionally, a film like *Reptilicus* or *Gorgo* would pop up from some other country, but now these productions skewed more toward the Japanese model.

Just like Kong, Godzilla's success spawned a quickly hammered together follow-up, known internationally as *Godzilla Raids Again*. Without Honda at the helm, the film lacks the same focus, meandering for long periods into how the monster affects the lives of Japanese fishermen, who become the film's martyred heroes. However, it introduced the idea of putting two big beasts in a movie together, as the personable Angilas battled Godzilla through much of the running time. When the original US distributor passed on a repeat performance, plans were made to incorporate the movie's special effects footage into a new feature called *The Volcano Monsters*, and the monster costumes were even shipped to the USA for additional scenes. But when financing fell through, a simple edited and dubbed version was released under the title *Gigantis the Fire Monster*, confusing legions of young G-fans in matinees across the country.

In the meantime, daikaiju pioneer Honda kept busy. Determined to create a flying monster movie, he directed two very different versions of that idea with *Rodan* and *Mothra*. He borrowed ideas from H.G. Wells for the science fiction epics *The Mysterians* and *Gorath*. And he created a somewhat difficult to define cinema subgenre in films like *The Human Vapor* and *The H-Man*—mutant monster movies that could almost be described as horror noir. But Mr Honda was inevitably drawn back to his most stellar collaborator.

Their experience thus far had taught Toho Studios that dealing with the Americans could earn them big profits, so why not go into business together? Willis O'Brien had tried and failed for decades to create another sequel to *King Kong* that would pit his big ape against another monster. This idea outlived him, evolving into a plan to bring the two greatest monsters in the world together. The very concept of *King Kong vs Godzilla* had an air of the ridiculous about it from the beginning, and was driven by sheer showmanship of the first order. Naturally, much was lost in the heavily edited American version, but when Honda was brought into the project he immediately saw in it great potential for farce. The film's plot, with a gigantic ape brought into conflict with the gigantic lizard at the instigation of a greedy TV sponsor, matched perfectly the film's marketing attack.

On a roll, Toho kept the monsters coming, pitting their star next against another from their own stable. *Mothra vs Godzilla* is one of the series' finest entries, contrasting science fiction horror with inspired fantasy. The script weaves together elements of both characters brilliantly, while Toho's special effects master Eiji Tsuburaya refined his techniques to reach a technical and artistic milestone. Naturally, the Americans didn't quite get it. Mothra was deemed to be not a recognisable enough monster, and was left out of ad campaigns for the US release entirely, while the title tried to confuse audiences into thinking another American beast costarred in the retitled *Godzilla vs the Thing*.

And the monsters kept coming. Honda had tried to introduce a more human-looking kaiju in the Bigfoot adventure *Half Human*, and was asked to take another stab at it. The result was *Frankenstein vs Baragon* (aka *Frankenstein Conquers the World*) and its sequel *War of the Gargantuas*. These two films may have played fast and loose with the Frankenstein story, and the continuity between the two features doesn't even match up very well, but they're both terrific monster movies. There was also an attempt to bring back Kong once again in conjunction with an American Saturday morning cartoon TV series, which resulted in the potboiler *King Kong Escapes*.

Meanwhile, the Big G, who nearly got involved in the first Frankenstein picture, was thrown into ever more crowded monster rallies at the instigation of hostile extraterrestrials. After facing off with Rodan, Mothra and a giant golden space dragon in *Ghidorah the Three-Headed Monster*, Godzilla led the *Invasion of Astro-Monster* (aka *Monster Zero*). In an effort to save money, Toho sent him to south Pacific islands to take Kong's place when the Big Ape's own series was abandoned, providing an entertaining change of pace in *Godzilla vs the Sea Monster* and *Son of Godzilla*. But then it was back to their "more is more" sentiment in a big way, culminating in the over-the-top monster mash *Destroy All Monsters*, in which all available daikaiju at Toho's command are enslaved by foxy females from another galaxy.

Destroy All Monsters was supposed to be the big finish for Toho's star, but his retirement was quickly delayed by two factors. First, *DAM* was a big international hit. Second, competitor Daiei had begun a monster series of their own a few years before, and were making good money by keeping them cheap and aiming them squarely at the kiddies.

Giant Monster Gamera was made to compete directly with Godzilla, and even came to America in similarly edited fashion, given added footage featuring US actors and retitled *Gamera the Invincible*. But the kid appeal was obvious. Gamera is a very large turtle of mysterious and ancient origin which can breathe fire and fly using jets that shoot from the holes in his shell. Intrinsically silly it may be, but also a whole lot of fun. When Gamera isn't destroying large cities he finds time to save the lives of young children. Gamera went on to star in seven sequels through 1980, each one cheaper and sillier than the one before it—but kids loved them.

In addition, a side project produced by f/x whiz Tsuburaya had taken off—his TV show *Ultraman* became a huge hit. Kids went ape for this shiny masked superhero, who would grow to enormous size in each episode to battle an exceedingly strange assortment of hostile daikaiju. The shows, and their many imitators, were very cheap, but again the kids loved them. And so, Godzilla was revamped into a sort of scaly superhero to defend puny humans from other monsters, using as much recycled footage as possible.

Taking a hesitant first step into the kiddie pool, *All Monsters Attack* (aka *Godzilla's Revenge*) wasn't so much a Godzilla movie as a child's fantasy ala *Invaders From Mars* or *Robot Monster*. A latchkey kid in horrible urban wasteland escapes regularly into dreams of Monster Island, where Godzilla's son Minilla is his best friend and Godzilla himself (mostly via stock footage) teaches him how to deal with bullies. Next, our hero took on a disgusting smog monster in *Godzilla vs Hedorah*. This interesting experimental monster movie (which played US theatres as *Godzilla vs the Smog Monster*) was unfortunately dismissed completely by adults, who had more "relevant" matters on their minds in 1971. The plots of the next few Godzilla films were assembled from comic-book elements designed to get him into wrestling matches with other monsters. *Godzilla vs Gigan*, *Godzilla vs Megalon* and *Godzilla vs MechaGodzilla*—they all have their points of interest, and are favourites among a generation of G-fans who were introduced to daikaiju movies through them, but lack the gravity of their predecessors. Honda returned to the series to direct *Terror of MechaGodzilla*, which was announced as (yet again) Godzilla's final film.

While the daikaiju genre was reaching its nadir in the mid-1970s, there came a glimmer of hope from the US. Two Hollywood studios had their lawyers haggling over who would remake *King Kong*. Both projects got a great deal of press for playing up how their film would be made using innovative special effects techniques. Unfortunately, Universal ended up dropping their plans for a period remake using stop-motion f/x, or the new motion control technology used in the *Star Wars* films might have been developed earlier, making for a better quality remake. As it is, though the updated Paramount *Kong* of 1976 boasted the studio's ape would be brought to life through amazing new animatronics techniques, their giant Kong robot was just a stiff prop used in a few shots. Much better use was made of a Japanese-style man-in-suit beast, specifically an amazing performance by makeup man Rick Baker inside an excellent costume. In addition, director

John Guillermin, backed by a memorable John Barry score, tried to give the project some class. But the entire film is remembered foremost as a slice of typical '70s cheese, lumped in with glam rock musicals and pet rocks.

GODZILLA RETURNS

But can you ever keep a good monster down? The 1970s brought the movie blockbuster era into being, with movies like *Star Wars* changing the way society thought about such escapist fare as monster movies. Several plans to make an American Godzilla movie were announced (one of them to be in 3-D during the process' early 1980s revival), but before any of them got made, Toho decided to take the superbeast out of mothballs themselves. For Godzilla's 30th anniversary, they planned to celebrate with a new film that would scrap all the bothersome continuity (much of which chronicled Godzilla's adventures into the next century) and get back to basics. The new *Godzilla* was even bigger than before, and was brought to life courtesy of modern animatronics and optical f/x, to tell the tale of the monster's return in modern times. And like the original, the US version of *Godzilla 1985* was altered with the insertion of often silly footage starring Raymond Burr, and re-edited by the distributor to reflect American political views.

New World Pictures' cut of *Godzilla 1985* bombed in the US, but was a hit throughout Asia, prompting Toho to keep the party going. Publicised as based on an idea submitted through a studio contest, *Godzilla vs Biollante* has a slightly muddled plot, but delivered a fiercer, beautifully designed Godzilla in combat with a terrifying plant creature derived from his own DNA. A solid hit, *Biollante* insured that there would be a new Godzilla film released every year or so for the foreseeable future.

Getting into a groove, Toho brought back one of their monster favourites for *Godzilla vs King Ghidorah*, which features one of the most difficult to follow plots in daikaiju history. But then, time travel movies are always tripping over their own plotlines. In brief, a group of time travellers from the future arrives in 1991 Tokyo to announce that they can get rid of Godzilla (who they say will eventually destroy Japan) by making sure he was never created. A group of citizens is invited along on a trip back to World War II, where the futurites transport a rare godzillasaurus from his island home to a location far from the coming atomic bomb tests. But the group's real purpose is to not only eliminate Godzilla, but to use (banned in the future) atomic weapons to create a new monster that they can control and to change the course of history in their favour. Fortunately, Godzilla is created anyway, and he's even bigger and more powerful. After he defeats King Ghidorah, the only way to stop him from destroying Tokyo is for more friendly futurians to resurrect their beast as MechaGhidorah. Another factor added to the mix is the return of Megumi Odaka as psychic girl Miki Saegusa, a favourite character from *Biollante* who would be back for every Godzilla movie for the next several years.

It may have been blatantly inspired by *Terminator 2*, but *Ghidorah* was a solid hit featuring wonderful special effects and music—and so another monster favourite was revived for *Godzilla vs Mothra*. By this time, new Toho f/x chief Koichi Kawakita was earning praise for the beauty of his monster movies, and here he takes advantage of Mothra's colours and grace to create some wonderful imagery. Her revival was such a hit that Mothra made guest appearances in a few more Godzilla pictures, and even spun off for a trio of her own juvenile monster epics. One of Godzilla's better foes from the 1970s was revived for *Godzilla vs MechaGodzilla II*, which also brought back Rodan and gave Godzilla a new adopted son. Deft handling of all these elements, along with one of the best ever scores from series regular Akira Ikufube, resulted in another series highlight.

Which was followed by a lesser light. Returning to the theme of monsters created from Godzilla's cells, a new foe arrived on Earth in *Godzilla vs Space Godzilla*. This invader from beyond a black hole has an unclear agenda except to throw his weight around as much as possible, so audience sympathy is sought by having the villain beat up and imprison the insufferably cute Little Godzilla. With Big G teaming up with robot weapon MOGERA (a recycled idea from *The Mysterians*) to take on the big blue invader, the destruction is sufficient to be satisfying, but the film falls short in all other areas.

Further damage was inflicted on the Godzilla series by the unexpected return of another old rival. Made for half the budget of the most recent Godzillas, Daiei relaunched *Gamera: Guardian of the Universe* to almost universal approval. Not only did the revamped Gamera feature f/x that were the equal of Toho's, but the serious attitude taken by writer Kazunori Ito and director Shusuke Kaneko took everyone aback. Making a new Gamera movie was one thing, but making one that was actually *good* was another. The film's viewpoint was key to its success—where previous monster flicks would cut back and forth between the monsters' story and that of the dull human beings trying to deal with them, here we had a tale told almost entirely in human terms, giving us a "realistic" street-level view of monster mayhem. Kaneko went on to direct two more Gamera movies (*Attack of Legion* and *Revenge of Iris*), making each one a little better than before.

GODZILLA IN NEW YORK

While the Japanese struggled with the destinies of their daikaiju, a new kind of giant monster was emerging in the US. Steven Spielberg's *Jurassic Park* brought dinosaurs to astonishingly convincing life through digital animation techniques and sophisticated animatronics, creating a whole new ball game. With this, the idea of an American Godzilla movie was revived and, with a contract in their pocket, executives at Toho planned to retire their monster star once again. The somewhat ambiguous ending of *Godzilla vs Destroyah*, did away with Godzilla for all time…at least temporarily.

While Toho sat back to see what would happen, Sony geared up to launch their own 125 million dollar monster movie. They hired Dean Devlin and Roland Emmerich, the producer/director team behind the sci-fi megahit *Independence Day*, to be in charge, then placed stars like Matthew Broderick and Jean Reno in leading roles. The best team of art directors and f/x technicians in the world were put to work creating a believable, awe-inspiring giant mutant lizard to invade New York, and Sony's advertising department went to work to make sure everyone knew that not only was this Godzilla a totally different creature than the familiar Japanese man-in-suit monster, but the movie would be the must-see event of the summer.

Well, just about everyone did line up to see it. And just about everyone left disappointed. Though a financial success, *Godzilla* was panned by the majority of critics, and it didn't take long for the finger pointing to begin. Most G-fans are content in hindsight to say that if the producers had retitled the same movie *Beast From 20,000 Fathoms 1998* then they would have been satisfied with it. The problem was that Devlin and Emmerich made a Godzilla movie without Godzilla—kind of like making a biopic of Martin Luther King and making him Caucasian. But how did this happen? It's a complicated issue, but if a scapegoat is needed, one would do well to look at the script. Sure, the screenwriting team of Terry Rossio and Ted Elliott had penned the smash Disney hit *Aladdin*, but a closer look at their résumés reveals they were also responsible for the dull adaptation of Robert Heinlein's *The Puppet Masters* and the god-awful juvenile fantasy *Little Monsters*. Who would think of those two to write a Godzilla movie?

Despite this dark cloud of public disapproval, plans have been put forth now and then for a sequel. This idea is not as bad as one might suppose—a Saturday morning TV series spin-off created by obvious Godzilla fans worked pretty well, and with the right script, a sequel might actually be fun. Hey, a good script—what an idea!

21st CENTURY MONSTER MAYHEM

While Sony's *Godzilla* toys were being carted back to the warehouse, Toho decided a breath of fresh air was in order. One would expect a movie studio to be conservative, continuing on with the story of Godzilla Junior into the new century. But they did nearly the exact opposite. The new Godzilla movies would start from scratch as a kind of anthology, with each writer and/or director free to pick and choose what elements from the monster's past would be incorporated into their vision. The results have been far from flawless, but the free reign given to the creators of the last six Godzilla flicks has made them a very interesting string of daikaiju movies.

First up was the director of three previous Godzilla vehicles, making sure that the new series didn't go *too* far from the familiar. Sony liked Takao Okawara's *Godzilla 2000* enough that they decided to give it an English dub and tighten up the editing for a US theatrical release—something that hadn't happened to a real Godzilla movie in 15 years. Either they thought that American audiences would think it was a sequel to their own *Godzilla* (which actually happened quite a bit), or they thought audiences would accept Godzilla's struggle with an awakened long-dormant alien invader on its own merits (which also happened, as even G-fans could appreciate the care taken by Sony's post-production team).

However, the box-office returns weren't strong enough to net the following Godzilla movies anything beyond a decent DVD release in the USA. Next up was Masaki Tezuka, second unit director of the final two films in the '90s Mothra trilogy. *Godzilla vs Megaguirus* is a relatively straightforward monster battle with one minor twist. It's established that the ingenuity of mankind is at last beginning to catch up with the immortal Godzilla, and an invention that creates mini black holes almost succeeds in making him disappear.

Batting clean-up was Shusuke Kaneko himself, with the re-inventor of Gamera getting a long-awaited crack at the Big G and swinging for the fences. *Godzilla, Mothra and King Ghidorah: Giant Monsters All-Out Attack* goes all-out to give us an alternative universe Godzilla that is still recognisable as presenting one side of the monster. Far from the nominal heroism shown in the first two millennium Godzillas, Kaneko casts the mutant dinosaur as evil incarnate, a seething force intent on wiping out mankind. In accordance with a prophesy, the only thing standing in his way are three great elemental monsters: Mothra, Ghidorah, and (surprise!) Baragon, the feisty monster nemesis from *Frankenstein Conquers the World*. This satisfying entry gives us Kaneko's trademark viewpoint and some truly spectacular monster mayhem, along with an interesting twist on the mythos.

Maybe too much of a twist. Toho apparently panicked at the prospect of artists messing too much with their biggest meal ticket, and returned to Tezuka for a much safer two-part story. Godzilla is still the villain of these pictures, but is replaced as the star in *Godzilla Against MechaGodzilla* and *Godzilla: Tokyo SOS*. This is the saga of the third MechaGodzilla, a robot at the command of both the Japanese military and, quite poetically, the soul of the original Godzilla. The G-skeleton is recovered from Tokyo Bay and used to create the heavily armed robot, but in using the creature's DNA as a programming shortcut in bringing the beast to cyber-life, the scientists leave a ghost in the machine that threatens to turn their last defense into their biggest nightmare.

But faltering ticket sales had Toho altering course in 2004. They decided to celebrate Godzilla's 50th anniversary with one last huge monster movie. Ryuhei Kitamura's *Godzilla: Final Wars* is his tribute to monster-on-monster action, putting the daikaiju in between a hostile alien fleet and Earth superheroes in a frenetic slugfest that has Godzilla grappling with a legion of monsters all over the world!

So Godzilla retires, and no one ever makes a giant monster movie again. Does anyone buy that premise for even a second? Didn't think so. King Kong is back for another adventure, and daikaiju are popping up wherever you look, from that slimy space god in *Hellboy* to the dinosaurs and giant robots of *Sky Captain and the World of Tomorrow*. After all, we're still trying to figure out why we love giant monsters so much.

And we're loving every minute of it.

CONTRIBUTORS

Chris Barnes lives in Sydney, Australia, with his lovely wife Louise. He's a graduate (aka survivor) of the Clarion South workshop, studies historical swordsmanship, and his alter ego is Captain Pudding. He can be found online at <members.optusnet.com.au/cdbarnes>

David Carroll programs computers by day, and writes games about *Angel*, demons and zombies by night. He's also written a number of published short stories and much non-fiction about horror, history and Australian genre, a lot of which can be found at <www.tabula-rasa.info>.

Dr Terry Dartnall teaches Artificial Intelligence at Griffith University, Brisbane, Australia. His speculative fiction has appeared in *Ideomancer, Oceans of the Mind, Planet, Aphelion, Worlds of Wonder* and elsewhere. He was a 2004 Glimmer Train finalist. He lives in Brisbane with his family and likes rockclimbing and red wine. His home page is <www.cit.gu.edu.au/~terryd>

Chris Dickinson is a Western Australian writer and film maker. He has written several screenplays, and has recently had one optioned by a North American producer. He is currently researching a documentary about the space elevator concept, and preparing to shoot a science fiction short film.

Bob Eggleton is a prominent US SF/fantasy artist, winner of 8 Hugo Awards and 11 Chesley Awards. His work appears on numerous magazine and book covers and, though he is something of a Godzilla specialist, deals with a broad range of subjects. His books include: *The Book of Sea Monsters* (with text by Nigel Suckling), *Greetings from Earth: the Art of Bob Eggleton, Alien Horizons: the Fantastic Art of Bob Eggleton, Dragonhenge* (with text by John Grant), and the upcoming book *The Stardragons* (co-authored with John Grant).

Paul Finch is a British-based writer, mainly for film and TV, but who is no stranger to the short story. His first collection, *After Shocks* (Ash-Tree Press) won the British Fantasy Award 2002, while his novel *Cape Wrath* (Telos Books) was shortlisted for the Bram Stoker award in 2003. "CALIBOS" sprang from his love of '50s sci-fi movies (and his favourite dish—dressed crab), though it would not have been written if the monster hadn't been suggested by his 9-year-old son, Harry, who follows directly in his father's footsteps when it comes to the serious aspects of life.

Adam Ford is a poet, novelist, 'zine-maker and comic artist. His first novel, *Man Bites Dog*, was published by Allen & Unwin in 2003. He has also released two poetry collections to date: *Not Quite the Man for the Job* (Allen & Unwin, 1998) and *From My Head* (Scientific Productions, 1995). He lives in Melbourne and works as a freelance writer and editor, while slowly gaining confidence as an animator. He recently learned how to make sourdough bread, and is pretty excited by the idea.

Anthony Fordham is a freelance journalist living in Canberra, Australia. His work appears regularly in *The Australian* newspaper. He has previously had fiction published in *Aurealis* magazine and continues to juggle his writing time between business and pleasure (which is, after all, just a different kind of business).

Cody Goodfellow lives in Southern California, and has written two novels, *Radiant Dawn* and *Ravenous Dusk*. He is banned for life from entering the local Model Railroad Museum, for trampling dozens of tiny buildings while researching "Kungmin Horangi".

Richard Harland's latest novel, *The Black Crusade*, is a prequel to his first published novel, *The Vicar of Morbing Vyle*. Gothic, black and bizarre, *The Black Crusade* won the 2004 Aurealis Award for Best Horror Novel and the Golden Aurealis Award for Best Novel in any category of speculative fiction. His short story "Catabolic Magic' was joint winner of the Award for Best Fantasy Short Story. Between Vicars and Crusades, he has published three SF thrillers in the 'Eddon and Vail' series as well as the 'Heaven and Earth' fantasy trilogy. He lives south of Sydney in Australia.

Robert Hood, an Australian writer best known for his abundant short stories and occasional novels (including *Backstreets* and the *Shades* books), has edited two other story collections, namely *Crosstown Traffic* (with Stuart Coupe and Julie Ogden) and *Bonescribes* (with Bill Congreve). *Immaterial* (MirrorDanse Books, 2002) is a collection of his own ghost stories. He shares his life with publisher, writer and artist Cat Sparks, and two cats. (Website: www.roberthood.net)

Trent Jamieson lives with his wife in Brisbane, Australia. He has had work published in *Agog! Fantastic Fiction, Agog! Smashing Stories, Nowa Fantastyka, Aurealis, Eidolon* and *Nemonymous 4*. His first collection of short stories, *Reserved for Travelling Shows*, is due to be published by Prime Books in 2005.

Martin Livings, a Perth writer, has inexplicably had twenty-odd (some very odd) stories published in a variety of places since 1991, including *Eidolon, Aurealis, Ticonderoga Online, Antipodean SF, AustrAlien Absurdities, Fables and Reflections, Shadowed Realms* and two *Agog!* anthologies. He has been nominated for the Aurealis and Ditmar awards for short fiction, and has won a Tin Duck. More information can be found at http://lonewolf.iinet.net.au

Rosaleen Love is an Australian writer who writes about science and the rest of life. Her short fiction has been collected in *The Travelling Tide* (2005, Aqueduct Press, Seattle), and in two books published by The Women's Press, UK: *The Total Devotion Machine* (1989) and *Evolution Annie* (1993). She is a research associate at Latrobe and Monash Universities, Melbourne.

Penelope Love lives in Melbourne, Australia, and this story marks the historic first time she has shared anthology honours with her mother, Rosaleen. Her first love is H.P. Lovecraft's Cthulhu in all his squamous and non-Euclidian glory, but she says she'd stay up late for any daikaiju movie. This story is the serendipitous prequel to a trilogy-length manuscript project set in the same world.

Michelle Marquardt lives in Sydney and works as a veterinarian. Her first novel *Blue Silence* (Random House 2002) won the George Turner Prize and was shortlisted for both the Aurealis and Ditmar awards. Every couple of years she writes a short story; this is one of them.

Chuck McKenzie was born in Melbourne, Australia, in 1970, and still listens to far too much disco music. He writes stories, and sometimes people publish them, which is nice. For a slightly more comprehensive bio, why not visit the Official Chuck McKenzie Infosite? Unless you're busy, of course... (infosite: http://members.optusnet.com.au/chuckmck1/)

Garth Nix has worked as a bookseller, book sales representative, publicist, editor, marketing consultant and literary agent. His books are published around the world and are translated into more than 20 languages. They include the award-winning fantasy novels *Sabriel, Lirael* and the *New York Times* bestseller *Abhorsen*; the novels *Shade's Children* and *The Ragwitch*; *The Seventh Tower* sequence; and his new *The Keys To The Kingdom* fantasy series.

Skip Peel is author of the long running "Journal of Dr. Rex Summeral" series in *G-Fan*, comprising over 45 daikaiju stories. His unpublished works include two novels, a children's book, and a play, and he frequently writes church dramas and educational puppet presentations for performance. A graduate in English from Liberty University in Lynchburg, Virginia, he currently lives in Lakeland, Florida, with his wife Lora, and is partner in an event company specialising in reptile shows.

Robin Pen is a founding editor of the prestigious Australian science fiction and fantasy literary magazine *Eidolon*. He is the author of *The Secret Life of Rubber-Suit Monsters*, a book of humorous criticism aimed at fantastic cinema. He has received four Australian Science Fiction Ditmar Awards for his writings.

Stephen Mark Rainey is author of the novels *The Lebo Coven*, *Balak*, and *Dark Shadows: Dreams of the Dark* (with Elizabeth Massie), three short story collections, and over 90 published works of short fiction. For ten years, he edited *Deathrealm* magazine, and in 2004 edited an anthology of reprinted stories, titled *Deathrealms*, for Delirium Books. He has also edited the anthologies *Song of Cthulhu* for Chaosium and *Evermore* (with James Robert Smith) for Arkham House. Mark lives in Greensboro, NC, with his wife Peggy and three kaiju-loving housecats.

Eric Shapiro's wide array of fiction and nonfiction pieces have appeared in over 75 publications, in print and on the World Wide Web, including *The Elastic Book of Numbers* (Elastic Press) and *Fedora IV* (Betancourt & Co.). Eric lives in Los Angeles with his wife Rhoda. He will not be satisfied with his fiction until the pages literally catch fire...

J M Shiloh's mind was warped at an early age by a week-long after-school Godzilla movie marathon on local TV. The result was an enduring fondness for all things daikaiju. He now writes strange stories from his home in Texas, under the watchful eyes of a small army of Japanese robot/monster figures. He might as well still be nine years old.

Petri Sinda currently lives under Fremantle, West Australia (which may explain his high quotient of monster stories—three in the calendar year). Hobbies include waiting for acrylics to dry, convincing people their favourite colour is orange and judging the heights of clouds from sea level—all, alas, perhaps resulting from missing his cat: RIP Boop.

Andrew Sullivan lives in Canberra, Australia, with his wife, two children and n goldfish (where, at any particular time, $0 \leq n < \infty$). He has published one novel, *A Sunburnt Country* (Ginninderra Press, 2003), and has had stories in such places as *EOD*, *Gathering Forces*, *Antipodean SF*, *Harbinger* and *AurealisXpress*. "Notes Concerning Events at the Ray Harryhausen Memorial Home for Retired Actors" is Andrew's first appearance in an anthology. He has recently commenced a PhD in theoretical physics at the ANU.

Todd Tennant has been a professional illustrator for over 25 years, but has only recently entered the world of Kaiju-Art, in spite of being a big fan of the giant monster genres of film, TV, and comic books. Through his website *American Kaiju*, Todd is attempting to make up for lost time by creating original giant monster comics of his own (*Retro Monsters*) and with his creative partner Mike Bogue (*King Komodo*). Todd and Mike also have created a tribute to the Toho Daikaiju genre with their comics series *King Kong vs Godzilla*.

Brian Thomas lives in Chicago, Illinois, where the state fossil is the Tully Monster and the world's largest T-Rex skeleton makes her home. A former comic-book artist and animator, he is the author of *VideoHound's Dragon: Asian Action and Cult Flicks*, a contributing editor to *Cinescape* magazine, and has been a freelance correspondent to *Now Playing*, *Playboy*, the *Chicago Reader*, and many other books and periodicals. Rumour has it he was conceived at a drive-in movie theatre.

George Thomas is a lifelong giant monster fanatic who gained notoriety with his "War against the Wild Gods" stories featured in *G-Fan*, and helped establish fiction forums at a number of kaiju-oriented websites. He resides in New York with his wife, his son, and his giant radioactive pussycat. Find more of George's fiction and art work at his online archive called *The G-Spot* at http://clik.to/thegspot.

Iain Triffitt has written for television, radio, theatre and the written page, but seldom for money. With his writing partner, Brett Danalake, he has had one live radio play and three short plays produced so far. His short short "Porn Again" was published in *Agog! Smashing Stories*. One day he hopes to have a story published that's over 500 words in length. He lives in Five Dock in NSW Australia, with his wife Llyn and no cats (so far.)

D G Valdron is a Canadian writer, whose publications include *Interzone* in England, and *Parsec* and *On Spec* in Canada. His most recent publication was an essay on the TV series *Starlost* in a book to be published by McFarland Press. In real life, he works as an aboriginal rights lawyer in the arctic north. He lives a quiet life with his wife and mutant cat, where he likes interesting people and boring food.

Sean Williams, a *New York Times*-bestselling Adelaide author (and occasional DJ), has over sixty published short stories and eighteen novels under his belt, but remains inordinately proud of the odd odd haiku he manages to produce between deadlines (and the fact that there are more syllables in his bio than in his entire submission to *Daikaiju! Giant Monster Tales*).

Doug Wood has contributed stories to the fan website Kaijuphile.com. He lives in the US and grew up in Cleveland, where an abundance of horror movie hosts consumed many a weekend probably better spent studying.

Frank Wu's favourite giant monster of all time is the bat-rat-spider concoction from *Angry Red Planet*. His favourite giant monster movie, though, is *Them!* Frank, who lives in Silicon Valley in California, won a Hugo award for his art, but this is his first published bit of fiction.

CPSIA information can be obtained at www.ICGtesting.com
Printed in the USA
LVOW08s0232150916

504707LV00001B/8/P